A

THE OX THAT GORED

THE OX THAT GORED

JAMES D. CROWNOVER

FIVE STAR
A part of Gale, a Cengage Company

GALE
A Cengage Company

Farmington Hills, Mich • San Francisco • New York • Waterville, Maine
Meriden, Conn • Mason, Ohio • Chicago

GALE
A Cengage Company

LIBRARY OF CONGRESS CATALOGING-IN-PUBLICATION DATA

Names: Crownover, James D., author.
Title: The ox that gored / by James Crownover.
Description: First edition. | Waterville, Maine : Five Star Publishing, a part of Cengage Learning, Inc., [2017]
Identifiers: LCCN 2017022949 (print) | LCCN 2017027005 (ebook) | ISBN 9781432834371 (ebook) | ISBN 1432834371 (ebook) | ISBN 9781432837068 (ebook) | ISBN 1432837060 (ebook) | ISBN 9781432834418 (hardcover) | ISBN 143283441X (hardcover)
Subjects: | GSAFD: Western stories.
Classification: LCC PS3603.R765 (ebook) | LCC PS3603.R765 O94 2017 (print) | DDC 813/.6—dc23
LC record available at https://lccn.loc.gov/2017022949

First Edition. First Printing: November 2017
Find us on Facebook–https://www.facebook.com/FiveStarCengage
Visit our website–http://www.gale.cengage.com/fivestar/
Contact Five Star™ Publishing at FiveStar@cengage.com

Printed in the United States of America
1 2 3 4 5 6 7 21 20 19 18 17

To Dusty, Michael, and Patrick,
Mentors All

PROLOGUE

If you think by reading this you'll find out the particulars about the fight me and my posse had with the Newman gang, you are going to be disappointed and you might as well put this book down now. The Judge has ordered me not to say a word about it until all the trials are over.

If, however, you are interested in how a maverick kid (that's me, Lee Sowell) come to be a U.S. deputy marshal trained by the famous Bass Reeves or how three of the best deputies and lawmen in Indian Territory come to be, namely, Gamlin Stein, Harmon Lake, and a Texas kid named Tom Shipley, then you've come to the right place; read on, friend.

One of the scariest things we ever done was take on a band of comancheros, a band of cattle thieves, and a band of Comanches all at once and by ourselves. Those were desperate times and times that called for desperate measures. A fellow did what he had to do to get the job done and live to tell about it. Sure, we bent some laws—sometimes to the breaking point— but we got our men. It was our duty to do so, and we did it, but I still dream about that little job and wake up in a sweat after. One of the saddest times was when we found the remains of a deputy and his men. Tracking down and catching their killer was one of the things I am most proud of in my career.

If you are interested in knowin' a little about the great Judge Isaac Parker, and if you want to know some of Deputy Bass

Reeves and how we fought black and white crime in Indian Territory, read on, friend.

When the good judge talked about the sixty-five deputies
killed in the I.T. in the line of duty during his tenure, he didn't
include the many posse members also killed. He might have
made cook's wages and he might have made prisoner guard's
wages, but his life was on the line as much as the deputy's, and
he had as much to do with law enforcement as the deputy, for
those men were the deputy's posse.

Our ancient law says that a man is innocent until proven
guilty. Now a lawyer's likely to tell you that means the
"defendant," as he calls him, is innocent until a court declares
him guilty. He's practicing law where the deputy is more
concerned about practicing justice. A deputy will tell you that if
he catches a man with his murdered wife's blood on his clothes
or a thief is caught with a bloody knife and his victim's posses-
sions on him, he has been proven guilty. Why in the world do
you think they have manacles and chains on that tumbleweed
wagon they're dragging around?

It was a hard life in many ways, but it was a good life in the
outdoors, away from stuffy courtrooms and stinking jails, and I
miss it most in the spring when the mild breezes blow.

That's about all I'm gonna tell you about our adventures in
the old Indian Territory. If you want to know more, then read
on, friend.

Chapter 1
The Capture of
Burt Eakin

1882

It took us awhile to find a place where we could get the wagon across the M.K. & T. tracks, and when we got to a good place we stopped for the night. Old Baz lay back on his bedroll, his bare feet propped up on his saddle. All I could see of him by firelight was the near white soles of his feet seeming to float there in the air.

"The M.K. & T. railroad is called the Dead Line. West of it, a deputy's life ain't worth a wooden nickel. We ain't s'posed to arrest anybody east of the tracks. I once carried a man three days on my wagon afore we could git across the line and I could arrest him proper." Old Baz chuckled. "The saying is that there ain't no law west of Fort Smith an' they ain't no God west of th' Dead Line."

Before bedtime, Bass pulled a sheaf of papers from his bag and handed it to me. In it were a bunch of notes that obviously had been nailed up to trees, and such. They were all addressed to Bass Reeves or Ol' Baz and were threats and promises of many forms of death to Bass. Several were signed, some by more than one man.

"I collect these wherever I finds them, don't bother to answer them, but I shore remembers those that signs." He tapped the sheaf of notes. "That's a good thing t' remember, Lee."

"Lee, oh Lee, *Lee,* I see his shirt; I can git a shot at him!" Gamlin Stein called in a soft whisper.

"Don't you dare shoot him. Judge wants him alive an' I aim t' deliver him *whole* and alive."

9

"I could just wing him . . ."

"Not even a scratch, Gam, not a scratch. Git 'round on th' far side of him and make him move thisaway, but *don't shoot him.*"

"Damn."

"I mean it, Gam."

Gamlin backed down into the gulley and crept up toward the hilltop. It took him a long time to get there, but our quarry, Burton Eakin, never heard a sound or moved from his hiding place. The *ka-rack* of Gam's gun startled me, and Burt Eakin screamed and writhed. I jumped up and ran to him, heaping curses and consequences on Gam's person. Our prisoner sat holding his bare foot and moaning. I didn't see any blood and that eased my anxiety some. Gam seized Burt's guns and knife and stood there grinning. "Looks like it'll be fifty percent this time."

If there is a reward for the arrest of a prisoner, I always split it with my help. The percentage varies with the amount of participation of the helper, but they never get more than half, regardless of what they did.

"I *told* you not to shoot him. You'll be doin' good t' git a penny from me."

"Didn't shoot him." He held up Burt's heelless boot. "Shot his bootheel. I knew if it came to a footrace, Burt would outrun you by a mile—might coulda done it on one foot if he'd tried."

"You shot my foot," Burt whined.

"Whur's th' blood, an' let me see th' hole," Gam demanded.

"I cain't feel my toes." Eakin rocked back and forth, rubbing his numb foot.

"Hop up and get some circulation in it," I said as I helped the man to his feet. It only took a moment to get the manacles on him, and he limped and groaned around in a circle.

"Chain him in the wagon, Gam, and take my horse with you

back to camp while I gather up his things. Where's your horse, Burt?"

"Back there in the woods." He pointed the way, and I wondered why he had that ugly sneer on his face. "I'll ride Burt's horse." We were sure he was alone but I watched for an ambush.

"Don't let him get away, Gam." If my words weren't strong enough, my look would convince. I ducked into the brush and found the horse down in a ravine, untied him, and led him to the trail. Just as we stepped into the open, that horse grunted and bit into my shoulder. He lifted me plumb off the ground and was just beginning to shake me when I shot up over my shoulder and hit him between the eyes. His grip relaxed its hold and he crumpled to the ground, taking me with him. I lay there a moment, fighting off pain and darkness. My shirt was wet front and back and I was afraid to feel what was left of my shoulder. Fortunately, it was my right shoulder and didn't affect my gun hand.

It was two miles to our camp, and every step I took made me madder. Before a half mile had passed, I had devised a good dozen ways t' kill that no-good Burt Eakin. All of them were slow and very painful.

My pappy named me Robert E. Lee Sowell but no one knows me by more than Lee Sowell—and that's the way it's gonna stay. If the Judge knew my whole name, he would have me in chains *under* that courtroom faster than a rabbit. I never speak "southern," and for sure never say damnyankee. For all they know, my folks are farmers in Illinois, not Liberty Springs, Arkansas.

The U.S. District Court for the Western District of Arkansas covered a goodly portion of Arkansas and all of Indian Territory. Some folks north of Van Buren took exception to how I took trade in livestock for my moonshine, probably thinking my prices were too high. One night in the fall of 1877, as I sat by the cabin door peacefully smoking my pipe, the biggest, blackest man with a silver star under the breast of his coat rode up and said politely, "Lee Sowell, come with me to Fort Smith."

It was an invitation I couldn't resist and Bass Reeves was so nice as to gather up and carry along my guns and knives for me. There was still a light in the courtroom when we got there near midnight. Bass invited me in, and there behind that big desk sat Judge Parker. He looked up as we entered and asked, "Is this him, Bass?"

"Yas, suh, in de flesh."

The Judge looked at me a long time and my gut felt quivery. "Your name is Lee Sowell?"

"Yessir."

"Where did you come from?"

"I been stayin' over at Rudy for . . ."

"Before that."

"Illinois."

"What did you do there?"

"My folks is farmers."

"I have here a complaint about your way of appropriating certain cattle and horses in and around Van Buren. Based on that, I issued a warrant for your arrest. Do you have it, Bass?"

"Yas, suh, right here, Your Honor."

"Well, sign it and give it to me."

Taking a pencil stub from his pocket, Bass laboriously signed the paper and handed it to the Judge. "Thank you, Bass." He glanced at it and laid it on his desk beside the charges against me. "Now, Mr. Sowell, you and I both have decisions to make. This warrant along with your presence says I can remand you to the jailer downstairs . . . or I can release you under bail or other conditions as I see fit.

"I will give you two options: One is to go to jail and await trial, the other is to go to work for me in the territory as a deputy U.S. marshal."

I opened my mouth to reply and he stopped me with a wave of his hand. "You should know that the bail for this offense will be so high as to be unattainable, and that the roster for this term of court is full and your trial won't come up until after June of next year."

I was starin' straight at a stacked deck. "Well, sir—Your Honor—I believe I could make you a good deputy, given time."

"If I didn't think so too, I would not have made the offer. For now you will be under the charge of Deputy Bass Reeves. He will teach you well." Then he swore me in as his deputy marshal. "Bass, I think it would be in Deputy Sowell's best interests if he only practiced his law west of Fort Smith."

"Yas, suh, 'at jist what we do," Bass replied.

And that's how I became a deputy U.S. marshal.

We stepped out into the fresh night air. The stench from the jail below the courtroom came up through the floor. I've seen times when court was adjourned until a breeze came up and blew through the building.

Bass looked at me and said, "I'm a'goin' home for the night and I'll meet you right here in the moanin'. You ain't here by sunup, I'll come lookin' for you, an' I jist might bring you back draped over my mule, Judas, an' tell Judge you fit me."

"You wouldn't shoot a deputy U.S. marshal, would you?"

He stepped down a step so's he could look me in the eye without stoopin', "On'y two people in this worl' know you a marshal."

I understood.

The ferry across the river to Van Buren stops early in the evenin', and I had to wake the ferryman to cross. The only thing he was cheerful about was chargin' me double for after-hours. I hurried to Rudy, loaded my gear on my horse, and rode back to the waiting ferry. It cost me th' price of one crossin' for th' wait an' double for man an' horse t' cross agin. Bein' dark, I gave the man one of my counterfeit silver dollars. He was so smug, he forgot to bite it to see if it was real. Bet he was mad in th' mornin'. I rolled up in my blanket an' slept under the court-house steps.

A small disturbance at the hitchin' rack told me someone had ridden up, and I emerged from the steps thinkin' it might be Bass. It wasn't and I got real acquainted with the muzzle of another deputy's .44. "Ain't healthy t' sleep under them steps, boy, that's where the trash hides t' ambush deputies," the shadow behind that gun said. I spent what little was left of the night sittin' on steps where comers and goers could see me plain.

Bass didn't break stride when he passed me, just said, "Come on." I caught up with him at the door to a small office down the hall from the courtroom. There were several other men I took for deputies in the room. They all were getting warrants from a little man behind a high desk. From the talk and joshin', I took it that he was Lyon Rankin, the marshal's clerk.

"Hey, Bass, I heered you stopped by widow Coughlin's," one of th' deputies called.

"I did for sure, Bill, but she didn't have anythin' for me. Said you left her somethin' th' last time you stopped that she wouldn't want t' give to anyone but you. Right nice of her, I thought, an' I paid her anyway."

Everyone who traveled in Indian Territory knew of the widow Coughlin or some woman like her. Left to fend for themselves and most likely with a bunch of kids, these poor women got along as best they could. "Entertainin' " men was one way to get along. I have t' say this, I never saw Bass Reeves take advantage of these women. He was married and behaved like he was, though when he got tired of camp food he would take a meal with one or the other and pay generously for it.

Bass stepped up to the desk with me stuck to his side. The little clerk looked up and said, "Looks like you'll be going out to the Cherokee Outlet this trip, Bass."

Bass took the packet of warrants and glanced at them, "Sho look thataway, don' it? Is Marshal Carroll in?"

"No, he's up at Vinita; lots of trouble there." Lyon gathered up papers for the next deputy and we moved to the door, Bass exchanging words with first one then the other. This was sure a different world than that outside this building. The deputies treated one another as equals, and there was none of the prevailing attitude of the day that Negros were inferior to whites and thus subservient. On the whole, black deputies were treated as equals by the white deputies, both knowing that at one time or another their lives would depend on a fellow deputy, no matter the color of his skin.

When I walked into camp, Eakin was chained in the wagon. He saw my bloody shirt and I thought for a moment he would laugh out loud.

"Your horse died, Eakin," I said.

His grin faded and he asked, "Was that what that shot we heard was?"

I ignored his question. Gam had picketed the animals and was cooking supper. It made me madder, 'cause he couldn't cook worth a tinker's dam. "Get away from that skillet an' git th' medicine kit out, Gam."

He looked up and saw my bloody shirt and drug the medicine kit out of th' wagon box while I took off my shirt. "What happened?" he asked as he wiped my shoulder.

"Eakin taught his horse to bite."

Gam gave a low whistle. "You got a perfect imprint of his

15

teeth—top . . ." he stretched to look at my back ". . . and bottom. Where's th' horse?"

"Layin' in th' trail with a big hole in his head."

He pulled our medicine whiskey bottle from the kit. "This is gonna sting."

I grabbed the bottle and took a long pull. "Go ahead."

I shoulda been drunk. It burned like the fires of hell and my knees almost buckled. I ran to the bushes and peed. When I got back to the fire, Gam said, "Now I gotta get th' back."

"You only did th' front? Good night, man, what you got agin' me?" He only grunted in reply and poured whiskey down my back. I would have gone back to the bushes, but I was empty. Another pull on that bottle didn't help a bit.

Gam looked me over carefully, poking here and there, laying a flap of skin back in place. "Don't know how t' bandage that, Lee, an' I think your collarbone's broke."

"Just lay a strip of cloth over my shoulder. A clean shirt will hold it in place. Get me a strap t' tie my arm down with." We got my shirt on over a thick bandage, strapped my elbow down, and with my hand in my belt, I was fixed as good as I could be. My head ached from the whiskey and my shoulder burned and ached somethin' terrible. "I don't feel like eatin', Gam, you feed yourself an' Eakin. I'm goin' t' bed. We're goin' in tomorrow."

I had to prop myself up as high as I could on my saddle and still couldn't sleep. Late in the night a horse came into camp and stood by the picket line with the other horses. I heard Gam get up and I pulled my gun to cover him if there was trouble. In a moment he came back for the lantern and by its light, I could make out a horse with saddle and bridle but no rider. Muttering to himself, Gam tied the horse to the picket rope, took off th' saddle, and put out the lantern. "That horse you kilt just walked into camp an' I tied him to th' line," he whispered, then disappeared into the night.

When I shot the horse, the bullet ran almost parallel with his face. My bullet penetrated the skin and ran right up his skull between his eyes and exited at his crown. It didn't even bleed much, but he must have had a heck of a headache. Later, Burt sold the horse to help pay his lawyer, and the man who bought him said the horse didn't bite anyone in all the years he had him. In that manner, he was better than his former owner.

"I never thought someone could burn coffee, but here you done it," Eakin growled at Gam at breakfast. "And how in the world can you burn an egg on one side and leave it raw on t'other?"

"It's just right in th' middle an' you kin eat or not, just shut up about it." Gam was sensitive about people criticizing his cooking. I hired him as cook because it paid twenty dollars a month, but really because he was a better shot than I was. I did all the cooking when I could. We were on the road, if you could call it that, by sunrise, all three of us in the wagon and me feeling every bump and jostle.

We caught Eakin in the Pottawatomie and Shawnee reservation where Jumper Creek runs into Pond Creek. It's a hundred and fifty miles from Fort Smith, and my body felt every foot of it. By midafternoon, I had reached my limit and called a halt for the night. Burt Eakin's mood had improved when he saw his horse tied to the picket line, and he had been obnoxious all day.

"Cain't take your punishment like a man," he sneered. It was too much for the mood I was in and my gun barrel on the side of his head made it a lot quieter in camp. It made me feel better, too. I hoped his head hurt as much as my shoulder.

Gam laid out my bed and I slept. A loud thump in the wagon jarred me awake, gun in hand.

"Was you asleep, Lee? I had to move this crate of hoss shoes an' I guess I must have dropped it." Eakin's evil grin told the truth of his action.

"Just restin' my eyes, Burt; go ahead with your redecorating."

"That's about all for now, you go on back t' sleep."

I was dreaming of a soft bed and clean sheets when a scream brought me up again. "Wasps is after me, they're stingin' me," Eakin yelled.

Gam trotted over and peeked in the wagon. "Don't see no wasps."

"They stung me on th' neck," the prisoner whined.

"We'll fix that," Gam scrambled into the wagon and back-handed the man across his face, rolling him over on his side. Before he could react, Gam had Eakin's right hand uncuffed and pulled behind his back where he refastened the manacles. Jerking the man upright, he stuffed a dirty rag into his mouth and tied it there with Burt's bandanna.

"Take his boots off, Gam."

Chapter 2
The Business Defined

Bass tapped his finger on his warrant folder. "Lee, we ain't in th' killin' business; we're in th' delivery business an' our 'goods' is bad men. Ever' time you kill one, it costs us money, less'n th' warrant's for 'dead or alive'—and that's troublesome, for we have to have witnesses to confirm th' death. Most of these people won't testify t' that 'cause they know it costs th' deputy money. Lee, if you have t' shoot a man, try t' wing him so he'll live at least till we git him to th' courthouse."

I awoke in the night burning up and my mouth too dry to swallow. Stirring around, I bumped the water bucket within my reach and found the dipper handle. The water was cold and sweet. I slept again.

The second day was no better than the first, but I gritted my teeth and we drove till dusk. Even one-armed, I was a better cook than Gamlin, and I cooked while he made camp.

"Looks like a mole been workin' up that hoss's face," Gam observed.

"You'd do better not to harm that horse permanent-like," Burt warned.

"Just consider that horse has come back to you from th' dead, Burt, an' any condition I left him should have gone to you," I replied.

"He don't offer t' bite me," Gam said over his coffee mug.

"He's a smart horse if he never offers t' bite anyone agin."

My shoulder ached awful and the bandage had stuck to me. I eyed the medicine kit with that bottle in it. "We gonna havta dress this shoulder, Gam."

"First thing after supper."

"Some whiskey on it now would maybe soak it loose by then."

"I could use a little of that 'medicine' myself; these irons are chaffin' me awful," Burt called from the wagon.

"We're savin' it for th' wounded, Burt." Gam uncorked the bottle, poured some over the bandage, and handed it to me.

That bottle was near empty and we were still a hundred miles from Fort Smith. "Gam, we're gonna have t' find a bootlegger."

"Just a little swig?" Eakin called.

"Don't give him the bottle, Gam."

Gamlin poured a swallow in a cup and carried it to the wagon. As he lifted it up to Eakin, the cup hit the sideboard and spilled its contents on Burt's outstretched hands. "E-e-yow-w," he screamed, "that stings!" He licked his arms and hands.

"Maybe you'll stop tryin' t' pull those things off now," Gam growled.

While Eakin was gnawin' th' gristly end of our steak, we changed my bandage and I stretched out on my bedroll. My shoulder was turning blue from my arm to my neck. In a day or two it would be black. It sure did hurt. Gam came over and sat b'side me. "Where we gonna find a bootlegger?"

We were camped on Elm Creek just east of Holdenville. "I heard Whiskey Horn was out of prison and back in business, but he makes the worst whiskey in th' country."

"I heard there's someone working the Flat Rock area . . ."

"Too far out of th' way, an' we don't know who's peddlin'," I said without opening my eyes.

"Well, there's always someone working Lake's Ferry on Deep Fork; maybe we'll git lucky there." Gam slung the dregs out of his cup and headed for the pot. "Hey, Burt, know anyone sellin' whiskey at th' ferry?"

"As if I'd tell you."

"Might be the only means you have o' gittin' some whiskey before jail. I hear they voted th' cells dry there."

"Drier'n O'Malley's cow—an' prisoners didn't git t' vote." Eakin spat.

"Such a shame. You oughta write th' President. Think on it, Burt; it's gonna be a long dry spell for you when you get to th' Fort."

I drifted off to sleep with those two jawin' and didn't wake until it was light enough to see. Gamlin was fixin' breakfast an' still jawin' with Eakin. Wagons work good out on the prairie, but in th' breaks and along rivers, you have your choice of deep sand or rocky hills. Both wear out animals and wagon, not t' speak of what it does to passengers. A wagon would last maybe a dozen trips in these hills and valleys, where you could get a hundred trips on the prairie. This third morning I rode my horse, and it was a much smoother ride. I was ok one-handed so long as he didn't get any wild hairs. The horse sensed my condition and behaved very well for me.

With Eakin chained to the wagon, he would make an easy target for the many people who would love to see him dead, so we called him John Smith when we got among people.

Gamlin worked on Eakin until he had talked him into a big thirst and he told us how t' get a jug at the ferry. We stopped a mile below the ferry. Gam tied his possibles bag to a stick and walked to the ferry while Eakin, aka Smith, and I waited.

Gam waited out of sight until he saw the ferry leave for the far side, then shuffled up to the dock where Jess Wimpee, a dockhand, idled away his time.

"Shore is hot an' dry 'round here; I could use a drink."

"There's th' river an' all you want if you don't mind chewin' it a little," the hand said. He didn't offer the dipper to the bucket of spring water sitting on th' bench by him. If too many drank from it, he would have to walk a quarter mile to the spring to refill, and it was just too hot for all that work.

"Been so long since I've drank water I plumb forgot what it tastes like. I might not like it an' sometimes it makes people sick. I'm lookin' fer sompin' a le-e-tle stronger."

" 'Stronger' ain't allowed in th' territory an' it's so scarce it's awful expensive." Jess yawned and pulled his hat down over his face."

After a quiet moment, Gam asked, "How 'spensive air it, friend?"

"Likely you can't pay six bits a pint," the hat said.

"Six bits! That'd git me a gallon anywhere else."

" 'Anywhere else' would hafta be east of Fort Smith, friend."

"I jist ain't that thirsty, I guess." There followed a long quiet spell where only the buzz of a hornet and whisper of crickets were heard. The ferry hand snored and Gam watched the ferry pull away from the far bank. He tossed a rock and it rolled across the plank floor. The hand stopped snoring. "So a gallon jug'd cost two dollars?"

Jess lifted his hat, eyed the approaching ferry, and dropped it back in place. "Two twenty-five, an' yuh git two bits back when you bring th' jug back whole."

"Hell's bells! Where's th' castle this thief peddler lives in, anyway?"

"Don't need t' go that far. I'm his clerk. I takes yore money an' gives th' goods."

"What's it taste like?"

"They's a sample jar under that tarp; try it."

Gam reached under the tarp and pulled out a pint jar full of an amber liquid. He swirled it around and it looked pretty good. Now, he had been around long enough to learn that the "sample" was a good quality whiskey bought in town and used to lure the prospective customer into thinking all the brew tasted this good. He had prepared for this moment. Of course, the whiskey he bought didn't taste that good, but by the time the customer discovered it, he didn't care enough to go back and get a *re*fund. After all, whiskey, no matter how bad, was awful dear in Indian Territory.

From his pocket he pulled a similar pint jar filled with amber tea and placed it under the tarp. *At least we'll have th' good stuff for ourselves,* he thought. The dockhand snored. "Not bad stuff, think I'll take a half gallon."

New life burst from the hand and he jumped up. "A dollar an' a bit for th' jar." He held out his hand and Gam counted out the money. "I seen a half gallon layin' ahind that stump up there. Has a bit o' hay layin' on top."

Gam walked up the bank to the stump while Jess busied himself docking the ferry. He saw the hand give the money to Owen Lake, the ferry owner. When he signaled, I drove the wagon down to the dock.

"He took my money an' gave it to Owen." Gam shook the jug at me.

The dockhand stared. "You a deputy?" he asked.

"I'm a deputy's deputy," Gam replied.

"Cook," I corrected. "You're both under arrest for peddlin' whiskey in th' territory."

"You can't arrest me, I gotta run this ferry," Owen whined.

"Better find that feller that run it last time you was caught. Tell him it'll be longer this time." Rumor had it that the man was very efficient running the ferry and just as efficient living with Owen's wife. She didn't even miss her child bearin', though folks say the child she birthed doesn't favor Owen at all. Owen came home unexpected, and last anyone heard of that feller, he was "Gone to Texas" somewhere north of Kansas.

"What's my family gonna do?" The man was near tears.

I got mad. "Why in th' world didn't you think of that *before*, Lake? Now you're tryin' t' put it off on me when *you* are the one responsible for the mess you're in an' *not me*. Why do you think I should put my job in danger for you?"

"I'm just tryin' t' make a . . ."

"You got a good livin' runnin' this ferry. You're greedy enough t' take advantage of th' Indians' thirst for drink without thinkin' o' th' consequences. *Then* you whine an' cry 'cause you got caught. You disgust me. Lock him up good, Gam. I'm goin' up to th' house t' tell his wife."

Down below the house a ways was a pig sty, an' it had a strong alcohol smell when I passed. The hogs were laying in the mud or staggering around th' pen. *They're drunk*, I thought, *Owen's brewing his own this time.*

With all our attention on Owen Lake, Jess Wimpee had disappeared. I found him sitting on the stoop of the Lake house. "Think you could run the ferry?" I asked.

"Better'n Owen, I guess."

"Then git in those bushes an' don't come out until we leave. Pour out all that whiskey. And if I *ever* catch you selling again, I'll arrest you and we'll *start* for Fort Smith. Might be only one of us gets there. *Do you understand me?*"

"Yessir."

He trotted off up th' hill and I turned t' find Mrs. Lake standin' in th' dogwalk, a half-dozen kids surrounding her. "I told him he would get caught agin, but he didn't listen." Her chin quivered, and I knew why I sometimes hated my job. She wasn't much t' look at, all used up with bearing children and work. *Must be she's a good cook*, I thought.

"Jess says he can run your ferry, an' it looks like one or two of those boys of yours are big enough to make a hand. Do you know enough cipher t' keep books?"

She nodded. "We'll git by, I reckon."

"Do you want t' come see Owen b'fore we leave?"

She shook her head, "Saw him at breakfast."

One of the boys and a young girl ran for the ferry.

"Where's th' still? I have t' destroy it."

"He wouldn't let us go in those woods ahind th' privy." She turned and shuffled into the living side of the house.

I made a detour around the privy and found a path down into the woods. There was a spring and a rough shed beside it with several barrels of mash souring. Boy, it stank. I took an axe that was stuck in a stump and beat up the still. When I looked up, one of the older boys was standing there.

"Help me dump these barrels, son."

"Yessir," he said, and I think he was strong enough to have done it alone.

"Don't feed your hogs too much of this at a time. You could kill 'em."

"Yessir, we done found that out. Won't be much of this left after a couple days, an' we'll have t' watch out for drunk bears, 'coons, 'possums, an' hogs for a while. Those pigs in th' pen were wild till they got too drunk t' run an' we penned 'em up. They won't try t' git out if we keep 'em drunk awhile."

"So men ain't the only ones t' git stuck on th' stuff."

"No, sir. I seen enough of it t' stay away from it altogether, an' so's my brothers."

"You're big enough t' help Jess and your mother run th' business. I reckon you'll git along OK."

"Yes, sir. Thank you, Deputy."

"For what?"

"For takin' my pa. I hope he don't come back—ever."

My shoulder felt better after Mrs. Lake put new salve and bandages on it. She agreed with Gamlin that the collarbone was broken and I should keep the arm immobile until it healed on its own. Two prisoners would hardly make the trip profitable. Even so, I felt pretty low and wanted to get to the fort as soon as possible. Driving down George's Creek the second day, we ran into a herd of horses. The funny thing about this bunch is that there were a half-dozen or more brands on the horses and the herders had run when they spied our tumbleweed wagon. Gamlin had prevailed upon me to chase the men. Considering our light load and the prospect of two easy catches, I agreed. We trailed them to a dugout in the breaks and had them trapped before they knew it.

"Hey, Deputy, supper's on, come on in an' les eat."

"You wants us t' bring in a bucket o' water when we come?"

"Wouldn't hurt none; this barrel water is pretty stale."

"You think they got a barrel o' water in there, Lee?" Gam shifted uneasily; he wasn't one to sit still long.

"Likely they filled one—a year ago—won't be any good now. These boys ain't too high on labor an' industry."

We had those two horse thieves holed up in their dugout for goin' on three days, an' no tellin' how much longer we'd be sitting out there waiting for somethin' t' happen. "If they do have good water, we're gonna be here a long time."

"Scooch 'round over there a ways an' see if you can see a barrel, Lee." I crawled one-armed down the gulley an' stuck my head over th' bank. A shot from the dugout sprayed dirt and grit in my face and I fell back. Gamlin was laughin' at me. "O-o-oh, they got me, Gam, I been shot in th' face," I shouted. "Gam come help me—Gam? You there? I can't see, Gam, an' I'm bleedin'." I started crying and carrying on, loud enough for those boys in th' dugout t' hear.

"Did you see anything?" Gam whispered.

"Yeah, there's a barrel half-hid in that hall to th' left, I think I can get a few shots into it."

"I'm comin' over there with the Sharps. You draw their attention away an' I'll get a shot off. This .50 ought t' make a pretty good leak in that barrel."

"Where are you, Gam? I'm comin' to you," I called in my panic voice and moved down the gulley, showing myself occasionally and drawing fire away from Gam as he moved to my old position. "Those fellers must have an arsenal in there t' be wastin' so much lead," I growled. Gam only grunted. I let my hat show a little and a bullet cut a groove across its crown. It let in so much light I had to sew it up later.

Gam laid his rifle on the bank and hazarded a glance. "Think I see that barrel. Draw their attention an' I'll take a shot."

Three quick shots from my rifle, and the fourth was drowned out by the boom of that .50.

Angry talk from the dugout told us the shot had been successful. "You got it, Gam. That flood may wash those boys right out of th' place." Of course, it didn't, but it would go a long ways toward shortening their stay inside. We sat out the long hot afternoon, and just before sunset, their milk cow came to th' barn down by the creek, lowin' in a sad voice. She hadn't been milked in three days an' she was gettin' uncomfortable. "Think I'll have me a little milk for supper, Gam."

"Mm-m it ain't buttermilk, but it'd shore go good with cornbread. Go on, I'll watch th' dugout."

Ol' Bossy was right willing that I relieve her, and she stood still while I milked one-handed. Of a sudden she raised her tail and started peein'. It was a bad habit some cows got into and she had never been broken from it. On a sudden inspiration, I shoved my bucket under her deluge and in a moment had a bucket full of milky pee.

She sure was disappointed when I left with our job unfinished, "I'll be back shortly, Bossy, you wait right here." At the mouth of th' gulley I motioned to Gam and circled around to the top of the dugout. Whoever had made the dugout had done it right. (It was sure the present occupants hadn't built it.) When they put the chimney through the roof, they suspended a large flat rock cover over it like a short-legged table so the smoke would be disbursed some and no critter—two- or four-legged—could get to it and cause mischief. From the amount of smoke coming out around the rock it was obvious the outlaws were cooking supper.

The big rock on top was heavy for one man to lift, but with a strong pole I was able to lift one edge enough to slide it off its supports and expose the stovepipe. I sloshed a little from the bucket down the pipe. If you've ever peed on a fire, you know how pungent it can be. Well, we learned that day that cow piss stinks twice as much. "Phew-ee." I dumped the whole bucket in and slammed it over the flue.

The reaction below was almost immediate. Coughing interrupted the flow of curses and yells. I ran to the front just in time t' see those two run out, firing as they came. When they were out far enough, one turned on me and fired before I could bring my pistol to bear. The bullet passed by without harm, but the man didn't get off another shot. He didn't feel the ground come up to meet him.

Gamlin had the other feller on th' ground cuffing him. "Come on down, Lee, we got 'em both." Halfway down I remembered the bucket and went back for it.

Yellow-tinted steam drifted from the dugout and out of the chimney. "Phew-e-e-o-o, that stinks. What did you put in there?"

"Cow piss an' milk. No one's gonna sleep in there tonight. Let's get to camp an' away from here."

"He's dead." Gam nodded at the body. The live prisoner sat up, legs spread, chin on his chest. Tears washed dust and dirt traces down his face. "You should have winged him, Lee." We both hated to lose a potential prisoner.

"He was sure determined, Gam, I don't think wingin' would have stopped him. Go ahead and finish milkin' that cow an' I'll take care of this prisoner." He nodded and trotted off. "You be sure t' wash out that bucket first," I called after him.

I picked the prisoner up by the nape of his coat and set him on his feet. I saw Bass Reeves do that once with one hand. He might be the strongest man I have ever known, certainly the strongest in the territory. "Come on, friend, we'll take care of th' other when that air clears some."

It didn't take long t'chain our new prisoner in Tumbleweed, wash up in spring water, and get the beans and cornbread going. It all vanished almost as fast.

While the prisoners ate, we went through the cadaver's pockets and put his belongings in a bag with his name. Then we carried him into the dugout and laid him out on the ground. I kicked the rock scotching the door open and locked it shut from the outside.

I always figured up about what we would be paid when we delivered a prisoner to the court jail. "How far is it to Fort Smith, Gam?"

"I'd guess it t' be about a hundred miles, wouldn't you?"

"Close enough. That's ten dollars at ten cents per mile plus six bits per day food allowance for, say, five days' travel time, considerin' no delays or detours. That comes to . . . about six dollars and a total of sixteen dollars, delivered."

Gamlin looked at me across the fire. "That's also how much we lost because you killed that other man."

Chapter 3
Medicine Jack and Caesar

Bass Reeves filled his cup and walked out into the dark where I sat with my back against a big log. He screwed his gun belt around until the gun was in front and sat down with a grunt. "Us deputy marshals is allowed to arrest people for assault with intent to kill or maim, murder, attempted murder, manslaughter, arson, burglary, robbery, larceny, adultery, incest, rape, and willfully and maliciously placing obstructions on a railroad track." *He ticked the offenses off on his fingers.*

"Now, manslaughter is accidental murder or killing someone unintentionally. Those folk are usually easy t' handle. The ones hard t' handle are the murderers an' would-be murderers, 'specially if it's a white man killing an Indian or black man. Gen'lly, they don't consider that murder and they are very upset that others do. Larceny is jist 'nother word for stealin'. Them other things, incest, an' rape, are the most disgusting crimes, an' a lot o' vermin that does them ought t' be strung up same as murder. I ain't worryin' too much about adulterers. 'Course, we don't want no train wreckin' or robbin'.

"If you runs across any of these fellers, you don't have t' worry about a warrant. They'll make you one at th' courthouse.

"Make friends with the Indian Police. They can be a lot of help at times."

Gam and I crossed the M.K. & T. late in the afternoon and drove until dusk before we stopped. My shoulder was really hurting, and my jaws were tired from chewing willow twigs. If they helped stop the pain any, I was afraid t' go long without one and let the pain increase. That stinkin' moonshine of Lake's didn't help a bit, and between me and Gam, his smooth "sample" was long gone.

"Gam, I don't know if we should go to McAlester to Doc Stewig's or go on to Fort Smith." The good doctor was especially keen on injuries such as mine—he was no slouch with bullet wounds, either.

"Doc Stewig's likely t' be out on a call an' you'd be stuck with that medicine man Simmons, an' you know you wouldn't take a sick horse t' him."

"Yeah, you're right, we'll make for th' fort an' hope I live that long. Make Burt dig my grave deep if I don' make it."

"Huh," Eakin said, "yo're too ornery t' die from a little ol' horse bite."

"That horse gits sick an' you'll say he got poisoned biting me."

"Could be, could be."

"Lake claims his 'shine cures a lot o' things," Gam added.

"Yeah, like healthy stomach linin' an' good eyesight," I replied.

Another night of fitful sleep, and we were on our way before sunrise.

We were camped under Wildhorse Mountain when three men rode into camp. They were Creek Lighthorse Policemen Caesar and Medicine Jack with a white prisoner.

"Light down an' have a cup." Gam shook the pot to make sure there was enough coffee.

The two Indians dismounted and dug out their cups. Gamlin poured both full and we squatted by the fire. The prisoner sat on his horse, ignored for the moment.

Though the Lighthorse Police are primarily concerned with patrolling and protecting the Indians, they will occasionally arrest a white man, especially if the crime is serious, like murder or rape. The disdain these two policemen showed for this man indicated to me that he had done something special.

After a second leisurely cup of coffee, Medicine Jack said, "We brought you a prisoner. His name is A.B. Chew. Folks call him Abe."

"What's he done, Jack?" I asked.

"Killed a young girl he was living with. Claimed he stole her from her family up in the Cherokee Outlet. One day he busted her head with a big rock and drug her off into the brush."

On closer scrutiny, the prisoner struck me as a weasel-faced little man you wouldn't give a second glance in a crowd—the sneaky kind you would not trust. He was dirty and smelly and stayed that way th' whole time I had him on the wagon. My other prisoners complained constantly about his smell.

Caesar handed me a folded circular and I opened it. The description matched the prisoner down to his dirty personal hygiene. The crime was for kidnapping a fourteen-year-old girl, and there was a five hundred dollar reward for his capture. In a perverse way, the poster had saved his life, for if that poster had said "dead or alive" the prisoner would have been riding that horse belly down. Creek Indians don't put up with vermin who kidnap, ravage, and kill children. The Lighthorse officers had kept him prisoner a long time while they looked for me. Few of the other marshals would split the reward with them, so they waited for a deputy who would.

"I'll get him to the courthouse and apply for the reward. Sometimes it takes awhile to get it, but when I do, I'll give you half."

The two men nodded. They knew who would keep his word. Jack handed me a much worn sheet of paper on which were scrawled a half-dozen or more names, depending on how they were interpreted. "Witnesses."

"Good, this will help the court a lot." I folded the paper and stowed it in my saddlebag, and after I had written down their statements, we ate. The men got no extra pay for feeding their prisoners, and since they had this man several days and were obliged to feed him several times, I paid them to cover that expense.

With the new prisoner secured, we slept, and the aroma of fresh coffee awoke me before dawn. Our two Lighthorse guests were just finishing their cups while their three horses waited, saddled and ready to go. We shook hands and they disappeared into the gloom.

I didn't know it at the time, but Abe Chew was the worst criminal I ever handled. Even in those days of little paperwork, he had a record of crimes several pages long. His latest crime sickened even toughened criminals, and the Lighthorse had plenty of help in locating him—could have had twenty men for a posse if they had wanted them.

We learned later that somewhere in Kansas he latched on to a family of pilgrims moving to New Mexico Territory and volunteered to guide them across the prairie. Instead, he guided them into the Cherokee Strip and there murdered the family, husband, wife, and three of the kids. He kept the fourteen-year-old girl until he tired of her and dispatched her with a rock. Even outlaws didn't treat good women that way.

He was a sneak killer who preferred a knife in the back or a rock in the head to a gun. Although he preyed on the weak and unsuspecting, no one was safe around him. If you didn't know him for what he really was, you would take him for a simpering cowardly little man.

His fellow prisoners in the basement avoided him as much for his aroma as for his deeds, and that's saying something from a bunch of unwashed men used to ignoring personal hygiene. One night someone dumped the honey pot on him and all the occupants set up a howl to get him out of there. While the inmates cleaned up the mess, a couple of deputies took Chew to the river and soused him good. Then they made him take his clothes off and wash again. They claim they never saw the like of carp and suckers come up and feed in the putrid water.

We turned our four prisoners in to George Maledon at the courthouse; Gamlin went upstairs to get Lyon Rankin to make out the warrants on Lake, Chew, and the horse thief and I headed to town to find a doctor. He smeared me with Dr. A.W. Allen's Southern Liniment, the most vile-smelling salve, and sold me a jar for a dollar. "Put this on the wounds twice a day and keep them covered until they heal," the good doctor said.

I wandered into the saloon next door and ordered a "bottle of the best" unopened and sealed. Barkeep fanned his nose and said, "Dr. A.W. Allen's Southern Liniment. Seems that man don't know anything else. It must be made from skunk carrion. I'll give you a discount if you take the bottle somewhere else t' drink."

I took the discount and poured the medicine in the spittoon. Snooty barkeep.

The court set Chew's trial for late fall, which would give the deputies time to gather up witnesses.

I lay around my cabin a few days until Gamlin showed up anxious t' be on th' move agin. This roamin' th' countryside gets into your bones an' you seldom see a deputy marshal in one place long.

"Gam, I'm firin' you from th' cookin' job."

He was startled an' looked pained at the thought of bein' fired. "I *tole* you I wasn't no cook when you hired me."

"I know, but I didn't know you were *that* bad. It's a wonder you didn't poison someone."

"Now see here, Lee, I—"

"I've hired someone I'm sure can cook to take your place . . ." The boy wilted and looked so downcast, I couldn't carry on anymore. ". . . and made you prisoner guard at three dollars a day."

"Really? Three dollars a day? Wowee."

It was a goodly raise and the boy deserved it. Besides, it eased my conscience considerable since our cooks ain't supposed t' be chasin' crooks. Three dollars a day is little enough for such work.

"I just come t' see how you was an' when we're gonna go out agin. Didn't know about th' promotion an' all." Gam beamed.

"Give me a couple o' days an' I'll meet you at th' courthouse th' third mornin'."

"I brung us a couple steaks cut fresh this mornin'. Want I should start 'em cookin'?"

"No!"

Chapter 4
Two for One at Vian

Ol' Baz handed me the folder of warrants as we walked toward the stables. "Mos' important thing you can do is know your warrants an' what men you are goin' after before you leaves town. Might be you know more than our marshal about th' whereabouts of a man, an' I caught more than one in saloons down on Garrison Avenue. You don't get mileage for carryin' 'em from the territory, but that marshal sure makes note o' yore efficiency."

We sat on the tailgate of the wagon and went through the warrants one by one. I read each one to Bass and he listened closely. When I finished with one, he took it and looked at the paper intently, repeating the name of the person described. The warrants were placed in his folder in the order that we read them, and that was the way they stayed. I seldom had access to the warrants, but when I did, Bass would always caution me to keep them in the set order.

Bass Reeves could not read, and the most he could write was his name, but he would arrest his man and pull the proper warrant from that folder and recite from memory the charges against him—and he never got the wrong warrant or made a mistake in his recitation so long as I was with him. His memory was phenomenal.

Gam was sittin' on the steps of the courthouse when I got there, and I sent him to get wagon and stock ready. He looked around, curious t' see our new cook. "He'll be along shortly." I didn't say more.

Lyon Rankin was in the marshal's office when I went in to

pick up my warrants. He came out with a hand full of papers, and I could see the marshal wasn't at his desk. "Some kind of big powwow with the Cherokee," he said by way of explanation. "He wanted t' put you on courthouse duty until you were better, but the judge said you was well enough to take care of these things." He handed me a folder of warrants from a basket on his desk.

Thank you, Judge Parker.

The mules were hitched to the wagon and parked in the shade. Gam had saddled two horses, and he sat on the tailgate waiting for our customary reading of the warrants before we got under way. I noticed he was more attentive while I read and would look over the paper before putting it in the folder. I made sure Gam could read before I hired him, since my education had been a little worse than haphazard.

"We goin' th' usual route?" Gam asked.

"Let's start that-a-way and we might make a detour or two. I think I know where Fish Thomas is hangin' out. He might as well go along with us to Fort Sill. We'll pick up our cook on th' way."

We crossed the Arkansas on the ferry down at the foot of Garrison and took the road to Vian. We stopped on Little Vian Creek east of town midafternoon the second day, and I pulled Fish's warrant out of the folder. "Think you would know him if you saw him, Gam?"

"Sure."

"Well, he knows me too well for me to git within a hundred yards of him. Word gits around a deputy's in town an' a lot of people disappear. Folks don't know you, so you can git in an' out without causin' alarm. Ride in and check out the pool halls. That's where he'll be hangin' out. Look th' places over. If you see him, don't mess with him; come get me. You can't arrest him."

"Yessir. Do I get pool money?"

I dug a half dollar out of my pocket. "Don't spend it all in one place—matter of fact, don't spend it all."

"Yessir." He grinned and rode out of camp.

I made use of my time takin' care of the stock an' makin' camp. Toward sunset, Gam rode in. He dished up a plate of beans and pork, poured his coffee, and sat down to eat. "He's there; found him in the first place I went in. He was drinkin' with a feller he called 'Wat.'"

"Was this Wat short with a scar runnin' from his left ear to his jaw? He usually wears a hard-boiled hat."

"Yeah, that's th' fellow."

"We're gonna git two for one, Gam." Fred Watson was called Stubby, mostly behind his back, because of a peculiarity of his anatomy, and he was wanted just as much as Fish. "You say they were drinking?"

"Yeah. Didn't make a secret of it, either. We gonna go git 'em?"

"*I'm* gonna go get 'em." It was necessary that one of us stay in camp, or else we would return to find the place cleaned out down to the firewood. Even staying in camp, we had t' pay close attention to the livestock.

"When's that danged cook gittin' here?"

"We'll pick him up at Lake's Ferry. I'm just as anxious as you are t' git him, Gam. Say, you said the *first place* you went into, how many places *did* you go in?"

"All of 'em. You didn't want me t' give it all away by runnin' straight back here from the pool hall, did you?"

"No . . ."

"By th' way, here's your fifty cents back. Can I keep my winnin's?"

"You played pool?"

"Couldn't let those two know what I was up to. They sure

can't play th' game."

"I'm goin' t' town. Have Tumbleweed ready for two customers."

"They got horses sommers there."

"If they're sober enough, they'll be walkin' back." After sunset I rode in and tied up at the back of the pool hall. It looked like the traffic through the back door was pretty heavy. There were plenty hitchin' racks there. The only thing that separated this business from a saloon was the visible presence of alcoholic drinks. I bet with the right words, a fellow could get anything he wanted, and this close to Fort Smith. It was vexing.

I was depending on getting to the place between sunset and the time to light lanterns, when th' place was just dark enough to make it hard for someone t' recognize me. Fish and Wat were halfway to the front sitting at a table drinking supper. I walked up and picked up the bottle.

"Shay, buddy tha's my bottle." Wat reached for the bottle and I clapped a cuff on his wrist. Before he could move, I had Fish cuffed with the other end. "Whash goin' on?" He was more puzzled than angry.

"Well, first of all, I'm arrestin' you two for introducing alcohol into Indian Territory."

"Didn' in'erdoosh it, was here b'fore us."

"Where did you get it?"

"Good ol' T—"

"Sh-h-h, Stubby, he might be a dep'ty."

"You a dep'ty, misher . . . sha-a-a-y you didn' call me Shtubby, did you, Fish?"

I looked at the two of them. It sure took more than an afternoon to get this drunk. When I looked around, the place was empty except for three men playing faro. "Hey!" I called, "How long have these two been drinking?"

One of the men looked up, "Oh-h, I'd say about a week."

I plugged the bottle for evidence. "Stand up, fellers, let's take a walk in th' cool of th' evenin'."

"O-o-hkay, lesh go, Fish." Wat struggled to his feet, fell back into his chair, tried again, and failed again.

Fish just sat there grinning. "Where you been, Sht—"

"Don' call me tha'. I seen yore'n an' it ain't a bit bigger'n mine." He almost sounded sober. "Stan' up an' I'll sho-o-w you." Wat stood and began struggling with his pants, impeded by the handcuff. "Stan' up, I say," he shouted. Fish succeeded after a try or two and fumbled with his pants. "Turn loose o' me, Wat."

"Sha-a-y, what is this, Mishter?" Fish held up his manacled wrist.

"Just something t' keep me from losin' you in th' dark; let's go. Not th' front door, the back." They tried t' spin around. The cuffs hindered them and they stumbled. I grabbed them before they fell and guided them to th' back door. I tied a rope to th' link b'tween the cuffs and mounted, "Come on, boys, we're goin' for a walk."

"Where to?"

"How 'bout th' creek?"

" 'S all right by me; how 'bout it, Fish?"

"S'long es I don' havta dr-r-ink it." Fish giggled at his joke.

I led th' way and hoped no one would fall down. The ford was belly deep to a tall horse, and when we got there I hesitated about taking the men across. They didn't notice my stop and walked right on past me into the creek. Three steps and they were waist deep. I don't know who fell first, but before I could untangle the rope from me and my horse, they were both yelling and thrashing around until I was afraid they would drown. My horse took a couple of steps following th' pull of the rope and I heeled him on across, dragging the prisoners up on the bank where they lay choking and coughing.

"I think I swallowed some," Fish said and gagged and threw up. Stubby Watson just lay there groaning.

A torch came jogging from camp and Gam called, "What's goin' on there? That you, Lee?"

"It's me and two prisoners. Nothin's wrong, they just decided t' take a bath b'fore bedtime. Help me git 'em up."

The dunking had sobered the boys a little, and we had trouble convincing them to accept our hospitality and spend the night on Tumbleweed.

I rode back and took their horses to the stable. They weren't much; the stable would keep them awhile and probably sell them to cover their board.

Eventually, Fish and Wat quieted down and we slept. Th' way they both turned green when they smelled breakfast cooking convinced us not to even offer them food.

"Why's Wat's belt unbuckled?" Gam asked over his last cup of coffee.

"He was gonna expose th' fact that his name, Stubby, was a myth. Thank heaven that's still undetermined."

We crossed the Arkansas below Webber's Falls and headed towards Lake's Ferry on the Deep Fork. Our two prisoners were having a hard time of it, and an hour beyond the river crossing, Fish asked, "Are we there yet?"

"Where?" Gam asked over his shoulder.

"Fort Smith."

"Nope, we're goin' t' Fort Sill. You got on th' wrong stage."

"I'll be dead afore we git there," Wat groaned.

Fish lay back down without a word.

"I thought a long time afore I taken this job," Bass said as he laid his plate down and leaned back on his saddle. "It's a good job an' one a nigger can get ahead on, earnin' good steady money an' all. When I studied about th' danger, I d'cided if I was gonna take th' job, I was

gonna come out t' other side alive.

"*They's some requirements for stayin' alive an' doin' your job right. My old master wouldn't let me learn readin' an' writin', but he 'llowed I could learn t' shoot, an' he made sure I was good at it. 'Good' ain't enough; you gotta be* better *if you makes it. So you need t' git better. Th' next thing is you can't hesitate t' shoot a man if he needs it. Them that hesitates is mostly dead. You gotta use your head when you go after a man. If you can git him without shootin', you avoid a lot of trouble. Take him unawares an' take him alone. You don't kill a wasp sittin' on th' nest with a lot o' other wasps, you wait till he flies off alone, then you gets him. It ain't always th' right time t' get your man first time you sees him. You gotta be patient.*"

When we nooned on George's Fork northeast of Dunigan Mountain, Gamlin got out our folder and read through th' warrants. "Isn't there someone else around here we could pick up?"

"Nothin' b'tween here an' Younger's Bend," I said

"What's at Younger's Bend?"

Where has this boy been not to know about Younger's Bend? "Not much but old Tom Starr's boys and Belle."

"Belle Starr? Is she wanted?"

"Don't matter if she is. We ain't goin' t' Younger's Bend without an army."

"Why for?"

"Boy, where you been all your life? Don't you know about the Starrs and the outfits they run with? Those are bad folks and they don't tolerate U.S. deputies nosin' 'round their range. If there's a warrant out for one of them, the marshal will send a big posse t' see into th' matter, or we wait until the wanted man leaves the Bend t' grab him."

"Are you deputies scared of them?"

"Not scared, just smart. One o' th' things you want t' do in this business is stay alive."

"Well, I reckon."

"Then get smart an' get t' know your enemies. I warrant they's already a price on your head an' you aren't even a deputy."

"For real?"

"Yes, for real, Gam."

Bass Reeves is the only deputy I ever knew that could ride into Younger's Bend alone and live to tell about it. Belle Starr had a lot of respect for him, and she always made him welcome. When the horse thief charges came up against her, Bass was given the warrant to arrest her. A week or so after Bass left town, Belle showed up at the federal court and surrendered to the U.S. marshal. She had said more than once that she "did not propose to be dragged around by some deputy," meanin' she wasn't about to ride in someone's tumbleweed. It was Ol' Baz's practice that when he had a warrant for one of his many friends, he would advise the friend to turn himself in to the marshal at Fort Smith, and I'm sure that is what he told Belle. Bass made that request only once. The second time, his friend took a ride in Tumbleweed.

More than once, I have used the same method to good effect with people I knew. A deputy didn't have many friends, and it was not good policy to lose any of the few he had.

Chapter 5
New Management at Lake's Ferry

"*I see you're carryin' your gun lower an' tyin' your holster down,*" Bass said as we sat outside the courthouse watchin' people come and go. This guard duty on trial days was sure boring.

"*Yeah, I figger I better get faster if I'm gonna be goin' after outlaws.*"

"*You think a gunman sees you comin' he's gonna leave his gun in his pocket an' try t' beat you to th' draw?*"

"*Well, I think they's gonna be times I need a quick draw.*"

"*It sure ain't when you're goin' after a man. If your gun ain't in your hand when you knocks on that door, you may as well already be dead.*"

"*You didn't have your gun in your hand when you caught me.*"

"*No, but it was a lot closer than you thought, wasn't it?*"

For all his talk against fast draws, Bass Reeves was the fastest man on th' draw I knew. The secret was that he had a gun in his holster in plain sight and another gun inside his coat. It was natural for a man t' watch that right hand of his t' go for th' gun in his holster. Th' look of surprise when the man saw a gun appear in Bass's left hand as if by magic was priceless. He could shoot just as well left-handed as right. If he chanced to meet his quarry on horseback, Bass would put both hands on the horn, always with the left on top. An outlaw noted such things as well as seeing the holstered gun still looped down and on his right side. It sure lulled them into false confidence and Bass got his man.

"*You'd do better learnin' to be a good shot, for there's always gonna be someone faster, an' sooner or later you'll run up aginst him. I usually can tell if a man is th' fast draw kind by th' way he walks."*

"I tell by th' way he carries his gun."

"Can you tell if he ain't carryin?"

"Why no, can you?"

"Shore. See that feller just comin' through th' gate? He's a fast draw artist."

"How can you tell that? He ain't armed?"

"I can tell, Lee, 'cause he's limpin'. Most o' th' time a fast draw's first shot goes into th' ground or his foot. Likely he's alive today b'cause th' feller he went up aginst shot his foot and fainted. Don't go into a fight unarmed, an' you're unarmed if your gun's in your holster or pocket."

"Still helps if you're fast, don't it?"

"Sometimes, but I seen a lot of men as didn't get off th' first shot win a fight b'cause he could hit his target better. Lee, if we ever get in a fight an' I don't see your gun in your hand before the first shot is fired, I'm just likely t' shoot you first thing."

I could swear that Tumbleweed had a sign on her fifty feet high that said, "Beware, U.S. Deputy Marshal," and it didn't take me long t' catch on to th' fact that *no one* wanted to travel with us. Obviously, the outlaws didn't, but neither did the few honest folk, for they were viewed with suspicion by their neighbors. If a deputy got to nosin' around, the honest man was suspected of snitchin', and he and his suffered the consequences, whether guilty or not. As a result, when we were near communities or home places, we hid Tumbleweed from sight. That's where she was at Lake's Ferry when we stopped by to pick up Harmon Lake, our cook for this trip.

I didn't know if Harmon could cook, but I for sure knew Gamlin Stein couldn't. Harm seemed to be a smart kid and would be quick to learn—I hoped. He wasn't too sure how old he was. His ma opined he was between fourteen and fifteen. If so, he was big for his age. I figgered fightin' want would be a little easier for a grass widow with one less mouth t' feed.

There were two strapping big boys older than Harmon, Bud and Nick, and they had taken over operation of the ferry. Jess Wimpe hadn't poured out the moonshine like I told him, so the three boys had ganged up and whipped him off th' place. I made a mental note to keep my eye out for him and give him a free ride to Fort Smith when I found him.

The place was cleaned up considerably: hog pen moved to the back of the house, new porch deck replaced the old rotten boards, and the front door didn't sag anymore. The boys had done a good job cleaning up. Even Mrs. Lake was clean and groomed and better dressed.

Ferries are a good place t' catch those that are wanted, as almost everybody used the ferry, especially in times of high water, so we lazed around a few days just to see who would show up.

I was sitting on the dock turnin' a stick into shavings when this feller rides up, a wagon following. Without so much as a "Howdy," he growls at Nick, "Git this wagon over th' river an' be quick about it." He slapped his quirt against his leg for emphasis.

I showed only mild interest, and the boy led the team onto the ferry and pulled it across. He waited while westbound travelers loaded and came back across. Our rude customer showed his impatience and when Nick docked, gave him a sharp blow with the quirt. "Don't you ever dawdle when I'm crossing. Those people can wait until I'm through with the ferry." He rode his horse onto the ferry and without a word, the boy took him across.

It was obvious even from across the river that the man didn't pay, just loped up the road after his retreating wagon. Bud and

Nick watched him go and had a short conversation before the ferry brought another customer across.

I didn't say anything; just watched as the boys continued their work. Gamlin punched me with his cane, "Why'd you sit there an' do nothin'?"

"I got a feelin' this ain't over. Let's watch an' see what happens."

Gam grunted in disgust.

Some people are mighty shortsighted when it comes t' treating people right. They don't think of the future and the fact that they might have t' pass that way again. A kind word and prompt payment of debt will go a lot further than a growl.

We had good fishing at the ferry, I picked up a couple more men on my list, and the Lake boys were looking askance at this deputy hangin' around and pickin' up outlaws. It might begin t' hurt business. And still I hung around.

It was a week later when the man I was waiting on rode up to th' far side dock. We could tell by his manner and actions that his attitude had not improved any. Soon Bud, with Nick, was ferrying him over. He rode off the boat, turned his horse crossways in front of the line waiting to load, and said, "Go get my wagon; these people will wait."

Nick had tied up the boat, brushed his hands on his pants, and nodded toward a pile of crates waiting to be picked up by other customers. A kid not more than twelve years old stood behind the crates with a double-barreled shotgun as tall as he was laying across them. The waiting crowd and I moved to be out of line with those muzzles.

Looking at the cursing man, Bud said, "Number two buckshot, hair triggers, an' a nervous kid can be pretty dangerous, mister. Maybe you should step down here where it's safer."

Gam grabbed the horse's reins as the man stepped down and moved the horse out of range. He was too good a horse to shoot, that being th' advantage he held over his master.

The man raised his ever-present quirt to administer his form of justice, but just as quickly Nick produced his own long-handled buggy whip and delivered a blow that tore the man's britches at his thigh and left reddening welts across his legs. Before he could react, the whip backhanded him and wrapped around his buttocks. A strong pull turned him around, and while his back was turned Nick reached up, jerked the quirt from his hand, and in the same motion threw it into the river. He threw down the whip.

"Now, mister, I owe you somethin' more for the way you treated us before. If I can't whip you by myself, my two brothers here will help me, an' I'm pretty sure you can't whip th' three of us." With that, Nick proceeded to give the man what was probably the first whipping he got in his life, and it was thorough. He didn't take many blows until he hollered "Uncle" but either Nick didn't hear him or he wasn't finished.

Bud had to step in and hold him off. "That's enough, Nick; we don't want him kilt. Now, mister, you owe us for three crossings, and you might as well pay us for that wagon over there crossing. As soon as these people are loaded and over, we will bring it back."

The man was a mess. In spite of wiping blood from his face and his rapidly swelling eye, he managed to produce paper to pay his bill. Bud shook his head, "Silver or gold, mister, not paper." More digging produced the amount in silver. He looked around as if to gather his things, and the shootist behind the crates said in a squeaky voice, "Yore quirt went for a swim, mister."

Gam brought the horse back to the man. Just as he reached for the reins, the horse jerked and trotted off up the bank. "Now, I wonder what that horse was thinkin'?" Gam asked.

The man glared at Gam and demanded, "Don't stand there,

you dolt, go get him."

Gam took on a subservient attitude, "I would, I shorely would, but th' rheumatism has got aholt my hip an' I cain't hardly walk. Anyway, he won't stop for me. You're probably th' only one he will trust."

The man raised his fist as if to strike, and Gam held up his hand, palm outward. "Hold there, friend, you ain't got your quirt. I could help you into the river t' git it, but don't think I could make it to the top of th' bank after that horse."

It was a thoroughly demoralized man who disappeared over the riverbank after his horse. You will note that I have failed to give the man's name. That's because his family became quite prominent in the young Oklahoma Territory, though the man mentioned here never made any good and was seldom referred to even by family. There is no memory that he ever used Lake's Ferry again.

"I can't believe you just sat there the other day and let that man abuse Nick, an' then you let them fight today," Gam said as we let our supper digest.

"We ain't charged with keepin' peace, Gam, we're t' catch lawbreakers. B'sides they didn't any of them break th' law. I can't sit here and protect those boys, they're gonna have t' stand up for themselves, and I'd say they did that right well."

From Lake's Ferry, we drove west on th' divide, such as it was, between Deep Fork and th' North Canadian. It was early June and already there was no dew of a morning and the grass was drying up. The Chisholm Trail must have been three quarters of a mile wide. We crossed behind one big herd and watched the approach of another herd from the south. Several deputies made good by hangin' around the cattle trails when the drives were on. There was always trouble between Texians and Indians, and it wasn't hard to find someone who had broken the law in some way. The hard part was getting the culprit away from one of the drives without fighting the whole outfit. One bunch stole the deputy's tumbleweed with all his prisoners on it. They got their friend back and hired a couple of the other prisoners to go up th' trail before letting the remaining prisoners go. The deputy spent four days finding his wagon and getting it out of th' gulley it was in. Patrolling the cattle trails was too risky for me to try.

CHAPTER 6
LEE SOWELL, CATTLE THIEF

Bass pulled his horse up just before we topped the ridge. "It's best not to hunt th' fellers you're out to get, but t' let them come to you. Sometimes you have t' seem to be what you're not. A crook'll run from th' law, an' avoid an honest man if he can, but he's attracted to another outlaw.

"Study how those fellers act an' look an' try t' imitate them. You'll be surprised what you learn just by talkin' to 'em an' listenin'. Out of about twenty thousand blacks and whites living on Indian land, I doubt if there's five thousand of them honest people, an' an honest man stands out like a sore thumb."

It turned out that Harmon was a good driver. Over the time he drove for me, he put a bunch of extra miles on ol' Tumbleweed.

We were west of the Pottawatomie and Shawnee reservation in the Unassigned Lands and made camp on upper Bad Creek. Bad Creek is alkaline, but there's a sweet spring comin' out of a draw on the west side of the creek, and that's where we camped.

I had warrants for unnamed white men who were working with some Shawnees to run off cattle from the herds coming through the I.T. They were holding their stolen cattle somewhere in the Unassigned Lands. If we could find the herd, we might be able to catch several of them and possibly others that had no business in Indian Territory.

As th' creeks dried up, they would move their stolen stock south toward th' North Canadian, and later on maybe south to

51

th' South Canadian if it got dry enough. As they moved south, they would naturally concentrate their many little herds into larger and larger bunches. Eventually, they would have one or two herds, depending on the numbers, and they would get nervous about getting caught. Too, th' number of herds going north would taper off and there would be less cattle available t' steal and less eyes t' see thieves.

That would be the time they would strike out up th' South Canadian for New Mexico, where few people questioned a herd with so many different brands. It was buyers who didn't ask questions that they sought, and New Mexico was full of them.

The hazards of getting caught increased across th' Texas Staked Plains where rangers and cowmen alike watched for stolen herds. Brave thieves who didn't run when they saw a posse ridin' up didn't live t' gather another herd. *Killed Trying to Escape* became the epitaph for many a stock thief in Texas.

"Lee, how we gonna catch that bunch of cattle thieves? There must be twenty or more, th' way people talk."

"I think we'll nibble around th' edges an' pick 'em off one or two at a time. Only one man I know of ever accepted our invitation t' come an' eat supper on Tumbleweed."

"That's another thing, Mr. Lee," Harmon said, "we ain't got enough provender t' feed a big bunch o' prisoners."

"Don't count your prisoners till they're caught, Harm. We'll manage."

"Do like I did, Harm, and put more water in th' beans." Gam grinned.

"I catch you listenin' to Gam tell you how t' cook, I'll make you a passenger on Tumbleweed."

Harmon grinned. "No danger of that, Mr. Lee."

"It's late in th' season and most likely the last big herds have passed. These thieves are gettin' close to gatherin' the herds and pointin' them west. If we can catch small bunches before they join up, we should be able to arrest them without too much trouble."

"How you gonna get close to them in this open country?"

"I was thinkin' 'bout just ridin' into their camp in broad daylight."

"Like a fish needs spurs, you were."

"Think about it, Gam. Small groups of cattle joinin' up and headin' for New Mexico, no one's gonna think much of it if a feller turned a bunch of cattle into their herd and joined 'em."

"Only someone that worked with Bass Reeves crazy e-nough t' do somethin' like that."

"But it could work. Do you think you an' Harm could follow me an' stay out of sight until needed?"

"That dang wagon don't have t' be in sight to be heard. We need to stash it somewhere handy."

"On th' move like we'll be, there ain't no handy stashes available. She's gonna havta be close by all th' time." I thought about it a minute or two. "Here's what we'll do: I'll be a cattle driver. Gam, you stay out of sight and trail me. Come evenin' when we stop, you go back and bring up Harmon and our wagon to another hiding place. When I see a good time t' get 'em, I'll hang out my shirt to dry somewhere you can see it. Come in after we've turned in an' arrest all of us."

It took me an' Gam a couple of days t' gather a few strays out of the brush along the creek. Early on the third day I struck out with them looking for one of those small herds. Upper Flat Rock Creek was dry down to where Battle Creek came in and a little south of that, I found a herd being kept by three men and a kid. I watered my thirsty bunch and turned them into the herd with a wave to the two men, keepin' an eye on them. At their camp, I hailed the third man and the kid. "Got any frijoles an' coffee fer a workin' man?"

"Shore, stranger, how many did you turn into th' herd?"

"Nine steers, 'bout two year old; an' a cow, 'bout a hundred."

"You shoulda left that cow go."

"She'd be a might tough, but better than eatin' a steer worth real money," I said between bites.

"Tweed didn't say anythin' 'bout some stranger showin' up with strays."

I looked up in mock surprise, "He didn't? Why he was writin' out th' telegram as I rode away. Yuh didn' git it?"

"Seen any wires out here, feller?" the man growled.

"Folks call me Pony where I come from. You're welcome t' use it."

"This here's The Kid and 'round here, I'm known as Cap."

"Well I'll be a horny toad, my middle name's Cap, cousin— say you wasn't raised in a Missoury cane brake by a ol' mama wolf, was you?"

Cap almost smiled. "Nope, it was a she-bear in a hollow tree."

"Never heard o' that branch of th' fambly. Back home, we ain't so high-falutin'."

"Kid, go out and spell Pete awhile. Tell him we got company."

"But we ain't s'posed to herd till . . ."

"It's just fer a little while, Kid, not th' rest o' th' night."

The boy shrugged and rode out to the herd. In a few minutes a man rode in, ground-tied his horse, and poured himself a cup of coffee. He studied me carefully, and I was glad I had never seen him before. "Name's Pete," he said and continued sipping.

"Folks call me Pony."

"Nice steers you brought in, that your brand?"

"Me an' my partner's. We got a spread in th' Cherokee Outlet north of here."

"Out o' yore range a bit, aren't you."

"Might say I got pushed this-a-way. Quanna an' his boys is out huntin' buffalo an' when they couldn't find any on th'

Llano, they come in to th' Outlet. Shore made 'em mad t' find nothin' but Longhorns an' cowboys—d'cided t' rid th' world o' both.

"Burned us out, scattered our herd hell west an' gone. One o' my partners was killed and t'other was last seen toppin' th' rise goin' north on his Morgan. Ain't no Injun pony gonna catch him this side o' Kansas.

"I was doing my annual inspection o' th' insides of our haystack until they fired it. When it got too warm, I hightailed it south."

"Lucky your horse was comin' this-a-way."

"It was my dead partner's. He was eatin' hay on th' south side of that haystack an' d'cided t' go with me."

"Them steers must be half deer t' run with you like that," said Cap.

"I'm beginin' t' think that ain't Pony's brand," Pete said.

"You're right there, Pete. I figgered th' safest way t' git into your camp alive was t' make a donation. I picked them up along th' way. I figgered we'd both have a chance if they was four or five of us an' you-all knew those Injuns was comin'."

"You brung them Injuns in on us." Pete growled and threw th' leavins' of his coffee into th' fire.

"It's more like I'm runnin' *ahead* of them as they head south for their reservation. If I weren't, you'd be sittin' here fat and dumb till they rode in an' collected your scalps."

Cap looked at Pete, "What you thinkin'?"

"Sounds fantastic, don't it?"

I looked at Pete. "Which is most fantastic, me ridin' in here an' lyin' to you about Injuns, or Comanches lookin' for scalps? I ain't much into suicide either way."

Pete stared at me a long time and I didn't blink. "How far b'hind are they?"

"Maybe half a day, I'd guess."

"Cap, looks like we'll be movin' tonight. Better break camp."

"OK, send The Kid back in with th' packhorses. We'll be ready in a flash."

"Come with me, Pony, I'll get you a fresh horse an' you can help herd."

We didn't wait on Cap and Th' Kid, just rounded up and started the herd down Flat Rock Creek. We drove all night. Those fellers didn't have much thought about keepin' fat on th' cattle. By daylight we had come ten or twelve miles and reached th' North Canadian flats. After watering them, we drove them up a gulley and camped in the mouth where they couldn't get out past us, not that they were interested in that after walkin' all night. They grazed awhile, then bedded down.

The fourth man in the bunch was called AJ. He seemed a little slow. There bein' no need t' tend th' herd, we all laid around and slept some. Late in th' afternoon, I washed my shirt in th' river and spread it over a bush t' dry. I shore hoped Gam saw it.

Just after sunset I put my shirt back on and joined th' others around th' bean pot. Pete leaned back aginst his saddle. "Soon's it dark enough, we'll round up our stock an' drive up th' river. Don't make any moves t' indicate what we intend before it's too dark t' be seen."

"I been gittin' tingly feelin's on back o' my neck all afternoon. I'd swear we're bein' watched," Cap said. I sure hoped I knew who was watching.

Supper was almost over and I had just stood, when we were frozen by a call from the darkness, "Sit down, cowboy, you're surrounded by a U.S. marshal's posse and th' first one t' move is liable to git enough holes punctured in his hide t' ruin it."

"What the—" Cap fumbled for his rifle and a shot sounded from opposite the voice, the bullet knocking the coffee pot over. The fire hissed and sputtered. Cap froze and lifted his hands. I slowly sat, being sure my hands were in plain sight.

"That's good," Gam's voice from the darkness said. "Now I'm gonna call you out one at a time, and I want you to take a very slow walk south and follow my instructions. First one t' go is you with th' green shirt."

Pete was on the south side of the fire and he took great care to stand. He stared at me, his anger showing, then turned his back to the fire and stood waiting for more instructions.

"Walk forward three steps, Green Shirt, and drop your gun belt—very carefully."

Pete stooped to untie his holster and Gam's sharp command stopped him. "Untie that last. Loosen your belt an' let it drop. Now with your left hand untie that string." The gun belt fell free and Pete stood still. "Now put your hands in your hip pockets and walk ahead until you are told to stop."

Pete disappeared into the darkness and we heard a soft command from another voice. *Tarnation, Gam, what are you doing with Harmon out there?* Sweat rolled off my face and stung my eyes. My tongue went dry, and a cool drink of water would have been very good about then. We heard the soft rattle of a chain and it seemed forever before Harm called "secure."

"You with the checkered pants, you're next." AJ went ashen and shook as he rose.

"It's OK, AJ," Cap said. "Just go slow and do as the man says." The poor man looked on the edge of panic. Cap said, "I should go next, Marshal. AJ's too upset and might do something bad."

"I see. You can sit back down, AJ," Gam instructed in a gentle voice. A relieved AJ sat down and Cap stood. "Walk to where Green Shirt unloaded and do th' same." The process was repeated with Cap, and after what seemed an eternity, Harm called "secure" again.

"AJ, do you think you can do what Cap did, now?" I was

surprised at the gentleness in Gamlin's voice.

AJ nodded.

"OK, now you take your time an' I'll tell you *everything* to do."

"Y-y-yessir." AJ's voice trembled.

"Stand up."

"Yessir." The poor man was terrified. We knew if he panicked, nothing good would come of it. He obeyed step by step until he had his hands in his pockets, then he froze at the command to enter the dark. No amount of coaxing could convince him to move until Cap called from the darkness, "It's all right, AJ, I'm here and you can come to me." With Cap coaching, AJ approached the man, his hands still in his hip pockets. I heard Harm speak softly and in a moment, he called "secure."

The Kid was next, and he hurried through the process and was soon secure. Now came my turn, and Gam was not at all the gentleman with me. Twice, he threatened to shoot me, and when I got into the dark, he was rough with me until I resisted with many a harsh word. "You come with me. We're gonna have a little talk," he growled, and he led me into th' brush.

"Gamlin, I didn't expect you would include Harm in this thing," I whispered.

"Couldn't figger no way without him. Shore done good shootin' that coffee pot."

"They's gotta be a better way o' doin' this without exposin' th' boy to danger."

"Well, I didn't know anythin' else t' do at th' time. Now we got time t' think about it, we'll come up with a better plan. Th' trick when you're learnin' a lesson is t' stay alive during th' lesson, an' I'm learnin' a lesson t'night. It's tellin' me I ain't gonna do this agin."

Something glinted on Gam's shirt. "Say, you ain't wearin' my star, are you?"

"Cain't say I'se a deputy without'n it."

"You lose it an' it'll come out of your pay."

"What we gonna do now?"

"Well, I think you ought t' shoot me an' leave me out here."

"Say . . . that might work. You can steal the horses an' we won't have t' worry 'bout keepin' up with 'em."

"Just leave mine saddled and th' others tied loose, now shoot me."

Gam shouted a couple of times and fired into the ground. The world paused at the sound. After several minutes, he returned to the wagon and I heard him say, "Dad-blamed feller tried t' run."

I lay down under a bush and dozed a little until I heard Tumbleweed driving up to the fire. It wasn't long until all quieted down and the fire died to coals.

Th' Big Dipper said it was halfway from midnight to daylight when I awoke, stiff and chilled. *What the devil were we thinking about? I can't steal those horses without stealing mules an' all, and what would th' boys do without them?* I thought; then finally I came up with a plan that wouldn't give away everything.

It's impossible to identify someone in the blackness of night, and I had taught Gam and Harm how we could do that by knocking on something. I was one knock, Gam was two knocks, and Harmon was three. When I was away, Gamlin always took first watch, leaving Harm th' last half of th' night, so I knew the boy was most likely keeping watch from his favorite spot under the wagon. Easing around toward the place I thought the wagon was in, I stumbled into the tongue and it fell off its perch with a thump. In a moment, three taps came from under the wagon. Someone stirred among the prisoners. "What was that?" an anxious voice asked.

There was soft scraping as Harm stood up and answered, "Probably nothing. Go back to sleep and I'll check it out."

"Sure, I'll sleep while you stumble around in th' dark lookin' for boogers an' maybe gettin' yore throat cut. An' me on this chain like a fish on a line, just waitin' for my turn t' donate my hair to some Comanche."

"Shut up an' listen." Harm moved my way and rapped softly on the tongue. In a moment, his hand brushed my shoulder and I pulled him away into th' brush where we could talk.

"I'm gonna steal the animals, Harm, but I'll leave th' mules an' a couple of horses somewhere in the brush upstream. It wouldn't hurt for you to take all day t' find them. It would give me time t' scout out our next move. I don't care to do it like we did last night, and the next bunch we run in to will most likely be larger."

"Yessir; are you gonna take the cattle?"

"No, they've most likely scattered too much without any guardin'. We'll leave them where they are and let someone else take care of them. About five miles upstream, the river turns north, and it's another two miles or so to where a creek comes in from th' north an' just past that is an oxbow lake. Camp somewhere there and I'll find you. It may be three or four days. Yuh got enough chow?"

"We can make it if we get some meat."

"That shouldn't be too hard, with beef, venison, and fish available."

"Yessir."

"Help me get these horses on th' trail."

CHAPTER 7
DEATH IN A NARROW PLACE

Bass sat in his saddle, his hands resting on his saddle horn. "Sometimes, Lee, the law and justice gits taken plumb out of our hands. When that happens, th' onliest thing you can do is clap your hands, shout 'halleluiah,' an' go on."

We had been chasing a wife-killer for six days as he ran "from pillar to post" and all over th' country. This morning we had run across his trail and deduced that for some reason he was headed for his home place. We could smell the smoke long before we rode out of the woods into his yard and saw the still smoldering ruins of the man's shack. And there, swinging lazily from the limbs of the chestnut tree in his former front yard was our quarry. His body was still warm. Our chance of collecting a nice reward for his capture had died with him.

"We git so caught up in this business of catchin' people for th' money in it that we forget that it's about what's right and just. That feller got judged by someone b'sides Judge Parker an' he got what he deserved. Halleluiah an' amen. I'm goin' to supper." And that's just what Ol' Baz did.

We kept the animals tied to the picket rope and I led them away from camp. A half mile up th' river, I tied our ridin' mule under a tree and hoped Gam found him. He hates ridin' mules. A couple of more miles and I left the other mule munching grass. About sunrise, I tied the end of the picket line to a tree and left the last three horses on it. They had plenty of room to graze on

61

the end of that fifty-foot rope. That left me four horses to drive, and we moseyed up the river flats, giving the horses time to graze.

As if they rose from the bowels of the earth, four men caught my four grazing horses and two more appeared either side of me, not fifty feet away. I didn't have to look behind me to know someone was there also. I didn't move, my hands on the horn. By their dress, I guessed they were Seminole. "Move on up there toward the middle of those horses." The man behind me slapped my horse's rump and we moved ahead into the middle of a circle of men.

"Why do you have our horses?" the man behind me asked.

I turned to face a tall turbaned man who held an old muzzle-loading Kentucky rifle. This could only be one man. "Because, Puma, I took them from the men who stole them from you."

The man showed no emotion when I called him by his name; he just stared at me a moment and said, "Get down."

My right foot had barely touched the ground when the reins were grabbed under the horse's chin and I jerked my left foot free as he was led away. Puma towered over me and stared. "I do not know you."

"I know you because it is the business of every U.S. deputy marshal to know the chiefs."

"Why do you have our horses?" he asked again.

"Because I have the four men who stole them on my wagon in chains. I am trying to catch the cattle thieves who run their stolen herds to New Mexico."

"You have no star," he said as he tapped my chest with his rifle barrel where my badge should have been.

"I can't wear my star in the middle of their camp and live long, but you can see the holes where my star has been worn." I opened my vest for him to see.

He barely glanced at them. "What is your name?"

"Lee Sowell." I saw from the corners of my eyes that a couple of the men who surrounded me nodded.

Puma showed no sign of recognition. "We have vowed to kill the men who stole our horses." I knew the implication of his words, but chose to ignore the fact that he meant me.

"I have them in chains on my wagon, and they will have to answer to Judge Parker first. Perhaps he will hang them for you." That wasn't likely, but I couldn't help throwing him a bone along with the fact that I was innocent and held the culprits. *And* I wasn't about to let them take away my livelihood without a fight.

"Deputy not get paid for dead men," one of the men in the circle said.

There were smiles and nods, except for Puma. "We have made a vow."

"I also have made a sacred vow to Judge Parker to bring these men to white man's court. It may be that both of us can keep our vows if Puma is as wise and patient as I have been told."

There was a flicker of amusement in his eyes. He knew bull when he heard it. "What does Lee Sowell propose?"

"There are too many thieves for one or two men to safely catch. If the Seminole would help, we may be able to catch them all and stop the thieving."

"More thieves would come," one of the men said.

"Yes, there will always be thieves, but if they know the chances of getting caught stealing Seminole stock are sure, they would not bother them. These things become known among thieves."

"We do not care about white man's cattle." Puma's dislike of white men was obvious.

"Ah-h-h, but the Seminole love their horses and the thieves have stolen their best," I countered, indicating the four horses.

"Do you have a plan to get these men?" Maybe Puma was interested after all. The Seminole love war and would fight just for the fun of it.

"I have no plans for a one-man attack on fifteen or twenty men, but if I had seven Seminole warriors, I would take on an army."

"Lee Sowell has smooth tongue," one of the men said.

"Lee Sowell speaks truth," I replied. "The Seminole warriors are feared among the people for good reason."

Puma had not taken his eyes off me as I spoke. Now he seemed to relax some and said, "We will talk more about this. You will come with us." He turned, and without looking back, strode into the woods and brush. I was urged forward with the muzzle of a rifle.

The brush thinned as we left the river bottoms and climbed the hill. Just inside the edge of the woods was the Seminole camp. Somewhere in the brush, I heard a horse snort. One of the men motioned for me to remove my saddle. When it was off, the five horses were led away. My rifle was in its boot on the saddle and there had been no attempt to disarm me. They did not think it was necessary so long as one or more of the men were near.

Puma sat on a blanket back from the fire some and motioned me to sit near. An elderly woman brought us cups of hot coffee. "Have you seen these men who steal our stock?" he asked.

"Only their tracks. I would guess there are between fifteen and twenty of them, and they probably have a couple hundred head of cattle and close to a hundred horses," I answered.

"There are seventeen men and one boy who herds the horses and they keep him tied up at night," Puma replied.

"Do you know any of them?"

Puma shook his head. We drank our coffee in silence for a few minutes and I asked, "You would kill all of them?"

He looked at me, and his answer was obvious without a word spoken. I didn't blame him, but I had to try to stop him or an army of U.S. deputies would be looking for him in the near future. "It may be that some of those men have a price on their head. I would share the bounty with you. I would have to take the men to Fort Smith to get the reward."

"Horses are my money. I need no gold."

"Gold will buy you more horses."

The chief shrugged. "Where are they now?"

"They camp at Sand Creek and argue about how to get to the South Canadian. Likely they are also waiting for another herd to join them," I added.

"They will go up Sand and by Chimney Rock over to Tiger Creek. Water will be much trouble to find."

"How will you catch them?" I asked.

"There is a narrow place up Sand Creek where we will wait."

I wondered if it was as narrow as the place I was in at the moment.

I was well acquainted with the North Canadian, but had never explored Sand Creek. I didn't know its meanderings and how far up the creek the narrow place was.

Just after sunset, an Indian rode into camp and over his cup told us the thieves were packing to leave their camp early in the morning. "We must be in place tonight," Puma said and the men prepared to leave.

We rode directly to the narrow place, and I was surprised that it was no more than five miles from the Seminole camp. It was still daylight when we got there. A better place for an ambush would be hard to find. The narrows were not more than twenty yards wide and a quarter-mile long. Bluffs lined both sides. When it ran, the creek took up a good portion of the bottom.

Without a word said, the men took their positions, one leading the horses off to a hidden place. Puma showed me a trap they had made by burying a rope across the downstream end of the narrows and tying it to a tree. On the near side, the rope was strung over a stout limb and tied to a deadfall log propped up on a forked limb. When the log fell, the rope would be jerked taut about chest high for a man on horseback. Should any try to turn and run, they wouldn't get past the rope.

As we walked along the top of the bluff, I noticed several boulders scotched with rocks, ready to be rolled off. Each man had built himself a little rock fort with a hole to shoot through just in case the fight lasted longer than they had planned. They knew the men they were going against would not give up easily and were well acquainted with warfare of any nature. It was obvious there was going to be a battle here, and the survival chances of the men I wanted were slim. Even those captured alive would not be for me, and there was no way I could steal them and, draggin' Tumbleweed, avoid these Indians. If I got any of those men, it would have to be by some means that would satisfy the Seminoles.

Way into th' night I pondered the situation, but found no solution. The thunder of hooves awakened me to a new day, and to the sight of a hundred horses running through the narrows, followed by the herd of steers and cows, urged on by a dozen men riding low on their ponies.

Somewhere beyond my vision I heard several shots fired. The cows milled about in confusion. More shots, and the cattle turned and began moving back the way they had come. A mill became a trot and the trot became a stampede. Cowherds ran for their lives. I knew the rope was up and ran along the top of the bluff. There was little confusion at the rope. The cattle ran on without impediment. The sight of one, two, or three riders and a half-dozen riderless horses running ahead of the cattle told another story and I turned away.

One of the Seminoles stood beside me and smiled. "The cattle have done our work for us."

I clapped my hands and shouted "Halleluiah, A-a-men," to the man's utter astonishment.

Me an' Bass Reaves got into a gun fight with these two Anglos wanted for murder and robbery. We had t' kill both of them, one in front of his wife and kids. There was a minute or two when I thought we would have t' shoot th' widow, but Bass got her calmed down. He set me to supervisin' tumbleweed passengers diggin' a grave while he talked to the woman. Neighbors appeared as if by magic, carrying covered dishes and helping prepare the bodies for burial.

When all was ready, Bass opened his Bible and quoted several passages of scripture. He said a few kind words about the two men, then sang "Amazing Grace" as beautifully as any I ever heard. It must have comforted the widow and congregation, for they all complimented him after the service.

"A deputy U.S. marshal has t' wear many hats, Lee," Bass said, returning his boxed Bible to his saddlebags. "You a religious man?"

"Not too much. Pa said we was Baptists, but we went to ever' preachin' that come along. I guess I'm as religious as anyone else in this country."

"Well, if you ain't, you're gonna hafta pertend you are, for a deputy runs into more than his share o' funerals. Nine times out of ten, you'll be th' only one present who knows how t' run one. If you ain't got one, git yourself a Bible an' mark out some scripture t' read. It's always good to have a few words t' say which would be a comfort to th' bereaved. You be thinkin' on these things, for th' next occasion we have, you are gonna preach th' funeral."

"Did you ever preach a wedding, Bass?"

Bass grinned, "Sometimes new deputies asks too many questions."

★　★　★　★　★

I've heard cowboys talk about men caught in stampedes and how they were stomped to rags, but it didn't prepare me for what I saw in that narrow place. Only two bodies were together enough to bury. The rest were trampled into the ground or scattered along the path of the cattle. There was even one man out in the more open ground who could not outrun the stampede. His horse had fallen and they both were trampled by the herd.

The narrowness of the canyon had caused the herd to be strung out and resulted in more damage to the victims than would have happened in open country. A small herd of less than three hundred head had done as much damage as a thousand cattle on the open prairie.

The Seminole paid little attention to the bodies. They had their horses back and that seemed to satisfy them. They drove them back through the narrow place and on down the river, leaving me alone with the dead. I rode back down the river until I saw Tumbleweed approaching, then turned and rode slowly back up Sand Creek to the narrow place.

While Harmon took care of the wagon and prisoners, Gam and I rode over the ground.

"Dear Lord in heaven, look what happened to these men," Gam said to himself.

The rope still sagged across the gap, and four bodies could be discerned within a few feet of it. The fact that there was not one horse carcass near them gave testimony as to how the men came to be on the ground.

Harm walked over and when he saw the carnage, he turned a little green and returned to the wagon. Gam helped him supervise a couple of prisoners digging a grave and gathering rocks to cover it. I caught up with one of the surviving horses and got a bedroll from behind the saddle. We rolled the two bodies we could recover in it and laid them out by the grave.

When all was ready, we gathered the prisoners, and I read from Ecclesiastes, chapter three, and finished with the Twenty-third Psalm. I couldn't say anything about the men, not knowing them at all. We lowered them into the ground side-by-side and buried them. It was a quiet evening around the fire.

"What we gonna do 'bout those bodies in th' canyon?" Gam asked. He always assumed we had responsibilities above and beyond gatherin' living outlaws.

"I've thought on that, Gam, an' decided t' just leave them alone an' let nature take its course. Next time we're this way, we'll pick up their bones an' give them a proper burial."

"Seems awful harsh t' just leave them there," Harm said.

"I guess it does, but do you want to go pickin' up body parts an' gore? And do you think we can persuade these prisoners t' do it? We'll miss a lot of body parts because they are buried under th' sand. Coyotes and wolves'll dig them up for us an' we'll come nearer gettin' th' whole that-a-way."

"Seems awful . . ."

"Tell you what, Gam, we'll go find you a long box an' dig a grave while you collect body parts and we'll have a proper buryin', what d'you think?"

"I was thinkin' th' prisoners could . . ."

"Gam, don't ever ask a prisoner—er anyone else for that matter—t' do something you wouldn't—lessin' it's cookin'."

Those outlaws that got away scattered north and east from the bottoms. We didn't stand a chance of catching them, so I decided to move on up Sand Creek, cut west to Snake Creek, and up over th' divide in hopes of running across more stolen herds. Along the South Canadian would be the place most likely to have cattle traffic.

We could occasionally get a whiff of th' putrefaction already going on in the narrow place as we passed by on the bank above. In places, the ground was black with flies, and we pulled our bandannas over our faces to keep them away. Even the stock were bothered by the smell and vermin, and we had no trouble getting them to keep up the pace.

CHAPTER 8
TUMBLEWEED RESCUE

Ol' Baz dipped the chunk of meat on his knife in the gravy and chewed it slowly. "We rarely have time t' plan out how to git a man— and if'n we did, it would rarely go like we planned. Th' best we can do is plan out carefully how we're gonna start, *then put it into action. Gener'ly a good start is all you need, for the rest of the action will depend on conditions you can't foresee. Git th' advantage first, an' if you can't start with an advantage,* don't start.

"Clean rags, a little salve, an' a little medicinal whiskey will take care of a lot of hurts. If it don't, that shovel we're carryin' will take care o' th' rest. Most o' our diggin's three-by-six holes. With luck, you'll have a tumbleweed passenger or two t' do th' diggin'.

"Trouble's always not far away from a deputy, an' if it's too big, another deputy is likely nearby. Keep track of their whereabouts as much as you can."

Little River was still flowing some and we followed it south until it turned east—must have crossed it a dozen times—then we continued south and west to the South Canadian bottoms. We set our camp up Negro Creek where there was water, and Gam and I rode down to the Canadian early next morning.

We found that only a small herd of cattle had passed up the river in the last week or so. They were driven by two men. There was nothing for us to do but keep watch and let the thieves come to us, so we made camp comfortable and kept watch on the river bottoms from the bluff northeast of the mouth of

Negro Creek.

As usual, Gamlin was restless and Harm worried about his food supply. The boy had become a fair cook and an efficient camp keeper. Things were much better than when Gam was cook.

The evening of the fourth day, six or eight cowhands drove four or five hundred head of cattle into the flats across the river from the bluff. The gloom kept us from determining an exact count of the men.

Gam was excited. "We could fill Tumbleweed to th' gills with prisoners, Lee, an' some of them would have t' walk."

"Don't count your chicks afore they hatch, Gam. We got to catch them first—*and* stay alive doin' it. Let's watch an' see how they operate. Somethin' will turn up."

We watched as they made camp back in the brush away from the river and listened as a wagon found its way to camp. I started involuntarily as it came into sight in the gloom, and Gam swore.

"That's a tumbleweed, Lee, an' they's four men chained in it!"

"I see that. Be still and watch. The question is, who are they? Do we have a crooked deputy or a deputy and his crew made prisoners?"

"Either way it don't look good . . . say, did you see that?"

"See what?"

"That lead mule on th' wagon has a white head."

"Are you sure? Only white-headed mule I know of is Trace Price's hinny. Gam, I *know* that man ain't crooked."

"Th' question is, if he's on that wagon, why is he still alive?"

"If he is, it's for sure his days are numbered. We gotta find out."

There was no use in watching anymore. It was too dark, and they were out of sight in the brush. At camp, I pulled out some of the weapons we had confiscated from our prisoners and cleaned and loaded fully the best four revolvers in the bunch.

Gamlin checked the loads in our shotgun. "This will come in handy close in," he said.

I had been studying the situation and what we were going to do, and had come up with a plan. "Gam, I want you and Harmon to get you a place on the bluff where you can cover the flat good. I am going to try to get to the wagon and see for sure who is on it. If they are our friends, I'll give them the guns and tell them to hold off until they are out in the open in the morning. We want to take as many of these fellers alive as possible. Don't shoot to kill unless you have to, but when things start, I want you to make yourselves known so the outlaws will see what they are up against. Maybe we can bluff them into giving up. Try not to let any of them escape. Kill the runner's horse, if you have to, and in the extreme, shoot the man."

"Where are you gonna be?" Harmon asked.

"I'm not sure, but I will wear this green bandanna around my neck. Most likely, I'll be afoot. It's in my mind now that I will go upstream and try to stampede the cattle back on the outfit. If I don't do that, I may be sitting on that tumbleweed with Price."

We watched from the bluff until we were sure there was only one man riding night-herd. I slipped off the downstream end of the bluff and crossed the river at the shoals where an island sat in the middle of the river. This put me in a position to come up on the camp from the back. My hope was that the brush would be thick enough to hide my approach. I had a pretty good idea where their camp was, but by the time I got close enough t' see, th' fire had died down and all I had as a guide was an occasional snort from the animals tied somewhere in the brush. It was dark—black dark—and I had literally crawled under the wagon before I knew it. After I stopped shaking, I backed out and very cautiously stood next to the wagon. The high sideboards were just below eye level, but that didn't matter since there was no way to see anything.

I could hear soft breathing from someone sleeping against the sideboard right under my nose. There was a crack between the sideboard and the wagon floor, and the sleeper's side was against it. I punched the body twice and the soft breathing stopped. After two more firm pokes, the person sat up and leaned against the sideboard, his head resting on the top edge. With my mouth as close to his ear as possible, I whispered, "This is Deputy Lee Sowell, who are you?"

"Ozzie Dabney." Osgood Dabney was Tracey Price's wagon driver and guard. I had encountered him a time or two around the jail. Trace was high on him and his abilities, so I believed he could be trusted. A light rattle of chains reminded me he was manacled and I asked, "Where are your spare keys?"

"Under the nameplate on the back tailgate."

I started to move, then hesitated.

"To the right."

"Don't move." I found the nameplate by feel, and with my knife pried it back a little. The keys were in a hollowed-out place behind it. I pushed the plate back in place as best I could and returned to Osgood.

"Don't move, Ozzie; I'll put the keys in your jacket pocket. Here are some guns with *all* chambers full and enough shells for another round for each gun. Don't start anything until you are out in the open so my sharpshooters on the bluff can help. I am going up the river and try to stampede the herd back against the cowhands. How many are there?"

"Eight."

"Let's try t' take as many of them alive as possible."

Without another word, I dropped to the ground and crawled back the way I had come. At the upper end of the flat we were on, the hills came right down to the river. The outfit would have to cross the river to the flats on the west side. I worked my way up the hill to a place where I had a good view of the flat and the best crossing. Hopefully, I could stop the herd there, but for sure, I wasn't going to let the men get across the river. We were in a great bend of the river, and when it was light enough, I could see that my position put me almost directly opposite the bluff. We would all have to be careful not to shoot one of our own.

Activity increased as the light did, and soon preparations were under way to move. Seven men were riding out to gather up the herd. The eighth would be driving the wagon. It moved out on the flat with that blessed white-headed mule in the lead team. The driver turned and drove along the foot of the bank toward the crossing just below me. All I could do was watch. As they neared, their speed increased until they were running ahead of the herd. The driver was Ozzie, and he turned the wagon so sharply it tilted on two wheels for a moment. He drove straight into the cattle, two of the occupants rising to fire into the air and shout. Instead of stampeding, the herd began to mill. Round and round they trotted while the riders tried to stop them. A lone rider galloped out of the campsite, his gun banging away at the outlaws. I cursed my luck, for all I could do was watch. The nearest two fell from their horses, and two men turned and ran down the river. A shot from the bluff felled the lead horse. He fell on his rider. Another shot knocked the second man from his horse. Why didn't I bring my rifle? I sailed off the hill and ran along the edge of the brush out of the herd's reach.

The remaining three riders milled about each other, firing now at the bluff, at the charging rider, and the wagon bearing down on them. There was no escape and, fortunately for us, no hero in that bunch to go down fighting. They threw down their guns and raised their hands.

No one was paying attention to the two riders who ran for it, and the man trapped under his horse was trying to dig his rifle out. He stopped and cursed me roundly as I came up. Leave it to me t' pick th' one to show fight, for his handgun appeared in his hand and I had to shoot him. My lucky shot hit his arm and he dropped the gun.

The man fainted, and I took the opportunity to relieve him of the pistol and an ugly-looking bowie knife in his belt. The other man's horse stood nearby. It only took a moment to catch him and pull the dead horse off the man. As the dead horse slid away, our friend grabbed for the rifle.

"Hold still there, or I'm gonna hafta kill you in spite of it all," I shouted.

He lay back, his good fist beating a hole in the sand. "My laig's busted; heard it snap." He was stuck but wouldn't squeal. His ripped-up shirt stopped the bleeding in his arm. Fortunately, the bullet had passed through without hitting bone.

"If you don't mind, lay still there, friend, while I tend to those others." His running partner was just a kid, too young to even grow a beard. He lay on sand darkened by his life's blood.

Already, the others had the three riders trussed into the wagon with their would-be wagon driver. The first two who had fallen under Trace Price's charge were both sitting up, their fight gone. It was a relief to see that their wounds were not of the serious kind. One shot had passed through a shoulder, probably breaking the collarbone, and the other man had been shot in the leg.

I had the bleeding stopped on both men when the wagon pulled up. "These are ready to ride, but we've got a leg bone t' set over there." I nodded toward the two forms lying on the sand.

Gamlin stood over the boy's body. "I tried not to hit him hard, Lee. He's just a kid, ain't he?"

"A kid doin' a man's job takes on a man's responsibilities,

Gam. He wouldn't have died if his bleedin' could have been stopped in a timely fashion."

Deputy Tracey Price stepped down from his horse and shook my hand. "Shore glad you boys came along when you did, Lee. You saved our lives."

"We didn't 'come along,' Trace, we was waitin' for these cattle thieves t' 'come along' to us. It shore surprised us that white-faced mule had allowed you t' throw in with this outfit."

"He was aginst it all along, but Winchesters an' Colts carried th' deciding votes."

"We'll give you boys time t' think up th' most likely lies t' tell about how you got caught. Right now, we got a leg t' set, an' we might as well set this camp back up. We'll take most of th' day up doctorin' an' buryin'," I said.

"Harm's gone for our wagon, Lee," Gam put in. "I should go help him, an' it would be good if some of you help us ford th' river."

Trace stood up and rubbed his hands on his pants, "Oz, you an' Jess keep this herd together. When the boys show up with their wagon, help them across th' river. Boog, pull up to the camp and set up. We got a big bunch t' feed an' not much t' feed them on—probably need t' butcher one o' these slow elk."

"And I guess that leaves you an' me t' set that dang leg," I growled. Ozzie turned away to hide his grin.

"Well, I guess it does at that." Trace grinned and slapped me on th' back. "B'lieve you me, this is one job I'm gonna relish." It was the first time I noticed th' bruises on his face and his split lip. The bloodstains on his dark shirt were hardly notice-able unless you looked close.

We walked over to our patient, who watched us with alarm. "You ain't gonna touch me, Price. Git away from here."

"Lee, I want you to meet Spider Sutton, cattle thief and would-be comanchero, a man not too good t' beat another man with manacled hands."

"I mean it, Price, don't you lay a hand on me." Spider crawled backward on his elbows and good foot, dragging his useless leg.

"You wouldn't squeal over a broke laig, an' yer squealin' now afore you're touched? You ain't been up to some kind of mischief have you?" I asked.

"He set himself t' deliver a U.S. deputy marshal an' his crew to Comanches for disposal at their pleasure."

"Naw, I don't believe you. Spider wouldn't do that. The very idea of a white man turnin' another white man over to them savages—why it just don't happen, Trace."

"I was jist funnin' you, Trace. I wouldn't do that." Still, the man couldn't hide the animosity in his voice. "My laig's OK; it don't need nothin'."

Trace nudged the man's foot a little and Spider turned three shades of pale.

"But he didn't squeal," I muttered.

"I shore hope we find some straight splints. I don't want you limpin' to th' gallows. Folks might say I done you wrong, Spider, an' that jist wouldn't do." Spider's leg had swelled above the knee so much that his overalls were stretched tight. Trace knelt and split his pants to his hip. "Gener'ly, a leg'll break below th' knee when a horse falls on it. Looks like you made the exception to that rule."

"Don't go anywhere, Spider, while we get the operation table ready for you. I'll get th' splints, Trace; you get th' other stuff."

"I bet Spider has all we need in his bedroll," Trace said as he undid the roll from Spider's saddle. Spider groaned.

"Say, Lee, you wouldn't have any o' that *medicinal* whiskey, would you?" Trace called. "I'll need a good bracer afore we set that leg."

CHAPTER 9
A CHANGE OF VENUE

It had been a rough trip, bad weather, broken wagon, and lost stock. Bass looked at the four hundred dollars in his hand. "Least I ever made on a trip, Lee, an' th' most expensive trip. You might expect they'd go t'gether. Nothin' t' do but t' keep on doin'. We're gonna git outfitted an' go agin as soon as possible; cain't quit now."

We gave Spider Sutton a good stiff drink, then sipped a little ourselves while that took effect, gave him another drink, and set to work on his leg. It took us some time to get the splints to hold on his upper leg without slippin'. Pulling the leg below the break was hard because of the swelling, but we finally got it stretched out to where we figured the lower break cleared the upper one. Sutton never made a sound, and we gave him another drink before we lined the leg up where we thought it should be and let the tension off so the break could come together. Sutton's clothes were soaked with sweat an' I suspect somethin' more than sweat and he passed out.

"Let him sleep right there, we'll move him later," I said.

"For sure ain't goin' anywhere for a while." Trace walked toward camp rubbing his hands together. Neither one of us was any drier than Sutton.

Our wagon was pulled under the shade of the brush and Boog and Harm were busy cooking. Booger Jones was a black man and one of the best camp cooks I ever knew. All the deputies were after him to quit Price and cook for them. The demand forced Trace t' pay extra to keep him, but he was worth it to a man who loved his food. I never cared that much for food myself.

Both tumbleweeds were brimming with prisoners. The two wounded men were allowed to rest on the ground, chained to the wagon wheels. The stock had been turned loose to the herders and were grazing in the flat with the cattle.

After we ate, Price and I moved off to ourselves. Seated where we could keep an eye on both camp and pasture, we talked about our situation.

"We were fresh out of Fort Smith an' had got as far at th' Chisholm Trail when these fellers attacked us in th' middle of th' night; had us without a fight. So we spent the last ten or twelve days as passengers on our own tumbleweed. I tell you this, any man that has t' spend time on that wagon in chains oughter have his sentence reduced and be glad he don't spend his whole term on that contraption."

"I could tell that without th' experience, Trace; what were these yahoos up to asides stealin' cattle an' horses?"

"They have a date with comancheros outta New Mexico. The only reason we are alive today is that they were gonna give us to those wild Comanches and Kiowas, then sit and watch them work on us. Sutton and a couple others have a right vi-re-al hate for U.S. deputies."

I picked up a stick and started carving a toothpick. "We've been on th' trail of cattle thieves that have been preying on th' trail herds and ranchers. They have a good business stealing cattle and running them to New Mexico to sell to ranchers and traders who don't know what brands mean. We knew they were gathering for the drive so came out ahead to welcome them when they got here."

"We're sure glad you did, Lee. You saved our bacon for shore. We got enough prisoners t' make a load for both of us if we started in today." Price scratched in th' sand with a stick and was silent for a moment. "Lee, these boys were on their way to meet those comancheros and trade cattle for silver. Now, those Mexicans have a price on their heads . . ."

"I ain't about t' go 'cross that Estacado desert, dodging hostile Injuns, on th' off chance we might catch a bunch of greasers with a price on their heads."

"No, no, Lee, it ain't like that at all; *these comancheros are comin' all th' way to Indian Territory.* They'll be in our jurisdictional territory, an' th' Texas cattlemen will pay us a bounty for 'em. All we got t' do is catch 'em—"

"*And* dodge Injuns all th' way back t' Fort Smith. Th' catchin' ain't sure an' th' rewardin' ain't sure an' reachin' Fort Smith with our hair ain't—"

"Listen to me a minute, Lee, hear me out afore you d'cides somethin'. They're gonna meet the Mexes on Sweetwater Creek *in Oklahoma.* I know th' place. Been all over that country. We can leave our prisoners and one wagon at Fort Sill, stock up and drive this herd to th' meetin' place, gather us up a bunch of those comancheros, and take them *and* the herd back to Sill, where Texas Rangers will take the prisoners an' th' Texas Cattlemen's Association will pay us for the prisoners and every Texas cow in th' bunch—an' they're 'bout all Texans."

"I'll think on it, Trace." I said it mostly to get him off my back. His scheme was outside the normal deputy routine an' I wasn't comfortable with it. It didn't seem right t' capture outlaws and turn them over to out-of-state lawmen for a reward. I hopped up at the thought of Sutton still lying out there on the sand. "Spider's gittin' hot in th' sun, Trace, we better gather him in. Hey, Harm, you an' Boog come here a minute an' help us."

Sutton was dry and that was a worry; he should have been sweating. We rolled him on his side and stuffed his bedroll under him, and the four of us carried him to the shade of a wagon. I expected t' hear a lot of cursin' from the man, but he was quiet, and that was more worry.

"Get him some water, Harm, an' see if he wants anything to eat." I saddled up and rode out to relieve the herders. I needed time to think away from distractions.

Price's proposal was bothersome because we would not be working for the Judge, and that had been my idea of what my job was to be. Except for a time or two when I had to take a prisoner to the Paris office in Texas, I had taken all my prisoners to Fort Smith. It was an easy routine and didn't require a whole lot of thinkin'. I guess I had built me a nice little cocoon to operate in, and gettin' out of it was not comfortable at all.

Still, we would be goin' after lawbreakers, and they were inside our territory. Our job was to catch people like that, put them out of business, and bring them to the law to be tried. I didn't remember anything in my oath that stipulated which law they were to be given to, and it seemed right for Texas state law to have them since the crimes were against Texans and their property. The comanchero trade had been focused on Texas cattle. It had fostered the Indian aggression against Texans in these latter years by trading guns and ammunition for cattle and horses. The practice of stealing women and children and bartering what was left of them to the Mexicans was especially distasteful. The Mexicans did not buy the victims back out of compassion; it was a business transaction to them. One way or another, this had to be stopped.

What was it Bass had said? *"We ain't in th' killin' business; we're in th' delivery business an' our 'goods' is bad men."* That is so-o right. We got paid for capturin' outlaws, and I'm sure Texas money is just as good as U.S. money. Fort Sill was a lot closer than Fort Smith and that was sure a plus. Trace said th' pay from th' state was better than what that federal marshal paid.

All things considered, the whole proposition wasn't too bad. I wrestled with it for quite awhile before I made up my mind.

It was midafternoon before someone thought t' come out and relieve me. I caught up a fresh horse and rode back to camp for a bite to eat. Gamlin came and sat with me. "Did you hear where these boys is headed, Lee? Trace wants us t' go with 'em."

"Trace Price has *ambitions* that go beyond his *ability*, Gam, an' we ain't gonna git caught up in them."

"We ain't goin?" The boy was incredulous.

"No, we ain't goin' less'n half th' Fort Sill army goes with us. They's still wild Comanches and Ki-o-ways out there, an' if that ain't enough, those 'tame' Injuns at th' fort'll steal away an' do us mischief. It'll be a fight all th' way there an' all th' way back, and no guarantee we'll catch anything but hot lead and arrows."

"But, Lee . . ."

"Don't 'but' me; we ain't goin'. We'll go to Sill, restock, an' turn right around for home. We'll hafta skip Fort Supply this trip."

"I can't believe you'd pass up a deal like that."

"Believe it, Gam, an' I'll sleep better not worryin' 'bout keepin' our hair. Ain't it true that a bird in th' hand is better'n two in th' bush? Well, our birdcage is full, an' I ain't riskin' it for no dreamer's big scheme."

Gamlin's feathers drooped, but he didn't say any more about it, just sat there scratchin' in th' dirt. I figured he was mullin' over th' idea of leavin' me an' goin' on his own.

"Gam, you don't git rich chasin' someone else's pie-in-th'-sky dream. Good things come a little at a time to a man who picks his own road an' travels it steady, day after day after day. Gradually, he realizes that he has become rich in his own way, be those riches counted in children, grandchildren, acres, cattle, or gold. Most people lookin' t' be sudden rich are constant poor, mostly livin' off other folks' generosity."

"I know, Lee, I know, but don't it sound like . . ." His thoughts trailed off. "Dammit."

Damn wild ideas in young heads, I thought—*and the idiots who put them there!*

Booger Jones and Harmon walked by, Boog with a rifle in th' crook of his arm and both with their knives. Harm carried a pan and a singletree.

Boog sang out, "Fresh elk fer supper, Mr. Lee, Mr. Lee; fresh elk for supper, Mr. Lee."

They had a long conversation with Trace about which "elk" to butcher until a cripple was driven to the brush and shot. I checked on the prisoners and refilled their water bucket. The wounded men seemed to be OK, but it was going to be a couple of days before Spider would be able to travel, and then the travel would necessarily be slow.

"Booger's famous son-of-a-gun stew for supper, boys," said I. It had been slim pickin's the last day or two, and we all looked forward to that.

It had always been my habit to patrol around our camps. I got especially observant when we stayed more than one night in a place. I found fresh moccasin tracks in the brush behind the wagons and followed them to the place the spy had tied his horse. True to my suspicions, the horse was unshod. Our visitor had not tried to hide his trail, and I tracked him down the river until he rode into the water. There wasn't any sign that he had crossed directly over, so I surmised this was his way of hiding his trail. Many times in this country I have found signs of visitors like this one. Indians—and cautious whites—know their territory, and it is just as important to know who is around and what they are doing. Probably nothing more would come of this visit, but it was prudent to stay alert. It wouldn't do to be set afoot out here, and I had a particular desire that my hair stayed right where it grew.

I caught one of the prisoners stealing a bite from half a carcass he was turning over a pit of coals and knew we would be blessed with the aroma of roasting beef as we slept. He was startled at my appearance and a little sheepish. "Do not muzzle the oxen on the threshing floor," I quoted, and he grinned.

The highlight of our stay there was Booger's bar-b-qued beef. We ate on it two days. How he came up with that sauce for the meat is a mystery. He must have had the dry ingredients on his wagon—and he had enough t' make a gallon of the stuff. It put us all in a good mood, even the prisoners.

We packed up and left midmorning of the fourth day and only drove ten miles or so. Two of our wounded suffered so that we camped early. A three-day trip to Fort Sill became ten days. We checked our prisoners into the brig and our wounded to the doctor. We had decided to return the herd to the Texans now instead of waiting until later. Trace Price disappeared and rode in the next morning with Evan Worth, the Texas Cattlemen's Association representative, and four Texas Rangers. They looked the herd over at noon, and the rep said they would like to count the cattle and number the cattle with the same brands.

Bein' rangers must have been just a sideline occupation with those four men, for they were sure proficient at handling cattle. Evan Worth knew his business too. He was older than the typical vaquero, and had obviously been around cattle a long time. "I'm just an old broke-down cowhand who was lucky enough t' land a job I can do from my rocking chair."

Well, the "chair" he rode was cinched to a big black horse with a blaze face and four white stockings—and that feller didn't have any runners on his hooves. Ev knew every one of the twenty-one different brands we found in the herd. Ten of the cattle were turned aside. They were unbranded, most of them being cows that were someone's milch cow in the territory. When the counting was over, there were four hundred sixty head with Texas brands.

We found some shade under a mesquite tree, and Evan looked over my notes and made some calculations. "The association has authorized me to pay a dollar a head for every association cow returned to us. That would come to . . ."

"Ev, we come by these cows the hard way, fought two battles, lost one an' won one. Then we herded them cows halfway across th' territory. A dollar a head won't near cover th' cost of all that." Trace must have had experience with returning stolen cattle to the association.

"What do you think would cover your expenses, Trace?"

"It comes to almost two dollars a head, near as I can figger."

"At two dollars a head, I could go out anywhere in Texas an' buy good cattle. I can't justify that. I'll give you a dollar twenty-five an' that's as high as I'll go."

Evan Worth was holdin all th' high cards in this play, for here we were with a herd of stolen cattle tryin' t' bargain with the owners over the price of returning them.

"We'll take the dollar twenty-five, Ev, an' be glad we got it," I said. With those eleven outlaws we had to take back to Fort Smith, we would come out pretty good on the situation.

The association rep made out two bank drafts on a bank in Fort Worth, half of the five hundred seventy-five dollars in my name and half in Trace's name.

Trace said th' bank in Fort Smith would honor the drafts. "We'll make up a lot when we turn in those outlaws at th' judge's."

"We shoulda got more than half o' that reward. Trace would be feedin' some ant hill somewheres if we hadn't rescued him." Gam said later.

"You're probably right, Gam, but you got to remember that

deputies stand on a level floor, and some day Trace Price or some other deputy may have t' come to our rescue. We don't want any sour notes played in that song."

"Yeah, I reckon," was all he said.

Price was still campaignin' for a trip west the next morning, and I was still set on returning to Fort Smith when Evan Worth and the rangers rode into camp. I eyed the leather case he was carrying with suspicion. Nothin' good came from those things, especially out on the job. We had a round of coffee and after the second cup was poured, Ev opened his case and pulled out a sheaf of papers and handed them to me. I looked at them and swore. They were warrants for cattle thieves. In the blanks where the name goes were written in the names of our seven prisoners plus Pete, Cap, AJ, and The Kid, the four I had previously arrested.

"What ya got there, Lee?" Trace asked.

"Warrants for our cattle thieves—for th' Paris court."

"Let me see." He looked at each warrant and handed them back to me. "We're takin' these fellers t' Fort Smith, Ev."

"You can if you want to, but you will only be paid for taking them to Paris from here, an' that's a set distance. You'll be out all that mileage and found from here to Fort Smith, *then* to Paris."

"We'll git our own warrants at Judge Parker's court," Trace vowed.

"Won't do any good; these were issued first and take precedence."

"Ev's right, Trace. I saw it happen before. We been served with these warrants and we're required to take those men to Paris." This was one of those times when bein' a U.S. deputy meant servin' more than Judge Parker's court. We had a tendency t' forget that.

"I won't go." Trace threw his coffee out in disgust.

"We-l-l, technically *you* don't have t' go since I served Lee with the warrants," said Mr. Worth. If the rangers hadn't been so intent on our conversation, I would have hit the man. I guess they had experienced this conversation before. Strange that we hadn't heard of this from the deputies who had this done to them . . . or maybe only *one* deputy knew about it and kept it under his hat. There was the smallest trace of a smile on Evan Worth's face and I glared at Trace. He was studiously watchin' an ant between his toes carry a crumb across the sandy ground. I stomped the ant and hit Trace on the shoulder—hard. "You knew you—"

"Now hold on, Lee, I knowed somethin' like this *could* happen, but I wasn't so sure in this case since the crimes were done in the territory. The two courts have been arguin' over this for some time an' they decided that th' court that issued the warrants first had jurisdiction."

"Of a truth, the wind doth also blow in San Juan, Trace, an' you just gave yourself away by windin' too much." I was getting madder and madder. The fact that the rangers were enjoyin' it all didn't help a bit. "I was tellin' Gamlin that deputies all stood on a level floor an' watched out for each other, but I don't guess that applies to you. When you cash that Fort Worth draft, you're gonna owe us a hundred dollars. You can pay it in silver and gold or flesh, I don't care which. Right at this moment, flesh runs a mite more valuable than gold in my bank."

"Now, see here, Lee—"

"See yourself, Price. I've had it with you." I had to get away before I got arrested for batterin' a U.S. deputy to a pulp. "Harmon, break camp. Gam, bring the wagon to th' jail; we're goin' to Paris."

CHAPTER 10
A.B. CHEW'S TRIAL

*The good ladies who carry flowers and jellies to criminals mean well.
There is no doubt of that. But what mistaken goodness! Back of the
sentimentality are the motives of sincere pity and charity sadly
misdirected. They see the convict alone, perhaps chained in his cell.
They forget the crime he perpetrated and the family he made hus-
bandless and fatherless by his assassin work.*

    Judge Isaac C. Parker

By th' time Gam drove up to the jail, I had all our prisoners
checked out and waiting. They were unusually quiet. I guess my
mood showed and no one wanted to give me cause. The doctor
didn't want me to take Spider Sutton, but I insisted—and
shouldn't have. There's a road of some kind for the two hundred
twenty government miles between Paris and Fort Sill, but it's
not much. Spider suffered the whole two hundred and *fifty*
miles to Goodland Academy siding, and I put him and Gam on
the train to Paris while Harmon and I drove the rest down on
Tumbleweed.

The marshal was glad to receive the prisoners and agreed to
keep my other prisoners while we rested up a few days before
heading back to Fort Smith. I paid Gam and Harm part of
their wages and they both disappeared, set on seeing the sights
of town. After a visit with the judge, I was able to get a couple
of warrants for Fish and Stubby and hand them over to the

Paris marshal as well. Now I relaxed without worrying about prisoners.

Three days later, I picked up Gam and Harmon at the courthouse and we drove to the Frisco station where I had a car reserved. We loaded Tumbleweed in one end, the stock in the other, and with us in th' middle, rode to Fort Smith at twenty-five miles an hour. Gam was a mess but Harmon was in pretty good shape. Gam had shown him the ropes without inducin' him to drink, but I think he didn't have much trouble convincing him to get roostered.

We checked in at the marshal's office on a Friday, then went to town, where I cashed all my bank drafts and paid the boys off. Gamlin disappeared with instructions to meet at the courthouse Monday morning, and Harmon borrowed a horse and rode for Lake's Ferry. We would pick him up there on the way out.

We went in to get our warrants early Monday morning. Rankin informed us that we both had to stay for A.B. Chew's trial, which would begin in two days. Until then, we were blessed with guard duty. Two days of guard duty were bearable, and the trial would be Wednesday, so we could leave town Thursday morning, or possibly even Wednesday afternoon if we were lucky. It was funny watching Gamlin with people. He knew a lot of them and greeted almost everybody, talking and talking. Then of a sudden, he would disappear and couldn't be found. I got to noticing that his disappearances occurred when anyone from around Greenwood showed up. Something untoward must have happened there to make Gam shy—an' Gamlin Stein was not a shy type of person.

I reported in to the marshal's office every morning. On Tuesday, a young assistant prosecuting attorney, Ross Scanlon, was waiting to see me. "I want you to go downstairs and look at Chew with me," he said as we walked down the hall.

My appearance in the jail caused a small disturbance. Several of the men who had ridden Tumbleweed greeted me with words that should never be spoken, much, much less printed.

Abe Chew was not among the prisoners and the lawyer asked me, "Do you see him?"

"Hold on; I haven't looked at every one of them." To my surprise, it took me several minutes to spot Chew. When it dawned that he might have altered his appearance somewhat, I began looking over the crowd again. Over in the corner of the room was a small group of men gathered around a man with a Bible in his hands, obviously having a preaching or Sunday school of some fashion. I concentrated on the back of each man, hoping to see something familiar or that he would turn his face so I could see him. Chew wasn't there. I started to look away when the young lawyer squeezed my arm and whispered, "Look at the preacher."

I stared and watched the man a few moments before I could convince myself I was looking at A.B. Chew. "Well, I'll be da—"

"Couldn't have picked him out of a can of sardines, could you?"

"No, I couldn't have. What's he done, got religion?"

"Got religion, cleaned up, and started preaching."

"That's not good."

"No, it isn't, and our chances for a conviction have dropped considerably," said Ross the attorney.

I got mad, madder than I should have because I had been paid for bringing Chew in, and my business with him was over. But here was a murderer not likely to serve a day of time for his crime. Our ambitious prosecuting attorney had seen chances of a successful prosecution slip out of his hands. Not wanting a lost case on his record, he had assigned the case to his assistant. Ross Scanlon must have known, but I couldn't tell by his demeanor.

I sniffed. "Let's get out of here afore this stench ruins our clothes."

Upstairs, Ross said, "You see what we're up against. I can only hope to make a good case, and hopefully the jury will see through the sham, but I don't have much confidence."

I didn't either, but didn't say anything that might discourage the young man. He needed all the confidence he could muster. "We'll have t' let th' chips fly, and they'll fall where they may, I guess."

As usually happens, Chew's trial got put off until Saturday. By th' time it crept around, I was in a fine fettle. That young prosecutor was nervous as a cat in a dog pen. When my time came to testify, the clerk swore me in and I took my seat on the witness stand.

After th' usual formality of identifying myself and swearing that I had arrested the defendant on such-and-such a date at such-and-such a place, the prosecutor asked, "Deputy Sowell, is the defendant in the courtroom?"

"Yes, sir."

"Please point him out for the jury."

"The defendant." I pointed to A.B., and he smiled the sweetest smile at me.

After the prosecutor asked me several other simple questions, he rested. The defense attorney was a pompous SOB that everybody around the courthouse hated. He condescended to cross examination as though it was distasteful for him to speak to a common deputy. "Now, Deputy Sowell, tell the court how you came to arrest *Reverend* Chew."

"The Lighthorse police brought A.B. Chew to me in the Indian Territory."

"Lighthorse Police. They are the Indian police for each tribe, aren't they?"

"Yes."

"They are not supposed to arrest noncitizens of the territory, are they?"

"They do—"

"Answer the question, 'Yes or No.' "

"It's not a 'Yes or—' "

"Your Honor."

Judge Parker looked at me, and I could swear I saw smoke coming out of his ears. "The witness will answer the question 'Yes or No.' "

"No."

"You paid them money when they brought Reverend Chew to you, did you not?"

"I paid them for—"

"Yes or no: did you pay the Lighthorse Police when they brought the defendant to you?"

I looked at the Judge with smoke coming out of *my* ears. He nodded. "Yes or No."

"Yes."

The SOB turned his back and did a slow strut toward the jury box. "So you have just testified that the Indian police have no authority to arrest the defendant and that you paid the Lighthorse when they brought the defendant, Reverend Chew, to you."

Silence.

SOB spun around, "Is that right, Deputy . . . ?" He paused as though he had forgotten my name.

"Sowell, my name is Deputy Sowell."

"May I remind you that you are under oath to the court and must answer my questions? Did the Lighthorse Police make an illegal arrest and did you pay them?"

"No and yes."

"No and yes? Which is it, deputy?"

"No, the Lighthorse did not make an illegal arrest, and yes, I paid them for the meals they had bought for their prisoner."

Ross Scanlon smiled and SOB glared at me. "No further questions," he snapped.

Scanlon came back and asked me the same questions and allowed me to explain my answers more completely. Later, he said, "The defense attorney is depending on the jury to remember the answers you gave him and hope they're not as likely to remember the explanations you gave later. We'll just have to wait and see."

Medicine Jack came for the trial and brought a couple of people who had known the murdered girl and Chew. They testified, and the SOB gnawed and shook them like a terrier killing a rat, preying on all the Indian prejudice he could dredge up. The result was that their testimony was mostly ineffective.

In the hallway afterwards, Jack was so mad he was shaking. "I will never again submit myself to the white man's justice. Creek trials for murderers will be more just for the white man than this." I never knew of him or any other Creek Lighthorse bringing in a white, and they tell me several graves at Boggy Depot bear the Indian names for white criminals.

There are a lot of unmarked graves across the west that contain the bones of men subjected to field trials and given field justice. It could be Texas criminals "killed while trying to escape" or a gang of robbers and killers hung in west Oklahoma by a Colorado sheriff's posse. These things were necessary in the beginnings of civilization where law had not taken hold and juries were too intimidated to execute the justice required by a strong society governed by law.

I watched the rest of the trial and boiled every time that pompous lawyer opened his mouth. He was like a little mouthy dog yipping and snapping at everybody. It seemed the whole court was tired of him at the end.

The jury went to deliberate and I went home by way of my

favorite watering hole. An agitated Gamlin found me in the marshal's office the next morning. "Did you hear what that jury did for Chew yesterday?" Without waiting for me to answer, "They convicted him of *manslaughter* and recommended *leniency* from the court. I can't believe it."

"It just shows what a bath, Bible, and rat terrier lawyer can do for you," said I. "Please talk low and walk softly, Gam."

The Judge sentenced the man to fifteen years in prison.

Some time later, the good ladies and some of the clergy of the city petitioned President Hayes for a pardon for the little shrew, and he commuted Chew's sentence to two years, with credit for time served. It meant that the man would be freed in less than a year after his conviction.

Rankin looked up as we approached his desk and said, "Marshal Carroll wants to see you, Lee. Go right in."

I knocked on the marshal's door and heard his "Come in" call. He was talking before the door closed behind me, "You were with Tracey Price in the Unassigned Lands, were you not?"

"Yes, sir; we were chasing cattle thieves."

"When did you see him last?"

"We went to Fort Sill and I left him there when I took my prisoners to Paris."

"Well, he's left there, and I understand he went west from the fort. Do you know what he had in mind?"

"He was talkin' about going after some comancheros."

"You don't mean he was going to *Texas*, do you?"

"He told me the comancheros were coming to the Indian Territory t' trade with the Comanches and Kiowas since they could not leave the territory. He was after me to go with him, but the Paris warrants forced me to go there instead."

"You were planning to go with him?"

"No sir, I had decided not to. I had thirteen prisoners, and it was my intention to bring them directly here until the Texas Cattlemen's Association interfered and I got warrants for eleven of my prisoners to go to Paris."

The marshal's mouth tightened and I saw his jaw muscles working, but he held his tongue. In a political job such as his, it was best not to say too much. Flies do not enter a closed mouth. "Lee, I've received rumors and reports that one of our outfits got into trouble out there and may have been captured or wiped out by the Indians. Trace is the only deputy I know of who could be in that area. I want you to go out there and see what you can find. Leave your wagon here and pick up another man or two for your posse. Be sure they have good horses. I want you to move fast."

"Yes, sir; do you have any specific information about where to start looking?"

"Somewhere north of the North Fork of Red River is all I know."

"He was talking about Sweetwater Creek, so I guess we'll start for there and see how it goes. That's right on the border of Texas."

He got my unstated question. "You have authority to enter Texas in pursuit of outlaws, Indians, or citizens who might be in danger."

"We'll be on our way this morning. I will pick up another man or two in the territory."

"All right; good luck." He turned back to his papers, and I doubt he knew when I left the room. Gam waved a fist full of warrants at me, "Got our orders an' plotted out our trail," he called.

"Does it go due west?"

"No, we go north from Lake's."

"We're goin' due west."

"What for?"

"To rescue a fool if he's still alive, or to bury what's left of him if he ain't. Price went to Sweetwater Creek from Sill an' got into some kind of trouble. We gotta go rescue the idiot."

"Sweetwater? Comancheros an' Injuns? They got Trace an' his bunch?"

"That's what we gotta find out. What is so attractive about th' *possibility* o' catchin' a bunch o' Mexican comancheros? If anyone thinks they're a pushover, they're plumb loco. These are men who have dealt with wild Indians and *lived to tell about it.* They're as tough as the Injuns an' probably twice as mean.

"You might as well put Tumbleweed back up an' see that our horses are in good shape. We'll need a couple of packhorses. Let's use the wagon mules for that. Get them ready and I'll go to town and get more supplies. When you're ready, come by the store and we'll load up and go from there."

"What do you want to do with these writs?"

"Give them to me and I'll put them in the bag. We may get to one or two of 'em."

Gam had to go by the blacksmith an' get worn shoes replaced, and we didn't leave th' ferry until midafternoon. At Lake's we picked up Harmon and Nick Lake. I swore the three of them in as posse members and we left early the next morning, followed by longing looks from Bud and an eleven-year-old who swore he could shoot a shotgun taller than he was. I believed him, and convinced him that someone had to stay and help Bud with the ferry.

His name was Tom Shipley, but with us, he was christened Tenderfoot because of the condition of his feet when he found us. We had finished supper and Nick had found himself a place in the dark for his first watch when we heard a call: "Hello-o-o, the camp."

"Hello-o, stranger; ride in an' let us see you," I called. There was a rustling of brush and a man *walked* into the firelight, his rifle over his shoulder, bedroll on his back and a rabbit carcass dangling from his belt.

People haven't believed me, and more than once I've had to call up Gam or Harm or Nick to bear me witness that we found a cowboy just west of the Chisholm Trail *walking* back to Texas. It's not such a fantastic thing; there have always been tales of outfits so poor they didn't have horses. Some that started out with them lost them in Indian Territory, and finished the drive afoot. One wonders what those longhorns thought of that and how many were lost because they could outrun the herders.

"Where's your horse, stranger?" Gam asked.

"Stolen three nights ago."

I looked at him closely. It wasn't hard to tell that he had been to town. His sunburned neck spoke of skin that had been exposed to sunlight by a fresh haircut. His clothes, though soiled and torn in a place or two, were new from his bandanna right down to his boots, which had recently been new and fancy. Now they were practically gone, and I knew their demise. When he first started walking, he knocked the heels off his new boots. When the soles had worn through, Tom had taken the fancy tops and made moccasins out of them. The Lone Star that had been stitched in the tops of the new boots now adorned the top of the moccasins, and I guessed the soles of the moccasins were quickly wearin' thin. Another day or two of walking would have rendered him barefoot. Hunger aside, he had a great thirst and must have drunk a gallon of water before bedtime—and he didn't have to get up in the night, either.

"I left Dodge a day after the other boys in my outfit and thought I could catch up with them, but I haven't," the newly christened Tenderfoot said. "So I found me a soft stretch of sand and camped. When I woke up, ol' Lightnin' was gone. Tracks around the stake told me some kind Injuns had spared me my hair. There I was with a useless saddle, my guns and boots. I believed I could walk fast enough to catch up with the boys, but it seems they are gaining on me and I am resolved to walk to Texas."

"Think you'll get there afore th' snow flies?" Harmon asked. He set a plate of beans on Tenderfoot's knees and the young man ate.

"Is this your first trip up th' trail?" I asked.

He shook his head, swallowed, and said, "Second."

"Then you should know that you don't stand much of a chance getting through these Indian Nations whole."

"A fellow has gotta do what he's gotta do," said he and he turned his full attention to his plate.

I admired his determination, however misplaced it was. He seemed the typical Texan, tough, stubborn to a fault, a hard and honest worker.

When he finished eating, I asked, "Tom, we're going west a ways, how about riding with us, and we might find you a horse to ride?"

He looked thoughtful a moment and said, "I got a little money left over. It would be a lot better ridin' than hotfootin' it all th' way—in th' snow." He grinned at Harm.

"In snow an' barefooted," Harm corrected.

"Sleep on it tonight an' we'll talk on it in th' mornin'," I said. "Our first watch, Nick, is out there somewhere, so don't be alarmed when he comes in an' wakes Harmon."

"Yes, sir." Tom could have mentioned that he had seen Nick before he left camp and knew exactly where the man was—if he had wanted to. He rolled out his bed, sat, and rubbed his feet a few moments, and soon dug into his covers and slept.

"Git to bed, Harm. Wake me about one o'clock." I didn't sleep good with a stranger in camp and neither did Harm or Gam. Our guest never moved, even snored a little.

To tell the truth, I was real wary of Tom Shipley for a long time. It seemed just as incredible to me that he could have been walking to Texas as it was to everyone else. The longer he stayed with us, the more I trusted him—but that would have been just what he wanted if he had been up to mischief—so my mind would run th' other way awhile.

We finally found a horse for Tenderfoot when we ran upon an old Indian with a small bunch of mustangs. I called for an early nooning, and we set up and made a meal. The old man looked as if he hadn't eaten in a while an' when the beans were warm, he ate like it, too. After the meal Tom and the old man got their heads together and the tradin' talk began. They were still palaverin' over one of th' horses and a wore-out old kack when we picked up and moved on. I figgered that might be th' last we would see of Tom Shipley. The boys must have thought th' same from th' way the three kept lookin' back. He caught up with us midafternoon, riding a nice-looking grulla stallion. It seemed he was gonna stay with us "a little while longer."

CHAPTER 11
CARRETAS AND COMANCHEROS

Eventually, I got over my "distrust of Tenderfoot" hump. One day Gamlin asked, "What you waitin' for, Lee? Hire Tenderfoot an' make him a tumbleweed driver." Harm nodded his approval. He hadn't realized how much time caring for the mules and wagon took away from his other duties—and he was really getting into this cooking business.

"If you haven't noticed, Tumbleweed ain't along with us on this trip."

"No matter, he could do that."

"I'll do th' hirin—*and firin'*—around here," I growled.

It was the very next day that as I was catchin' up to the boys riding single file under cottonwoods that I saw Tom draw and fire over Gam's head. A huge headless snake flopped off a limb of the tree he was riding under and fell on Gam's horse's rump, which caused some interesting gyrations from the horse and amusing bronc riding by Gam.

"What'd you do, Tenderfoot? Throw that snake on my horse?"

"Naw," Tenderfoot drawled as he reloaded, "I seen that snake was gonna fall on you an' thought it would be better if he was dead when he fell."

"More likely, you seen he *wasn't* gonna fall less'n you encouraged him," Gam accused.

When Harmon could quit laughin', he said, "I seen more black snakes fall out of trees. They seem to be like a kitten that can only climb *up* a tree an' can't figger out how t' climb down.

One fell among Ma an' th' kids ridin' in th' back of a wagon once. It caused th' fastest wagon e-vac-u-a-tion ever seen. Then th' mules got wind of that snake an' had a runaway. Wasn't a whole lot left o' that wagon when th' snake fell out and th' mules finally stopped."

"Driver baled too?" Tom asked.

"Not until that snake tried t' climb over th' back of th' seat. Guess he had some idea he could drive better than me, so I let him have a hand at it."

Gamlin had gotten down and picked up the still twitching body by th' tail. Holding it high over his six foot tall frame, at least a foot of the other end still lay on the ground. "A big one," he grunted. "Are they as good t' eat as rattler?"

"Don't know; wanna try?" asked Harm. "You clean 'im an' I'll cook 'im."

But when they found a big field rat rotting in his stomach, they threw that snake away.

Tom Shipley demonstrated he knew something about guns with that shot. Not only had he seen a snake stretched out on a limb that two others had missed, but he had neatly shot the snake's head off from seventy-five feet. Whether he did it for serious concern for Gam or for mischief, I won't venture an opinion, but Tenderfoot was not at all beyond a good prank once in a while.

The so-called reconstruction of the south completed its destruction. This was particularly so in Texas, where law was made by Yankee soldiers and carpetbaggers and enforced by black policemen. Their mishandling of things extended the war a long ways beyond Appomattox. Rebel Texans held a deep and abiding (and I might say justified) distrust of lawmen. It was somewhat of a surprise to me that Tom stayed on with us after he learned who I was.

October first, 1877, I hired Tom Shipley as wagon driver, and from that time on he took charge of the packhorses. I also swore him in as posse member, and he was eager to tangle with Comanche or comanchero—maybe too eager.

This short-grass country had already turned brown, but the grass was nutritious for the stock and, as a result, we made good time. Meridian Creek runs roughly parallel to the state line about a mile inside Oklahoma. We set up camp in a gulley just east of the creek, well hidden among the brush and cedars. I gave the boys a little schooling on how sudden death came when a man encountered a Comanche or Ki-o-way and impressed them with th' need t' stay alert and hidden as much as possible. When things were set up to our satisfaction, Gam and I rode out about sunset the second day and scouted down Meridian Creek. It was too dark to see anything on the Sweetwater flats, so we turned and let the horses guide us back to camp.

The next morning we rode over th' divide to the Freezeout Creek drainage and rode below the ridge down to overlook the Sweetwater. The darkness last night had hidden the carreta tracks running down the flats. Even from a distance, we could count the trails of a half-dozen carts. "It could be a half-dozen carts or th' tracks of three goin' an' three comin'," Gam said.

"We won't know that until we go out and look, an' I ain't in th' mood right now."

"Wanna make a bet on it?"

"Shore, Gam; I'll be bettin' it's six carts, a yoke o' oxen each, an' two men to th' wagon."

"Huh," Gam grunted. "That'd been my bet too. Guess all bets are off."

"I like your way o' thinkin'."

"You don't suppose they went down on th' Red River, do you?"

"I would think that's too far into th' territory an' too busy for their comfort. Most likely they are holed up in a gulley here in these breaks. All we got t' do is keep our eyes open an' live long enough t' find 'em."

"We still lookin' for Trace, Lee?"

"That's our goal, but I'm startin' at th' other end of that trail an' workin' backwards. If they are still alive, they would be with the cattle thieves or the Indians. Pretty soon, they will be with the comancheros. It's not likely anyone else but Spider would hold them to give to the Indians, Gam, so I think we will most likely find them under a pile of rocks or their bones scattered over th' ground somewhere. Let's hope neither of those things have happened to them, and their trouble was somewhere they would be most likely t' survive."

Mortality troubles young people. Gam was extra quiet going back to camp. By th' time a man's forty in this country, he's seen enough death to accept it, though I never did make peace with it.

After supper, I laid out our plan for the next few days, "Tomorrow, Tenderfoot and Nick will go with me. We are gonna cut across the heads of the creeks that run south and see if we can cut any trails of cattle or Indians. If we haven't found anything, we'll spend th' night on one of the branches of Buffalo Creek and come back. Harmon, I will take you on our next scout if there is one. In the meantime, I want you two to stay around camp, guard our stock, and pretty much stay within sight or holler of each other. This ain't country a lone man oughta be roamin' through."

Crossin' breaks is all up or down and very little flat. It is hard on man and beast, and we took our time. Th' only tracks we saw were those of deer and an occasional buffalo. Less than ten years ago, there would have been so many buffalo, tracking cattle would have been impossible. Things have changed, and it was as sad and bewilderin' to the white man familiar with this country as it was to the Indian. We didn't even build a fire above Middle Fork, just rolled up in our blankets and, with our horses tied to our wrists, slept.

It has always been my practice to never return to a place the same way I went, so in the morning we rode up the creek to where it wasn't so broken and rode west, still looking for any sign. There was nothing.

"Well, we've established that the cattle thieves haven't come here from the north and east. Most likely, they left the Cimarron east of here an' drove down some easy divide to the North Fork of the Red River and up th' river to their meeting place."

"Not much challenge to Harm t' follow cart tracks. Bet he'll be mad." Nick grinned at the thought.

We rode into camp just at sunset and found the boys eating supper. After we ate, I said, "Harmon, you and Gam saddle up, we're gonna do some night riding. Bring your moccasins." I threw my saddle across one of the mules while the boys got ready. Harm tied a greasy sack to his saddle and we rode south.

We emptied that greasy sack and waited for full dark on the flat before we left Meridian Gulch. "We're gonna find one of those cart tracks out there and follow it. We'll have t' walk and let our toes guide us till moonrise."

It was actually easy to trace the carts in the darkness, and we made good time at it. South of Freezeout Gulley a couple of miles, the tracks turned left up the wide flats of a nameless gulley. By the light of the moon, we saw where they turned left again directly for the black maw of another gulley. Somewhere to our left up the main gulley, a cow bawled.

"We found 'em!" Harmon whispered.

"Shore enough, let's scout up to that bawling cow and see how many there are. It would tell us if those cattle thieves have arrived."

The gulley quickly turned narrow and steep, and we scrambled from the flats up the hill and walked the ridge. In the moonlight, we could see a small herd of cattle grazing the flat ground above the gulley.

"Ain't big enough for a herd, are they?" asked Gam.

"Looks like oxen, don't it?"

"I guess the question now is where the cattle herd is an' how close are they?"

"It also means we have some work t' do and right away, too," I said.

The cool air settling to the ground flowed down the gulleys and across the flat to us. It carried the scents of smoke and food cooking. We had to find out where the outlaws' camp was and get an idea how many men there were. "I'm going to creep up th' left side of that gulley and see if I can find out a little about them. You two take the horses and wait in the brush over there." I pointed to the hillside opposite the gulley. "You can come out when you see me returnin'."

I reached the hillside almost the same moment the boys disappeared into the brush with our animals. I couldn't have picked a more gravelly hillside to try to climb quietly. It was one careful step at a time, an' I would have sworn the sun would be up afore I finished my scout. An occasional word or sound from below told me I was opposite at least part of their camp. Getting down that slope quietly was impossible, so I would have to be satisfied to observe from the top of the bank—and most of that would be by ear and not eye. I lay on the brink of the bank and listened.

There was very little to be heard: an occasional word or two, some clanking tinware, a dog growling over his supper. I had no idea how many men were down there or just where they were. Most likely in that narrow arroyo, they were scattered some. I did make out two fires about a hundred feet apart. Dogs would make it almost impossible to sneak up on the camp. We would have to rely on speed and surprise to carry the day. It was useless to try to be quiet going down the hill, so I stood and ran, hoping I would sound more like an elk or deer running down the hill. It must have worked, for no one followed me.

Gam and Harmon met me and we rode back toward our camp. Nick and Tenderfoot met us at the bottom of the arroyo, and we found a dark spot to talk.

"Here's our problem, boys; we have twelve or more comancheros in a gulley with their carts of trade goods. We know a bunch of thieves are bringing a herd of cattle to trade, and we also know that Indians are coming to trade. Right now they are in three separate groups. If they get together, we don't stand any chance of getting them. We have to capture the comancheros and fast, but what do we hold them with? If we're lucky enough, we'll catch the outlaws and really have our hands full. It may be that they will have some knowledge of what happened to Price. If his wagon is near, we can put it to good use; if not, those prisoners have a long walk ahead of them."

"Then the question comes, how do we get away from those Indians?" Nick asked.

Gam added, "I packed twelve pair of manacles, Lee, but they would be a lot more useful if we had a chain."

"We could use the carretas for our wagons," Harmon offered.

"We'll have to at first, but that's gonna be a slow haul with oxen." Tenderfoot was at least looking ahead.

"We will take the prisoners to Fort Sill, so the trip will be shorter." I wasn't about to try to haul that gang all the way to Fort Smith.

"Say, maybe one of us could ride to Sill an' git those Texas Rangers t' help."

"We might could, Harm, but I want credit for catchin' those

thieves. Else we are just donating our time to the state of Texas."

"Gotta capture first, *then* call for help, right, Lee?" Gam agreed.

"Our problem is that we don't know where the cattle herd is. It could be here tomorrow, or it might be a week before they show up. If the Indians show up before the outlaws with the herd, we're plumb washed out o' th' deal. It would take an army."

"We should get the Mexicans as soon as we can," Harmon said.

I nodded, though no one could see me. "Yes, but the most dangerous thing is for us to go in blind."

"Any way we could lure them out o' that canyon?" Nick asked.

"They must be plannin' to set up trade on th' flats or else only let a few Indians into the gulley at a time. I would think they trust the Indians enough to set up in the open, myself." I was pretty sure that would be the case. As long as I knew, the Comanches had never attacked or misused the comancheros or the New Mexicans. Some ancient treaty had made them allies, and the two cultures worked together in a mutually beneficial way. "I'm gonna sleep on it awhile. Wake me before sunrise and we'll ride over and do something."

I suppose a man could get tired enough that any problem would not deprive him of sleep, for I fell into a dreamless sleep and only awoke when Gamlin shook my shoulder. "Near sunrise, Lee."

Maybe in th' Atlantic Ocean, there sure wasn't a sign of it in the western Indian Territory. Breakfast was strong coffee and venison jerky, and we were saddled up to go. I left Nick to watch camp. The cicadas had been singing for several days and were making enough noise that at first I didn't recognize the song of the carretas moving. We rode up the last point of land before the gulley opened up and looked over. There were four carts out on the flat, positioning themselves in a partial circle. The last two carts had not appeared. The men unchained the oxen from the carts and two men drove them, still yoked, up the main gulley to the grazing ground. I counted seven men within the arc of the carts. By our reckoning, that left four men in the gulley with the remaining carts.

"Why don't the other two carts come out?" Harmon asked.

"They probably have the whiskey and guns on them," I answered. "They'll want to keep them secure until the end of the trading. No one wants t' be around a bunch of drunken Indians."

The men with the carts gathered in the center of the circle and built a fire. They sat and smoked while the coffee boiled.

"Now's th' time for some coffee, boys. Tenderfoot and Harmon, you ride out on the flat and come through between the carretas. Gam and I will ride to cut them off from the gulley they came out of. Gam, cover the gulley when we get there, and I'll help th' boys with those men by the fire. We'll wait until Tenderfoot and Harm are in position to go. If they see us, that means t' go after them as hard as you can."

It took a couple of minutes for the two to get behind the carts. When they dismounted, we went in fast. The men at the fire saw us and a couple jumped up and ran for the carts only to be brought up short by the guns of Harmon and the Texan. The others stood around the fire, uncertain what to do.

"Estar sentado, por favor!" I called, roughly meaning "please be seated." Before the two Harmon had stopped could sit down, two shots boomed from the gulley. I felt my hat tug and heard Gam shout. As I turned, one of the standing men bolted again for the carts.

Gam's horse was down, and the boy was scrambling to get behind him. Other shots were coming from the gulley and I heard a shot behind me as I spurred to Gam's rescue.

"Shoot back, Gam," I yelled as I galloped by. Me and that horse raced right up the middle of that gulley, shots coming from both sides. A man rose up to my left and there was another time my left-handedness came to my rescue. I fired and the man fell. We stopped at the first carreta. When I jumped off my horse, I noticed a long bloody streak down his rump. I ran back down the trail a ways until my brain caught up with me and made me dive into the brush, just as shots clipped branches around my head.

I lay very still and listened. Men spoke low in Spanish: "Did we get him?"

"I do not know, be careful."

There were four men between me and Gam, one shot. A steady fire was coming from his area and I surmised one of the Mexicans was holding Gam down behind that horse while the others were stalking me. I prayed there were only two of them.

This was a ridiculous situation. There were four groups of men in a line firing at each other. Gam's shots whined over me and the man shooting at him could hit Harmon and Tenderfoot or the men they were holding. Surely those boys had moved their prisoners out of the line of fire.

The only men who didn't have to worry about accidental hits were stalking me—and I didn't know where they were.

"Do you see him?" The whisper came from my right. There was no answer, just a gentle swish of leaves on my left. I turned to look and, as I did, a man rose up not ten feet away, a grim look of triumph on his face. As we both were bringing our guns to bear, two shots, then a third came from behind me.

I'll not soon forget the look of complete surprise and shock that came over the man's face as he looked at two red spots forming on his chest. Slowly, he sank to his knees, gun falling from his hand, and his body falling after it.

"I have shot him, Tito. He has fallen." And I turned to see

the second man stand and walk toward me, his full attention on the fallen man. "Tito, he has fallen. Come out."

"Tito is dead, señor; you have killed him." His shock could not have been greater if I had slapped his face. He dropped his gun and ran forward.

"Tito, Tito, is this you? O-o-oh, I have killed you, my friend." He wept bitterly and I was affected by his sorrow. How tragic it would be to accidentally kill a friend. It gave me some idea of what Wild Bill Hickok felt when he shot Mike Williams, his best friend in Abilene. I picked up his gun and left him there with his friend's body. He would do no more harm today.

As I stalked the fourth man, I heard a single shot behind me and realized with a start that I had failed to take the dead man's gun. Gam's shots clipping off limbs above me were coming less often as his ammunition diminished. The answering shots were coming from my left as I faced them, roughly opposite the place where the first man had fallen. It only took a moment to locate the man and stop his firing.

CHAPTER 12
PADRE SOWELL

"It's all clear, Gamlin, you can come out now," I called.

"It's about time," came the reply. I marched my prisoner down the trail to the flat.

The boys had indeed moved out of the line of fire and were holding the prisoners behind a pile of boulders. They all looked whole and by that, I deduced the shot I had heard when I started my charge was a warning and nothing else.

"Gam, you and Harmon stay here with these prisoners. You will find three bodies in the gulley. If these men dig the graves, we'll have a Catholic mass when I come back." There was a stir among the prisoners and looks of sadness. Most likely all the men had some kin to the others in the group and a loss was keenly felt when one fell.

"Tenderfoot Tex and I are going to see what has happened to our two drovers. Keep your eyes open; they may be sneaking around here." We mounted borrowed horses and rode.

The oxen were still yoked and the drovers were gone. Their tracks showed them running away from the arroyo on up the hill. "They wouldn't be running away, would they?" Tom asked.

"I wouldn't think so; let's follow them a ways and see." We followed them only a little way across the flat until I was sure of their destination.

"Tom, they're heading for the gulch the carts are in. You follow them. I'm going back to warn the others and go back up the arroyo to meet them. They will probably be armed, especially if they get to the carts, so be careful. Remember, I will be in front of you, so don't shoot me." I turned and trotted back down the hill. On the slope, I kicked my horse into a run. The last part was the steepest, and he was almost on his haunches sliding in the gravel.

Our prisoners were digging a grave large enough to hold three bodies. I warned Harmon and Gamlin about the two drovers. They sat among the boulders where it would be hard to get a shot at them and I turned to the gulley. I tied my horse in the brush at the toe of the slope and slipped around the point into the gulley. A light breeze coming down the hill would carry any sounds to me, but there were none. Somewhere between here and the top of the gulch were two armed men who would love to get their sights on me. Where were they? And where was that Tex? Ol' Baz used to say, *"Let them come to you."* I waited, and waiting was always the hardest thing for me to do.

It was the faintest of sounds you pay no attention to, but it persisted. I realized with a jolt that it was someone moving through the brush off to my left. A sound from behind told me I was between the two men. I prayed they didn't know I was there. Sweat seemed to pour from me, and I constantly dried my hand on my pants—until the sound came to my ears and I stopped. All movement stopped. Had they heard too? It was a foolish thought; no one could have heard that, but it worried me.

Now the sound of their movement recommenced, and they moved on by me without discovering where I was. I listened to them move away until the sound died and I knew they were at the verge of the brush. The view of the flats must have been puzzling to them, for there was not a person in sight and the sounds of the prisoners digging—if they were still digging— would not carry to them.

At the sound of Tenderfoot approaching, I stood and waited

for him to discover me. He mouthed, "Where?" I pointed to their two positions. Being at the edge of the brush was a big advantage to us, and we waited to see what they would do. An occasional movement of the brush tops told us they were moving together. Tenderfoot moved away from me so we could have them in a crossfire. The stalkers became the stalked as we crept toward them. Now we were close enough to hear them whispering in Spanish.

"Where could they be, Beto?"

"I do not know; perhaps they too are dead."

"There was much shooting. I fear for them."

I turned my head away and through cupped hands whispered, "They are all safe, amigos, and we can take you to them."

They both turned to the apparent place my voice was coming from. "Who speaks?" the one called Beto asked.

Before I could answer, Tenderfoot replied, "Those who surround you. If you lay your arms down and step into the open, you will not be harmed, and we will take you to your friends.

I spoke again, "If you choose to fight, you will quickly join Tito and his friends on the other side."

There was a long pause, then the unnamed man said, "We cannot fight so many we cannot see. It would seem better to join the living instead of the dead, my friend; let us go with them."

"Step into the open and lay your weapons down," I commanded.

The two moved out on the sands a few feet and laid down their guns. One laid his machete beside them. "Do you have any knives to add to that?" asked Tenderfoot.

"*Sí.*" And they both laid down their Green River butcher knives.

"The others were over there behind those boulders, Tom. You start that way with them and I'll get my horse." Shade from the hills had reached far out on the flats, and I suddenly realized it was late afternoon. We hadn't eaten since sunup, and it had been hours since I had a drink. I had stopped sweating and my knees felt weak. My canteen hanging on the horn was a welcome sight, and I drank half of the water. Too tired to mount, I walked to intersect the path of Tenderfoot and the prisoners, where I handed the Texan my canteen. He drank most of the water and handed the remainder to the Mexicans.

"We'll get you more water in a few minutes," I said. "Tom, mount up and see where those others are, and I'll take care of these two."

He found them essentially where they had been, behind the rocks all day, and waved his hat at us. We rounded the rocks and I motioned the two to join their friends. Gam and Harm had gathered all the foodstuffs they could find, and over against a big boulder had supper cooking. Harmon's experience feeding this many was limited and he was nervous about running out, but one look at the pots assured me he had enough for this meal, and maybe a little more.

Four men, ten prisoners, four yoke of oxen still yoked, Tenderfoot's horse at the top of the gulley, the carretas scattered, our camp unattended, and a funeral mass were too many tasks to attend to before dark overtook us. Tenderfoot grabbed a cup of coffee and rode off on my horse to retrieve the two horses left in the arroyo. Gam and one of the drovers ate a hurried meal and trotted off to see to the oxen. While the rest of the prisoners ate, I sent Harmon around to the carts to gather up bedding for the men. At one of the carts, he untied a couple of dogs who were panting in the shade. They ran directly to the stream and drank and waded out and lay in the cooling water before they returned and found their master among the prisoners. The man greeted the dogs and fed them beans wrapped in tortillas.

I talked to the men about who we were and what we were going to do with them. We discussed a funeral mass for their friends and decided it would take place the first thing after breakfast in the morning.

I was in a real quandary about what to do with the prisoners for the night until Harm mentioned the chains on the carretas and reminded me of the manacles Gam had in his saddlebags. Harmon guarded two prisoners as they gathered chains from the carts, and we set about preparing one long chain for our prisoners.

The oxen, having grazed enough, were driven down and drank at the stream. Then the drover and Gamlin drove them into the arc of carts, where they contentedly settled for the night. A rope corral across the open end would be enough to hold the gentle giants.

A manacle around their ankle and through a chain link would hold the men. We collected their sandals, and they soon had their blankets around them and slept.

Two hours of sleep in thirty-six hours such as we had gone through began to tell on me, and I was really dragging. I set the watches and lay down without eating and slept. I can't say I was rested when Gamlin woke me for the last watch, but I did feel better—well enough to be very hungry. The prisoners still slept. I could count ten forms wrapped in their blankets, so as quietly as possible, I set about fixing coffee, beans, and rice with salt pork. A can of tomatoes kept me until the food was ready.

The camp awoke gradually. I prepared for the funeral while the others ate. Tenderfoot and Harmon unloaded a cart while Gam hooked up a yoke of oxen, then he and Tenderfoot went up the arroyo to fetch the bodies. I warned them not to mention that one of the men had shot himself. According to Catholics that man was not to be buried with the sanctified, and we would have had to dig another grave, to say nothing of the angst the knowledge would cause these friends and kinsmen.

I know what you are thinking about me holding a funeral mass, but in this wilderness a priest was not available and this was the best we could do. I had taken the trouble to learn the funeral mass in butchered Latin and read scripture and say a few words of comfort to the congregation. It helped. The Mexicans were very affected by the deaths, and more than one shed tears as we buried their friends, neighbors, and kin.

"Let's get these men up the gulley where they will be cooler and easier to keep," I said. We moved them up to where the two carts were still parked, rekindled one of the fires, and put on a pot to boil.

"What now, Lee?" Harm asked.

"I been thinkin' we were awful lucky catchin' ten outlaws without an injury of some kind. I doubt we'll be so lucky with that bunch of cow thieves. Th' five of us handlin' ten prisoners this far out without a tumbleweed wagon is a real chore. On top of that, we haven't accomplished what we came for, and that is t' find that Price outfit."

"These men haven't seen anything of them—I asked," Harmon said.

"Wouldn't expect them to, comin' from the west," Tenderfoot allowed.

"The ones most likely to know is them cow thieves." Gam said. "What if we could catch just one of 'em for questionin' purposes?"

"We need t' clean up things here afore we go after somethin' else. We have t' gather up all th' whiskey an' arms and hide them. One of these carts emptied should carry it all. We'll keep one keg of whiskey and one keg of powder for evidence and load the rest and hide it."

It didn't take long t' empty another cart, but going through the carts in the valley took time. Every cart had, among the other things, a keg or two of Taos Lightning and a keg or two of powder or some bricks of lead, caps or needle gun ammunition, and a needle gun or two. We kept one gun for evidence and left the rest. They wouldn't be any good without bullets and powder. It was after noon when Harmon and Gamlin drove up the river to our campsite.

Tex spat a stream of tobacco juice and looked at me. "These *peons* wouldn't have enough money in a lifetime t' buy th' stuff on one of these carts."

"You're right there, Tenderfoot. Someone else is footin' th' bill. If you followed th'money, you would find either a man makin' an investment in a business or a New Mexico rancher lookin' for cheap cattle. They are greedy, dishonest men who think nothing of profitin' off their fellow Americans."

"Damnyankee soldiers, lawyers, and ranchers stealin' off of poor Texas cowmen tryin' t' make a honest livin'." Tenderfoot Tex spat the words.

"Still North against South, is it? Not entirely, Tex. They's crooked southern men just like they's honest northern men. You cain't paint them all with th' same brush, son."

"I guess I know that, Lee, but down here when I shoot a damnyankee, nine times out o' ten, I've shot a crook."

"How many have you shot, for gosh sake?"

Tenderfoot laughed. "Th' only ones I've shot *at* were black an' mostly wearin' a star over their hearts for a target. I ain't sayin' how many got hit, but they's a few rapers o' white women that won't do it agin."

It seemed th' world was upside-down with honest folk fightin' crooked lawmen an' bein' branded outlaws. People in high places incitin' others with inflammatory words, then sittin' back safe and sound, givin' tacit or even spoken approval of lawlessness and violence. They know the lawless ones will never be brought to justice because the Big Man controls the law and who gets prosecuted and who don't. It was still a rich man's war and a poor man's fight.

Harmon and Gamlin didn't get back until midafternoon. They had spent a lot of time erasing their tracks up the gulley where we had camped. The squeal of those wooden wheels on a wooden axle were heard a long time before they came into sight. I sure didn't relish listening to that at close range from there to Fort Sill.

CHAPTER 13
A PLAN GONE BAD

*We sat our horses on a bluff overlookin' the Arkansas River an' saw
smoke risin' from chimneys 'way southeast at Tulsey Town. Bass
backhanded my shoulder and said, "Knowin' th' territory ain' jus'
knowin where th' creeks, rivers, hills, an' towns is, Lee. It's knowin'
who's livin' there an' what they's doin' there. Most o' th' time if
they ain't white or nigger black, they jist honest Injun tryin' t' git
along.*

*"You ain't out here t' roam 'round th' countryside pickin' up
crooks. When you leaves th' river, when you crosses th' Dead Line,
you better have a plan on where you goin' an' what you plan on
doin'. Don't never catch yo'self wanderin' without a plan. Don't
never know what th' nex' two, three, or four steps is; you gotta think
ahead. And for de Lord's sake, don't never let your posse think for
one minnit you ain't got a plan or notion of where yo're at!"*

I had violated one of Ol' Baz's "Don't Nevers"—W-e-e-ll,
maybe two or three, for at that moment on Sweetwater Creek, I
didn't know th' territory. Oh, I knew th' geography well enough,
but I didn't know the people in th' sense that I didn't know
who an' where those white cattle thieves were, an' I didn't know
where those Indians were. I only knew they both were bearin'
down on us, an' here we were with their allies in chains—not
the thing t' instill confidence in your guests.

Step one had t' be to get our comanchero prisoners out of
sight and quickly. "Gam, you and Nick hook up two yokes of

fresh oxen an' load up those prisoners and take them up on top of Freezeout Canyon. Make a camp somewhere out of sight that we can defend, an' roll up th' tracks b'hind you.

"Harm, they need food enough to last a couple of days—make it three. Gam, you can cook for these men if you want a mutiny, or you could elect one of them t' cook for you. I suggest—"

"I got your point, Lee, an' we'll git along jist fine," Gam growled, and Nick grinned.

At least he didn't say "without you" out loud. "Tenderfoot, you an' me an' Harm are goin' to yoke up that other empty carreta an' th' rest of those oxen and drive them up behind Gam, then we're goin' on a scout. Get our horses ready an' see to your needs. Harm can pack food for us."

"How come I cain't go scoutin'?" Gam whined.

"You were hired t' be prisoner guard an' you have th' experience t' get that done without gittin' killed or losin' prisoners, that's 'how come.' "

"Seems t' me you went on th' last scout anyway," Tenderfoot said.

We saw Gam and Nick well on their way and drove the empty cart and oxen behind them. The campsite Gam chose pleased me an' I told him so. Nick returned down the gulley to erase tracks. Harm took his four oxen down the creek to water while Tenderfoot and I made a rope corral in a grassy spot against a canyon bluff. We left Gam and Nick busy makin' camp and rode down Freezeout Canyon in the gloaming.

Tenderfoot was a Texas cowman, and he would be best able to handle himself with the cow thieves. He would be just as likely to take on th' whole Indian delegation if he encountered them. It was best that I search the most likely paths for the Indians, and Tex and Harm look for the herd.

We rode until it was too dark to see, found a corner, and

slept. Daylight showed that our "corner" was the mouth of a gulley with overhanging bluffs that looked like they could crumble any moment. The boys moved out in the open t' cook breakfast. From that time on, they made it a point to select a night's camp while there was still light to see by. After we ate, I laid out the plan for our search. "We will ride down the North Fork of Red River until we meet one of the bunches we're looking for or until we get to Buffalo Creek."

It was an easy ride until Sweetwater turned southwest and we turned southeast up over the breaks and worked our way down the steep hills to the North Fork. There was no sign of man or beast traveling up the river. Three miles of river flats brought us to Buffalo Creek.

"I want you two to ride up Buffalo and see if you find the herd. The first stream entering Buffalo on the left is West Buffalo. The second, about three miles up, is Middle Buffalo Creek. It is the only good route for a herd to travel. A goat would have trouble comin' down Buffalo proper, so go up Middle Fork and look for sign or cattle. I will go on down North Fork and see if I can find the Indians.

"Try not to be seen, and get a count of how many men are in the group if you find them. Our object now is to find Trace Price an' his crew, not catch cattle thieves. I'll meet you back here at the junction of Buffalo with North Fork at sunset tomorrow night."

They turned up the creek and I continued on down North Fork trying to stay out of sight as much as possible. The hills to the north came right down to the river bottom, ending in bluffs and steep slopes, but the south side was broad, gently rolling land. The Indians could be anywhere there, saving several miles by cutting across a big curve in the river. They probably would be traveling near the divide where travel was easy and water still available.

I turned south and rode up toward the divide, watching for a sign. The Indians, being a large crowd, would not try to hide their trail. There was no sign of their passing.

I found a shady spot and let my horse rest and graze a little while I thought. There were too many ways the Indians could come—up Salt Fork and turn north to the Elm Fork that ran north and south along the Texas line, much like Meridian Creek did further north. If they left Salt Fork at Mulberry Creek, the traveling would be easier. Then they would travel up almost the whole length of Elm Creek—and we would miss signs of their passing entirely! The thought brought me up short. Those Indians could be on Sweetwater Creek right now, and it wouldn't be a chore for them to find Gam and Nick with their prisoners.

I rode hard for Buffalo Creek and got there midafternoon, long before Harm and Tex were expected. The only way to leave them a message was to write it in the sand, so with a big stick, I wrote "Gone to camp," then stuck the stick in the sand with my shirt tied to it with the hope they wouldn't tromp around and wipe out the message before they read it.

I still remember how relieved I was that there were no signs of the Indians passing up the creek ahead of me, but something still tugged at the pit of my stomach and made me hurry on as fast as my tired horse could go. We were almost to the parked carretas near sunset when Hoss stopped, ears erect, and turned forward. I listened, but heard nothing, and urged the horse on. He resumed his walk, all his attention on something ahead that he heard or smelled. It was some distance on before I heard the faint bawl of a cow. The herd was here!

Now my stomach really did turn over. Here I was facing an unknown bunch of hardcases that were between me and our camp; Harmon and Tom were off somewhere without any knowledge of the whereabouts of anyone but Nick and Gam—if

they hadn't been discovered and taken care of already. I had to
think, but thinking didn't do any good. I had to *do* something,
but what to do? It was as if my mind was torn into two or three
parts, each pulling in its own direction.

*I had a plan, Bass, but it's blown all to pieces and my people are
scattered. This thing has gone bad and is probably goin' t'go worse.
What can I do? He would look at me, shake his head in disbelief,
and say, "It's time for a new plan, Lee."*

Squatting behind some brush, I drew myself a map. Gam,
Nick, and prisoners hopefully were up Freezeout; the herd at
the carts; Indians somewhere south of here; and Harmon and
Tenderfoot either behind me, or they might be up on the herd's
backtrail following it or even watchin' them from somewhere
above. The thought struck me that they could easily have cut on
over to Gam's camp at the head of Freezeout Canyon. I couldn't
count on them for anything; it was all up to me at this moment.

The herd had only been here a part of the day. The drovers
might be puzzled by the absence of the comancheros, but probably not alarmed enough to make much of a search. What I
didn't know was how many there were and *where* they were.
Most likely, they would have one or two riding nightherd and
the rest around their camp. They could have a guard at the
camp, depending on how many there were. The best I could do
from here would be to wait until dark and try to get close
enough to determine how many men there were and their locations. I only needed one of them to find out if they knew
anything about Tracey Price. The easiest thing would be to grab
someone on nightherd.

Before the blackness was complete, I rode the last mile across
the flats toward the carretas. The herd was bedded down to my
left along Sweetwater, and I could smell smoke and food cooking. I tied my horse in the brush opposite the camp and crept

across the flats to the carts. There was only a small fire; by its light I counted five men sitting around it. If there were two on nightherd and possibly one watching the camp, there could be eight men in the bunch. When I counted bedrolls, there were only six, so there was most likely one man on nightherd, and I had accounted for all members of the crowd.

Somewhere up the valley a ways a horse snorted and reminded me to check on the drovers' horses. As I approached, I could see dark shapes grazing and someone called, "Is that you, Sam? A little early, aren't you?"

I grunted something unintelligible and moved toward the man. All I could see of him was his light-colored hat. When it was in reach, I buffaloed him hard with the barrel of my pistol. He went down with a groan and I was on him and taking his gun. His tie-down thong made good wrist-wraps, and I had his hands tied behind his back and his bandanna holdin' the gag in his mouth before he came to. After a little struggle, he relaxed and I helped him sit up.

"My name is Lee Sowell, dep'ty marshal for Judge Parker," I whispered in his ear. "I'm here looking for Tracey Price, another dep'ty marshal, and his outfit. Now, friend, I'm gonna undo your gag, but before I do, you should know that I have a knife b'tween your ribs." I poked him with the point. "And at the first loud sound you make, it's gonna go into your lung. You won't even be able to finish your yell, understand?"

"Umm-humm," the man mumbled and nodded. He was gagging a little.

"OK," and I loosened the bandanna. The man spat the gag out and coughed.

"Now, friend, tell me what you know about Dep'ty Price? Don't be shy and *be truthful.*"

"We ain't seen no dep'ty."

"Where'd you come from?"

"We been along th' Chisholm pickin' up strays."

"And yo're takin' 'em back t' Texas to their rightful owners, aren't you?"

"No, they're our'n now, an' we gonna sell them to some Mixicans comin' t' git them."

"Ya got a bill of sale? They got your brand on 'em?"

"No, but, ain't possession is nine tenths o' th' law?"

"Not on branded cows an' horses, friend." I pricked him a little with th' knife and he flinched. "Now tell me exactly where you were on th' trail."

"We started out on th' Canadian an' worked north nearly to Kansas."

"How long have you been in this area?"

"Man, we ain't been in this area till t'day."

I asked him a hundred other questions until I was convinced he was telling the truth. As far as I could determine, this bunch had not been involved with any deputy posse disappearing in this area. We knew that Trace had come toward th' vicinity of Sweetwater Creek in anticipation of gathering a bunch of comancheros and cattle thieves. Somewhere between here and Fort Sill, he had disappeared—or that's what was rumored.

Paying so much attention to comancheros and hardcases had wasted valuable time when we should have been looking for Price. Still, here we were in th' middle of a cattle-thieving ring with th' chance of catching the whole bunch. I remembered Bass's lesson on what we were here for, and decided that as long as we held the upper hand, we would try to capture the whole gang. Perhaps the Texas Rangers and the Cattlemen's Association would like t' take th' whole shebang off our hands— for a price, that is.

"How many horses do you have here, feller?"

"Twenty, an' we have t' pickit ever dad-burn one of 'em."

"Well, after tonight you won't have t' picket a one." I hoisted him up on his feet and marched him to Hoss, where I replaced the gag and cuffed him to the right stirrup of my saddle. Then, leading my horse, I returned to the horses and collected as many as I could by pulling up the picket stakes and tying them head to tail, leading eight of them out of the valley—all done before Sam the relief man appeared. I didn't know what the alarm would be when he found no one on guard. All I could do was rely on the darkness to hide our trail until morning. By then we should be safely put away. It looked like a small herd as we passed. My prisoner said there were less than two hundred head, a bunch being lost and more confiscated by deputy marshals. Some of his buddies were at this moment sitting in Judge Parker's jail. I didn't mention that I was th' one who put them there—or that they were GTT, Gone to Texas. He could find that out for himself.

We would never have found Freezeout Canyon if the moon hadn't come up. About halfway up the canyon a stream flowed into Freezeout from the east. It was from an ever-flowing spring, coming from under the high cliffs at the head of the box canyon. Once committed to the canyon, the only way out was the way you came in. I led the horses up the canyon a ways and turned them loose one at a time, hazing them up the canyon. Their trail would be plain. When the searchers followed them, they would be trapped. We returned to Freezeout, and on up the canyon after I had erased a hundred feet or more of our tracks.

Gam was sittin' by a dying fire, his chin on his chest, his rifle across his legs, and Nick slept nearby. All I could see of our prisoners were lumps wrapped in blankets.

At my first call, three Mexican heads popped up from their blankets. At my third call, Gamlin jerked awake, and I had to call again before he comprehended what was goin' on.

"Where you been?" he growled. "Been on guard duty long enough."

"We only been gone a day an' a half, Gam, an' Nick had half o'that time guardin'.'"

"That means I been a' eighteen- er twenty-hour guard." He stared hard at our new prisoner in the light of the fire and said, "Hello, Rube."

"Howdy, Gam, how you been?" this Rube said.

"You two boys been neighbors or in th' same cell t'gether?" I asked.

"Lee, I suppose yo're th' last man in th' whole U.S. t' know Ruben Hale from th' South Fork o' th' *Little* Red River of Arkansas."

"Well, Gam, I'm not the last man, but I'm th' *first* man t' tell you he drove in a herd of stolen cows to th' carts t'day."

"Anyone livin' within four counties of th' Hale clan knew of them and their sticky fingers. Ain't shocked a bit, Lee. Ol' Rube been makin' pets outta other folks' stock since he could straddle a hoss, ain't ya, Rube?"

"Cain't say I haven't an' set by it long, I guess." Ruben grinned, and I think he was a little proud of the fact.

"Gam, have you seen Harmon or Tex?"

"Not since you-all left, a week ago."

"You're gonna perceive a shortfall when you get a check based on *my* accountin' o' yore time."

Gam grinned and handed me his guns. "I'll show our guest to his room, an' you kin he'p yourself to Manuel's beans an' tortillas. Coffee's hot."

I don't know how many miles we had walked beside that horse, and my feet were sore from stepping on rocks in my moccasins. I unsaddled and rubbed the horse with some fists of grass before stumbling to the picket line with him. "You'll get some grazin' in th' mornin', fella; time t' rest a little."

"You know, that Rube was plumb upset that I took his shoes off." Gam threw a stick on th' fire an' sat down. "Says he ain't

128

slept barefoot in years, an' from th' smell o' things, I don't think he was exaggeratin' one bit. Whur's yore shirt?"

"Left it with a message for Harm an' Tex. I sent them up Buffalo Creek lookin' for sign and had t' leave our rendezvous before they got back. I don't know where they are now. They surely found the herd's trail. They could be watchin' their camp or backtrailin' to our meetin' place. They could have come here from the cattle trail if they had chosen."

"Ain't seen 'em. Wish you wouldn't risk our cook that-a-way."

"You admittin' he's a better cook than you?"

"I'm jist admittin' I don't relish that chore."

"Best I can figure, there were six men with the herd. Now they are down to five, an' I'm hopin' they don't realize we got Rube an' think he run off chasin' those horses I brought and hazed up that box canyon off Freezeout."

"You thinkin' o' catchin' men in that canyon?" Nick asked.

"Yeah, but I don't know how effective that's gonna be. With ample water an' horsemeat, they could spend th' next year in there."

"At least we'll know where they are."

"It ain't findin' Trace an' his posse, Nick, an' that's our job now. Accordin' t' your man over there, they haven't seen them. I tend t' believe him, 'cause it would have been in th' last few days if Trace came this way from Sill."

"It's easy enough for one man t' disappear out here, but a wagon an' four men should be a lot harder t' hide from ever'one," Gam observed.

"I'm givin' us two days t' mop up this mess, an' we're leavin' whether we're done or not," I said. "You get some shut-eye while I sit here and think a bit."

"Won't even argue with you on that." And Gamlin rolled up, drew his feet up t' fit his blanket, and slept. I always felt crawly sittin' in th' light of any fire at night and moved into the dark where I could keep my eye on prisoners and camp. When my thinkin' got t' runnin' in circles, I got up and checked on the horses, then walked all the way around camp without scarin' up any boogers. When I could see my hand in front of my face, I threw fuel on the fire an' started a new pot of coffee. Two or three prisoners and Nick sat up and began talkin', an' Gam fought his way out of his blanket. "Can't git a bit o' rest 'round here without someone interruptin' it."

"Y'know what, Gam, I think sleepin' makes you grumpy. It might be you shouldn't do that anymore," Nick said.

"*Not* sleepin' is th' problem, an' if'n you don't back off, I'm gonna cook breakfast."

I laughed. "Ain't never seen a man cook with a bullet in his gizzard, Gam."

Rube raised his head an' peeked over his blanket. "You ain't lettin' Gam cook, air ye?"

Now Nick laughed. "Your cooking is known far an' wide, Gam."

After coffee and cold beans rolled in a Mexican spoon, I was saddling up a fresh horse. Hoss eyed my tortilla and I gave him my last bite. "Gam, Nick and I are ridin' down to that box canyon an' see if we catch anything. If those boys show up, send them down to me."

"Shore thing, boss."

CHAPTER 14
THE BOX CANYON TRAP

Our fugitive had gotten plumb away without a scratch an' we sat and pulled cactus spines out of our legs and arms after we had despined our horses. Bass hitched his britches up and buttoned them. He tossed me th' pliers and poured another cup of coffee.

"When you go out on your own, Lee, you gotta have people you can trust t' do what you tell them. Don't fool with someone who's always strayin' from th' task at hand. On th' other hand, don't keep anyone around who don't think for they's self an' change th' plan when conditions requires it. Convince your men that the objective is most important—an' gittin through it alive is more important. These woods is full o' outlaws, an' lettin' one go only makes room for th' next."

A ride in th' cool of an early morning is one of my favorite things, and that ride down Freezeout was one of th' best. We didn't talk much, just enjoyed the morning. Beans must have made ol' horse thirsty, for he had t' stop an' take a long drink. I wondered if beans did horses th' way they did people. He hadn't enough in that one bite t' cause harm. Tied in a shady spot a good ways above the side canyon, our horses seemed content to stand and stomp flies off their legs. Walking down the valley was pleasant, and I wished there wasn't so much business at hand. The north side of the canyon came to a point of rocks at Freezeout, and we scrambled up and found a cedar t' crawl under on top where I had a good look at the layout below.

It surprised me that there was such little cover in that spring-fed arroyo. There were few trees. Button willows grew along the edges of the stream, and there were no more than a dozen live oaks scattered up and down the canyon. 'Way up by the boxed end were a few cottonwoods.

Most of the ground was covered with a good stand of grasses and those horses were sure enjoying it. One had his picket rope tangled in a willow. He had eaten all the grass in his circle and laid down to digest it.

With a man on the bluff opposite us, anyone caught in the arroyo could be captured easily, for then there would be no place to hide. The sun in my eyes made me blink, and closing my eyes at this moment would not be good. Soon it was above th' rim of my sombrero. The shadow of the east bluff slowly crawled across the little canyon, urging the horses to seek shade. They were the first to sense the approach of horses. Two riders came into view tracking the strays. The sound in that arroyo carried so well that I could hear their conversation clearly.

"Lookie here, Josh, them horses found a good place t' graze."

"Shore looks good, don't it? Think I'll let my hoss graze a little. No hurry getting back to camp."

Both men slipped the bridles off their horses and let them graze while they lay in the shade and talked. Soon both had their sombreros over their faces and were asleep. If I could slip up on them now . . . I backed down the rocks, leaving Nick on top to watch, and started around the point when I heard a hoof clink a rock. Out in the open with no cover near, there was nothing to do but stand my ground. A man rounded the lower point of the canyon, eyes on the ground. I raised my rifle and sighted that sombrero when a second rider appeared. It was Harmon. I had come so close to killing Tenderfoot, it made me mad and shaky. "Don't you two know the lead man is to watch the surroundings while the second man does the tracking?"

Tex's hand simultaneously went for his gun as he looked up.

"We tried that, Lee, but he kept followin' my tracks an' sayin', 'We're gittin' close, Harm, we're gittin' close.' "

"Where have you two been?"

Tenderfoot frowned, "We been comin' back, boss. We found the herd's trail an' came down to tell you an' all we found was yore shirt on a stick and scribblin' in th' dirt—"

"At least *I* could read it," Harm interrupted.

"Quit yer jawin', you two; we got a couple of hardcases t' catch. Tenderfoot, climb up there on that point of rocks where you can see those two men sleepin' in th' arroyo under a live oak. Harm, bring your durn rifle and come with me. Nick is up there watching. We'll see which one o' you is th' first t' wake a sleeping crook an' get shot at. We're walkin' up there with th' vague hope we can catch them still sleepin' and not have t' dodge lead."

I was talkin' to Harm and the horses by th' time I had finished. That boy only got half of my wisdom an' instructions. We mounted and hurried toward the mouth of the arroyo.

A little rustle of a bush down the way told me Nick was still in place, and when I rounded the point of rocks, there sat that Tex swingin' his legs over the edge of th' bluff. He grinned and lifted his sombrero in salute at the same instant a rifle slug jerked it out of his hand. His ass-end sure made a fine target divin' into th' brush. Just before I pulled th' trigger, my brain caught up with my hands and shoved the barrel high.

The whoosh of a bullet by my ear brought me back to the business at hand. Harm fired and someone yelled in the canyon. *Don't kill our cash crop, Harm.* I still didn't have sight of the two men and now Tex, still bareheaded, was firing. I yelled, "Don't kill 'em, Tex!" and rode hard. Firing stopped, and I found the two men standing out in the open, empty hands held high. "I'm

Deputy U.S. Marshal Sowell. You two are under arrest. Don't move."

Nick stood on the edge of the bluff, gun ready. There was no sign of the Tenderfoot. I turned the men around and tied their hands behind their backs, being careful not to get between them and any of my assistants. As we marched out to Freeze-out, the Texan met us, a little more sober than usual, wearing a hat with two bullet holes. "You didn't shoot at me, did you, Lee?"

"Did you need shootin' at? Did your antic take my mind away from th' job at hand an' nearly get *me* shot? Another fool trick like that, an' someone liable to be writin' yore mama a sad letter." I handed him th' reins to his horse and marched the prisoners up the creek.

I heard Tex whisper, "I think he shot at me, Harm."

There was no answer, but I'm pretty sure Nick and Harmon both knew I had.

We used the last two manacles to attach the new prisoners to our chain. I got my book out and wrote a description of them by what they gave me as their names. One was Josh and the other was Isom. Neither one had a last name they wanted to give me.

Gamlin was pleased we were back, and we were pleased he had one of the Mexicans cooking. Tenderfoot was awful quiet; while they ate, I talked to the four of them. "Marshal work is tedious and tiresome and it's good t' have a little diversion in camp, but when we're after people is no time for horsing around. It could get someone killed. I would feel bad if the prankster got killed and worser if he got someone else killed, or even hurt, for that matter. When I give instructions, listen carefully and do as exactly what I tell you as you can. Remember, most of the people out here would like t' see you dead, even th' women.

"We got three of the six with that herd. I would like to get the other three before we have t' leave, but I'm worried about the Indians. It won't go good for us if they found us with their friends chained up. I think it's time to use one of Ol' Baz's tricks. Gam, you and Harm get the hats and everything from th' shirts out off these three an' bring them down to us. Tenderfoot, let's go round up those horses. Nick, you stay with the wagon."

Gam met us at Sweetwater when we drove the horses out with two outfits from the prisoners. He had already put on one shirt and hat. "I expected t' see Harmon an' not you in disguise."

Gam shrugged, "We flipped for it an' Harm lost."

We drove the horses back down the creek in our new disguises. Our quarries were scattered over the flat, moving their remaining horses to fresh grass. The man to our far right gave a shrill whistle, and a buckskin horse pricked up his ears and trotted toward him. I held up a fistful of picket ropes and rode toward the man who watched closely. When his pet horse got to him, the man jumped on his bare back and, bending low, galloped for the creek with me close behind. Well, I *started out* close behind, but that buckskin was stretched out so low his belly nearly dragged, and he began putting distance between us at an awesome rate. By the time we were halfway to North Fork down Sweetwater, the dust of his passing was settled before we got to it, and me an' hoss quit th' race.

I hadn't heard any shooting. By that I surmised the other three had better luck. Still, I hurried back as fast as my winded horse could hurry. It was a real relief to see two prisoners trussed and walking my way.

"Where's your man?" Gam asked with a big grin.

"Already trussed up on the chain. I was wonderin' what was holdin' you-all up."

135

The two prisoners were grinning and one said, "Only thing can catch that horse has wings."

"Yeah, an' only thing you gonna do when that boy gets back here with those Comanches is trade places with us on that chain—if you happen t' be breathin' at th' time," said the other.

"Might as well start loosenin' your hair so's it won't hurt so much when they lift it," the first man said.

"Not much chance o' him feelin' it, Red," said the man who gave his name as R.P. Black. His common name was Rip. Red was born without a last name.

"Gam, you and Harm take our new friends to th' hotel an' put 'em up in our luxury rooms. Tell th' girls t' be extra kind to 'em. Tex and I are going to throw out th' welcomin' mat for our Injun guests." It sure did feel good to have all the outlaws and comancheros in hand. Now all we had t' do was deal with the Indians, and I had a plan. I caught up one of our packhorses to go with us.

At our cache of likker, lead, an' powder, we loaded the lead and powder and buried it in a gulley far up the Sweetwater where the bank caved off on it right nicely. I was sure the Indians would not find it after the rest of my plan was in effect.

We had six kegs of that Taos Lightning, and we hauled two of 'em up Freezeout Canyon a ways. I took one and rolled it down the hill. It hit a big rock, bounced high, and shattered in a shower of liquid.

We dug a hole by the five kegs left and buried one of them there with just a skim of sand over the top. With two kegs loaded on the packhorse, we led him down the gulley and turned left over to the next gulley that ran down into the little flat. Halfway up, we laid out another keg in a depression and covered it with rocks. We couldn't go far with that lopsided load on the pack, so at the bottom of the gulley we buried the fifth keg. I took the last keg, poured out half of it, and loaded it on the horse.

At the creek, I filled the half-empty keg with water with the hope that it would make the poison a lot less potent and still give the taste and just a little bit of buzz.

Tex grinned. "I know what you're doin', now, Lee. It sure oughta work if we live long enough t' see it."

"Th' lucky ones of us will be a long ways away from here makin' tracks when it happens." We spent th' rest of our day erasing all sign that we had gone up Freezeout beyond the box canyon, though without a good rain, it wouldn't be hard for an Indian to see our trail. I was hoping they would not be looking.

CHAPTER 15
A TAOS LIGHTNING WELCOME

The cattle must have been driven hard, for they didn't stray much, just stayed in the bottoms and grazed and waded the creek. Tenderfoot, Nick, and I spent a restless night laying out away from the carretas where we were not liable to be found by any night-wandering Indian. The next two days were full of nervous waiting. All we did that first day was drive the whole cavvy and the oxen to that little box canyon, wiping out cart tracks, and closing off th' canyon mouth to discourage them from leaving. So long as the grass held out, they were not likely to wander.

The second day we made a fire pit and butchered a steer. The aroma of that meat cooking was a wonder. If Indians showed up, they would have a feast. If they didn't, Harm would have something t' feed his prisoners.

I hardly slept that third night for worry about where those Indians might be. If they intended to attack us, it would be just as the sun rose, but there was no attack and I was relieved. I wouldn't have waited on them except for the fact they were coming from Fort Sill and might know or have seen sign of Tracey Price's outfit. We rode out, gathered the cattle a little, and herded them up the creek to fresh grass. The sun was a little past its zenith when we rode back, and I thought I could detect a little cloud of dust downriver. "What do you make of that, boys?"

"Looks like we're fixin' t' have company," Harmon said.

Tenderfoot showed his concern. "Hope they're in a good mood."

"We'll have t' see that they are. Stoke up that fire an' put the other beef quarter on. Then you can drive up that other steer we been holdin'." The boys hoisted that watered keg onto my saddle, and I hurried toward the approaching dust cloud. When I could see it was Indians, I set our keg up, knocked the top in a little, and laid a dipper on top. When they were in sight, I fired my rifle in the air and hollered while I rode in a big circle. The warriors gathered in a group and watched. I whooped again and fired and circled one more time, then trotted off toward camp. At a faint yell, I turned to see the Indians charging. I circled and whooped again, then rode on. I wanted to keep as much distance between us as possible until I could see if my plan worked.

As I watched, the van of the charging warriors passed the keg; then, as if they recognized what it was, skidded to a stop and turned around. The laggards didn't run past, and there was a rush for the keg. Soon they were whooping and firing their guns in the air if they weren't grabbing for the dipper or trying to drink from the keg.

Cattle swirled around them, being driven by women and children. Only one or two women stopped at the keg. The rest plodded on wearily, carrying their packs and driving cattle and children ahead of them.

As they entered the little valley, Tex shot the steer and clumsily began to bleed him out and skin him. The women, seeing the carcass and meat turning on the spit, dropped their loads and hurried to us with renewed strength. They shooed Tex and Harmon out of the way and took over the camp. We stood aside and watched as they fed the children. Cups magically appeared, and even children drank coffee. Soon a fresh second pot was coming to a boil and ground coffee was poured in.

They discovered our two big pots of comanchero rice bubbling away, and steaming spoons of cooked rice replaced coffee in children's cups. Some dug into that hot rice and others waved the cups as if to cool its contents. Harmon marveled. "They're awful hungry, Lee."

"Yes, game must be scarce."

"And no buffalo," Tex whispered. His eyes were a little misty, and I wondered that a Texian who had suffered much pain and privation from these very people would miss the buffalo or show any pity for the Indians. Maybe it was just sympathy.

Gradually, the men trickled in, a few at a time, mostly pleasantly tipsy, and found a place around the fire. Steer number two lay on his peeled-off hide, ready for the fire when needed. A young boy was turning the spit while other children gathered wood and stacked it by the fire. We were totally ignored, and I rode out to see what was going on at the keg. It lay on its side, empty and abandoned. There were four men scattered along the tracks to the valley, sleeping off their overindulgences. A couple of women stood over two of the inert forms, scolding and abusing. I rode back to the boys and watched.

Gradually, peace and reason settled over the little valley. Two or three tipis arose in the gloom and other family groups settled without their shelters. The women brought us three plates of meat and rice. I marveled that any was left. As we finished and refused seconds, a man approached. He was obviously a man of some authority, and he addressed us with surprisingly good English, "Thank you for welcoming us into your camp. We had been told that you would make war with us."

Did I notice a little disappointment in his tone? "No, we are at peace with our friends the Comanches and Kiowas. I am Lee Sowell, deputy marshal from Judge Parker. We are after the white man thieves that have stolen cattle from the herds moving through."

"I see. I am Son of Stone Calf. My people are tired and will rest tonight. Tomorrow, we will talk of many things."

The sun rose on a miniature Indian village in that now crowded little valley, and a dozen fires were cooking breakfasts. Few warriors could be seen, and those who were out didn't move around too much.

"I don't think we want to deal with a bunch of hungover Injuns, Lee," Tenderfoot said as he drank his morning coffee.

"Me neither; it might be that we can call a holiday and dicker with them tomorrow."

Son of Stone Calf looked over his village and, I'm sure, noted the absence of warriors and readily agreed to my suggestion. "We have traveled far with little rest and food. It will be good to rest and prepare for our parley tomorrow. Tonight we will feast and dance."

"I would like a little feasting and dancing—without firewater."

"You probably wouldn't know th' steps to their tunes, Harm," I said.

"He's got that feastin' part down purty good, don't he?" Tenderfoot observed.

We spent the day visiting with the people and watchin' their work and play. Those children were everywhere, especially in the creek. Though there wasn't a lot of water, they were in it most of the day. Several women went down to bathe and wash clothes, and they shooed the kids downstream so the water could clear enough for the laundry.

Living near that valley was hazardous for fat steers. Three of them ended up on spits and in bubbling cauldrons that afternoon. Women streamed down from the hills with arms or bags of mysterious herbs and leaves for the stews. The whole valley held the aroma of good things cooking, and we all looked forward to a great feast.

Tenderfoot was interested in the horses and dickered with the owner for one he fancied, but didn't make a deal. In the afternoon the women laid out their trade goods, and it was a pitiful lot. There was not a buffalo robe in the bunch, and that was the main thing the comancheros were after. Deerskins were abundant and well finished, but robes of buffalo hides and the cattle held the highest attraction for the Mexican people. I wondered if they would ever return; the buffalo, I mean. It made me think of them and the wild life of the plains Indians. Even the open range was disappearing. Son of Stone Calf must have had the same thoughts, for as we sat and watched the dancers, he said, "The comancheros wanted so much to trade with us that they came all this way, but I fear the thing they wanted most will never be again. We have so little to trade on the reservation." After a long pause, he said softly, "And the buffalo are gone."

I thought of the last line of a hymn the old folks used t' sing: "Sad, sad the bitter wail, almost, but lost."

The drums played all night, and we Anglos slept but little. I awoke in the early morning, startled at the sudden silence, and looked down into the valley to see if anyone was there. A soft north wind blew the smoke of the tipis away, and only one or two old grandmothers stirred around. The great fire was deserted, reduced to white ashes and an occasional wisp of smoke. It looked like our parley would be late in the day.

Presently a crier went through the village, calling his message, and a young man rode up with a message from Son of Stone Calf that we would parley at the big fire when the sun was halfway to the zenith. When the time came, we joined the Indians at the rekindled fire, though it was plenty warm without it. Stone Calf was seated at the head of a half-dozen elders on his right. He motioned for us to sit on his left. A circle of warriors surrounded us, and the women and children found places behind the line of men.

If sitting in the middle of a bunch of warriors who felt no love for the white man was intended to intimidate us, it did a good job. The Texian sat with his hand always near his gun. The Indians might eat his lunch, but he was determined to have a bite or two.

We smoked the usual ceremonial pipe of kinnikinnick, its delightful aroma wafting around our heads. I fervently hoped it was a peace pipe. From the looks from some of the warriors, I wasn't sure.

"We have been wondering at the absence of our friends, the comanchero," Son of Stone Calf opened by way of questioning.

"They waited for you, but had to leave suddenly. They have given us permission to trade with you with the request that we be generous," I replied—mostly truthfully—well, maybe partially truthfully. A stir rippled through the crowd as my talk was interpreted to them. There was more than one exchange of glances among the men, and I wondered how much they knew about our "arrangement." Our lives hung by a thread. I forced my mind away from that thought and concentrated with all my mind on the business at hand. Any show of loss of nerve or fear would bring violent judgment down on our heads.

We agreed to let the women trade their wares first, then the men would take their turn. Comanche women are rather shy and withdrawn as a whole—until they start bartering. Then they are harder to work deals with than the men. Of course, they are trading items they have made with the labor of hands and back, and those things are dear. Our negotiations were mostly word-less, since we had little common language save for some sign language.

I had all the wares from one cart laid out on a couple of blankets. A woman I judged to be of middle age led a delegation to me, laid out a blanket, and arranged her tradewares on it. We sat facing each other, almost knee-to-knee, between the blankets. In addition to several fine deerskins, she had some possibles bags with beadwork, a couple of pairs of moccasins with fine beadwork, and some worthless trinkets.

She handed me a deerskin and I pretended to inspect it—pretended, because I didn't know a danged thing about what made a deerskin good. I folded the skin and placed it on the ground between us. Pretending to consider carefully, I selected a nice tortoiseshell comb and a black rebozo and laid them by the skin. A groan from the spectators told me I had grossly underpaid, and I pretended I was not through selecting items. I added a small pot and metal dipper.

"No," the woman said and put the dipper back. She pointed to something else on my blanket, but I didn't know what she wanted.

"This?" I touched the item I thought she meant.

"No," she pointed to the left of it.

"This?"

"No."

"This?"

"*Si! Si!*" she nodded emphatically, so I exchanged the dipper for a large serving spoon. She looked at me expectantly.

More merchandise. I added another comb and a hand mirror and looked at her. We were close. The woman picked up a small paring knife from my stock and laid it by the trade pile. I pretended reluctance and, looking over her wares, selected a small trinket of some kind and laid it on the deerskin.

A murmur went through the cloud of witnesses and the woman frowned. She put back the knife and pointed to a Green River butcher knife. "No." I shook my head and put the paring knife back into play. Again, she pointed to the big knife.

I shook my head and considered a moment, then placed the

big knife on the stack. Putting the trinket back, I pointed to a pair of moccasins.

"Oh, no, no," the woman exclaimed. She selected another trinket and put it on the deerskin while I exchanged the knives again.

"Sí?" I asked.

A reluctant "Sí."

That was the first of three deerskins. By the time we were through with all her trading, I was exhausted. I needed a drink and there was none; walking around helped. When I got back, the next woman had laid out her wares, and beside her first folded deerskin was a pile of my merchandise she had chosen as adequate for her fine work. Of course, it was too much and of course we dickered—for an hour, until the trade was mutually acceptable. This trading business was killing. I regretted capturing the comancheros before their trading was over.

Even with Tenderfoot running a trade and Harmon keeping our blankets stocked, it took us all day with the women, and we had stock left over.

Harmon looked at me after supper. "You know it will be slower with the men, don't you?"

"It couldn't be any slower."

"Oh, yes it will; the men will want to trade one cow at a time. We'll be two or three days with them."

"No, we can't have that; the longer we stay here, the more we are likely to be found out. I'll go talk with the chief." My conference with Son of Stone Calf was fruitful. We tried to set prices for the man stuff, but couldn't come to an agreement. In the end, we made a mass trade, all remaining stock including the likker for the whole herd, delivered to Fort Sill. Soon all the carts were empty and the Indians were happy.

My questions about the Price posse brought some response. The tribe had followed the wagon tracks from Sill for several days. When they left North Fork south of Barton's store, the wagon trail turned toward the Granite Mountains. Several of the young men had followed the trace and found the wagon parked near one of the sinks at the foot of the mountains, apparently abandoned. They didn't think anyone had been around the wagon in several days. I groaned, *Not the Granites, Lord;* those bare, hot, waterless hills would be hell on earth this time of year. Why Trace would go there, I don't know.

The warriors now were impatient for the rest of their booty, and the longer I delayed, the more valuable my scalp became—to them.

"I am the only one who knows where that firewater is, and I won't tell you until the camp is broken down and the herd is on its way back to Fort Sill."

While two menacing men guarded me, the others hurried off to get things going. I talked to Harmon and Tenderfoot, "You two go with the herd to Fort Sill. I will stay here and show the warriors where the kegs are, then go help Gam and Nick get away. When you get there, find Evan Worth and sell him the herd. Try to get a dollar two bits a head, but no less than a dollar. When you are through, get what supplies you need, Harmon, and come back to the Granite Mountains. Looks like we will be there, looking for Price and his posse."

"We don't know where the Granites are, Lee," Harm said.

"You will pass them on the way to Sill. When the Indians leave the river and cut across country, you will be able to see them on the right. Ask one of the Indians to point them out to you."

Camp was broken down in record time, and by midmorning the herd was gathered and sent on its way, boys herding and the rest of the camp following.

CHAPTER 16
STARVATION AND SLOW ELK

The time had come. There would be no more delay without bloodshed—and I knew whose blood was most likely to spill. Only the threat of losing their end of the trade kept me alive this long. Gathering the men, I led them to where the keg under the rocks was hidden. While the Indians were preoccupied, I told my two guards where the other two were buried. They went off with a yell and some of the other men followed them. I waited a few minutes for the alcohol to take effect, then slipped off, driving the Indians' ponies with me. At the Sweetwater, I ran them down the creek; when I was sure they would keep running awhile, I turned back.

I picked up the horses and oxen on my way up Freezeout Canyon and rode on up to the top.

"Where you been?" Gam growled. "We been here with these prisoners expectin' t' get our heads peeled any minute. We're runnin' out of food. I was about t' shoot that loudmouth Red an' cook him for th' others to eat."

"Don't do it, Gam; he's too tough t' chew," Rip Black called.

"Hook up two of these yoke to the wagon an' let's get out of here. Those Indians are goin' on a big drunk an' we got to make tracks," I whispered. It would not do to tell these prisoners what was going on.

"Deputy, reckon we could tap one of those kegs o' likker? I'm gittin' awful thirsty jist drinkin' straight water," Red said.

"You know, Red, I had th' same idea an' started down th' hill with one, but I fell an' that barrel rolled down that hill an' busted on a big rock. Only got a lick er two afore it soaked into th' sand."

It wouldn't have caused any more sadness on that cart if I had said one of their buddies had died. Come to think of it, some had—died, that is.

The boys must have been pretty nervous, for they had all the camp gear piled in the spare cart, and about all we had to do was hook up oxen and move. We drove all night and all the next day, staying above the rivers on a flat divide. At dusk, we stopped and made a dry camp. Before dark I rode a couple of miles down to the North Fork where an unnamed creek ran into the river. Tracks of the cattle and camp passing were plain on the flats across the river, and that eased my mind some. The north side of the river wasn't too steep for the carts to descend safely.

Gam met me as I returned to the camp. "We just ate the last of the food except for the dried beans and rice."

I thought a moment, "We are too close to the drunks to burn a fire all night. Some of them might not have gotten very drunk and could be looking for us right now."

"Coffee will have to do for breakfast, I guess," Gam said.

"We'll be on the flats tomorrow and I could do some hunting. Deer sign has been good."

"Lee, we ain't got much sleep the last few days an' we're both dead on our feet. I've gotta have some sleep," Nick said.

"OK, you two, get some shut-eye and I'll keep watch."

"Sorry, Lee."

"That's all right, Gam, you've done a good job." I didn't mention that I had not slept much for some time also. This bunch was my responsibility, and it was my job to see that we were all safe.

The only way I could stay awake was to walk. I must have circled our camp a hundred times that night. The light of dawn burned my eyes.

"Gam, make that coffee strong; it's the only thing that will keep me alive today."

"Ain't none o' us gonna be alive if we don't eat," the one called Josh grumped.

"We'll be on th' flats today, Josh, an' I'll get a deer, or would you prefer a buffalo or elephant?"

"Elephant would be fine, but what are th' rest of you gonna eat?"

"We'll get along jist fine smellin' th' meat cookin'," Isom said.

"He's gonna wait till it's cooked t' eat? I doubt *that.*" Red was skeptical.

"When I get some meat, we'll stop and eat. We're just as hungry as you are, but we ain't ridin' a chariot like you are; we're working."

There were caustic remarks made about that, too vulgar to be revealed in genteel company. We broke camp and squealed down the divide to the river.

The stock stopped to drink and we refilled all the canteens with fresh water from the creek.

"Deputy, what's th' name o' thet creek there?" Red asked.

"It doesn't have a name that I know of, Red."

Rip lifted his hat from his face, "Does now."

"What is it?"

"Starvation." The hat settled again.

The funny thing about it is that the name stuck, and that little creek is called Starvation to this day. Hunger doesn't lend itself to relaxation and sleep. Almost all the prisoners stayed awake, though not much conversation could be carried on above the infernal and eternal squealing of those wheels. I rode along the edge of the herd's tracks looking for the signs of deer returning to the brush from their watering at the river—and I wasn't doin' too good at it. I kept nodding off.

The day wore on and it was after noon when a yell, then a bunch of yells, from the cart jerked me alert. The whole crew was yelling and pointing to an arroyo. I looked just in time to see something big disappear into the brush. No one had to urge me to hurry; I relayed that message with my spurs. We hit the brush on the run and almost ran into a steer that had been overcome by curiosity and was peeking out at us. I shot him between the eyes.

Now, I don't know of anything living that will stay alive when shot between the eyes at close range with a rifle, but that steer just stood there, legs apart, staring straight ahead. I levered another shell into the chamber and hesitated. It was risky enough to fire one shot. Anyone within hearing would have trouble deciding where that shot came from, but the second shot would find him with ears perked, and the direction would be greatly narrowed down.

Still, that steer just stood there staring at me. I heard footsteps behind me and the Mexican cook trotted up, butcher knife in hand, "Iss he dead, señor?"

I pointed to the hole in the animal's head. "It didn't bleed."

"A-h-h, no blood, no live," he said and walked by me. The steer didn't move and he pushed his shoulder. No movement. The man laid his shoulder against the animal just behind the front shoulder and pushed hard. Slowly at first, the animal toppled over on stiff legs. There he lay as if made of stone, stiffened body just like he had stood.

The Mexican looked at me and said in Spanish, "I have not seen this before, señor; does the gun do this to the animal?"

"I don't know; I have never seen it before, either. It's very strange."

The squealing stopped somewhere nearby and we pulled the steer out to where the carts were parked in the shade of the west bank of the arroyo. "Slow elk for supper, boys."

Two Mexicans were gathering wood. There would be no worries about escapees before they ate. Beans and rice and coffee were simmering on the fire in record time and another fire was building in a pit.

"Jist hand me one o' them laigs with th' ham on it an' I'll take care of it without th'bother o' cookin'," Rip said.

"You gnaw one side an' I'll gnaw t'other, an' we'll meet at th' bone," Isom drawled.

Suddenly we had a dozen expert cooks givin' advice an' issuin' orders until Gam yelled, "Shut up, you rannies. I'm givin' th' first plate to th' quietest one on th' cart."

Silence and peace descended upon camp.

The beans on the fire had been soaking in an olla on the cart all day. Gam dished them out when the meat was cooked.

"These beans air a le-etle chewy, Gam," Rube said gently.

"Go ahead an' eat a good bait an' I'll give you hot coffee for breakfast. You can swell all day tomorrow an' won't need enythan' t' eat till supper," Gam shot back.

We hadn't paid much attention to the two dogs traveling with us. They trotted along or rode in one of the carts when tired and assumed guard of the camps. Their master shared his food with them, and whoever was cooking made sure they had enough. The cook gave each a bone from the steer and they were contented to chew and eye the other warily.

The three of us were in a lot of strain; one slipup and we would be fortunate to merely trade places with our prisoners. We were in a real tight spot and we needed rest. With sunset, the prisoners were all settled. I took the two dogs and tied one close to me and the other close to a complaining Gamlin. We had to sleep and the dogs had to watch if we were to survive. I slept.

Green eyes reflecting the firelight, lips peeled back from huge white fangs, and the low growl of the wolf of my dreams disturbed me. I stirred, the wolf disappeared, and I was again falling into a deeper sleep when the low growl came again. I snapped awake, eyelids opening the only thing about me that moved. Under the cover, I gripped my gun and waited. The dog beside me growled low in his throat. Turning my head slowly, I stared at the fire. Only an occasional spark lent any light, and it took me awhile to locate a darker shadow near the fire and out of place. Another step and the creature would be among the cooking beans and meat. I sat up and yelled, and the two dogs charged to the ends of their tethers barking and growling. The dark thing disappeared. Of course, the whole camp was aroused. "It's nothing," I called, "just a prowling coyote after our breakfast. Go back to sleep." And they did.

I awoke with the rising sun in my eyes, rested some, but I could have rested more. We turned our dogs loose. After sniffing around where the creature had been, they resumed chewing their bones, though I think they had traded just to see if one got something better than the other.

It took awhile to feed and store our meat away, and we didn't get away until almost midmorning. I wondered how the warriors were getting along. Not good, I hoped, and not very fast. We were on the trail between two potential enemies, the ones behind and following us more dangerous. That tiny thread our lives hung on still held.

CHAPTER 17
A DAY AT THE BATHS

The creeks were fast drying up, and we were forced to follow the river closer than we would have a few weeks before. The breaks were rougher near the river, and we finally gave up and followed the river down on the flats.

"Why don't you just put your saddle on backwards an' ride like that?" Gam asked as we broke camp the third morning. I had spent a lot of time covering our back trail. Any Indian—or anyone for that matter—afoot could have caught up with us easily, and I expected them any time. My neck was stiff from looking over my shoulder so much, and my mind was tired of thinking of all the reasons they had not shown up.

The herd followed much closer to the river and we followed in their tracks. They cut across the big loop in the river that curls around the Granite Mountains, and we followed until we found the faint tracks of a wagon going toward the mountains. Those tracks ended where the Price tumbleweed sat at the foot of the pass between Flat Top Mountain and Soldiers Peak. It was a good place to camp in the summertime, being on the northeast side of the Soldiers Peak and shaded by the mountains in the hot afternoons. In these mountains, "hot" is a relative term, for it was hot everywhere. Even here on the flats, we could feel the heat radiating off those rocks like an oven. They are no place to be in the summertime.

Our cavyyard with the spare oxen mixed in had behaved well, following the bell mare. Now they scattered a little across the plain, seeking to graze on the browning grasses.

Gamlin and I scouted the Price wagon carefully. "Don't seem like they left in a great hurry; th' harness is in th' toolbox an' there's still food in th' safe," Gam called from the wagon bed. He got out the wagon sheet and we spread it over the hoops for shade in the wagon and moved our prisoners from the carreta.

"You don't often see a bunch of fellers anxious t' mount a tumbleweed, Gam."

"That depends on where th' feller's comin' *from*," Red observed. "I don't ever want t' see one o' them damned carts again."

"I don't ever want t' *hear* one o' them blasted carts again," I added. "That screech is still in my head. At least we have our firewood gathered for a few days." The grins on the tumbleweed showed they understood what I meant.

Rip Black agreed, "Best use them things can be put to."

With the camp settled, we made a closer inspection of the area. Of course, any tracks were long gone, and it was significant that there was no cooking fire. It was as if they had pulled up, unhitched, and rode off to who-knows-where.

"What now, Lee?" Nick asked.

I scratched my head. "I guess the next thing we could do is ride plumb around these hills an' see if we can see any sign that might tell us where they could be." Gam's face fell some, for he knew who likely would be doin' th' riding. "Get supper ready; after that you can catch up th' horse you want t' ride an' get ready t' leave before sunrise in th' morning."

His grin almost split his face and he jumped to it. I took the axe and began breaking up the side posts of one of the carretas to the cheers from the Anglo prisoners and the consternation of the comancheros. Though the shade of the mountains was blessed, we could still feel the heat radiating off those cursed rocks. By full dark when the desert-like plain turned cool, that heat would feel good.

I got a fire goin', Nick got th' cook goin', and Gam trotted out to catch his horse. He came back hot and sweaty, a smug-looking horse in tow.

"Nick, we're gonna have t' get a lot of water. That sinkhole around the corner is good enough for the stock, but too green for us."

Gam's face fell a little, then he said, "I'll go right now an' get some."

"Now don't go off half-cocked; it's a long ways either way you go. One of us will go in th' morning when we can see what we're doin'. Matter of fact, *I'll* go jist t' be sure we get good water. You'd stop at th' first water no matter how bad it was, 'cause you wouldn't be drinkin' it."

"Aw-w-w, Lee, I wou—"

"You would an' you know it. Let's git busy an' feed those yayhoos so's *we* can eat."

After supper, we sat down, and I drew out the outline of the mountains and the rivers. "We're sittin' here in this notch between Flat Top up there and Soldiers Peak over there. When you start out in the morning, go around th' foot of Soldiers till you get to th' river. It's best you cross as soon as you can, then up here, you'll have t' cross Elm Fork. Th' rivers are low an' you shouldn't have any trouble crossin' if you watch for quicksand.

"You cain't cross North Fork after Elm b'cause it's in a gorge you *can not* cross. Watch the mountains for any human activity and watch the ground for any sign of passing. North Fork comes through th' mountains in a gorge—here."

"Can I get through there?"

"No, don't bother with it, no one is likely t'get in there; it's river from wall to wall. About a mile north of th' gorge is a sort of cove in th' mountain. Injuns use it for a camp, an' I think there is a spring there—at least there used t' be.

"On around, you'll pass b'tween a baldy rock to your left a ways an' come to an end of th' mountains. Your problem is that th' river can't be crossed until you ride to the head of that gorge up near this mountain that sits off by itself. That's Walsh Mountain. We passed it this morning."

"Reckon we better look at it?"

"Not now; it's not likely they would leave their wagon here and ride or walk all the way up there. Concentrate on the gorge and mountains until you git back here."

"That's a lot of ridin' if I have t' go all th' way to Walsh Mountain t' cross."

"I expect that if you do any lookin' as you go, you'll spend th' night somewhere along th' way."

"I'm gonna take another horse t' carry my bedroll and chow."

"I want you to be here by sundown day after tomorrow. If you have to, leave off scouting an' be sure you get here by then."

"We can backtrack an' pick any I have t' skip."

"Now, git ready an' git t' sleep. You got a big day ahead—and tie that dog close to you. I don't care if he stinks an' has fleas; at least with him there, you'll be awake when that Injun slits your throat."

Gamlin was gone when I woke next mornin'. His companion was tied to a wagon wheel. I suspect he left long before daylight. I jist hoped he didn't fall into a hole stumblin' 'round in th' dark. I got our cook up early an' we finished breakfast early.

"You fellers're smellin' awful gamey. What say we ride around to th' river an' take a bunch of baths?"

Isom grinned. "I don't need one yet, but I dreamed last night I was layin' atween a couple o' skunks that had been dead awhile."

"Dead skunks'd smell sweet next t' you," Red said. "Fact is I wouldn't be surprised if those dead skunks got up an' moved away—somewhere upwind from ya."

"Damn these chains, anyway," Rip declared, "they shore ain't no de-moc-racy 'er we'd of voted you off a long time ago, Isom."

"Nick, get these fellers on th' wagon an' lock them up an' I'll call up a couple o' yoke of oxen. This train's movin' out."

When they were secure, I caught up four oxen, an' when we tried t' hook 'em up, found I had three gees an' had t' let one go an' catch one I thought was a haw ox. Luckily, I remembered right, an' we were soon on our way. It was two miles to the river. It took a little time for the boys t' choose a spot just right for bathin' an' washin' clothes where they could hang them on bushes t' dry.

Nick had the key to the locks. While I sat my horse, my rifle across my lap, he brought the prisoners down an' locked both ends of the chain to two wagon wheels. The men sat in the shade under th' wagon. Nick loosed one Anglo and one Mexican from the chain. "Now, boys, here's th' rules of this game: you both can take a bath, wash your clothes, and hang them on th' bushes. Then, you two bein' first, get th' privilege o' cleanin' out ol' Tumbleweed an' settin' up residence in a clean wagon—"

"I ain't gonna clean up that wagon *after* I taken a bath," Red declared. "Ef'n I git thet priv'lege, I'm gonna do it first." His Spanish partner nodded agreement.

"That makes good sense, Red; where'd you learn t' do that?" Josh asked.

"Got it sleepin' next t' me." Rip sniffed.

Soon, the two were cleaning the wagon. When they started sweeping, the men under the wagon were showered with dirt and had to evacuate the premises and stand in the warming sun. There was no small amount of advice given, most of it ignored by the two workmen.

Finished, the two jumped down and came around to me. "Just because I say this only once don't mean it ain't important, so listen close. When you are off that chain, I will be payin' very close attention to you. If you get a notion t' run, remember this horse is faster than you and a bullet is even faster. It'll pain me t' have t' shoot you, for by that I will be losing money. However, I *will shoot* if you make me. And another thing; the river is shallow enough that a bullet can reach you with effect even underwater. Just don't try anything, an' we'll git along fine. Any misbehavin' will cause this party to end, and the unwashed will remain that-a-way.

"Nick, Gam said there was a box of Pears soap in that storage box. Get us a couple of bars."

Nick opened the box and rummaged around a moment, "Don't see any, Lee."

"Is there a box in there with a man's picture on it?"

"You mean Henry Ward Beecher's pichur?"

"Yes, that's th' soap. Open it an' git us two bars—come t' think of it, bring that whole box down. I'm sure we'll need more than two bars t' git this bunch clean.

"Nick, I meant for you to git Cookie washed first so he could be cookin' us up a dinner. Put that man back on an' get th' cook off first."

"No, no, Señor Lee, I should be first. I have cleaned thee tumbleweed and I am most dirtee."

"A-h-h, you are right, Beto; you earned the right to go first and I forgot." I chuckled. "Go."

Nick tossed the two men a bar of soap apiece and off they trotted to the river. Off came Red's boots and he waded in with his clothes on. The naked Beto watched in wonder as Red began vigorously washing his clothes while still on his body.

"Yuh cain't wash th' seat o' yore pants with them on," Isom called. "That's where yo're gittin' th' most wear-n-tear."

"You jist tend t' your own laundryin' an' I'll tend t' mine, thankee."

"I'm only givin' you half an hour t' git done," I called. "We only got about twelve hours o' daylight left, an' it's gonna take all of it to get everyone washed."

Rube found Booger's alarm clock in the safe and brought it to me. I set it for twenty minutes for these two and gave it back. "Time's up when the alarm goes off, boys. Unless there's any strong opposition, Nick will be timekeeper."

The many boisterous objections were ruled frivolous by the judge on horseback, and his ruling stood. Nick rummaged in the toolbox again and came out with a checkerboard and two well-used decks of cards. Soon three games were going under the wagon: the checkers made of dried brown and black beans; a poker game; and on the end of the chain, the remainder of the Mexicans were playing some form of faro. Matchsticks were used for money.

Nick sat on the riverbank or in the water, keeping time an' offerin' unwanted advice to the bathers. I thought it was prudent of him that he took pains t' stay within my range of vision at all times. It was nice t' know he took my talk to heart.

Rube and Cookie, the last two to bathe, were in the water after sunset, and we elected to stay the night right where we were, in spite of the mosquitoes. Yes, Cookie got two baths and deserved them the way he kept us in food all day.

CHAPTER 18
TEXAS PERDITION

"Did you know they weren't no jails in th' Bible?" Bass Reeves sat
back contemplating our catch as the men were eating their meal on
Tumbleweed. *"When someone broke th' law by killin' or hurtin' their
fellow man in some way, th' people dealt with it right away. It was
just a lot easier t' deal with a killer when he was standin' b'side his
victim with blood on his hands. We feel a lot of sympathy for th'
deceased an' his grievin' kin* there, *but take th' body away an' in
some perverse fashion, th' sympathy gits transferred to that sorry
killer. In this business you gots t' remember th' victims even when
they're out of sight. They* are *th' ones derservin of our sympathy.*

*"An' here's another thing you needs t' keep in mind all th' time,
Lee. Lots of guilty fellers brought b'for' th' judge shows remorse—they
say for their crimes—but if that was true, why didn't they turn they-
selves in? It ain't remorse for th' crime, it's remorse for gettin' caught
an' their sins brought out in th' light o' th' law. Don't waste no
sympathy on those fellers."*

By midmorning we were on our way back to the notch.
Tumbleweed smelled much better, and the men were more
comfortable being clean and on the roomier wagon. I took off
the upright poles from a carreta and made a shelter by stretch-
ing the tarp from the wagon to the poles at each corner. The
prisoners now had plenty of shade under the wagon and shelter.
By sunset all was back in customary order.

I worried about Gamlin. There were a hundred—no, a

thousand—things that could go wrong for a man out there alone and it was getting late, well past the time I had expected him t' arrive.

His hail to the camp was a great relief. He rode in with two lathered horses. "That was too long a ride t' make in two days an' look for sign too, Lee. I didn't git half o' th' east side looked out b'fore I had t' give up an' ride."

"Don't worry about it, Gam, we'll pick up where you left off an' you can nursemaid this bunch tomorrow. I'll take those horses an' you git some chow. Cookie left things on th' fire for you."

We didn't talk much while he ate and the horses cooled some. Before Gam finished, I walked the two horses around to the sink and let them drink. Gam was on his bedroll when I returned, and I unrolled mine nearby so we could talk. "I take it you didn't find anything."

"Not a scratch, Lee. It's as if they had disappeared off the face of the earth."

"About the only thing you've accomplished is determine that they haven't left these mountains—well, I should say probably haven't left; it's been so long since they got here, any sign has disappeared."

"You can see a lot of th' mountainsides from down here, but there were places a man would have t' climb to t' make sure no one was there."

"Yeah, but even at that, those places are mostly too small t' completely hide a posse with a half-dozen horses an' mules unless they were hiding for some reason. I can't figger out what in the world Trace was or is up to."

"Any hopes of treasure around here?" Nick asked

"They's always stories of 'gold in them thar hills' for every hill west of th' Mississippi, Nick. I'm sure these hills have also been crowned with that curse."

"It's the only thing I can think of that might attract them. For sure, no outlaw on th' run is gonna pick these rocks to hide on in th'middle of summer."

My watchdog whined and nosed my face as if to say, "Will you shut up an' let a tired dog sleep?" The two of them had spent the day romping in and out of the river, and he was still damp from his last dip. Gam didn't say anything for a while and when I heard his soft snore, I turned over and slept. Dog was happy.

After breakfast, Nick and I rode north along the foot of the mountains. There is a pass between Flat Top Mountain and King Mountain to the north. We searched the sides of Flat Top all the way up to the divide, then crossed and rode down the foot of King and Mount Lugert.

The north side of Lugert was eroded away by the North Fork, and we rode up to the abrupt chasm of the gorge. My horse shied away from the hole, and I dismounted and walked over toward the rim. Now, I don't like great heights nor deep holes, so at a distance that felt safe, I got on my knees, crawled to the lip of the canyon, and lay on my belly. That one hundred-foot-deep gorge would have been just as scary to me if it had been twenty feet deep. It was still deep in shadow and hard to make out details. The roar of the river as it raced through the narrows to my left made an echoing sound up and down the gorge, and mist from the rapids drifted upstream in the breeze, making things even more indistinct in the gloom. Searching the gorge from above would have to wait for the noon sun. I crawfished back away and we rode on until I was sure our search overlapped Gam's.

Though it tempted me to cut across the plain far away from the gorge, we stayed close in order to see it in the sunlight. Nick saw nothing of note until our third stop; he called me to the rim. Even then, there was no evidence of human presence, past or recent. I was about to crawfish away when something about the rocks directly below caught my attention. The bottom of the cliff was covered with piles of loose rock that had fallen from the bluff. Over time, it had piled against the side and aged until it was nearly black, but directly below us, there was a streak of very light rock, much like I had seen at the foot of mines in the hills. Someone had recently removed a large amount of rock from the cliff and dumped it over the slope. No matter how long we looked and stared, there were no other signs of activity. I backed away and we rode back to camp in the gloaming.

It's really amusing how much my arrival at camp after being gone all day was like coming home to a bride with young children. She was always ready to tell of her trials with one child or the other or with th' whole lot, an' Gamlin was just like that at the tumbleweed: "First thing this morning, Josh got into it with one of th' Mexicans next to him, an' th' two trussed up either side of him; 'most beat him to a pulp afore I could stop 'em."

The arrangement I had put them in after their baths had a comanchero on either side of an Anglo. It seemed to work good for a couple of days. Josh had won almost all of his two neighbors' matchsticks when he was caught dealing off the bottom. That ended the card play and commenced the war. The fellow lay under the wagon, both eyes swollen nearly shut and a new gap in his front teeth. He grinned at me. "Got a chunk of ear an' a good portion of nose afore we got separated." I glanced at the prisoners on the wagon. It was no trouble picking out the two, one with a sizable piece of his right ear missing and th' other with a bloody nose. I just shook my head and walked away. "You got th' cards, Gam?"

"Both decks and th' checkerboard."

"We need to investigate the bottom of the gorge; do you think we could move in th' morning?"

"Yup, but why don't we go t'other way an' unload these scalawags at Fort Sill, then come back, and I can help you look the place out?"

"It would take us most of a week, round trip, t' do that. Still, these prisoners have spent enough time on Tumbleweed in this heat. We probably ought t' git them relief."

"Lee," Gamlin said softly, "I don't think a week delay will hurt our search for Price one bit."

"I'm beginnin' t' think th' same way, but we don't know that for sure. Still, unloadin' the prisoners would free up four of us to look the country over and possibly discover a reason for Trace's disappearance. I'll sleep on it, Gam."

The only thing clear in th' morning was that the sooner we got rid of the prisoners, the sooner the Tumbleweed Race War would be over. We had to separate Anglo from Mexican to avoid more bloodshed. Right after breakfast Gam hitched up four mules and pointed the wagon tongue toward Fort Sill.

It was with some relief that we found evidence that the Comanche warriors had passed us by. We followed the cattle's trail knowing we would meet Harmon and Tenderfoot some-where along the way. They appeared the second day, and Gam was talking to them well before they were within hearing. By the time they got to us, he was in a fine fettle. "Tex, you can have these mules an' welcome to them." He turned to the prisoners, "And I'm *not* talking about th' mules pullin' this wagon, I'm talkin' about the jackasses *ridin'* this wagon. Anybody, *anybody* clumsy enough t' git caught dealin' off th' bottom oughta git horsewhipped. Give me that horse." The exchange was made without the mules breaking stride, and the only delay with Gam on the horse was the changing of his direction.

"What's this all about, Gam?" Harm asked.

"I been ridin' herd on this bunch of rannies till I'm sick of 'em, that's what. They're yours for a while."

"In so doin', Harm, you will probably save one or two of us from gettin' lead poisonin'," Rip muttered.

"Don't go feelin' so smug about that, feller. I can still administer doses of poison from horseback," Gam called. He rode off to help Nick with the horse herd, glad to be away from tumbleweed chatter. I didn't blame him.

We nooned on West Otter Creek; after we ate, Harmon told us about his trip. "We only got a dollar fifteen a head for th' cattle. There were nine head he wouldn't buy, an' we drove them over to the Comanche camp."

Tex spat. "That long-haired Injun agent had a fit over us doin' that. Said we should have give 'em to him for 'proper' distribution. I told the SOB we just wanted those Injuns t' git th' meat, not some fat-assed politickin' agent. He's nervier than a busted tooth."

"You know what, Lee? A couple of those cows had come fresh with calves an' I showed th' squaws how t' milk them," Harmon said. "They took right to that."

"You ain't gonna tell them what they did to you?" Tex asked.

Harmon blushed, "No I ain't gonna tell, Tenderfoot."

"Then I will. Them wimmin watched him milkin' an' got t' chatterin' an' gigglin' an' Harmon asked them by motionin' what was funny. Then one o' th' young ones with a papoose came up an' dropped her top an' squirted Harm in th' face with her milk. You never heard such laughin' an' carryin' on."

Harm grinned.

We had been talking about Trace and his posse in terms of the past, and gradually we became convinced that we were looking for corpses and not living people. Nick was concerned about the family at the ferry and requested he be released to return home when the prisoners were delivered. It seemed reasonable, so we agreed that four of us without prisoners could carry on our search without him. He was going to look at Fort Sill for a chance to go home, or to Fort Smith with any group that might be going that way.

I wrote out a note about our search for Tracey Price. "Nick, take this note an' put it in a telegram to Marshal Carroll in Fort Smith. While he's doing that, Gam, you find Evan Worth an' tell him t' meet us at Cottonwood Spring. We have a string of Comancheros and thieves and Texas horses for him. I don't want soldiers nosin' around in our business, so stay mum about what we're up to. We should be to th' spring tomorrow evenin'." They rode out when we resumed our journey.

Cottonwood Spring was a pleasant place, a popular camping place. Gamlin rode up to the spring th' morning after we got there and said the Cattlemen's rep would be there later in th' day. Nick had found a wagon train headed for Fort Smith and latched on to it.

I hadn't said anything to the prisoners about what we were going t' do. When Evan Worth rode up with four Texas Rangers an' several vaqueros, they began t' realize what was afoot. "You'd never have taken me alive if I knowed you was gonna turn me over to those Texicans," Red said between clinched teeth. He knew there would be no wrist slapping in a Texas court—if he lived long enough to get there. The Comancheros became very upset. They had a real fear of those monster Texicans, and with some justification.

Harmon showed his concern but didn't say anything. It didn't take us long to make the trade. Worth wrote out a draft right there and handed it to me. "We sure could use that prisoner wagon, Lee."

"It ain't mine t' sell. We're headin' back out t' find th' owner, be he dead or be he alive."

"We been hearin' somethin' about one o' Judge Parker's posses gone missing. His name's Price?"

"Yeah, we found this wagon sittin' out in th' middle of th' plain an' no one around. We're gonna go back an' see if we can find somethin' of him an' his men."

"Well, good luck. I hope you have a happy ending," Worth added, then said his farewells. "By th' way, Tex, I never caught your last name," he said as they shook hands.

"That *is* his last name," Gam said. "His first name's Tenderfoot." We hardly ever used th' Tenderfoot handle anymore.

They marched their prisoners off on foot. "Texas Rangers ain't known for their fancy equipment like wagons an' such," Gam observed.

"Ain't used t' havin' prisoners—long," Tex mumbled.

"I got attached to some o' those Mixicians, an' those Anglos weren't all bad," Harm said.

"They was pretty human, weren't they, Harm? Most outlaws are most o' th' time. It's easy t' sympathize with them an' forget their victims, th' ones deservin' of our sympathy. Gatherin' stray cows ain't wrong in itself, but spookin' a herd in th' night t' pick off a bunch of them is. More often than you think, those cows are stolen at th' expense of some honest cowhand runnin' through th' night tryin' t' save his herd an' gettin' killed by tromplin' or runnin' off a bluff or wreckin' b'cause of a gopher hole. In my mind, those boys got blood on their hands, only we can't see it."

Harm nodded and Gam asked, "What about those comancheros, Lee?"

The Texan spoke up, "They're in th' middle of a whole lot of sin. If they didn't trade with the Comanches, th' Injuns'd have no market for stolen cattle, wimmin, an' children from Texas farmers an' ranchers. Th' trade got th' Injuns guns an' powder t' keep up their war on decent folk—and rotgut t' feed their weakness.

"Then those comancheros turn around an' sell their cattle to ranchers in New Mexico who do not care that they were stolen. In fact, they buy th' more gleefully b'cause they are Texican stolen beef."

"It's th' market for stolen cattle that drives th' whole operation," I added.

Tex spat. "You might think the comancheros were drinkin' th' milk o' human kindness by ransomin' captives th' Injuns took, but it's a business with them. If they don't think they would profit by th' transaction, they leave those captives to their fate with the Injuns." If Tex ever spat b'for he talked, you knew it was somethin' important or he was mad.

I threw th' grounds of my coffee in th' fire. "That's enough jawin' for th' day. Git busy, an' let's make tracks afore that feller comes back an' wants his money back."

Chapter 19
Granite Mountain Gorge

An old mountain man told me this tale about the North Fork and the Granite Mountains: "They's a Injun legend about the river you folks call North Fork of the Red River and the Granite Mountains. It goes somethin' like this: That river were born with a perverse nature. In all that flat plain it began t' run through, it could have gone around either side of them Granite Mountains. But no, there weren't anythin' fer it to do but turn right into those mountains. I s'pose if we could have heerd 'em, thet river would heve been a-hollerin' at those mountains, 'Git out o' my way!' And them mountains woulda been yellin' right back, 'Go 'way, we ain't a-budgin'.'

"Well, that ther river didn't go 'way an' those mountains didn't budge, an' there musta been a mighty collision. Water is mighty persistent in findin' its lowest level. Pretty soon, it found th' least little crack in th' shoulder of Quartz Mountain an' started pushin' its way through to th' plain west of th' mountain. First water run out over that rock an' th' rock laughed, but it didn' know water. Le-ettle by le-ettle it started eatin' down into that crack and makin' it wider an' wider till thet whole river just bust through. That mountain, she squoze back, an' th' hard bedrock of ol Quartz Mountain wouldn't let th' river dig down th' last few feet or go no wider, an' there they were when first man found 'em, river roarin' an' tryin' t' dig through thet mountain an' mountain squeezin' river through a little gap on its shoulder. Course, now ol' Mother Nature hes cooled th' argument a bunch by not givin' thet ol' river es much water es afore, an' mountain an' river purty much quit ther fightin'."

Now that we were shut of comancheros an' cattle thieves, it seemed the disappearance of Tracey Price and his posse weighed heavier on our minds. It was our constant conversation around camp, and we made sure we didn't dawdle on the trail to the upper end of that cañon.

We set up camp just across the river from th' mouth of what is now called Armstrong Creek. "Only fair way I know how t' do this is t' draw straws t' see which one o' you three gits th' privilege o' keepin' camp first." I held a fistful of straws of varying length.

Gam frowned, "You ain't gonna draw with us, Lee?"

"It's an insult, Gam, t' think that I would be dumb enough t' sit around camp watchin' th' stock sleep an' let you three loose on this canyon. I'd be buryin' one er two o' you or patchin' up broke bones an' wonderin' if you'd live long enough t' git you to a doctor."

"So you'll be goin' in ever' time?" Tex grinned.

"Quit yer jawin' an' draw a straw."

"Ha, I got th' longest," Gam crowed, "looks like you two gotta figger it out . . . an' th' loser is . . . Tenderfoot Tex!" Harmon grinned.

We started down the canyon. Within a quarter mile, th' trail ended abruptly and we were scrambling over rocks and rubble that went right into the river the rest of the way.

"If I'da knowed how rough this was gonna be, I'da volunteered for permanent camp keeper," Gam complained.

"Shore wish we had a boat," Harm sang out from th' top of a house-sized boulder.

If I heard that "Wish we had a boat" song once, I heard it twenty times. May have sang th' chorus a couple of times myself.

We were so intent on our trip, we passed our destination a ways before I looked up. "Hold up, boys, we been havin' so much fun, we ran right by that rock dump."

The rock dump I had seen from the top had been thrown over the edge of a narrow ledge halfway up the cliff. It was made up of quartz, a very pretty stone some folks use for gravestones. We couldn't see where it had come from on the ledge and looked for a way up to it.

"I say agin, Lee, they ain't no way up there from down here 'lessen yuh got wings," Gam called from under the cliff.

"OK, Gam. Harm, look down th' wall to your right, an' I'll look behind us an' see if there's any way up we passed by." But look as we might, there was not even a remote way we could climb up to that ledge from the bottom of the cliff. "I'm about t' subscribe to your wings theory, Gam," I said as I dropped from the hundredth lookout boulder.

We were trudging back to camp hot, dusty, and dry, when Tex called to us from above, "Hey, fellers, where you goin'?" There he stood, hands in his pockets on the very ledge we had worked all day to reach—and he wasn't a half mile from camp.

"Blamed if I ain't gonna shoot 'im," Gamlin threatened.

"Wait, Gam, he ain't suffered enough," Harmon warned.

"Tex, how th' . . . how did you get up there?" I called.

"I didn't git *up* here, I got *down* here—through that little wash there." He pointed to a very steep and narrow crack in the rock that ran from the plain above down to the ledge he so casually stood on. "My only problem is it's too steep an' gravelly for me t' git back up, an' there ain't no way on down from here."

"You can jump now, Tex. I'll catch you," Harm called in a sweet voice.

"I got a better chance flyin' down."

"Don't worry, Harm, I can hit him on th' wing," Gam said.

"How long have you been there, Tex?" I called.

"Oh, 'bout three days, I figger. Ain't a drop o' water up here, an' they's a whole lot o' sunshine in these rocks."

171

"I suppose next you're gonna tell us you followed a stray horse down there."

"Fer a fact, Lee, how'd you deduce that? I choused him back up that draw an' forgot t' grab his tail as he went up, an' he left me flat."

"I'm gonna grab your tail an' twist it plum off," I threatened. "The idea that I left you t' watch th' place an' you go explorin' instead. I suppose there's no dinner cooked, an' th' stock is scattered plumb t' hell an' back."

Tex contemplated the toes of his boots.

"Since you're there, go down that ledge a ways an' see if there's been anyone else there an' if you can tell what they been up to. We'll go to camp an' see what's left of it an' th' stock. If we don't forget, we'll be by eventually t' help you out o' there." I turned and trudged after the other two.

Camp seemed in order except our beans had boiled dry an' burned and Harm was scraping the Dutch oven out. "Think I'll just run down to th' store an' buy another oven an' throw this one away."

"Hold on to it, Harm, we can put Tex's ashes in it an' take him back to his grievin' ma."

"What makes you think she'd grieve, Gam?"

Even an hour baking on that ledge would be hard on a body, an' Tex had been there longer. I caught up his saddled horse and a couple of canteens, one only partially full of water, and rode the rim to the wash. After I had lowered the partial canteen to him, Tex tied the rope around his waist, and me and the horse pulled him up. His clothes were dry as dust and I wet his bandanna and he washed his face and neck, then drank.

"That ledge has a muddy stretch on it a ways down, and there are a lot of boot and moccasin prints in it. Th' thing that worries me, Lee, is that there's only one set of boot prints coming back with those moccasin prints. Lee, it ain't gonna be good if they left people on that ledge without water."

"We'll find out tomorrow, Tex, let's get back to camp an' see if anything's fit t' eat." Harm had made biscuits and we all had a can of tomatoes with our fatback bacon. Gam lost the morning straw drawing, and I was a little relieved to know I wouldn't have t' corral two wild colts. Harmon was a lot calmer and less impulsive than the other two. We fixed us a permanent rope with knotted handholds down the little gulley and walked the ledge. In one spot, the ledge was muddy; in another, it was only a few inches wide and we had to hug the rock. It wasn't wide enough anywhere for two to walk abreast. We were in the deep morning shadow of the bluff, but the rocks around us still radiated heat they had absorbed over time, and we were soon soaked in sweat.

Folks, especially rock hounds, will tell you there are no caves in granite rocks, but what we found that day put th' lie to that tale. I could see the lighter dirt crossing the ledge where the dump was below, and as we approached, we could see a hole in the face of the bluff. Where limestone caves are made by water dissolving rock, this granite cave was made by the underlayer settling in such a way that the rock split and opened a crack like an inverted V. Someone had recently enlarged the opening to the crack. That was the explanation for the new rock on the talus below.

The lighter dust on the ledge had lots of footprints in it, both moccasin and boot. There were some drops of blood, burned black with sun and age. "What you suppose is in th' cave, Lee?" Tex's voice in my ear made me jump.

"Don't know; let's have a look."

But to look, I would have to be peering over Harm's shoulder, for he was already standin' in the doorway, "Just letting my eyes git used t' th' dark, Lee, I ain't goin' in till you're ready."

"Yuh can go anytime, Harm, but don't fall into any hole

more'n a hunnert feet deep, 'cause that's th' longest rope we got," Tex said from behind.

I grunted. "You fall into *any* hole, we're leavin' you there."

Harmon took a step or two inside and we followed, soaking in cooler air.

"Whut's that smell?" asked Tex.

I sniffed and became conscious of the smells of th' place. "That's th' smell o' death, old *and* new, Tex."

The boy moved to the wall, "Make good targets standin' in th' doorway, don't we?"

I felt foolish, but said, "Anyone set on shootin' us woulda already done it, don't you think?"

"He could have a slow fuse," Tex mumbled.

Harmon had squatted on the floor, peering into the gloom. "There's something over there against that back wall; looks like bodies." He pointed to the left wall back against the rubble that had fallen into the room. The inverted V widened as it penetrated the rock, and I could see that rubble from the top had fallen into the room. It would probably eventually fill the whole void. A couple of moments more and I could make out the forms Harm was indicating.

"Looks like people, don't it, Lee?" Tex was leaning forward as if straining to see in th' gloom.

I reached for my matches. "Believe so, Tex; let's get closer an' look. Watch your eyes." I struck the match and the flare blinded me for a moment. When the fire settled down, we walked across to the forms and looked them over. "There's your old death, Tex." Harm drew a sharp breath. This dry climate had for the most part preserved them after the fashion of dried apples. Their skin had turned very dark to such an extent that you could not determine what their natural coloring was in life. There was a fine coating of dust over them.

Two of the four bodies wore rusted armor from helmet to

spats covering th' tops of their shoes. One of the other bodies was that of a friar or priest, whichever you want t' call him. The hood of his robe was over his head, which looked like it had been partially shaved, leaving a wreath of hair just above the ears. The third body was that of a young woman. She had been placed with more care than the other three. Her costume gave evidence that it had been very elaborate when she wore it in life. With my second match, I inspected the bodies more carefully.

The two soldiers had not died natural deaths. "Look, this one had his hand cut off," Harm observed.

Tex nodded, "Yep, probably bled to death."

"Is that a knife handle stickin' out of that other man's chest, Lee?"

"No, it's the short shaft of an atlatl spear."

"Wow, it went through the armor right into his chest."

"Looks like the thrower wasn't too far away," I said as I stood up. The strong sickening odor of rotting flesh assaulted my senses, and Tex gasped. I turned to the wall and there, just before the match burned out, was the contorted face of a man, his eyes staring into mine, his nose not twelve inches from mine! "Look out!" I hollered and ducked back down, reaching out to assure myself that there was rock between me and that man. The rock was there, thank heaven.

"What was that?" Tex asked.

"I don't know," I said, then, "Who goes there? Speak up."

Silence. Harmon knelt beside me. "I don't think he will ever talk to you, Lee."

"He was dead, wasn't he?" Tex was more hopeful than sure.

I struggled for a match and struck it on the rock. The image of that face being illuminated from below as I rose haunts my dreams still. I can't count the times I have dreamed that vision and awoke soaking wet in sweat, heart pounding. I stood eye to eye with the head of Osgood Dabney, this time with more distance between our noses. His dull eyes held my attention. They didn't reflect the flame of the match. To his left sat the slightly cocked head of Booger Smith, and the flare of my next matched revealed Tracey Price, a neat round hole in the middle of his forehead.

Harmon began retching, "Get out of Harm's way, Tex." A glimpse of Tex's blanched face told me he wasn't far behind Harm. My stomach was rolling. "Let's get out." I followed the two out the entrance. Harm wet his bandanna and washed his face and neck. I tasted bile and rinsed my mouth with water and spat it over the edge.

Our signal for Gam was to fire three shots. Soon he was peeking over the edge of the bluff. "Hey fellers, your servant awaits."

"Gam, go get us a couple of those candles and a hand full of matches, please." I didn't feel good enough to growl at him.

"Did ya find somethin'? Did you find out where Price is?"

"Part of him, Gam. Now git th' lead out an' git goin'." I was feeling a little better.

I could hear his horse galloping away and very soon galloping back, but it seemed like a long time to me. He swung a canteen of fresh water, three candles, and a box of matches down to us. While the three talked, I lit a candle and reentered the cave. There on a shelf chiseled out of the rock were the heads of Tracey Price and his posse, eyes staring ahead and lips drawn back from teeth as the skin dried. The odd shape of Ozzie's face caught my attention. I turned the head to find that the back had been crushed in. Dirt and sand indicated the weapon of choice had been a big rock. Booger's head had the same damage. I didn't have to turn Trace's head to know there was nothing there. He had been shot at such close range that his face was pocked with powder burns. If the killer got that close without resistance, Trace must have been asleep or restrained in some fashion. I fervently hoped he was asleep. Most likely his two partners were not so fortunate as to be asleep when the final blows came.

"Look over here, Lee," Tex called from the very back of the cave. He pointed to a piece of buckskin and the mummified shoulder and arm of someone mostly buried under the dirt and rocks. Just a little bit of removing rocks uncovered what looked like an ancient mummy that must have been there a very long time.

"There's caves in th' limestone hill country of Texas that the Lipan 'Paches call burial caves where they lay out their dead. I'll bet this is th' same thing here, but it's a long ways from hill country."

"Those hill country Lipans got pushed out here by Kiowas and Comanches, so I bet you're right, and this is a Lipan burial cave."

"Why put those heads in here?"

I rubbed my chin and thought, "Maybe they were killed too far away to bring th' whole bodies an' they just brought their heads."

"They wouldn't kill them an' then bring their heads t' bury in their cave if they were enemies," Harm said.

"That's right. Trace's grandma was Lipan an' he spoke th' language well—practically grew up in their villages," I said. "No, they buried him here because he was Lipan and they brought Ozzie an' Booger b'cause they died with him. Those Indians are around here somewhere, and we need t' talk to them."

"What are we gonna do with these heads?" Harmon asked.

"Nothing, Harm; this is their burial. Let's get out of here and go hunt Indians and killers."

CHAPTER 20
INTO THE MOUNTAINS

"Cruel they have said I am, but they forget the utterly hardened character of the men I dealt with. They forget that in my court jurisdiction alone sixty-five deputy marshals were murdered in the discharge of their duty."
Judge Isaac C. Parker

I don't even remember squeezing through that narrow place on the ledge on the way back to the gulley, my mind was so full of what we had just seen. Harmon took Gam back to see the tomb. He returned in a very rare solemn mood. We were all saddened by the discovery, and many a memory of our times with the three men were expressed in somber tones around the fire that night.

Gam struck his fist on his knee, "I'm ready t' broach hell t' git th' ones that did this. What's your plan, Lee?"

I thought a moment before answering, "I think our first step is to find where the men were murdered. And the quickest way t' do that is t' find the Indians who brought the men here." I avoided saying "their heads," and we never alluded to the fact that the entombment did not include bodies.

"I don't think th' posse drove that wagon here," Harmon said.

Tex nodded, "No, if they had, their whole bodies would be in the tomb, wouldn't they?"

"Well, we only got about a million square miles o' plains t' cover. How you boys propose we do that?" asked Gam.

I started to speak, then kept my peace. It would be an education for the three to figure out a plan of action. Besides, it seemed I was left out of this discussion. *And I know what we are going to do. Let's see what they come up with,* I thought.

"Think we could find any trace of the ones leavin' that brought Trace, Booger, an' Ozzie here?" Harmon asked.

"Anythin' we find won't give much detail after this long," Tex said, "but it might tell us what *direction* they took."

"Well, even if it didn't give us a direction, we know th' wagon came from th' southeast an' likely that's where the Injuns came from."

"Ain't necessarily so, Harm; that posse would have to been foolin' 'round ah awful lot not to be a good distance *north* of here. They was in a big huff t' git t' Sweetwater Creek when we last seen 'em." Gam forgot that the Indians said they followed the wagon tracks until it turned off for the mountains.

"If we ever could find some fresh tracks, we might determine if one of those horses was shod, an' that might tell us if Boots was an Anglo or a half-breed that preferred boots to moccasins," Tex said.

Good point, Tex, I said to myself.

"I'm bettin' on all Injun," Gam said.

"Me too," agreed Harmon, "but that still don't tell us who killed them."

"We got t' find out what th' Injuns know afore we determine that." Tex lay back as if that would help his thinking.

Harmon nodded and Gamlin agreed, "Just like you said, ain't it, Lee?"

"Yup, an' if'n you three are gonna jaw all night, movin' out in th' mornin's gonna come awful early."

★ ★ ★ ★ ★

The notch where we first found Price's wagon was at the foot of what's called Devil's Canyon. It was here that the U.S. Government had its first powwow with the plains Indians in 1834. The famous Colonel Henry Dodge was in command, but he had some distinguished men in his dragoons, like Nathan Boone, ol' Dan'l's son, Jefferson Davis, and David Hunter, who would be a Union general. George Catlin was along with his paints and Governor Montfort Stokes, chairman of the Federal Indian Commission. The old boy was seventy-two at the time. I saw his grave at Fort Gibson. Don't know who the Indians were.

We made a big circle from the foot of the mountain around the notch, an' found the tracks we and the Indians had made following the wagon. Then on the south side of the canyon, we found very faint tracks of several horses heading east.

"Got t' be our friends," Gam said.

"Well, lead on, scout; let's follow them," Tex commanded.

They camped at the north bend of the North Fork and from looking at their camp, we guessed there were six of them and probably all Indians. From there, they turned southeast, aiming for the north end of the Glen Mountains.

"Bet we find them in the mountains," Harm said.

"And *I'll* bet we follow them until *they* find us, Harm." I had been in th' hunt for Injuns enough times t' know that a white man seldom found an Indian except by accident.

A man not knowing better would say it was only about two or three miles from the river to the Glens, but in this clear air distances are awful deceiving. It is over ten dry miles from the river to the hills.

"What are we gonna do for water, Lee?" Harm was always concerned about givin' th' stock good care.

"Don't worry, Harm; as long as we stay on the Indians' trail, they will lead us to water," I answered. True to my prediction, we found their camp on Glen Creek where there was still a trickle of water running. Harm and the horses were relieved. When we readied for sleep, I cautioned the watch, "Keep your eyes open; we are liable to have visitors anytime. If they come around on your watch, show them goodwill, unless they have our horses in tow, then try not to shoot one of us or a horse when you make war."

The night passed quietly, and by the time the sun stuck his nose over the horizon, we were under way again. Our trail passed down the front of the mountains and across to the mouth of Boggy Hollow on Otter Creek.

"They're gonna go up that creek into th' Wichitas, an' we're gonna lose 'em," Gam worried.

For the umpteenth time, I informed him, "Gam, we ain't found 'em; we only found their tracks. We'll follow them until they disappear on us, which they will sooner or later, then we'll find a nice place t' camp until *they find us.*" And that's just what we did.

It was the fourth morning that we had company. A Lipan named Nicasio walked in for breakfast, took a plate, filled it with beans and biscuits, poured lick over all of it, and sat down to eat it with his fingers. After he licked plate and fingers clean, he looked longingly at the empty bean pot, and Harm gave him the last biscuits covered with molasses. On top of that, he drank about a gallon of coffee. When the last cup was finished and Harm tilted the coffee pot to show it was empty, he rubbed his distended stomach and sighed. Before his droopy eyes could close for a nap, I asked about the burial. "Nicasio, we are most grateful for the burial of Tracey Price and his men."

Nicasio nodded, his chin lowering to his chest, "Trace was good Lipan." His eyes began to close.

"Did you bury him?"

"No. Others did." It seemed I was talking to a dead man—and it was a sure bet the man was talking in his sleep.

I slapped his foot and he jerked awake. "Where did you find them? Tell me now, for we will hunt his killer."

"Tepee Creek."

"Tepee Creek? What's he doin' over there?"

Nicasio shrugged.

"Whereabouts on Tepee Creek, Nicasio? That thing's *miles* long." I slapped his leg again.

He roused up and said, "Me not know, me not find, me not bury." Then taking my face in both hands and pulling it till our noses almost touched, *"Me sleep now."* And that's just what he did.

There was a soft laugh behind me. "You should not feed Nicasio before you talk to him."

I turned and there stood Walks With the Wind, laughing.

"I suppose you are right, my friend. Welcome."

"And welcome to you to our mountains," Walks replied.

"Do you know where Tracey Price was killed? We would find his killer."

"Yes, it is I who found White Fox and his wagon." His face reflected anger and sorrow. "He had been long dead, and we surprised the white killer going through their things at the wagon. He jumped on his horse and no one in our group could catch him."

"I will find him, Walks With the Wind, and take him to Judge Parker's court."

"That is good. White Fox was killed on Tepee Creek as Nicasio said, north of the Tepee Mountain. The killer had joined them just west of Fort Sill. He smashed the black man in the back of the head with a shovel and he fell into the fire. The other two were still sleeping and he busted the one called Ozzie with a rock, then shot the sleeping White Fox in the head. The black man was burned up when we found him. Only his head and feet did not get burned. We could not move him. It was a long journey to the tomb, so it was decided to bury their bodies there and take their heads to the Tomb of the Fathers."

We were all silent for a few moments, and Harmon handed Walks a steaming cup of fresh coffee. "Nicasio has eaten all our food, but I am cooking more," he apologized.

Walks smiled. "We have a saying, 'Sad is the man who comes to the fire after Nicasio.' "

"What did this killer look like, Walks?" Gam asked.

"He was a small man, very dirty, and his hair was long and not cared for. He rode there"—pointing northeast—"on a large roan horse with a white blaze—a very fast horse."

"Sounds like half th' whites in th' territory," Tex, who hadn't had a bath in weeks, said.

"No, he is *very* dirty," Walks said. "Stinks like striped cat."

"Seen some o' them, too." Gam nodded.

"I think he would go to Rainy Mountain." Walks With the Wind was not a guesser. If he said something, you could count on it being right, even if he said "I think."

"Then if all is well with you, Walks With the Wind, we will go to Rainy Mountain and see if the Kiowa know anything of this man."

Walks smiled. "All is well here, Lee Sowell, but would be much better if you take the Comanche and Kiowa away with you."

"It would be easier to catch the clouds, my friend."

CHAPTER 21
A KIDNAPPING AT RAINY MOUNTAIN

The longer you camp in one place, the more you make yourself at home, and it always takes longer to pick up and move. The sun was going down before the wagon was loaded and we were ready to move.

"Bank th' fire, Harm, an' get some sleep. We'll be up b'fore th' sun in th' morning." He had been hard at work cooking enough food to get us through the traveling days ahead.

"I'm on my way, Lee, soon's I bank coals around this pot of beans."

Nicasio had hardly moved all afternoon. The last thing I saw as I lay down was his moccasins pointed to the fire. Morning came well before dawn. I stepped over the still-sleeping Lipan and threw buffalo chips on the fire, added water and coffee to the pot, and went for the stock. Men ain't the only ones t' get comfortable in a long camp. Those perversive horses knew we were packing to move; they determined to stay where we were by disappearing.

It took over an hour to find them, and I was in a fine fettle when we got back to camp, dusty, sweaty, and thirsty. Gam was abusing the still-sleeping Nicasio over something and Harm was fussing around the fire. Tex was sitting on a boulder a safe distance from the activity, taking it all in with an amused look on his face. "Better sit out here, Lee, where you're safe from th' blast when Harm blows up."

"What's going on, Tex?"

"Did you hear Nicasio get up in th' night?"

"No, I slept until you got me up for the last watch, then I had t' chase down this blasted stock."

"Well, some time in th' night, that Injun got up an' ate half th' pot o' beans, an' Harm is fit to kill."

"*Half th' pot?* Don't he know that crossin' th' cook is as risky as braidin' a mule's tail?"

"Short rations today, I'll bet." Tex was enjoying the scene before us.

"Guess I'd better go in afore something bad happens. If they puncture that Injun, he's liable t' explode and hurt someone."

"Don't worry about the beans, Harm," I called. "We'll eat 'em all for breakfast an' that Injun'll know we got nothing for dinner an' not follow us." I tried to make light of the situation, but Harmon was too proud of his work to get much comfort from my talk.

"I'm sorry, Lee . . ."

"Don't worry about it, Harm; if you'da set on that pot with a shotgun in your arms, that Injun would have found a way to those beans, believe me. His eating is legendary among the Indians, and that's saying a lot, considering how much any Indian can eat." The Indian is a natural binge eater because of the inconsistency of his food supply. He moves fairly easily from famine to feast, but even among the Indians, ol' Nicasio is legendary.

"Look at that stomach, Lee," Gam said. "I'm thinkin' he's gonna blow any minute."

"Let's eat and get goin' before he wakes up." And that's just what we did. Our last view of the old camp showed Nicasio unmoved, sleeping off his overindulgence.

The food was awful shy at the noonin', and Harmon was still upset about it. I tried to convince him it wasn't his fault, but it was little consolation to him.

Gamlin disappeared while the stock were feeding on the sparse grass. He strolled in chewing on a peeled prickly pear. "Purty bad when a feller has t' rustle his own food."

"Even worser when he has t' pick birdshot out o' his rear while he gnaws on a pear leaf," Harm growled.

We camped at a spring on the north side of Unap Mountain that night. I was concerned that we had been too occupied with the Price massacre to pay attention to the overall reason we were out here, which was to "harvest" outlaws. Marshal Carroll would look askance at us not bringing in any prisoners a second time in a row, after we had to leave that load at Paris. The Judge would know about it too, and I didn't want t' get on the bad side of either man. I studied our warrants until it was too dark t' see, and we slept with the aroma of beans and roasting meat disturbing our rest.

I awoke quite suddenly with the realization that I really was smelling roast meat, when there was no meat in the camp when I lay down. Easing over on my side, gun in hand, I looked to see a shadow squatting by the fire, turning a little spit with a leg of antelope on it.

"Nicasio, what are you doing cooking at this hour?" And I didn't even know what the hour was. The big dipper showed that my hour to start watch was at hand.

Tex whispered, "Came in about th' middle of my watch with an antelope over his shoulder—an' I was sure he would not leave with it afore we had a crack at it."

Nicasio turned to us, "Me help you find Booger's killer."

"*Booger's* killer? Might have known." Tex chuckled.

"Th' man's heart is in his belly, ain't it?" I couldn't help laughing. "That is good, Nicasio. You will be of much help, but stay out of the beans until breakfast."

He grunted and turned back to his cooking. "Bet he's already been in 'em," Tex whispered and resumed his guard duty.

People in th' know will tell you that our diet was not healthy, but I disagree. We did well on beans an' fat meat. An occasional bait of pigweed and poke greens with a little fatback thrown in would keep us regular, and there was always sunflower seed, plums, grapes, and chokecherry in season. We would add rice and dried fruit, canned goods like peaches and tomatoes for variety, but it always seemed the end of the trip was made on beans and fatback.

Rainy Mountain was some sort of spiritual place for the Kiowa people, and the government had established the Rainy Mountain Indian School Reservation around it. We rattled into the settlement around to the superintendent's office and residence. While I looked up the superintendent, the boys drove Tumbleweed over to the blacksmith shop for some needed repair and maintenance.

"It's about time you showed up. What took you so long?" was my introduction to the man.

"What do you mean?" I asked.

"Aren't you the one sent here to investigate the kidnapping?" he asked.

"No, I am on the trail of a murderer who might have come through here a few days ago."

"I don't know anything about that." He dismissed the subject with a wave. "I want you to go after that kidnapper and get that child back here before the Kiowa get on a rampage about it."

The man's attitude was beginning to wear thin. "Well, mister, why don't you tell me about it, and just maybe I can help you if you can help me find my man."

The man's arrogance seemed to melt away a little and I realized he might have been scared. The kidnapping of a child in his care meant he would be held accountable by the tribe and even more so by the child's family. In most tribes the loss of a child carried the penalty of death. "Take a deep breath and tell me the whole story," I commanded.

The man looked at me and stammered, "I-I'm sorry. This thing has put much pressure on me, and I am very worried about the child's welfare." I could well imagine how he felt about his own welfare out here without a white settlement in fifty or a hundred miles and surrounded by angry Indians, not far from the wild state.

"About a week ago—"

"It was nine days ago, on June thirteenth," a young man I took to be some sort of clerk interrupted from his desk.

"—a white man rode in here and asked the blacksmith to shoe his horse. He stayed around a few days in spite of my hints that he should leave, then of a sudden he was gone. It wasn't until that night that we discovered Amanda was missing. The children said they had last seen her over by the creek picking plums. We searched, and the boys found where she had been and where a horse with new shoes had ridden up and there had been a scuffle. Then they had both mounted the horse and ridden off."

"They rode north, and the boys traced them to the Washita, but lost their trail and returned," the clerk added.

"What did this man look like?" I asked.

"He was small, kind of mousey, like someone you would not trust," the clerk continued, "very dirty with wild hair under his hat . . ."

"He stank," the superintendent interrupted.

"Did he go by any sort of name?" I was sure he was the man we were looking for.

"Called himself 'Brother Abe,' said he was a preacher." I took it that the superintendent had little direct contact with the man since he was not interfering with the clerk's talk.

"This sounds like the man we are chasing, and we will follow him right away. We need to purchase some supplies. We have added a tracker to our posse and will likely run short of food before we get to another store."

The clerk opened a drawer and grabbed a ring of keys. "Store's open." He unlocked a door and entered the store.

"I will send my cook over to get th' stuff he needs." I hurried to the smithy.

"Harm, run up to the super's office and get what you need from their store. I'll be back to pay for it later."

If a town doesn't have a barbershop, the next best place to get information is from the blacksmith. His shop is generally an open shed, and he sees everything that moves within sight. This smithy was small and wiry and talked as much as a fiddler's clerk. He knew everything and everyone. "Shore, he came in an' wanted his horse shod. I made him show me his money first, he was so raggedy and dirty. Rode a fine horse; wouldn't be surprised if he didn't have some Kentuck Purebred in 'im. Roan with a blaze face, he was, an' leggy too, a real runner, I bet.

"An' watch th' girls, you bet. He'd sit here by th' hour, just lookin' at 'em. No doubt what was on his mind. I told him what these Ki-o-ways did to a white caught messin' with one of their wimmin, but he paid no mind. Told ol' Super about him, but he don't mind me much.

"Now, that Amanda was right purty, only about fourteen or fifteen summers, but all woman. I shore hope you-all catch up to him an' that girl ain't been harmed—much."

Lipans and Kiowa mix like vinegar and oil. I was curious about where Nicasio had got off to. Tex found him squatting over a map drawn in the sand, deep in conversation with several of the male students. Conversation over, they all rose and Nicasio hurried past Tex, saying as he passed, "We go now, much hurry." He mounted and was riding north alone.

"Tex, stay with Harm an' follow us. When it starts gettin'

dark, set up camp and we will find you. It's only about twelve miles to the Washita, and I imagine you will camp somewhere along it. We're going with Nicasio." I mounted and hurried to catch up with Gam, who was following the Indian.

CHAPTER 22
THE STILL BUSTERS

We were tiny specks on the prairie when Harmon finally got his supplies and Tex paid the clerk from the money I had given him. "Come on, Harm, move that wagon; we gotta catch up," Tex called.

"You know darn well we ain't gonna catch up to men ridin' horses with this wagon, Tex. You might as well relax and save your bile for somethin' worthwhile."

They drove on north at a reasonable speed for the mules, Tex riding miles more than necessary, circling and returning to urge Harmon on.

"Tex, look at your horse. You near run him t'death for nothin'. Tie him to th' tailgate an' let him rest. You're th' one impatient to go. *You* do th' runnin' an' let that poor horse alone." Harm stopped the wagon. "This wagon ain't movin' till that horse's tied to th' tailgate an' your feet are on th' ground."

"Come on, Harm, I ain't hurtin' this horse."

"You're wearin' him out for no reason other than your own impatience. What'll it be? I'm waitin'."

Tex spat. "I'll jist leave you sittin' here."

Harmon picked up his Winchester. "This is a big flat plain, an' you gotta long ways t' go afore you'd be out of rifle range."

"You wouldn't shoot me."

Harmon grinned. "Wanna try me?"

Friend Tex lifted his hat and scratched his head. "You know, I'm thinkin' you *would* shoot me or waste a lot of ammunition

191

tryin'." He couldn't help grinning back at the cook.

"Wouldn't take over one shell," Harm replied.

"Oh well, I guess you have a point about the horse. I'll let him rest and ride with you awhile. Hold on until I tie him on." He tied his horse and trotted around to the wagon seat. Harmon scooted over, and Tex noted that the rifle was on the far side of the driver. "You wouldn't o' shot me, would you?"

Harm clucked at the mules. "We may never know."

They moved on at a mule's pace, which Tex compared to that of the proverbial snail. "You're in so much of a hurry, hop down an' run a ways. You'll run off some energy that-a-way an' find out how your horse felt."

"That may be a good idea; think I will."

"I ain't stoppin'; me an' th' mules er in a hurry."

The breaks of Oak Creek gave the boys troubles, for the trail became dimmer and went where no wagon could go. They did a lot of detouring, and Tex decided to ride ahead and locate the trail. "Ground's so broken I wouldn't havta be far t' be out of range of that rifle less'n it can shoot around corners an' over hills."

"Anything more than fifteen yards'd be fatal for you," Harm replied.

"You can't afford to miss, an' you'd only git one shot."

"Buckshot won't miss at that range, Tex."

When they got to the bottoms of the creek, Harmon turned the wagon upstream. "Find where they crossed th' river an' we'll camp there," he called to Tex.

Tex rode back to the wagon. "This ain't th' Washita, if that's what you're thinkin'."

"If it ain't, what is it?"

"I don't know, but it ain't th' Washita."

"Sez you."

"Harm, think about it. This here stream ain't five yards wide.

Th' Washita starts 'way over in th' Texas panhandle, a hundred, hundred thirty miles from here. It's gatherin' water from other creeks an' streams over that hundred miles, an' it'd be fifteen yards wide, maybe more, by th' time it got this far."

"Maybe you're right; where did they cross?"

"Up there sommers." Tex pointed upstream, and Harm turned the wagon and followed. Fortunately, they found the crossing where the climb out of the bottoms wasn't so steep. They were able to follow the trail fairly easily until they hit th' breaks of what turned out to be another creek that was so full of gyp the stock wouldn't drink. Two miles further brought them to the headwaters of another creek with good water, and men and animals drank. Another mile put them over the divide and into the Washita drainage. By now, it was too dark to follow a trail, and the two concentrated on getting the wagon to the bottoms of the river in one piece. This they did, the last half mile in almost total darkness. Grass was good, and they picketed the animals close to the wagon where they could be watched. A little venison jerky, and they crawled under the wagon and slept.

"My, my, don't that air smell good?" brought Harmon out of a sound sleep. A sniff or two cleared his head and made his eyes water. Tex was sound asleep and talking. "Pour me a double shot o' that tanglefoot I'm smellin' an' keep that bottle handy; this vaquero's mighty dry."

"Tex, wake up. Yer dreamin'." Harm threw his boot.

"Huh?" When Tex awoke, he was sitting up, gun in hand. "What's goin' on? Harm, you there?"

"I'm here, Tex; what's that you smell?"

"You got whiskey, Harm?"

"No, but I can almost taste it when I breathe."

Tex inhaled. "Me too. Where's it comin' from?"

"I don't know, but we better find out b'fore we're too drunk t' do anythin' about it. Throw me my boot."

"You throwin' things at me agin?"

"You talkin' in your sleep agin?"

"No, I *do not* talk in my sleep. Git it yourself, you know where you threw it."

It took a few moments of head bumping and growling for Harm to find his boot. Tex was up and waiting when Harmon finally came out from under the wagon, hopping on one foot and pulling his boot on. "Where's that smell comin' from?"

"Don't know, but I can almost taste it."

Harmon shook his canteen and found it empty. Stepping to the river, he filled it and took a long drink. "Sa-a-ay, this water's purty good, 'bout eighty proof, I'd say."

"What? What you talkin' about, Harm?"

"Here, take a shot."

Tex took the canteen and sipped a little. Smacking his lips, he tasted the alcohol and then drank some more. "Harm, we done found th' fountain of youth an' paradise. Soon's it light enough, we're gonna find the big rock candy mountain. Dump that water barrel, we gotta refill it." And that's just what they did. By the time Tex could get his canteen filled, the water had lost its flavor and tasted like . . . water. He went running downstream, water splashing from his inverted canteen. Scooping up some water, he sipped. "Too weak." And on down the river he ran until he found a drink to his satisfaction. "Wait till Lee hears about this; he'll cuss an' rare."

"Cussin' an' rarin' won't be all he does when he tastes that water," Harm said.

"A-w-w, we just took that for ev-i-dence," Tex asserted. "Wait'll he sees that tumbleweed loaded with bootleggers an' their still."

"Just when do you propose that t' happen?"

"Why, soon es we catches 'em, Harm, soon's we catches 'em."

"First, we gotta find 'em," Harmon said as he walked up the river.

Now it so happened that they had camped on the river just below the mouth of Boggy Creek and by taste testing, they found that the tainted water had come down Boggy. Further testing determined that the dumped mash was coming from the second arroyo on the north side of the creek. It was just light enough to see that there had been a lot of activity in the creek bottoms. The boys retreated to the brush south of Boggy to plan what they were going to do.

"We need t' find out how many there are," Harm said.

"Don't matter; we'll just catch them gathered up an' march them off to Tumbleweed."

"I'm thinkin' it'll be about a half-minute arrest afore th' lookout they got hidden in th' brush throws down on us an' we become fertilizer for th' grasses of Boggy Creek Bottoms."

"Harm, you worry too much."

"And Tex, you don't worry enough; it's gonna get you an early buryin'."

"Just what d'yuh propose, Mr. Caution? Callin' down that vulture an' askin' him how many men are in that gulley makin' tanglefoot?"

"All I'm sayin' is we ought t' do some spyin' afore we goes blastin' in there blind."

"Tell you what. *You* go spy an' I'll wait right here polishin' up on my draw-an'-fire."

"Instead of practicing, why don't you go get that shotgun and a hand full of two-ought shells an' beat it back here without bein' seen."

"OK, Harm, I'm doin' it—and I'm keeping th' scattergun fer my own personal use."

"You do that, Tex, you do that." Without another word, Harmon crept through the brush to a point above the gulley where the brush came down to Boggy Creek and he could cross without being seen. The hard part of the climb up the opposite bank was not the steepness of the slope, but the sparse cover that made for a meandering assent. It took Harm quite awhile to work his way back to the top of the gulley, only to find that the brush was much thicker down the slope, an indication that there was a good source of water there.

He could see as he descended the gulley that the wash had exposed a layer of limestone. Water was seeping out where the limestone lay on a thick layer of granite. He heard the water gurgling over the rocks before he found the secondary wash coming in from his left where there had to be a goodly spring coming down to join the main gulley. It was just a few feet past this junction that he heard voices and decided it was time to retreat a little and climb the side of the arroyo for a better view.

The camp could not have been a hundred feet beyond where Harm stopped and retreated. Though it was hard to see through the brush, he could see the fire pit and bedrolls spread around. There were three of them, one shared by two people. Four men. With a little luck, they would be no trouble to round up.

The breeze brought the odor of soured mash, strong enough to make his eyes water, and Harm looked for the still. It seemed it was downstream a little from the camp, and as he watched a man came from that direction. "Hack, go down an' help Otis chop up some more firewood."

His order was answered when a rangy looking youth rose from the brush above the camp and clumped down to the gulley. Soon the sounds of wood-chopping came softly through the trees. The man giving the order picked up a rifle and climbed to Otis's lookout station. Harm shuddered inwardly when he realized he had been within a few feet of stumbling into the lookout stand.

In a moment, another man came up the little stream, drew a

cup of coffee from the fire, and sat on one of the bedrolls. Two chopping wood and tending the still, one in camp, and one on lookout accounted for four men. Harmon waited another three-quarters of an hour to be sure there were no more men in the camp, then slipped away and back to his rendezvous with Tex.

The Texan was leaning against a scrub oak pretending sleep and asked, "Is everything good, Captain Caution?"

"I found the camp, and there were four men in it. They have a lookout up above the camp, and the still is down below it."

"Good, let's go get 'em."

"Sure, Tex, you go up above th' lookout and herd them down that gulley, an' I'll be waitin' t' escort them to our wagon. Better yet, why don't you go get those boys, an' I'll be cookin' a big feed for us all an' we'll have a little party. Be sure t' bring a jug er two for dessert. Let's go."

"All right, Harm, it ain't gonna be a cakewalk, but it shouldn't be so complicated to catch four men."

"How good are you at actin'?"

Tex stroked his beard, "Don't know; what you got in mind?"

"If we could draw them out of that gulley they're in and into the open down here, it would be an easy thing t' get the drop on them."

"Dream on, Captain."

"When that mash came down th' river, it was enough t' make a man drunk if he drank enough of it—"

"About ten gallon to th' shot, I'd guess," Tex interrupted.

"If you was to pretend you got drunk on it and was lookin' for th' source, makin' a lot of noise about it, they might come down t' see what it's all about. I could go back up and capture the lookout and come down behind them. We might take them without firing a shot."

"Might."

"Got a better idea?"

"No, I don't. I guess that might work all right. We could try it, maybe."

"All right, you go get your horse, and I'll work myself back up behind the lookout. Give me about an hour, then ride up Boggy and make a lot of noise. When I hear you, I'll gather up the lookout an' march him down behind the other three. Bring some manacles with you so we can truss 'em up good."

"I'm on my way, Captain." Tex gave a salute and trotted off. Harm retraced his steps up the hillside and down into the arroyo. The wait was longer than he expected, but eventually, he heard a shot away down the river, then another closer, this time with some faint shouting.

There was activity in the bootlegger camp. The lookout rose to a crouch only twenty feet from where Harmon lay and called, "What's that noise about, Dud?"

The man called Dud sat up from one of the bedrolls an' said, "I don't know." He sat a few moments, then picked up his rifle and walked down the path to the still. The lookout settled back down for a moment, then, as the noise continued, rose and walked to the camp. Harm followed as far as cover would allow him. He could hear Tex a little plainer, now.

"Ya-a-a h-o-o-o." And he fired his gun again. "Ya-a-a h-o-o-o."

The lookout took a few more steps toward the noise and Harm called softly, "Lay that gun down and put your hands up."

The man whirled around, his rifle coming up, but he froze when he could see no one. Again, Harm whispered, "Put the gun down, friend, or die."

Still, the man searched for the source of the voice. Sweat ran down his cheek and dripped off his chin.

"I'll count to three, then you die." Harm could hear Lee's voice in his mind, *Don't kill th' money crop, Harm.* "One." Long pause. "Two." The man slowly crouched and laid the rifle down. "Now the handgun and knife."

Again, the man crouched and laid the pistol down by the rifle. He reached for the knife and, as suddenly and swiftly as Harmon Lake had ever seen, threw the knife with such force it split the little elm sapling ten feet away from where Harm was hidden. Just as swiftly, the man turned to run and Harm shot him in the leg. "Didn't kill him, Lee," he muttered as he ran for the fallen man.

"Ya-a-a h-o-o-o!" Tex called as three men came running out of the arroyo. "Howdy, boys. I've found Whiskey River down by th' big rock candy mountain! Trouble is, I've placered th' river out, an' now I'm lookin' fer th' mother lode. Hev you boys done staked yer claim on it?"

The three relaxed a little, and the two younger boys laughed. "He got drunk on that mash we dumped in th' river last night," the one called Hack crowed.

"Can that stuff be that strong in th' river, Dud?" the other boy asked.

The elder man had separated himself a little from the other two and stood watching Tex, his hand on his pistol grip. "Don't know, but I'd think he would have t' drink an awful lot of water t' git drunk on it."

"If you boys have th' mother vein claimed, I'm gonna go find Gin Lake an' build me a cabin right there. Yessiree, my wanderin' days is over!" Tex was in a sweat, for he had heard Harm's shot and didn't know what it meant. For all he knew, Harm could be out of the game. He delayed a little more. "Sa-a-ay, you boys wouldn't let me in on your claim, would you? I'll let you stay th' winters in my cabin on Gin Lake, an' we could all share in th' bounty."

"We might share with you, friend. Just git down off'n that

horse an' we'll go up to th' mother lode." Dud was wary. He had heard the single shot from the arroyo too.

"Cain't," Tex said. "My legs is so wobbly I needs this horse's legs t' git me anywhere. He didn't do any placerin' in th' river."

"I don't b'lieve yore 'placerin' would get you that drunk, friend," Dud said.

"Ya don't? That's funny, 'cause somethin' was mighty powerful in that water. Horse wouldn't drink it till it was all petered out." From the corner of his eye, he saw a man emerge from the brush of the arroyo. It was Harmon.

"Well, lookee here; it's Mr. Harmon Lake, fellers. I'll thank you to put your hands on your sombreros. We have some nice jewelry for you t' wear on your wrists."

Dud made to draw, and Tex's double-barreled shotgun rose. "Don't do it, Dud."

Now Dud was no coward, but he was no idiot, either. He had never seen anyone win an argument with a shotgun at this range. He cautiously raised his hand to touch his sombrero.

"Boy, I'm glad you didn't draw. I forgot which barrel had birdshot in it an' which had buckshot." Tex grinned. "I was gonna hafta give you both barrels."

In a few minutes the three bootleggers were disarmed and manacled. A miraculously sobered Tex asked, "What took you so long? I was running out of things t' say."

"I had to shoot the lookout."

"Boy, Harm, Lee's gonna be—"

"He ain't dead."

"Good. Let's get this thing over with and these fellers secure on Tumbleweed."

"OK, you ride over and bring Tumbleweed here and I will guard the prisoners."

"You ride over and git th' thing yourself. I'm too shaky t' do much right now."

"I'll go. You make sure things stay in hand here. The one I shot won't be going anywhere, so you don't have t' worry about him."

"You just hurry back."

Hurry as he did, Harm didn't get back to Boggy Creek for nearly an hour. Tex was nervous the whole time. He had never participated in a capture alone before. His mind was occupied with worry about what he would do if he were left alone with four prisoners and one of them shot. He had just about decided that he would let the men go and run for it if Harm didn't return. It was a great relief when he heard the wagon approaching.

They got the prisoners situated on Tumbleweed and went up the gulley to get the wounded Clay. Although Harm had gotten to him quickly, he had lost a goodly amount of blood, and there was a chip of bone where the bullet exited his leg. They determined that the bone wasn't broken, but that chip meant it was going to be very sore for a while. The boys took turns practically carrying the man down to the wagon.

"It's gonna take us th' rest of th' day t' break their camp down," Harm complained.

"We could burn it."

"Yeah and they could sue us for th' damages if they lived past th' trial."

"They could?"

"Sure could, Tex, an' most likely they would win. Besides, they're gonna need their bedding for a while."

Tex turned pale and his eyes got big. "Harm," he whispered, "where's their horses?"

Now it was Harm's turn to go pale. "Holy crap, Tex, we plumb forgot . . . I knew those boys didn't look too worried when we chained 'em up. Stay calm and mount up and look for them or where they went. We got another man t' catch."

Tex mounted as casually as anyone who expected a bullet any second could, and rode around the flat looking for any indications of where the horses might be.

Someone muttered something on the wagon and the others laughed. Harmon looked up at the men and said, "You fellers think we forgot about your horses? Ha, that was th' first thing we took care of."

"Izat fer real?" Dud asked. "I'm a-thinkin' you tinhorns forgot."

"Maybe he thinks we took th' trolley cars." Otis grinned.

"You boys go on jawin' while I cook us some grub. It ain't often I get t' hear such stim-u-latin' talk. Such culture's hard t' find out here in th' Nations."

Tex had completed his circuit of the flat and rode up to the wagon, "Might as well go up an' bring that horse wrangler down to his buddies. He's probably gittin' purty lonesome sittin' up there all alone."

Harm noticed a flicker of disappointment across Hack's face, but the rest showed no emotions. "Don't be gone too long or your supper'll be cold."

"Yes, Mother." Tex turned and rode up the dry first gulley they had passed. It showed promise of not being too steep and rocky to ride. As soon as he was out of sight of the wagon, he looped the shotgun over the horn and drew his rifle out of its boot. Satisfied with its load, he chambered a shell and rode on, the rifle across his knees. Near the top, he dismounted and slipped to the edge of the brush. To his great relief, there sat two wagons, both containing several barrels. A coffee pot sat among the coals of a small fire, but there was no one visible anywhere.

Tex studied the wagons. Those high sideboards could easily hide someone, and the shooting of a few minutes ago would have given an alarm. The horse herd was bunched a couple hundred yards across the flat near the brush on that side. Tex thought the wrangler could be hiding in the bushes behind the horses—if he wasn't in one of those wagons with a scattergun, waiting for him to ride up.

"Nothing like a load of buckshot in th' face t' ruin your day," he muttered to his horse. "You got any suggestions as to how we can ferret out this feller?"

"For starters, mister—"

Tex jumped, and for a second he thought the horse had spoken.

"—you might just step away from that hoss an' raise yore hands to th' Lord above. He's th' only one kin keep you alive."

Tex stood perfectly still except to slowly raise his hands. "I didn't know you was armed, old hoss, an' I for shore thought you was on my side."

"Turn around, durn you, an' you'll see this ain't no horse talkin'."

Tex turned and looked down the maw of a rifle barrel not eighteen inches from his nose. At the other end of that long Kentucky smooth bore flintlock rifle was a slim kid, holding the rifle as far along the barrel as he could reach, the stock hugged close to his side by his elbow, finger on the trigger.

Tex moved his head out of the line of fire and the muzzle followed. "Son, you got me, but that barrel in my face makes me mighty nervous. Just point it by my head an' you can swing it in place when you fire."

The boy hesitated, then said, "Not on your life, mister. This gun stays right here till you tell me who you are an' what you're up to."

"Well, I'm a U.S. marshal here to catch murderers, thieves, and bootleggers, an' I just caught a passel of bootleggers at their still down there. I was just comin' up t' git their horses. They didn't tell me there was another man up here."

"I ain't no man. I'm a girl!"

Tex peeked around the barrel and glimpsed a freckle-faced kid before that barrel retook the center of his attention.

"Did anyone git hurt in all that shootin'?"

"Just one man got shot."

"Who was it?"

"I think his name was Clay."

"O-o-oh." The kid jumped, the flintlock fell, and in that instant before the powder in the chamber ignited, Tex shoved the barrel away and up. The boom of the blast was the last thing he heard in his left ear for a long, long time. Burning black powder showered his clothes, setting his shirt and hat afire and burning into his arm and cheek. The brim of his sombrero had shielded his eyes from the fiery missiles. Stunned, Tex fell to the ground, even while feebly trying to brush the fire from his shoulder.

The next thing he became conscious of was the blackness and horrible ringing in his ears. When the blackness went away, he could see a perfectly blue sky speckled with cottonwood leaves and drifting cottony catkins from the trees. Pain shot through his left ear, and he felt to see if it was there. His hand came away bloody. A dull ache signaled from his shoulder. It was covered with blisters from the fire. When he tried to sit up, he discovered his dizziness and lay back down. He was alone.

CHAPTER 23
TEX MEETS BABY KAY
(HARMON'S TALE)

They raced around the point of land, straight for me. I could tell it wasn't Tex on his horse; beyond that, all I could tell about the rider was that it was a small person in a big hurry. They skidded to a stop, showering the fire and food with sand and gravels and this *girl* jumps down yelling, "Where is he?"

"Where's who?"

"My papa!" Her face was streaked with muddy tears.

"Who's your papa?"

"Clay Stone. *Where is he?*"

I motioned to Tumbleweed. Before I could speak, she clambered up the wheel and tumbled over the sideboard right on top of the poor man. Fortunately, his injured leg was pointed the other way and she landed on his chest.

"Papa, Papa! Are you alive, Papa?"

Clay Stone grunted for his breath and managed to get out, "I'm alive, if I can ever breathe agin."

"He said you were shot; are you, Papa?"

"Just through the leg, Baby Kay; I'll be OK."

The girl sat up beside her father and wiped her face. "I was scared, Papa."

I looked cautiously over the sideboard. "You still alive, Clay?"

"Barely." He grinned up at me. "This here's Baby Kay, my daughter."

"I surmised by th' way she come roarin' in here, callin 'Papa,' that she was someone's daughter. Where's Tex?"

The girl must not have been over twelve years and fifty pounds. She looked at me defiantly and said, "I kilt him."

"Atta girl, Baby Kay," Dud crowed. I glared at him, a promise of dealin' with him later on my face.

"Why did you kill him?"

"Cause he said my papa was kilt."

I was all shaky inside. "Git down here. We have to go get him."

"I ain't goin' back up—"

"The hell you're not," I gritted, and pulled her over the side by her shoulders and sat her on the horse. "Now *stay* there." I led the horse over to where mine was tied and mounted up. Tex's horse was winded from his run down the gulley, and we made a slow assent back to the top. "Now, where did you leave him?"

"Over near th' wagons in th' brush."

"Show me, dam . . ." I had to pause to reclaim my composure. "Show me exactly where you left him, girl."

With a defiant jerk of the reins, the girl turned and walked the horse to the spot where Tex lay. The gun lay where Baby Kay had dropped it.

Tex looked a mess. His sombrero smoldered in the grass, his shirt was burned off, and his shoulder and neck were blistered. Black spots speckled his jaw and neck where burning gunpowder had burned into his skin, and blood oozed from his ear canal. His eyes were closed and he was breathing. "Tex, can you hear me?"

"Uh-huh. You don't have t' whisper."

I couldn't find blood or a bullet hole on him and I asked, "Are you hit anywhere?"

"Huh?" It was to become a common word in his vocabulary for some time.

Louder: "*I say*, are you hit anywhere?" From this time on, I had to talk loudly in order for Tex t' hear me.

"Blowed my ear off, and I cain't see." All this time he had not opened his eyes.

"Try openin' your eyes."

They opened and he said, "There you are, Harm, plain as th' day you was born."

It was a great relief that his eyes had not been damaged. I coaxed him into sitting up, but he was so dizzy, he had to lean on me. The girl knelt beside Tex and began wiping blood away from his ear and neck and gently pulling powder fragments from his skin.

"Git away, girl; ain't you done enough damage to me today?"

"I'm tryin' t' help you now," she replied. She stopped her work and sat back on her heels, looking at the damage she had done. "Does it hurt?"

"Huh?"

"Does it hurt?"

"You don't have t' yell." But she did—have to yell, that is.

With much coaxing and holding up, we got Tex up on my horse, and I managed to mount behind the saddle and hold Tex. Baby Kay took my reins and led us down the arroyo to camp. She was a great help in getting Tex's bed laid out and him into it. Tex had a time finding a position he could lie in. The blistered shoulder wouldn't let him lay on his back, and to lie on his right side caused the blood to pool in his ear. He finally found that he could lie on his left side with his arm extended over his head, the only discomfort coming from the blisters in the fold of his shoulder.

Baby Kay found some burn salve in the medical kit and put it on the burn. A good stiff drink of medicinal whiskey let Tex relax enough to sleep. Supper was gritty, and there were gravels in the beans. All complaints I got were referred to Baby Kay. The girl turned her full attention to her papa. At bedtime, she refused to leave him, and I agreed to let her stay only after she agreed to being manacled to the chain.

I settled by Tex and spent a restless night without much sleep, between worrying about him and watchin' the wagon tenants. This was the second night we had spent without Lee and Gam, and I really hoped they had noticed. It was not likely that we would be moving for a day or two. Toward morning, I finally slept—only to be awakened by plaintive calls from the wagon, "Mr. Mr. *Mr. Harmon.*"

"What!" I was answering even before I was fully awake,

"I've got t' *go!*" The little girl voice was urgent. Unshackled, she ran for the brush and I stoked the fire and began fixing breakfast. This one-man tumbleweed operation was no good.

After breakfast I sent Baby Kay to tie the remnants of Tex's shirt to a bush at the mouth of Boggy Creek in case the two returning lawmen missed the abundance of tracks leading up Boggy. Tex looked better, actually said he felt better, but he was so dizzy he didn't feel like lifting his head. His ear had stopped bleeding, and he let the girl pick the burned powder grains out of his skin. She tried to wash out the black left in the burns, but could do little good. Tex would wear those scars the rest of his life.

Midafternoon, Lee and Gam rode up the creek, Lee ready to explode and Gam grinning from ear to ear at our predicament. Lee was somewhat mollified when he saw the prisoners, mad again when he saw Tex, happy to hear about the still to be busted up, and almost softened when he saw Baby Kay. He assured her it was Tex's fault for getting shot and not hers.

Tex was sure he would have to kill Gam to ever put an end to talk he had been shot by a girl. I think he is right.

These bootleggers showed a lot more ambition than their competition, bringing a still all the way out here in the reservations for the Cheyenne-Arapaho, Comanche, Kiowa, and

Apache lands. Their hope was that they would be far from the trodden paths of the deputies, and that they could operate a long time without being detected—hope based on ignorance of the paths of some deputies in their circuits from Fort Smith to Fort Sill to Camp Supply and back to Fort Smith. When we ran that route, we seldom reached the marshal's office without a full load of prisoners. I heard Lee say it was his most profitable route in the territory.

The next morning, Lee had us take the prisoners down from the wagon and marched up to the still, where he spoke to the prisoners. "I brought you up here to witness the destruction of the still. This is not to punish you, but it is so you might be witness to the fact that we do not keep the still for ourselves and that it is certain that it will never operate again."

That said, he took the axe and proceeded with a most thorough destruction of the still. In all the time I worked for Lee, he never let any of his posse destroy a still. In case someone held a grudge and sought revenge, only Lee would be the one they sought. "I've already got a target on my back, and one more man looking for me isn't gonna matter much."

We had become convinced that we were looking for A.B. Chew as the killer of Tracey and his crew. "It was only because we had lost Nicasio and his trail that Lee returned to look for you," Gam told us. I don't think we ever after made a trip that Lee didn't caution us that we should ever be on the lookout for Chew or rumors of his whereabouts.

Baby Kay stayed with her papa and us, a help and bane to th' whole crowd. She insisted on sleeping with her father, but had the run of the camp otherwise. We could set watches by her nature call in the predawn morning. It became the wake-up call for me to begin breakfast. Even after she was gone, time to get up in our camp was called Nature Call.

Tex recovered quickly except for his hearing, which never got back to normal in that left ear. We learned to speak up when addressing him; else we were condemned to repetitions. "Huh?" became his most commonly used word.

We picked up two more bootleggers at Camp Supply. A Reverend Chew had passed through alone, but no one knew where he went from there, except for a rumor he was headed for Dodge City. Lee was determined to follow him and send us back to Fort Smith with the wagon, but we convinced him to go back with the promise we would give the Reverend Chew our full attention.

At the marshal's office, Lee's report put Chew on the most-wanted list, which was easy because the man had murdered a deputy and his crew. One of the deputies—I think it was Mayberry—actually captured Chew, but Chew killed the cook and escaped. His capture stock rose to unprecedented heights, but nothing was seen or heard of him in the I.T. for a couple of years.

Lee Sowell never forgot him.

We don't know how far Nicasio followed Chew, but we do know that Nicasio found the girl's body and returned it to Rainy Mountain, where she was buried. Even through their sorrow, the family of Snow Flower (Amanda) showed their gratitude to Nicasio and he was always welcome at Rainy Mountain, though they sometimes groaned about his prodigious appetite.

CHAPTER 24
TAHLEQUAH

Me an' Bass had been havin' a runnin' quarrel with ol' Bob Dosser, the outlaw, for some time—three or four years—when we run across his trail in th' Cookson Hills, and it was fresh. We took up th' trail, just him an' me. All day we followed, all th' time gainin' on Bob. We figgered we weren't more'n an hour behind him about sunset when th' darnedest thunderstorm struck us with enough rain and lightnin' for two storms. That trail was washed out in thirty seconds, and we sloshed down into a gulley to try and find a dry place for the night.

We weren't ridin' five feet apart when a bullet sang between us, and we abandoned those horses like they was on fire. I lay behind a big stump an' Bass found a spot between two big trees that gave him cover. We waited an' waited. The long wait paid off when a figure stepped out of the trees, got caught in the flash of lightning, and Bass shot him. That gave away his position and the other man made it hot for him. I got in a couple of shots, then had to duck lead and move.

When I looked again, Bass was down! There he lay, facedown in the mud, his gun still in his hand. Now I was in a sweat, having lost track of the shooter, an' him knowin' just where to find me. You can bet my eyes were big as saucers lookin' for that feller. Presently, I heard him laugh an' he stepped out into the open, walkin' straight to Bass's body. "Gonna git me, were you Bass Reeves? Well, look who got who."

When he was close, that Bass raised up and said, "Bob Dosser, you're under arrest."

211

Dosser brought his gun up, but before he could fire, Bass shot him in the neck. Bob Dosser fell dead.

Workin' through the Indian Nations, a deputy hears of "wars and rumors of wars," and often some man's name comes up again and again until the deputy gets a strong urge to meet that fellow. Feed that urge long enough and it becomes an obsession, and said deputy makes it his personal goal to "get his man."

It's best not to let those obsessions happen, for it tends to make a man one-purposed to the neglect of his many other duties. It almost come that-a-way with Bass Reeves a time or two and it almost—maybe mostly—became that way with me about a couple of outlaws. When an outlaw gets wind of a deputy's feelings for him, he either makes tracks for the unknown like A.B. Chew, or takes up the challenge like Tavener Hunter, and a search becomes a feud.

Tave Hunter was into a little bit of everything: introducing alcohol, land swindling, road agent, train robber. If anyone got in his way during the course of his activities, he shot them. It seemed like every crime committed in the Nations was perpetrated by Tave, until I was sick of the name and determined to eliminate it from the equations.

Tavener Hunter had two families, one up at Scraper on the Illinois River, and another at Big Cedar on the Kiamichi River. He operated out of one until things got too hot for him there, then he went to the other wife. Between him and the two women, he only had eleven children, but he was still a young man when all that ended.

We were in Fort Smith, just finishing a run, when we heard he had robbed a stage in the Winding Stair Mountains. Knowing he would be heading north, I kept Harmon with us and instead of taking a few days off, we set out to get Tave Hunter.

His favorite route was through Van Buren, where he usually found a market for any stolen goods he might have.

His features had become too well known on the trains, so he had been taking the Fayetteville Road to Evansville, Dutch Mills, or Cincinnati, Arkansas, then turning into the Cherokee Nation over to Scraper.

Evansville was right on the border, and her saloons provided ample refreshment and entertainment for the Cherokees who developed a thirst for such. The Starrs and Sixkillers were among the frequent visitors. If Tave didn't feel pressured by any pursuers, he would stay at Evansville a few days and usually left broke and with a headache. He considered Dutch Mills and Cincinnati dull, for they were more farming communities than places for entertainment. If he could get past Evansville quickly, he would generally get to Scraper with a little jingle for the wife.

"Th' way folks treat lawmen, you'd think we all have leprosy er somethin'," Gamlin groused as we sat about eating a little supper. We had gone in to Evansville to see if Tave had passed through and got nothing. Even when I bought supplies and asked old Phil Barnes at the hardware store, I got a mean reply. "I ain't seen him, an' even if I had, there's no way I'd be tellin' *you* about it." He said it loud enough for all in the store to hear. "The receipt is in the package." He handed me my package, and turned to help another customer.

"Did you get any soda today, Lee?"

"Yeah, Harm, it's in that package on th' tailgate."

Harmon opened the package and brought me the receipt. "Somethin's written on th' bottom, but it's too dark t' read it."

I leaned toward the fire and read the note: *left here 2 days go north*. The note was hurriedly scribbled and hard to read. Barnes had let me know about Tave and hadn't drawn the wrath of the outlaws living around Evansville. Good people caught in such rough circumstances lived a tough and sometimes dangerous life. I appreciated the chance he took and made a note not to put him in such a predicament again.

Dutch Mills was first named Hermannsburg for the German that started the town back before the Civil War. It was quite a German settlement at one time, but their Union sentiments made them such a target for Confederates and bushwhackers that the whole settlement packed up and left for St. Louis one night. After the war, new settlers renamed the town Dutch Mills. "Yes," the miller told me over the noise of his grist mill, Tavener had come through, mostly sober, and bought a sack of cornmeal and a sack of flour. He was pretty sure Tave left on the Baron Creek Road.

"He's headed for Scraper. There's no way to get ahead of him unless that wagon sprouts wings," I said. It seemed we were always behind our quarry, a place Bass said never to be if you could help it.

"What in th' world does Tave do in Scraper?" Gam asked. "Th' biggest thing about th' place is its name; it ain't even a town."

"His wife's folks live there and feed his family when he's on th' run," Harm replied. He held little regard for a man who neglected his family, and less regard for a man who had two families at th' same time. Most of Harm's wages went to the care and upkeep of his own fatherless brothers and sisters at Lake's Ferry.

I began drawing a map in the dirt. "Gam, the Illinois runs through th' country like this. Scraper is here. New Springplace Mission is just a few miles northwest, about here. Tahlequah and Park Hill are down here on th' river. Row is north of Scraper . . . what's that new name for Hico?"

"Siloam Springs, Lee."

"Well, it's here. Scraper's just in th' middle of all these places, an' Tavener can get into any kind of mischief he wants to."

"Yeah, an' if he wants t' branch out, there's all those towns in Arkansas he can do mischief in," Tex added. "So what we gonna do, Lee?"

"We're gonna have t' get ahead of him an' let him come to us. The question is; where is he gonna go from Scraper?"

"Was he me, he'd go lookin' around close for somethin' t' git into," Tex mused. "Maybe he would go up to New Springplace first."

"He'd have t' be a real hellraiser or awful careless t' cause trouble that close t' home," Harm said.

"I think he is, Harm."

"You know, regardless of anywheres else he goes, he *will* sooner or later go to Tahlequah."

"You're right, Gam. I suppose our surest bet would be to go hang aroun' Talequah until he shows up. We're always sure to get good pickin's there, an' th' Lighthorse will probably have a list of characters we could give transportation t' th' Fort."

It seemed the plan to go to Tahlequah brightened th' mood in camp, and we were on the road early next morning.

Baron Fork isn't the straightest route from Dutch Mills to Tahlequah, but it's the easiest in those bottoms, and we made good time.

Lighthorse officer Ben Nakedhead met us at the Illinois River ferry east of town. "Hello, Ben. How did you know I was coming?" I asked.

Ben chuckled. "Tela-Indian faster than telegraph. We have some white prisoners for you. It would be best for us to give them to you before you cross the river. Too many dam' lawyers in town."

"These are fellers I caught before getting here? Think I could house them in the Lighthorse jail while I'm here? I'll pay for their stay."

"Shure, Lee Sowell. We will be glad to keep your prisoners

for you. Anyone special you are looking for?"

"No, just makin' a sweep pickin' up trash for Judge Parker."

"Camp on the river side off the Eldon Road. We'll see you tonight."

"All right, Ben; nice seein' you agin." We turned around, to the consternation of the boys, and headed up the Eldon Road. There was a nice campground halfway to the river from the road, and we set up camp there.

My posse had griped about standing nightly guard up until we found Tracey's head with a hole in the middle of his forehead. Since then, there had been no complaints. I told them to expect company in the night and not to shoot any Lighthorse policemen. About an hour before he changed the first guard, Tex woke me. "They're here."

"Good. Stir up the others."

I don't know why they called their policemen Lighthorse, but all the tribes did. Police in each tribe operated differently. The Cherokee, being most independent, paid little attention to the white man's laws and enforced their own law as they saw fit. If they caught a white or black man breaking either law, they arrested them and sorted out the laws later. The result was they almost always had a few whites in custody waiting for a deputy to come by with vacancies on his wagon. It didn't take long for lawyers, both Anglo and native, to discover they had green pastures in Tahlequah defending inmates against "unfair and illegal police tactics." Thus, the sham of taking prisoners from some tumbleweed out of town so they can be "kept" in the city jail if the deputy plans to stay around for a while. Deputies certainly didn't mind the trouble.

People of Tahlequah welcomed U.S. deputies to town, for it meant a general exodus of the black and white trash that infested the town and things would be quiet and orderly for a time. We deposited our prisoners at the jail, parked Tumbleweed in the wagon yard, and rode into town.

"Here's some spending money, boys. Look around and don't get into any trouble. If the police get you, you'll have a long stay until the next deputy comes to town. They won't release you back to me."

"Good gosh, what's there t' do in a town that ain't got no saloons or loose wimmin?" Gam asked.

"For starters, try a shave, haircut, and bath. That way, these people won't smell you approachin'."

"Won't do any good, Lee, if'n he puts th' same clothes back on," Tex observed.

"Al-l-l right, see that mercantile store over there? I'm gonna set up an account there an' you boys—all three of you—are gonna go over there and buy new clothes—nothing fancy now—and I'll pay for them out of your wages to come; how's that?"

Gam frowned and Tex hooted. "Fine by me. Wonder if they got any Levis without bibs."

"Don't need no new clothes," Gamlin snarled.

"Fine with me, Gam. Just don't complain if these people keep their distance from you. They hate t' smell dirty Anglos."

"Com'on, Gam, let's go see what they got. You might change your mind," Harmon urged.

We dodged traffic across the street, and I set up an account with the store and left the boys to their own devices while I ran some errands. It was good to let people know I was in town and available if they had any news for me. Park Hill with its female seminary was more sedate, but white crime knows no boundaries, and I picked up a couple of tips about goings-on east of the river. A trip that way might prove fruitful.

217

CHAPTER 25
THE ARREST OF TAVENER HUNTER

None of us ever mentioned Tavener Hunter's name, and I wanted it kept that way for two reasons. One, of course, was because he would get word that we were looking for him; and two, because there was a small reward for his arrest and I wanted to keep that for my posse. I made one arrest of a horse thief in town and narrowly missed another man as he galloped out of town. The next morning we made a small show of heading west out of town, making sure enough people saw us leave that the word would get around. Our unfortunate prisoners were going to have to endure Tumbleweed while we waited for Tavener to show up. Late evening, we circled around the north end of town to the ferry on the east side and went merrily on our way until dark, when we turned north and set up camp in a gulley off the bluffs. It wasn't a comfortable camp.

The chances of catching Tave before he got to town were slim, but it was a sure thing we would know when he passed. A week went by without signs of his passing, and the prisoners were getting restless. I couldn't say that I blamed them, but I also couldn't say that I cared a whit for their comfort. The problem was that the more restless they got, the more dangerous it was for us to handle them, so we packed up one morning and drove downriver to the Tahlequah Ferry.

I rode ahead of the wagon and had a listen to the ferryman. "Quite a mix-up in town last night. Tave Hunter drove in with a wagonload of whiskey an' had it all sold afore th' police that

cared got wind of it. The rest of the force was already drunk."
He chuckled. "Got a swig er two myself. Can't say it was bad
an' can't say it was good, either."

"Where did Tave get his whiskey?" I asked.

"Didn't say, but he came down th' Tulsey Town road."

I rode back to the advancing wagon. "Tex, you and Harm
take the wagon to the campground we used when we came to
town and set up camp. Harm, give me that list of goods you
need, and Gam and I will ride in and get them."

Tex turned the wagon and Harmon fished out his list. The
kid had been with me long enough to know that something was
up. I could see it in his eyes. "We should be back by sundown.
Anything else you need?"

"Nope." And he turned away.

Alcohol is truly devastating to the American Indian. The
introduction of a wagonload of whiskey to a town is almost
equivalent to setting off a load of powder in the middle of the
place. Going up the hill before we got to town, we began seeing
signs of trouble.

"That's not a hog in th' road, Lee. That's a big fat woman,"
Gam exclaimed.

She was hugging a jug to her side. "Looks like that's where
she decided to sleep it off. The ferryman said Tavener drove a
wagonload of whiskey into town last night. We're going to find
him."

"Knowed somethin' was up." Gam pulled his rifle and
checked the load, then slipped another round into his hip gun.

There were areas of town where it was quiet, either because
the whiskey hadn't gotten there and the people were staying
indoors, or because they were sleeping off their debauch. It was
the noisy parts we were interested in, for it was sure that would
be where Hunter would be.

We found his wrecked wagon, horses still attached, in the

middle of the street on the north end of town. "Looks like he didn't get too far into town afore he was caught," Gam observed.

"Looks like it. Help me unharness these horses." An anger was building in me. I hated to see animals neglected or mistreated. Truth be known, I would arrest a man quicker for cruelty to his animals than for introducing alcohol into the territory. Unharnessed, the horses headed straight for a watering trough.

"Hey, feller, you stealin' my horses?" Tavener stood on the stoop outside of a doorway to a noisy party.

"Tavener Hunter, you are under arrest," I called.

"What for—is that you, Sowell?"

"First, for cruelty to animals, an' second for ever'thing else you done t' break th' law."

A bullet slammed into the sideboard of the wagon inches from my head.

Gam whirled and fired at a shadow disappearing into a building behind us. "Why is it these imbeciles aim for the head when th' gut's a much bigger target?"

Tavener had taken advantage of our distraction to run down the boardwalk to an alley. "Cover my back, Gam. I'm goin' after him." I ran to the alley, drew a shot as I passed, and ducked into the open door of the next building. I counted three bodies on the floor as I ran to the back door. It flew open and Tave was silhouetted for a moment. My shot was too late and I stopped. I had a decision to make. The half-glass door swung back to close, and in its reflection I saw Tave standing against the wall by the door, gun held head high. I spaced three shots into the board wall and heard the man grunt. *I don't want him dead, Lord,* I thought.

I heard him fall and moved cautiously to the door. There he lay, pistol pointed at my head. I shot into the dirt beside his face as he fired at me. He missed. *Someday someone isn't gonna miss.* The thought was worrisome.

Tave was down, gut-shot somewhere, and blinded by dirt and gravel in his right eye and face. He wasn't goin' anywhere. Sporadic firing from the front of the building told me Gam was occupied, and I moved left around the building. Gam was taking fire from at least two shooters in the buildings across the street. As I watched, a rifle barrel appeared from an upper window of the store closest to me and I fired two quick shots. The gun fell out of the window. *One down.* Bullets were suddenly spattering all around me, and I dove for the ground and rolled under the porch. "Good gosh, how many of them are there, Gam?" I called.

"Three left an' growin'."

Shots were boring into the boardwalk above me. "I'm holed under th' porch, Gam. Run out back an' see if you can flank them, and I'll hold them off from here." Truth was, I wasn't goin' anywhere without some relief from somewhere. Gam fired three quick shots, and I heard him running for the back door. I squirmed around and saw smoke from a window across the street to the right of the porch. When the barrel was extended to fire again, I put three shots into the wall beneath the window. The barrel tilted skyward and slid into the building. *Two down.*

This business of being caught under a porch in a crossfire is no fun. My cartridge belt was nearly empty, and still no Gamlin to the rescue. The best I could tell from my *dis*advantage point, there were only two shooters left, the others being put out of order, out of ammunition, or lost interest and wandered off.

The sound of two quick shots came from the left, and that shooter quit shooting at me. *Thank you, Gam.* A few minutes later, Gam called from the shooter's position on the right, "It's all right, Lee, you can come out now." I checked the alley behind me, rolled out from under the porch, and stepped to the boardwalk. Alleys to my back give me the chills. Gam came out of the building with a man walking ahead of him, hands high. "Only one prisoner, where is the oth—"

"Here he comes." Gam nodded, and I turned to see a man limping toward me, hands high. Tex was guiding him with his gun barrel. "Found him shootin' out of his window in violation of City Ordinance 'Thou shall not shoot out thy window.' " Tex grinned.

"What the devil are you doing here? I left you with the wagon."

"Harm forgot something he was in need of."

"Why didn't he come himself?"

"He lost the coin flip."

I looked at Tex a moment, but couldn't stay mad. After all, he had stopped a man from shooting at me. "OK, let's clean up here."

Tex dug into his shirt pocket and handed me a folded note. Inside, Harm had written one word: *soda.*

We cuffed the two prisoners in hand, and Tex guarded them while Gam and I checked the other shooters. I was anxious about Tavener and found him where I left him. He had a wad of his shirt pressed to his side, and it didn't seem to be bleeding much. The bullet had gone in the back of the fleshy part of his side and traveled six inches before it exited the front. It didn't seem like it could have gone through any organs. The side of his face was bloody from a couple dozen pock marks where sand had hit him, and there was a large cut by his eye that had caused it to swell shut.

Tavener cursed me soundly. "Might have known you would back-shoot a man—"

"I'll back-shoot any man waiting behind a wall t' ambush me—or any other man, for that matter. Only sissies whine about fair play when *they* don't play fair. Now shut up; we got a trip t' take." I helped him up, but made him walk up the alley on his own. Any sympathy would be wasted on him.

Gam had returned with a wounded prisoner. When I asked about the other shooter, he shook his head. "He's dead; took two in th' chest."

"Let's get these three to a doctor. Which one of you wants to go get Harm?"

"I will." Gam turned before anything else could be said and caught up our horses, tied mine to a rail, and rode out toward the ferry.

"Tex, there's three bodies layin' around in that store; see if any of them are alive. If you find a white man sleeping his drunk off, bring him out. We'll give him a ride to Fort Smith with Tave here."

In a moment he stuck his head out the door and said, "They's all alive, an' one of them looks white, but he won't say."

"If he don't say he's Injun, he's white; drag him out here."

There was a doctor on the next street over, and we limped the men over there. On the way, we met Officer Nakedhead. "Coming to our rescue after th' shootin's over, Ben?" I shouldn't have been testy. That's the way they generally do it when deputies are concerned.

The Indian grinned. "Been looking for Tavener."

"I'm all sold out, Ben," the bootlegger said with a grin.

"By the way, Tave, where's your loot? I have to confiscate it as evidence." I didn't, but we usually confiscated it so the prisoner couldn't use it to bribe or buy himself out of trouble. He usually got most of it back—eventually.

"It's in a safe place, an' you ain't gittin' it," he vowed.

"Hope it's a good enough place t' stay safe eight or ten years." A glimmer of doubt flickered in his good eye.

The good doctor was in and busy patching up those injured in their debauchery, but he gave priority to gunshots and stabbings. We were next in line after a cut-up Indian with about a hundred stitches about his body. Doc looked the patients over and put them in the order of priority. When he learned one was Tavener Hunter, his demeanor hardened, and he put the man last in the order.

Gam's capture still had a bullet in his leg, and he was first in line. Doc got the bullet, cauterized the wound, and turned his attention to the other wounded man who only had splinter wounds in his thigh. Both these men were Indians, but they had attacked a deputy and his posse, and thus earned a ticket to Fort Smith on Tumbleweed.

When Tave's turn came, Doc had him lay on the operating table, which was at one end of the long room that served as waiting room and examination and treatment room. Turning to the waiting patients, he beckoned to a mother with a young boy. As they approached, we could see that the boy had been severely beaten, as well as the mother. Taking the boy gently, he sat him on Tavener's stomach. The man grunted in pain and tried to sit up, but I firmly restrained him in his place. "I thought, Mr. Hunter, that you would like to see what your whiskey has done to one of our residents of this community." That said, the kindly doctor treated the child for his many injuries, stitching in places and treating broken skin and bruises where he found them. The child hardly whimpered, though great tears ran down his face. When he finished with the child, he left him seated where he was and turned to the mother.

"Get this kid—" My slap across his mouth stopped Tave, and he didn't finish his sentence.

There were severe cuts on the woman's forearms where she had shielded herself and probably the child from her attacker. Doc removed the bloody rags and treated the arm with disinfectant, stitched where needed, and bandaged. I had not seen her bloody back until Doc turned her around and cut away her bloody blouse. The boy, still sitting on Tave's stomach, sobbed. It took ten stitches for one long cut, and I made sure Tavener Hunter saw each stitch applied. Not a sound came from the woman as Doc worked. I marveled that the woman could even stand, much less walk to the doctor's office for treatment. When he finished with her, he wrapped a light blanket around her shoulders and instructed his assistant to take the two to his quarters where his wife would care for them.

Doc turned and looked closely at the prone patient before him, "Look at me, Tavener Hunter." Their eyes met. "There's a little girl at their home, not three years old, whose wounds will never heal. Laid out on a board next to her is her father who, most unfortunately, was not killed before the child's spirit left this world. His blood is not on the hands of the policeman who shot him. He did what he had to do. I wonder whose hands are stained with that man's blood and that of the little girl's." He grabbed Tavener's hands and waved them in the man's face. "Why, there they are, Mr. Hunter. There's the blood of that baby and the blood of her father! That's not all. There's blood from many others on these hands, people poisoned by your vile drink. How are you gonna live with that, Mr. Hunter, how?"

Tavener's face was pale, but he set his jaw and jerked his hands away. "It's not my—" My slap stopped his sentence and split his lip. I was glad my gun was in my holster and not my hand. "Shut up, Tave, and be a man. Stop whimpering."

"I have taken an oath, Mr. Hunter, and I am bound to treat you as best I can. I will do so only because that oath compels me."

When he finished, he turned away as if from a distasteful chore. I paid the doctor for treating my prisoners, and taking Tave's wallet, paid for the woman and boy's treatment and the little girl's burial.

We were with the doctor long enough that Harm and Gam

had found us and waited in the street. As I chained Tave to the wagon, he said, "You had no right to spend my money that way."

I marveled at his hardness. "Tave, I am sincerely sorry I didn't kill you the first time I ever saw you."

His puzzled look told me that he was not able to comprehend the consequences of what he had done.

Chapter 26
The Ox That Gored

"It is not I who hung them. I never hung a man. It is the law."

Isaac C. Parker

We stopped by the mercantile and I settled up our bill, which included a ten-pound carton of baking soda for Harm. "This time, maybe you won't run out so soon." Tex and Gam grinned at his discomfort.

The best way to get to the east side of the Illinois River is to cross the ferry east of town, then turn south, the canyon south and east of Park Hill not being passable by wagon. We were headed that way when a well-dressed man stepped into the road in front of Tumbleweed. I rode up to him and asked—as if I didn't already know—"What can I do for you, sir?" I didn't dismount.

"You have prisoners who are citizens of the Cherokee Nation and must be tried in our courts." He handed me several warrants that had obviously been blank until he had hurriedly scribbled in the names and charges. There was no judge's signature. Of course, Tavener's was the top warrant. "Tavener Hunter is a white man. I will take him to Fort Smith."

"Mr. Hunter is married to a Cherokee woman, and thus a citizen of the Nation. He will be tried here for his crimes." The man could have finished by saying that most likely Tavener would never see the inside of a cell and never be tried for his crimes after he had generously spread around some of his bootlegging money.

"I wonder if Tave is a citizen of the Creek Nation too, since he also has a Creek wife and family down there."

"It does not—"

"My warrant predates yours," I interrupted. "And since Mr. Hunter has broken United States laws, he will be taken to Fort Smith for trial. You may petition the court to hold him for you upon his serving his sentence in the States."

The rest of the warrants named Cherokee men who had fought us. "These men fired upon a U.S. deputy and his posse in the course of carrying out their duties. They are subject to U.S. law and will go to Fort Smith with us."

"You cannot take citizens of the Chero—"

"I can and will if they fire on United States deputy marshals and live to tell about it." One warrant bore the name of Wid Alvroe, a man I did not have. The charge against him was "The Illegal Manufacture of Alcohol."

"I don't have Wid on here, but it looks like I should. Gam, I saw Wid Alvroe sitting on the bench in front of the barber shop when we went by, go get him and we will arrest him for this man. He was wearing a green checkered shirt and no hat." Then to the lawyer, I added, "We'll stay right here until Gam returns with your prisoner."

The fact that Wid was openly free confirmed my suspicions that the Cherokees had no intention of prosecuting him. The same would go for Tavener and my other prisoners. "Do you have any witnesses who will testify against Wid?"

"I do. In fact, I am witness to his crimes myself," the lawyer answered. I dug out a pencil and wrote the lawyer's name on Wid's warrant. "A deputy will come for you when Wid's trial is scheduled so you can testify." I carefully folded the warrants and packed them away. "I will give these warrants to the judge so he can notify those in authority that the Cherokee Nation wants these men when they have served their sentences." I didn't mention that since they were not signed by a judge, they were invalid and would not be honored. I'll bet Mr. Lawyer already knew that, but he didn't say anything.

Gam returned with the prisoner walking ahead of him. Wid was walking awfully close to the ground, his toes kicking up dust with every step. He looked very much the worse for the wear. "Big night, Wid?" I said loudly.

Wid winced. "My head—"

"A ride in the fresh air of th' country will improve your health greatly. Tex, give this man a de-luxe seat on Tumbleweed."

"Wait," the lawyer cried. "He isn't supposed to go to Fort Smith, he's a citizen of this Nation—"

"Who broke U.S. laws against the production and introduction of alcohol into the Indian Territory. I thank you for your help in arresting this man, and I am sure the judge will take note of your good citizenship when you testify at his trial. Now if you will step out of the way, we have to get these prisoners to the court."

"I will not allow you to kidnap Cherokee citizens."

"The word, sir, is 'arrest,' and that I have done legally. If you impede me any more in the pursuit of my duties, I'm gonna give *you* a ride to Fort Smith." He stood there long enough to convince himself that he had done his duty, then stepped to the side. Tex and Gamlin flanked the back of the wagon, rifles across their knees. I nodded to Harm and he slapped reins. The mules started with a jerk and brushed the lawyer as they passed. He had to step back to avoid being run over by a wheel, and again when Gamlin rode by. We rode on without another backward glance.

"Why don't we let the Cherokee Nation try these criminals?" Tex asked as we relaxed around the fire that night.

"Because their court is subject to the influences of hard cash," Gamlin said.

"And they have a stubborn and perverse idea that they do not have to obey white men's laws and morals. They would let a guilty man go free to prove their point," I added.

"Why don't we have our own trial an' give Tave what he deserves?" Tex asked.

"You weren't a Texas Ranger, were you, Tex?" Harm was aware of the ranger's propensity to write off prisoners as "shot while trying to escape."

"We'll get him to Fort Smith an' th' court will decide his fate." I leaned back on my saddle couch and sipped coffee.

"Maybe they'll hang him," Gam said.

"I don't understand why they have to hang," Harmon said.

Tex and Gam were almost in harmony, "An eye for an—"

"Jesus changed that; said we should love our enemies."

"Harm, if someone sneaked into your house an' killed your ma an' th' rest o' yore fambly, would you love him?"

"No, but other people might, like his wife or ma or kids."

"It's like we said, 'An eye for an eye—' "

"No, no, no!" I sat up, sloshin' my coffee dangerously close to th' rim. "That rule does not count for New Testament people anymore, but there's one Old Testament *principle* that does." I rummaged around and pulled out my Bible box and moved closer to the fire so's I could see to read. "Here it is . . . Exodus 21:28; '*If an ox gore a man or a woman, that they die: then the ox shall be surely stoned, and his flesh shall not be eaten: but the owner of the ox shall be quit. But if the ox were wont to push with his horn in time past, and it hath been testified to his owner, and he hath not kept him in, but that he hath killed a man or a woman: the ox shall be stoned, and his owner also shall be put to death.*' "

After a moment of thought, Harm asked, "What's a goring ox have t' do with hanging a man?"

"Yeah, I don't git that," Gam said.

Tex stirred. "Me neither."

"OK, let me explain. It says, *'If an ox gore a man or a woman,'* meaning if he gores for th' first time, *'that they die: then the ox shall be surely stoned, and his flesh shall not be eaten: but the owner of the ox shall be quit.'* That means that if the ox gores to death the first time he gores, he shall be put to death, but since there was not any warning that he would gore, the owner should not be held accountable for it. Now listen to verse twenty-nine: *'But if the ox were wont to push with his horn in time past—'* To push with his horn means the same thing as gored in the past. You don't have to have a horn stuck in you to be gored. I was gored once by a old mamma cow when I was treatin' her calf. She just took her old dull horn an' pushed me away—didn't break th' skin, but I was gored in th' strict meanin' of th' word. *'And it hath been testified to his owner, and he hath not kept him in, but that he hath killed a man or a woman: the ox shall be stoned, and his owner also shall be put to death.'* What does that say to you?"

"Well, it says that if your ox gores an' kills someone, he's to be killed, but you are not responsible b'cause you didn't know he would gore." Gam said.

"Yeah, but if that ox gores an' th' owner knows it an' don't pen him up, *then* he kills someone, th' owner is just as guilty as th' ox." Harm was beginning to understand.

"I see that," Tex said. "Any cowhand knows that an animal that gores will gore again, an' it's best t' do away with him soon's possible . . . only we usually dehorns or eats 'im." He grinned.

"So much for oxen, but how does that have anything to do with us?" Harmon asked.

"Do you think th' Lord's talkin' only about oxen here?" I asked. "An ox that gores will gore agin; don't a dog that bites bite agin? If a man murders, is he likely t' murder agin?"

"Where'd you git 'murder'?" Gam asked.

"Think about that gorin' ox agin. He didn't gore 'cause someone had it in for him. He murdered someone."

"An' if he murdered, he'll likely murder again." Tex got it.

"An' if a *man* murders, he's likely t' murder again, ain't he?" Gam added.

Harmon was quiet for a moment. "So-o-o, we ain't punishin' th' murderer, we're riddin' our society of a dangerous person who is disposed to murder people for one reason or another."

"Or for no reason at all," Tex mused.

"Who is th' owner of *our* ox?" I asked.

"The 'owner' of the man is society . . . and the laws that govern us."

"You could be a lawyer, Harm."

"An' I would be his murderer if'n he was t' become one," Gam warned.

"The murderer has blood on his hands. If we catch him and let him go and he murders agin, they's blood on our hands."

"I can see that, Lee, and if we take that murderer to court an' th' jury turns 'im loose, an' he murders agin, that jury has blood on their hands," Tex added.

"And if some governor or president lets him go, he could have blood on his hands also." Harmon was deep in thought. "Our laws and our courts are set up to handle such situations—"

"So are most societies, Harm. Look at the tribes; they have laws t' handle murderers, even th' so-called wild Indians identify and deal with murder within their people. In their minds, most everyone else outside their tribe are at war with them, an' to kill them is not murder."

"Yeah, but th' other side calls it murder," Gam asserted.

"Out here, where there is no law or people who feel they are not governed by any law, a man has to be a law unto himself. And sometimes in the extreme, he becomes law, jury, and executioner. It no longer becomes 'An eye for an eye,' but it may become 'an eye for a wrong look,' or a life for a wrong word."

"Like them A-rabs cut off a hand for a stolen loaf of bread," Gam pointed out. "Th' punishment's worser than th' sin."

"So you could say that the Lord's 'eye for an eye' made the law more just?"

"Looks that-a-way to me, Harm. I'm goin' t' bed. All this thinkin's give me a headache," Tex said.

"You'll haveta catch up with me. I been talkin' in my sleep fer a half hour," Gam said through a yawn.

Harmon was deep in thought. When I rose to make my bed, he asked, "Can I see your Bible, Lee?"

"Shore, but don't lose nothin' out of it. I got my funerals an' masses in there."

After a moment or two, he said, "What's this . . . a *wedding*?"

I pretended to be asleep.

CHAPTER 27
BASS IN THE CROSSFIRE

1886

"Sometimes it's hard to git witnesses; harder gittin' 'em t' testify. More'n once I've had t' bring 'em in trussed up on the wagon. When you go after witnesses, it's best you don' show your hand till yuh got him surrounded. I usually gits me a disguise an' make sure they're cornered afore they knows who I am an' what I wants.

"It's hard to testify against a defendant, knowing that things ain't settled with the trial. If the defendant's declared innocent or receives a light sentence, it's fo' sure he would go looking for the witnesses that spoke aginst him. Then there's also friends and kin that'd be offended and seek revenge. Most of the time it's healthier for the witnesses to disappear—before or after the trial."

We had hung around Tahlequah long enough for the word to get out, and our trip down the east side of the Illinois River was a bust. The roads to Fort Smith in Arkansas were better than the territory roads, so we drove to Evansville, where we had the good luck to pick up—and that quite literally, since he was dead drunk—a horse thief who specialized in stealing Cherokee Ponies. He had a good market in Arkansas and Missouri for the horses until we interrupted his business.

It was a relief to be rid of Tavener Hunter and collect the reward. I told the boys the two hundred fifty dollar reward was a five hundred dollar reward and they could split two-fifty between them. I didn't want them worrying that I had gone soft.

There was a buzz around town about goings-on in the marshal's office. Two years before, Bass Reeves had accidentally shot his cook, Bill Leach, in camp one night. Marshal Carroll and the Judge had both accepted Bass's explanation of the circumstances, and life had gone on. Bass had many enemies among the cat-eyed and curly wolves of the territory, and the rumors didn't stop there. So persistent were they that it began to trouble the marshal and Judge Parker. They got their heads together and decided that the best thing to do was to charge Bass with murder and let a trial clear it up. Bass lost his badge, and a few days later Deputy Fair applied for a writ and arrested him on the charge of murder. The list of witnesses would have served well as a roll call of the prisoners residing on Bass's tumbleweed at the time of the incident. These upstanding citizens had all served time as a result of being arrested by Bass.

Presentiment and prejudice swirled around the issue, not to mention the political leanings and ambitions of the men involved in determining Bass's fate. After hearing all testimony, the commissioner placed Bass in jail, and it took the best lawyers in town to eventually secure bail being set. Bass was in jail six months before he was freed on bond.

1887

"Lee, Marshal Carroll doesn't seem to be concerned about the welfare of one of the best deputies he has." It was another one of those late-night consultations with the Judge in the court-room, a visit I usually dreaded. It was a relief to hear that the subject of this visit wasn't me.

"It's that Southern Democrat prejudice against th' dark man, Judge." If I'd been talkin' to anyone else, I would have been more descriptive, but the Judge didn't care for those words.

"They have finally gotten him out on bail, but now it seems that the people Bass needs as witnesses can't be found or they disappear, some after they are subpoenaed. This is his latest list of witnesses his lawyers submitted to me today, and here are the subpoenas filled out by my hand and unseen by any other person aside from the lawyer, myself, and now you. I want you to go find these people and ensure that they are here for the trial."

I took the papers and looked them over. "It looks like the bulk of them are around Fort Reno and Wewoka. I shouldn't have any trouble finding them."

"Just be sure they are here for the trial. I don't intend to have any railroading of a man because the criminal element thinks he does his job too well."

"Yes, sir." I could have added more, but for once my better judgment held the upper hand.

He took the papers back and sealed each one in a numbered envelope. "The number corresponds with the numbered name on this list. I trust that you will be the only one to see this list before these are served."

"Yes, sir, I will."

"Good. Now be on your way; you don't have a lot of time."

Gam was sitting on the courthouse steps. "We in trouble agin?"

"No, he wants us to do a special job." We headed for the stables.

"Secret?"

"Yeah, the subpoenas are sealed. I want to leave before daybreak."

"That's mighty sudden, Lee. We ain't got any provisions on th' wagon, Tex is off in th' unknown, an' Harm's at th' Ferry."

"Well, I'll tell you what, Gam, *I'll* leave before daybreak, *you* get provisions for th' wagon an' find Tex. Hogtie 'im if you have to. Go by Lake's an' . . . no, I'll go by Lake's an' get Harm. Anyone asks that has a right t' know, we're goin' by McAlester to Fort Sill. Anyone else asks, keep mum. Start for McAlester, and as soon as you are sure you ain't followed, make a beeline for Fort Reno. We'll find you somewhere along th' way. You got all that?"

I could feel his disgusted look in the dark. "Shore do, Lee. I ain't no idjit."

"Well, quit talkin' like one."

"I swear, Lee, I ain't said ten words, an' they weren't idjit words."

"Be sure we have plenty of shells and coffee. We may have ten passengers t' bring back." Gam disappeared into the dark and I saddled up, grabbed my bedroll and a can of coffee, and rode for the ferry. The river was low, the Poteau down to a trickle. Instead of waking the ferryman, I swam the ford. The water was still warm from the summer, but the September air was plenty cool. Horse trotted until he was warmed and I just shivered in wet clothes and cool wind. Sunrise and I arrived at Lake's Ferry together.

Bud was already ferrying folks across. "Howdy, Lee. Out afore breakfast, ain't yuh?"

"For a fact, Bud. Is that Harmon at th' house?"

"Left him a-snorin' away. Th' kids'll be tickled t' see you. Go on up. Ma'll have breakfast goin'."

"Believe I will, Bud; good t' see you agin."

Nick was sitting on the steps lacing his boots and finishing his last cup of coffee. "Hey there, Lee, step down; how you doin'?"

"Fine as frog hair, Nick; how're you-all?"

"Doin' good 'cept for keepin' these little ones fed. They'd eat a cow a meal if we let 'em."

"Well, don't stunt 'em; they'll taper off after a while. Harm up yet?"

"Better be—Tom come get this horse."

In a moment, Tom came through the door—without his famous shotgun. "Hello, Mr. Lee. How are you?"

"Hungry. Don't make too much fuss over this horse. He's gonna be on th' road soon, I expect."

He stood a couple of steps above me and solemnly offered his hand. I noted with satisfaction that his grip was firm. "I'm doin' fine, Tom; how are you?"

"Nick! Tommy! Where are your manners? Mr. Sowell hasn't eaten, and you both do nothing about it." Mrs. Lake stood in the door. "Come on in here, Lee. I have breakfast ready for you to dig in to, if you don't mind takin' it away from the kids." She laughed; it looked like the life of a single parent agreed with her, or maybe just life without Owen Lake. She led me back to the breakfast table on the back porch, which was now screened in. The hum of small voices stopped as I entered, then almost as one, they stood and tilted over the long bench and ran to me. "Mr. Lee's here! Mr. Lee's here," they called.

I sat down so I could get all the hugs coming my way. The youngest one they called Butterball climbed up on my knee, leaving egg smeared on my pants. He jabbered away, but I wasn't familiar with the language. The last hug I got was from Baby Kay Stone. Harm had brought her to live with them while Clay, her dad, served his horse-thieving time.

"It seems to me, Mrs. Lake, that you have one more child than the last time I was here."

"She surely does, but I'm not a child; I'm a *girl*, Lee Sowell," Baby Kay scolded.

"Well of all things, is that you, Baby Kay?"

"I'm not *Baby* any more, just Kay."

"You'd think I would know that by now." I laughed and sat

her on my vacant knee. She avoided contact with Butterball. "How have you been doing, Miss Kay?"

"Just fine, thank you. I like it here."

"She has been a godsend to me, Lee." Mrs. Lake set a brimming plate before me and filled a cup with steaming coffee. She relocated the plate out of Butterball's reaching fingers. "Get down, Butterball, and let Mr. Lee eat his breakfast."

Butterball climbed down, his hands considerably cleaner than when he climbed up my leg. He padded back to his seat in his sleeping gown, and Baby Kay lifted him onto the bench.

Harm appeared at the screen door carrying the slop buckets. "Hello, Lee. You've come out early."

"Sorry, Harm, but the Judge has a special mission for us. Says we're th' only ones t'git th' job done."

"I'll be ready in a few minutes; where's Tumbleweed?"

"Gam's bringing it out after he's provisioned it."

Harmon grimaced. He had struggled with Gam's provisioning before. "I hope he goes by the list I gave the store before I came out."

"If he doesn't, we'll both baptize him." I laughed.

I spent a pleasant hour with the family before Harmon was ready to go. After we had been a ways down the McAlester road, we turned off and rode for Fort Reno. "What's our job this time, Lee?" Harm asked.

"We've got to round up witnesses for Bass's trial. The ones Bass wants keep disappearing."

"That whole thing's a put-up deal; can't they see that?"

"Sure, they can, but a trial is th' best way t' squelch it, though it won't stop all th' talk."

"I can see that, but why did they wait two years?"

"The marshal and Judge Parker were satisfied with th' explanation Bass gave, but the jackals kept howling until they felt it would be no good t' wait any longer for a trial. I have sealed subpoenas with numbers on them. The numbers correspond to the numbers on the list in my pocket of people we are to arrest." It was always good for the posse to know what we were up to in case something happened to me. "I intend to take these witnesses into protective custody and deliver them to the court."

Harmon nodded. "We're gonna have some unhappy passengers."

"Looks that-a-way, Harm."

CHAPTER 28
THE SEARCH BEGINS

I know it sounds fantastic, but nearly every white person we saw in the I.T. in those days was dodgin' th' law. We were not set up to take prisoners on this trip and didn't want to be encumbered with them. After the third fugitive we saw and left alone, Harm started a list of the violators and their locations. He kept it for two days, and when he filled up the second sheet, he quit. That night I asked to see his list and went over each entry. At the bottom of the second sheet, the last entry was: "All Of Them."

I had to laugh, "Not much use in takin' notes, is there, Harm?"

"No, and it's a shame, too."

"They're here b'cause they think they can live without law. Trouble is, the law has followed, and eventually it will catch up to them. You and I get impatient when we see them apparently free to do their mischief, but their time to pay comes either by the hand of man or by nature."

There was not a single person on our list in Wewoka, most likely because they had seen us coming and made themselves invisible. Asking around was futile, the people being intimidated and scared to talk. We didn't waste any time staying there.

We waited for the wagon on Sixmile Creek east of Fort Reno. Tex drove in about noon the second day, and Harm immediately went through the chuck box to be sure Gam had bought everything. It was the extra things not on the list that I was concerned with, and sure enough, there were a few.

There were ten names on my list, names I didn't want broadcast back then, and names I don't want to mention today, for most of them are still living, and some people would still condemn them for testifying in favor of a lawman. So, for this purpose, I am going to refer to the people by their number, in that way keeping them anonymous. All witnesses will be referred to in the male gender, although there are females on the list. I let all three of the posse read the list, even though Tex would not know any of the people.

Bass had last seen Number Four at Fort Reno. He could testify that the prosecutor's witnesses—Hill, Jones, Grayson, and others who were prisoners of Bass at the time—all declared that the shooting was an accident.

"He's not likely to be around the fort, but most likely down in Hogtown," I said. "Spread out and look around."

"I'll take that side of th' street, Lee, an' you take this one." Gam turned and ambled up the boardwalk.

"Harm, you an' Tex check out th' cribs out back there—and *don't* sample th' merchandise."

Gam found our man in the third saloon, pouring his last dollar down a rathole called faro. He couldn't resist Gam's invitation to dinner, and we had our first passenger.

Meanwhile, back at the cribs, Tex and Harm were stirring up the ladies. Each knock on a door was answered by the same refrain or some variation of the theme, "Go away, I'm restin'. It's not time to play."

As they approached another door, a commotion two houses away caught their attention. A figure wearing nothing but boots appeared, hastily gathered clothes trailing from his arms. Close behind, wielding a broom quite effectively, bounced and jiggled another disrobed figure of the opposite gender. "Pay me in shin plasters, will you? I'll take my pay in flesh, you sorry four-flushing piece of—" she suddenly stopped, her bare feet having come in contact with a healthy clump of sand spurs. "Dad-blast it."

The man stopped also—half a block away. "That's why I wear my boots, Kat. It's a lot less painful if you have to move of a sudden." He was hopping around on one foot trying to pull his pants leg over a pointed boot.

For the first time, Kat looked up from pulling sand burs from her foot and noticed the two boys standing there staring. "What are you two bums staring at? You're both old enough t' know better. Ain't you gonna help a woman in distress? *Come here!*"

Well, how do you approach a naked woman? Tex would tell you ver-r-ry carefully, for when he was within reach, the woman, really not much more than a girl, grabbed his arm and jerked him to her, at the same time yanking his gun from its holster. "Now, you sorry thief, I'll teach you to steal from me!" she yelled and quite expertly placed four quick shots around the escapee, who crow-hopped out of sight between two cribs.

"What's wrong with this gun? You got th' sights messed up?" our horseless Lady Godiva asked.

"That's a hundred yards away, lady, an' you was wigglin' 'round on one foot," said the Texan.

"B'sides, it was sighted in for a cross-eyed man," Harm added.

"It sure isn't a straight-shootin' gun." Kat didn't seem to be at all conscious of her bare-bottomed condition. "Reload. I may need it again."

The boys tried not to stare, but the fascination of seeing . . . well, you understand.

"Is there a gentleman here who would help a lady in distress remove these sorry spurs from her feet?"

"Yes, ma'am." Harm hesitated, then hastily went down on one knee. The woman plopped her foot on his other thigh, her hand on Tex's shoulder for balance. Harm diligently concentrated on his chore, afraid to look up.

"Take your time there, son. I can stand on th' toes of one foot all day."

"That one's done." Harm looked up at the face peering at him over two rounded mounds. The other foot was loaded with spurs, and Harm had to get his knife out to remove several spines that broke off their spur when he removed them. "That's th' last one, ma'am." He glanced up one last time before rising.

"Well, thank you, young man; I'm grateful. Come by th' House of Dance tonight and I'll give you a free dance, maybe two." She picked up her broom and glided away, skipping and dodging likely sand spur locations. The two boys watched, fascinated.

"Say, lady, what was th' name o' that man you shot at?" Tex called.

"That sorry flesh thief was—"

"Who happens t' be Number Nine," Harm whispered. As they turned to pursue the man, Harm felt a tug on the knee of his pants. He had knelt in a clump of sand spurs, and they covered his bloody pants.

"Come on, Harm, we gotta catch him b'fore Lee does." Tex rounded the corner of the house Nine had disappeared behind and ran into the man. He was peering in the window of the house, buttoning up his shirt. "Peeping Tom, you are under arrest." Tex had him. A muffled scream came from the house. The window shade swiftly descended, failed to lock, and rolled to the top, spinning around a few revolutions before stopping. Harm glimpsed bare shoulders and arms above a tightly clutched sheet as the shade descended again, this time to stay.

The men kept out of sight as they marched their prisoners

back to camp, where they found Lee and Gam securing their prisoner in Tumbleweed. Harm busied himself cooking.

"Got us a peeping Tom, Lee," Tex said as he hopped down from the wagon, his prisoner secured.

"You ain't gonna haul me all th'way t' Fort Smith just fer lookin' in a window, air ye?" Nine called.

Lee rubbed his chin, as in thought, "Well-l-l, we might not have to. You bein' caught wide-eyed and all, we wouldn't need a trial. We would have t' call a jury to set sentence . . . sa-a-ay in this case, an *all-woman* jury."

"What you think about that, Nine?"

"Shore; it's gotta be better than a trip in this."

"I'll go select a jury, and we'll have a trial as soon as possible."

All pretense of secrecy had now slipped away as the opportunity for entertainment was seen by the posse. Word of the pending trial got around like a grass fire on the prairie. The problem Lee had was keeping the jury *down* to "twelve women, good and true."

In a preliminary hearing that evening at the wagon, now parked at the end of the one Hogtown street, Nine pled for bond. The jury conferred and set bond—at five million dollars—to howls of glee from the assembled male crowd and applause from the female contingent.

Judge Sowell pounded the barrelhead with his blacksmith's hammer for order. "Because of the danger of the defendant fleeing, I am setting bond at five million dollars as suggested by the jury." Cheers and applause from the audience were squelched by the rap of the hammer and a scowl from the judge.

There ensued a hurried conference between the judge and the court clerk, Gamlin Stein, and the judge addressed the jury. "Ladies and gent . . . Ladies of the jury, because of the crowded docket of the court, trial is set at eight p.m. the day after tomorrow. You are charged, under penalty of the law, not to discuss or read anything pertaining to this case until such time as the trial begins. Should anyone approach you about the trial or mention the trial to you, you must immediately report the attempt to the court bailiff, Mr. Tex Shipley."

The judge looked at the audience and said, "Any person attempting to influence any member of the jury will be arrested and charged with jury tampering, and *this* court will prosecute that person to the full extent of the law." With two booming raps on the barrelhead, the jury was dismissed and solemnly paraded off to their respective places of employment. Court was dismissed and the crowd dispersed to their favorite watering holes or dance halls.

No one came forward with bail for the unfortunate prisoner, and he had to spend his time on Tumbleweed or around camp in chains. All arrangements were soon made for the trial, which would be held on the high loading dock of the general store, the wide street providing ample room for the large crowd expected to attend.

CHAPTER 29
THE PEEPING TOM TRIAL

Duty in forts of the frontier was deadly dull. Even in such places as Hogtown the "entertainment" was dull and routine for the people who worked there night and day after night and day. The opportunity of a diversion such as a mock trial was as anticipated as a Fourth of July celebration. Everyone had two days to set his affairs in order and prepare for the trial. Word would go out to the surrounding countryside, and many a cowhand and farmer would be in attendance. It would be a great time for the posse to look for the men they wanted.

Although the trial was all in fun, there was a serious side to the matter, for the vastly outnumbered "entertaining women" on the frontier were in such constant demand that they hardly had any time for rest and privacy. Any infringement of that precious time was greatly resented by the women.

Lee secured substitutes for court clerk, bailiff, and camp guard so his three possemen could circulate through the crowd looking for their witnesses. They devised a method of signals so Lee from his vantage point could signal the presence, number, and location of any of their wanted men. There would be a strong contingent of soldiers in attendance, as well as those on guard for any trouble that may occur.

Earlier, two officers from the fort had presented themselves to the judge, volunteering to act as prosecutor and defense lawyer in the trial. After due consideration, the judge ruled that no person with more law experience than the judge could serve.

247

He had decided to conduct the trial without representation from either side.

Early in the afternoon, people began to trickle into town. An hour before court time, people appeared with chairs borrowed from various places and formed a half circle around the dock. There they sat, and no one was allowed to stand between them and the dock. A half hour before the trial time, the standing area behind the chairs began filling. The crowd was relaxed and convivial, greetings and laughter most commonly heard. Twelve ladies in their best array exited the store and solemnly took their places in the jury chairs.

Promptly at eight I entered the "courtroom" in a long black frock and rapped on the barrelhead. "Let the trial begin."

The first witness was called, and Miss Kat took the stand:

Judge: "Miss Kat, tell us where you were early on Tuesday just past."

Miss Kat: "I was in my room entertaining *him* (pointing to Nine)."

Judge: "What happened?"

Miss Kat: "We were settling up our business and that sorry, no-good tried t' pay me what he owed in shin plaster."

"O-o-o-o," went the crowd.

The judge's gavel raised and quiet was restored.

"Jedge, I swear I didn't know that money was counterfeit. I had just won it in a faro game at Big Bend's," Nine the defendant called.

Judge: "Counterfeit money? What did you do then, Miss Kat?"

Miss Kat: "I ran his sorry naked a—hind end out of my house, and he ran up the street and stopped to put his pants on when I stepped on sand spurs and couldn't chase him no more."

Judge: "You were barefooted?"

Miss Kat: "Judge, I was barefooted *all over;* I was *so mad.*"

Testimony in the trial was delayed until the judge could

restore order in the "courtroom."

Judge: "You may continue, Miss Kat."

Miss Kat: "There were these two gentlemen standing near, and one loaned me his pistol and I tried to put new ventilation in that scoundrel, but the gun was off some. He hid between the houses, and these nice boys helped me rid my feet o' those spurs an' I went back home."

When the hoots and laughter from the audience subsided, the judge dismissed the witness and called the next witness.

Judge: "The court calls Miss Sue to the stand."

(*I must insert here that "Miss Sue" is an alias. "Miss Sue" is now the respected wife of one of the most successful ranchers in the region, and we would not sully that good name.* Lee S.)

Judge: "Miss Sue, tell us what occurred at your house last Tuesday morning."

Miss Sue: "I had not arisen yet, having spent most of the night dancing, when I heard a noise outside my window. When I looked, there was that man (pointing to the defendant) looking at me and unbuttoning his clothes. This nice deputy came and arrested him. I don't know what happened after that because I covered up and lowered my blind."

Judge: "This man saw you sleeping in your bedclothes and was caught in the act of undressing at your window?"

Miss Sue: "Yes, your honor, only it was too hot t' wear bedclothes."

Judge Sowell's dismissal of the witness was drowned out by the laughter and calls of the audience. When quiet was restored, the court called Tex Shipley to the stand.

Tex was sworn in to establish the defendant's guilt:

Judge: "Tell the jury what occurred leading up to the arrest of the defendant."

Tex: "Harmon Lake and I were canvassing the area of the cribs looking for a wanted man when this man come bustin' out o' this house wearin' nothin' but his boots. Right b'hind him came Miss Kat wearin' nothin' but a smile an' swattin' th' man with a broom. He ran up th' street, an' Miss Kat ran after him till she stepped on sand spurs. When we went to help her, she grabbed my gun out of its holster and shot at the man four times. She couldn't move for the spurs in her feet, an' Harm volunteered to remove them. He got down on one knee and Miss Kat propped a foot on his other knee. He was real concerned that he might be too rough and kept looking up t' see if he was hurting her."

Tex grinned as the crowd howled, and Harmon glowed.

Judge: "Continue, please."

Tex: "When the operation was complete, we saw Miss Kat to her door and turned to pursue the man. When I rounded the corner of the house he had disappeared b'hind, I found him peeking in Miss Sue's window and we arrested him."

After the witness was dismissed, Judge Sowell addressed the jury. "You have heard the testimony, and there is no doubt that the defendant is guilty. Therefore, it is your job as a jury to establish and recommend to me proper punishment. A table has been set up inside the store and the bailiff will escort you there for your deliberations." The jury rose as one and entered the building to the applause and calls of the crowd.

The judge pounded his gavel. "This court is adjourned until such time as the jury notifies this court that they have come to a decision."

The crowd didn't have to disburse far, for all the saloons had set up "boards on barrels" outside their saloons and served their customers there in the street. The crowd was mellow and swirled and visited; no one seemed to be overindulging.

The posse gathered around Lee and Gam said, "I found

Number One over on the left side. He was with some cow outfit."

"Number Six is sitting in the second row of chairs, nine or ten in from my left on the dock. He's wearin' a white shirt with a black vest and a red sash," I said. "We will have to separate th' cowboy from his buddies or take on th' whole bunch. We won't nab them until after the doin's and there isn't a crowd around. Both of them have warrants attached to their subpoenas and we will use them to justify the arrest. That way, they won't suspect our real mission."

The bailiff walked out on the dock and rang the fire bell. I could see the jury standing inside the door waiting to return to the "courtroom."

"Keep your eye on the two we have found and watch for others. I can't imagine we would have more luck than we have now, but you never know." I returned to the dock and began banging the gavel to start the sentencing session.

The jury paraded in; when they were seated, I asked, "Ladies of the jury, have you reached a decision?"

The jury forewoman stood to scattered applause and calls; the judge frowned. "We have, Your Honor."

"The defendant may rise." Then to the foreman, "What say you?"

"We, the jury, recommend that the guilty party run the gauntlet composed of the good women of this community—and that he run it naked."

It was some moments before the judge could restore order. Banging the gavel did not work, but when he rose and pointed his pistol to the sky, the crowd quietened down.

"Is that the decision of the jury?" There were twelve emphatic nods.

"Very well, I hereby sentence—"

"Judge, Judge! Your Honor!" The guilty party was waving his hat.

"Does the defendant wish to address the court?" The judge's impatience showed.

"I . . . He does, Yer Honer."

"Speak."

"I ain't . . . The defendant refuses to run the gauntlet—"

Here he was interrupted by boos, hisses, and catcalls by the crowd, and the rest of his statement was lost in the noise. When order was restored, the judge said, "You may continue."

"The defendant refuses to run the gauntlet unless the women are naked too." He hurried through the last to stay above the protests again arising from the audience. The hubbub died and a murmur arose from the audience until the import of the defendant's statement was fully absorbed, then shouts and cheers rose to the point of pandemonium. The defendant had won the crowd over.

Judge, jury, and defendant held a protracted conference, during which messengers were hurriedly sent to the four board and barrel saloons. While the crowd calmed down and after a few moments of silence, relatively speaking, the judge rapped the barrelhead. "The jury and defendant have reached an impasse on the nature of the punishment. Therefore, the defendant had no other option than to appeal his sentence. He will be transported to Fort Smith for trial."

After a few moments of boos and hisses, the judge continued, "We have agreed, therefore, and I hereby rule, that the defendant be fined four kegs of beer, to be consumed by the jury and audience within this courtroom." As he spoke, four of the small barrels were rolled out, set in blocks at the edge of the dock, and tapped, to the hearty approval of the crowd.

The jury, each with a mug, descended the steps and filled their cups. A filled mug was handed to the judge. Standing and holding the mug high, he rapped the barrelhead. "This court is adjourned!"

Four board and barrel bars, laden with empty mugs were quickly emptied, and the crowd proceeded to empty the four kegs. Other than the usual sots, there was little drunkenness, the gregarious crowd able to secure little more than one mug apiece. Witnesses Number One and Six were quietly escorted to the wagon with peeping Tom, and by daylight, the posse was miles away from Fort Reno and Hogtown.

CHAPTER 30
LAVENDER COWBOY

I had just finished a funeral for an infant that had died of cholera, and we were heading for our next campsite. The saddest of times is when we have t' bury a child, and it always affected us and made us sad. Gamlin and Tex were drivin' Tumbleweed, and Harmon and I rode either side of th' wagon.

"That was a nice sermon, Lee. Was it one of your'n or from Ol' Baz?" Gam asked.

I opened my mouth to answer when Harm interrupted. "*Gam,* did you know he has a *wedding* ceremony?"

Gam nodded. "Seen him use it once out to th' Canadian."

"How can you do that, Lee, and look them folks in th' eye?" Harmon asked.

"T'ain't hard t' do when I'm makin' a couple already livin' t'gether honest. Now, let me ask you a question: What makes a wedding legal?"

"I never thought about it . . ."

"Is it a license issued by th' state, or is it some piece of paper signed by some preacher? Maybe it's what's written in th' family Bible that makes it a marriage."

"I-I-I don't know . . . th'. . . . th' Bible says, 'What God hath put together, let no man take asunder . . .' " Harm's voice faded as thoughts crowded into his head.

"Did God marry your folks?"

"Come on, Lee, don't hassle th' boy so much," Tex urged.

"Well, what do *you* think it takes t' be married?"

"I don't know an' I don't give a tinker's dam." Tex shrugged.

"I didn't take you-all t' raise, but I'm gonna show you this anyway an' let you d'cide what makes a marriage in th' sight of God, who is th' highest authority in th' whole scheme of things." I reached around in my saddlebag and pulled out my Bible box. "First Corinthians 6:16 says, *'What? Know ye not that he which is joined to an harlot is one body' for two, saith he, shall be one flesh.'* So, what does God recognize as a marriage?"

"When you go t' bed with 'em?" Gam asked. "I never knowed that."

Harmon stood up in th' stirrups. "You mean that when we was in Paris I got married to that . . ."

Gam and Tex were laughing. "There's you another polygamist, Lee," Tex hollered.

Gam slapped his leg. "Don't worry about it, Harm. She was eddicated an' sophisticated. Didn't she shave her laigs?"

"Shaved her legs?" I hollered.

"Yeah, Lee, an' under her arms too!" Gam barely got it out between hoots. "But she said that's es far es she was a-goin'."

"As far es she's a-goin' on *her.* Did she say anything about yore beard?"

Harm thought a moment. "Said I'd look better without'n it."

I hooted. "See? She got herself all shaved up but couldn't stop there. Women start shavin' their legs an' underarms—"

"An' some o' them, upper lips," Tex interrupted.

"—th' nat'ral thing for them t' do is t' start in shavin' on men."

"A-w-w-w, Lee, I don't think that had anything t' do with leg shavin'," Gam said.

"You wait an' see. If this leg shavin' becomes ep-i-dem-ic, men's faces is gonna start goin' naked. Next thing they'll be want us t' shave our chests."

"*Shave our chests!*" Tex yelled. "Why that's our manhood, I'm not gonna shave my chest for anybody."

"Never?" Gam asked.

"Never!"

"Can you live without a woman?"

"I'll get curried by someone what don't shave her legs . . . if I have to."

I laughed. "It don't happen that-a-way. You gonna git stuck on one o' those smooth legged gals an' she's gonna git you thinkin' 'bout a permanent arrangement. You'll git your boots polished, your hair cut, your beard dyed black, an' put on a tie an' git married. Then one mornin' she's gonna look across th' breakfast table with those big eyes an' say, 'Oh, Tex, you'd look so-o-o much better without that beard. Your mustache *tickles* when we kiss.'

"An' soon after that you're gonna appear at th' table naked-faced. She's gonna be thrilled an' 'reward you accordingly.' Then one chilly night, she's gonna snuggle up to you in bed an' lay her cheek on your chest an' giggle a little an' say, 'Your hair tickles.' And so it goes."

"I ain't shavin' my beard an' I ain't shavin' my chest er any other parts o' my body fer no woman," Tex yelled over hoots from Gam an' Harm.

"That's jist th' way it happens, an' it's a-gonna happen to you too, Tex," Gam hollered.

"Never!"

"Women are in-sid-ious that-a-way. Give 'em a little an' they'll take th' *whole* pie," I said. "They're campaignin' for th' vote now. I'd rather let a nigger vote than a woman. They git th' vote an' next thing you know, they're wantin' t' be president, mark my word."

"Women already got th' vote in Wyoming, Lee," Harmon said.

"You know why they give wimmin th' vote?"

"No, why?"

" 'Cause they ain't hardly any wimmin *in* Wyoming. Them boys is hopin' by givin' them th' vote, they'll attract a bunch o' them t' move in an' hopefully they'll be th' marryin' kind."

"An' I s'pose when they git enough o' them in, but not enough t' vote it down, them good ol' boys'll vote out wimmin voting?" Gam laughed.

I laughed. "Ain't gonna work that-a-way, boys. You see them men are gonna call it too close. They ain't gonna factor in that for ever married woman, they'll be *two* votes agin' 'em an' only one gen'ral vote to dis-in-fran-chise wimmin will ever be taken. Them boys is already caught, an' don't know it, an' next time it comes around, some woman's gonna run for governor o' th' great state of Wyomin'."

Harmon took off his sombrero an' wiped his face with th' tail of his bandanna, "I see now why you ain't never married, Lee."

"An' ain't likely to in th' future." Gamlin laughed.

CHAPTER 31
AMBUSHED

We found the deputy's two-wheeled tumbleweed cart empty and his body in his bedroll under it. He had been shot at very close range. His cook/driver was a hundred yards from camp, shot and scalped. "White man's scalpin'," Bass said. "You can tell by th' sloppy job he did."

They had been dead several days. We dug their graves where they lay and rolled the bodies into them. It was the best we could do.

Bass Reeves has a set of rules for campin'. "We lay out our bedrolls an' we cook an' eat afore dark. By dark, th' fire's banked an' there ain't a light in camp. After dark, we move our bedrolls so's any prowlers don't know where we are. We never sleep close to anyone else unless one is sick or needs some special attention. Once we lay down, we don't stand up. Anyone layin' on th' ground can see better than someone standin', an' standin' will make you a nice target. Don't ever sleep under the wagon. That's th' first place a prowler looks. Talkin' gives away our position, so no talkin' after dark. Don't let a snorer sleep in camp. I'll let a prisoner go afore I'll let him snore in my camp.

"Where to now, Lee?" Harm called as he pulled the wagon out on the road. We were two days out of Fort Reno and going east, trying to find more of Bass Reeves's witnesses.

"The luckiest thing I can think of is us findin' four of the men we are lookin' for so easily. I don't know if we'll find another one, so let's head for Fort Smith by way of Cherokee

Town to pick up Number Two who lives there. A couple of these boys is said t'be at Boggy Depot, but I'm not sure we need to go that far south. We might just make a beeline for the Fort from Cherokee Town. Bass thought another one of his people would be around there. If we get to court with five prisoners, we'll be doing good. Any more than that would be gravy."

Gam groaned. "We're gonna hafta cross that quick-sandy Canadian River. I *hate* it."

"Don't worry, Gam," Tex said with a straight face. "This time o' year th' quicksand's only about neck deep—standin' on your horse's back."

"I hate sandy creeks and rivers. You never know when you will step into quicksand. Sometimes you will be walking on what looks like dry ground and it will be that darned quicksand." Gam groaned again.

Harm turned the wagon a little east of south until we hit the Canadian bottoms. We crossed the river to a new settlement called Purcell, where whites were waiting for the opening of the Unassigned Lands. We camped by the river south of town and Gam, Harm, and I went in to look around. Not seeing anyone on our list, I returned to the wagon and let Tex go. Daybreak found us already on the road south.

"Why would anyone want that land for any more than grazin' an' not too good for that?" Tex asked.

(*Actually, this is some of the best farmland in the territory. I rode through on patrol a couple days after the run in '89 and found two-day-old gardens with the corn a foot high and beans ready for pickin'. Amazing soil! Probably get six gardens a season out of it.* L.S.)

"Lee? Why don't they arrest these people an' make them leave until th' land is *legally* opened?" asked Harmon.

"B'cause they ain't no law aginst them livin' on th' *edge* of the Unassigned. If we find whites living in there, we're sup-

259

posed t' run 'em out. I didn't see any when we came across, did you?"

"No, but I shore seen a lot of *tracks,*" Gam said.

"To tell you the truth, Gam, we got more important things t' do than trackin' down Sooners," I answered—and we did; maybe even Bass's life depended on what we could do about getting his witnesses.

Smith Paul's Valley was an old community, and we were welcome there, the local folks watchin' a general exodus south out of town as Tumbleweed drove in th' north end. So long as we were visible, th' town was pretty quiet. We set up camp in th' wagon yard and Tex and I rode on south four miles to Cherokee Town to see Number Two. William Leach was Bass's cook and had stayed with Two for several days, being very sick. It was only a couple of days later that Bass accidentally shot William while working on his rifle.

"Why, of course, I'll be glad to testify for Bass Reeves. He's one of the few good deputies Judge Parker has," Number Two told us as we sat on the front porch of his house. "One thing I won't do is ride that tumbleweed wagon," he vowed.

"If I hired a buggy, would you drive it?" I asked.

"Without a doubt and gladly," he assured me.

"By the way, have you seen Number Ten lately? Bass thought he was staying around here somewhere."

"He certainly was, but last week he went to Boggy Depot on business. We expect him back here tomorrow. I'm sure he will be glad to testify for Bass. We will meet you in Smith Paul's store day after tomorrow."

There was nothing for us to do but look for others on our list and wait for Two and Ten to show up. Two drove the buggy into the yard early the second day—alone. "Ten hasn't showed up, but I left word for him to catch up with us on the way to Fort Smith. I'm sure he will," he reassured us. Ten never did catch up with us, but he did show up in Fort Smith just in time for the trial.

Two led us out of town and stayed in the lead the whole trip, far enough ahead of us so that his dust was not a bother. As we approached the end of our trip, I grew more and more apprehensive and nervous. If there was any place for ambushes, it would be here, close in to Fort Smith where enemies of Bass could waylay us.

When I talk about heading straight from Smith Paul's to Fort Smith, I'm not talking about a straight line. That would take us into that bottomland between the Arkansas and Poteau rivers. It's a swampy, overgrown, boggy land, and we would not likely get Tumbleweed through. There's people in there that can't get out. They drove as far as their animals could pull them and when they couldn't go any farther, they built a shack and stayed right there. Goin' straight to Fort Smith meant going northeast to the road from Lake's Ferry, then east to Fort Smith—not the shortest distance, but the quickest and surest by far.

At Lake's Ferry, I hired Bud Lake to go with us on into Fort Smith. We had not been bothered so far, but I was sure we wouldn't get to the courthouse without challenge of some kind. There were a goodly number of travelers on the road. I kept my eyes on anyone approaching from either direction. A mile or so behind us was a wagon and one horseback rider. They had crossed on the ferry behind us and stayed back all day. They worried me. That night, we camped under the bluffs on the southeast corner of the Rattlesnake Mountains. As was our custom, we ate before sundown, and the fire was down to coals and banked before dark. I warned our prisoners that we expected trouble before we got to Fort Smith and they would have to sleep in Tumbleweed from here on into town. They were to stay below the sideboards as much as possible.

It had been threatening rain all afternoon. Now it began, a soft, dense, and cold rain that had everything exposed soaked in no time. We folded down the canvas on the wagon and tied it down tight. At least the passengers would be mostly dry.

"That'll be th' first place a prowler would look for us, Bud," Harmon said, and a sheepish Bud crawled out from under the wagon.

"You got a slicker, Bud?"

"Got 'er on, Lee."

"Good; I want you to set up by th'end of the tongue back agin' th' bluff. Tex, you set up camp at th' back of the wagon agin' that bluff. I'm runnin' a string from Bud around the outside wheels and back to you. Any tugs on that string means trouble, Bud, so stay close to the ground so you can see better, an' for gosh sake don't shoot any of us.

"Gam, you and Harm get either end of the picket line an' don't let our stock get stolen. I will be between picket line and wagon, against the bluff. No talkin' and no movin' around. Stay where you are even if we have visitors. Anyone you see standing is fair game for a lead injection, and I don't want any of us gettin' shot by his own man. Keep your guns dry and ready."

Sleep didn't come to me. I sat and watched and listened to the soft whisper of rain on the leaves and strained to hear anything out of the ordinary. There was nothing. I was beginning to feel that any premonitions I had were misleading me— until a gravel rolled down the hill behind me. Then there was another one that bounced off the cover of the wagon. It could be a coon or 'possum out scouting about, or it could be a two-legged varmint out for no good.

Slowly, I slid down until I was on my back. I crept out a

ways, then turned around until I was on my back, facing the bluff.

For a long time, nothing happened. That told me we were dealing with something b'sides 'possums or coons. Someone was up there. I lay in water, rain in my face, and my shotgun under my slicker. Slowly, I moved my right arm, and by laying my forearm over my forehead, I was able to shield the rain from my eyes.

We called the hillside a bluff and for all practical purposes it was, but it wasn't a vertical bluff, just very steep—so steep it could not be climbed. A sure-footed man could descend the hillside easily, though I could not imagine that being done with only two pebbles falling because of his movements. This man, if he wasn't a ghost or could fly, was an expert stalker. Without some diligence and a little luck, we would never expect an attack from behind us. My next worry was how far up the hill the person was. My buckshot had a definite range, and it was not very far.

Even though the wagon was pulled up close to the slope, it could be seen from the top of the bluff. By climbing down the slope, the stalker told me he wasn't interested in the passengers in the wagon. He was looking for the posse, and with us against the bluff, he had to descend the hill to get sight of us. *Well, you helped him out some here, Lee, crawlin' out here in th' open like this,* I thought. It was right that I should be the target instead of one of the boys. Even so, I wanted to move, to get back under the shoulder of the bluff. Knowing that any movement on my part would be seen, I forced myself to lie still.

My eyes were in constant movement, looking for my enemy. Every bush, every dark lump lying on the hillside was a body, not an old log. I started counting the possible hiding places until I lost count. My mind envisioned an army of men rising up at dawn to fill the camp full of lead and death. The thought jolted me: *could there be more than one?* Those two pebbles seemed to come from one place on the bluff, and it wasn't possible that any one intruder could get up there without giving himself away in some fashion. *Think about it, Lee, there are more than one out there, in front and behind. The thing you have to figure out is which one starts th' war . . . No, that doesn't matter so much. The one on the bluff won't be expected; he's th' dangerous one. Let the others take care of what's in front of them; you take care of the one above.*

Dawn came creeping through the clouds and rain. Objects became clearer on the bluff, and soon the shadows would descend to uncover me lying in plain sight. I could feel myself the target in the sights of the man above. He was waiting for something, maybe to be sure I wasn't a log, or maybe for someone else to start the fight. Well, here's th' signal t' start, feller, and I raised my shotgun and fired at the most likely target, instantly rolling away from my position. Almost instantly, two shots rang out, one from above and one from behind. I felt a searing pain go through my back as I desperately rolled and looked for my shooter. My right arm went numb and I couldn't move it.

He was there above me, nowhere near where my blast had destroyed a buckberry bush. I fired the second barrel. It was a long shot for a shotgun, but enough to make him flinch and duck. My .44 came up and I fired four quick shots. The pistol had the range, but not the accuracy of a rifle, and my shots only had the effect of making the man duck again.

There was firing from along the base of the bluff and behind me, and I knew the boys had engaged whoever was out there. Desperately, I grappled with the tarp for my rifle. Another bullet struck my bed where I had been a second before. There, I had it! As I came up with the rifle, there was a cr-a-a-a-ck of a black powder rifle behind me. The man on the hill slumped down, his rifle slipping from his hand and sliding down the hill until it lodged against a bush.

I turned to behold Number Two (who hadn't slept in Tumbleweed) calmly reloading her *muzzle-loading* Kentucky rifle. "Get down, Lizzie! They're still shootin' from behind you!" I yelled, running to shield the woman from fire and forgetting all about keeping my witnesses anonymous.

It seemed I couldn't move fast, and it seemed like it took me forever to reach the woman crouching by the wagon. I crouched in front of her, searching for a target. All was quiet for several minutes, then Gam called from somewhere out in front. "It's all clear; this one's dead. Don't shoot. I'm standing up."

We'd killed our "produce" again.

Slowly he stood and the rest of us stood with him. Lizzie resumed reloading her rifle. "Granpa's ol' Kaintuck still shoots straight, don't she?"

"She does, an' you better be glad that bushwhacker behind you was busy shootin' at someone else instead of you standin' there in th' wide open," I chided.

I turned to see how the others had made it. "Been wallerin' in th' mud agin, Lee?" Gam asked.

"There was someone on th' bluff, an' I was lookin' for him." I tried to move my arm, but it wouldn't do what I said t' do; just hung there and shook a little.

"Was you hopin' that yeller slicker would mark your target when you shot your coattail off?" Tex asked.

I hadn't noticed the coattail hangin' over th' shotgun muzzle when I fired. It was clear of th' second shot.

"Gosh, Lee, you're drippin' mud," Harm observed.

"And blood!" Lizzie exclaimed behind me. "Here's two bullet holes in your slicker." She took my rifle from my hand and pulled the slicker off my left shoulder. I could pull my left arm out of its sleeve, but that right arm wouldn't move for all my effort. Lizzie clucked. "You been back-shot, Lee."

I felt weak and my knees buckled, but someone caught me from behind and I didn't fall. "Get him over here on the tongue, an' let's see what has got him." Now a woman was in command. I sat on the tongue by the wagon bed where I was sheltered somewhat from the rain. Someone took my shirt off.

"You got two bullet holes in your back, Lee, an' by th' looks of them, you should be dead right now." Gam was talkin' from somewhere far off.

There's nothin' like sleepin' in a feather bed listenin' to rain on a tin roof, I woke up thinking. But when I opened my eyes, I was layin' in my bedroll under a tarp stretched over the buggy. Someone was talking. ". . . must have been turnin' over, an' that bullet skimmed up your shoulder blade an' busted out th' other side. If they had been goin' straight in, we'd be shovelin' dirt over you."

"Comfortin' words, Gam; you ever thought 'bout b'comin' a preacher or doctor?" I mumbled. I was lying on my left side and my left hand was asleep. When I tried to roll over off my arm, pain shot through my right side, seemingly from my fingertips to my toes. I got my arm free and the feeling slowly crawled back down my arm. "Where are we?"

"We ain't moved yit," Tex said from behind me. "Gotta dig a two-man grave first."

"Are you diggin' yet?"

"Bud's takin' his turn. We're down 'bout three feet,"

"Deep enough. Put 'em in an' let's get on th' road. Less chance of harm if we're a movin' target."

Harmon was peekin' over th' sideboard. "Lee, *Gunn's Domestic Medicine* says—"

"Don't quote me any scripture from that book, Harm. That quack don't know th' half of what he's talkin' 'bout, an' I ain't gonna subject myself to his mistreatment."

"We got a horse an' team an' wagon t' take along now, Lee," said Tex.

"So it was them."

"Yup, you'da knowed one of 'em, too," Gam said. "Had th' pool hall at Vian."

"You mean he come after us after I paid him for th' supposed damage we did to his place?"

Gam chuckled. "Business is business, Lee. That mountain goat you an' Lizzie got was Injun. We never seen him b'fore."

"Harm, get my Bible an' read th' short sermon for outlaws an' let's get out of here. Tex, bring up their wagon. I can lie out straight in it. You fixed breakfast yet, Harm?"

"We done et, Lee. Miss Lizzie said you could have half a cup of coffee if you wanted it b'fore she got back," Gam said.

"Where'd *she* go?" I raised my head, then regretted it.

"Huntin' herbs for your pain. We done got a prickly pear poultice on your holes," said Tex.

"Tex, you're s'posed t' be haulin' that wagon up here, an' there you stand, hands in your pockets."

"I'm down three an' a half feet on that double-wide grave. It's someone else's turn." Bud had walked up. "Say, Lee, your nap over?"

"I ain't th' only one been sleepin'. I wake up an' looks like nothin' been done 'cept pilin' me in this buggy. You git out there an' guard Miss Lizzie till she gits back here. Gam, you an' Harm see to th' buryin' till they get back for th' readin'.'"

Bud grunted. "Shot in th' back an' still givin' orders."

"Ha! He gives orders in his dreams all th' time an' wakes up wonderin' why they ain't done yet," Gam growled.

I must have drifted off to sleep then and didn't hear anything until the other wagon rattled up. "Blamed stubborn mules," Tex was muttering.

"Watch yourself when th' lady's around, Tex."

"I will, Lee; she's still 'round th' corner there. You should see th' junk in this wagon."

"Go throw what's no good in th' grave. Maybe th' Injuns won't bother th' bodies if they think we just buried our junk—and while I'm thinkin' about it, have the boys go through their pockets and put their valuables in a sack for th' next of kin. I know that pool sharp had a family."

"Shore 'nough, Lee." His voice faded from my comprehension.

"Here's some more broth for your pain, Lee." Lizzie bent over me with a dipper in her hand.

I was stretched out in the wagon. "How'd I get here?"

"You don't remember?"

"No."

"Well, never mind. I'm driving the wagon, and the buggy got left at Childer's Station. Take this. We'll be in Fort Smith tonight."

I drank the bitter stuff and drifted off to sleep, barely realizing that we were moving again.

It took some fortification, but I was able to walk into the marshal's office with my witnesses, who all gladly went into protective custody until the trial came up the next week. Harmon and Bud went home and Gam, Tex, and I watched the trial. The jury was given the case Saturday, October fourteenth, and it wasn't until Sunday evening about seven that they returned a verdict of not guilty.

Bass had hired the three best lawyers in Fort Smith for his defense. He had to sell his nice home and move into something less than nice to pay for them. They did their job well, but Bass was broke. He was soon back as a deputy, but as soon as he could, he transferred to the Paris office. His family stayed in Fort Smith.

CHAPTER 32
CHEW'S TRAIL WARMS

1888

We heard Chew got run out of Dodge, and when he did, the backstabbings and robbing stopped. Now, Dodge wanted him back, but he had changed his name from A.B. Chew to Abe Brown, shaved his head, and grew a beard.

He popped up at Clarendon, preaching, and the good folks ran him out for preaching apostasy. There'll be no free love among the Methodist gentry. Word was he passed through Mobeetie on his way to Fort Supply, but he had not arrived there.

"He must be somewhere south of there," Tex said

We were at the community of Grand, I.T., north of the Canadian, where we picked up a prisoner wanted for bigamy. "Why would a man marry more than one woman out here where th' white variety is so scarce?" Gam asked.

"Maybe he's oversexed," Harm offered.

"Dumb," Tex asserted.

"Mormon," I guessed.

"He don't look oversexed to me, an' he says he ain't Mormon," Gam said.

"Just leaves dumb," Tex mumbled through a mouth full of biscuit.

I threw out my coffee dregs, "Now then, we have that settled; let's get to bed. Tomorrow we'll go to Norice an' see if we can pick up Chew's trail there or at Gage. We'll go into Woodward from there. Someone has to have seen him somewhere. He ain't th' kind t' stay in th' wilderness long."

Norice, which is now named Shattuck, was a watering point on the new A.T. & S. F. railroad. Gage, a little ways toward Woodward, was a laid-out railroad town named after some big muckety-muck in Chicago. There was little activity around Norice, the only excitement being an Indian woman wailing and crying about her lost girl. Tex got the girl's description and we drove up the road the railroad built when they laid the tracks.

A couple of miles out of Norice, a young Kiowa Indian brave joined us. "I help you track girl," he said in tolerable English.

"We welcome your help," I responded. "Where are the tracks?"

"They are here." He pointed to a set of horse tracks in one of the wagon wheel traces. "They go this way."

"They?"

He nodded and pointed to a parallel set of tracks in the other wheel trace. "White man lead her horse."

I felt a chill on the back of my neck. "White man?"

"Sí, only have hair on face, no scalp."

"How tall?"

"He short, like so," he said, holding his hand a little above his shoulder.

"Sounds like A.B. Chew, Lee," Tex said.

The Indian, whose name was Blue Earth, shook his head. "He called Abe Brown."

"Two names, one man, Blue," I said. "We must hurry; the girl is in danger."

Blue Earth nodded and led the way at a lope, Tex struggling to keep the mules and wagon apace. Soon the tracks veered north into the brush and we followed, leaving poor Tex sitting in the road cursing his luck.

We spread out either side of Blue, looking for any other sign. "Here, Blue, they're coming back to th' road," Harmon called.

We gathered around the tracks of the same two horses going back toward the railroad. Blue Earth knelt down and studied the tracks. He shook his head. "Only one rider come through today. Other tracks made yesterday."

I shuddered. Harm turned pale and Gamlin's jaw was set, his eyes hard. With an air of resignation, Blue returned to the day-old tracks. They led down to Wolf Creek and up the bank to a stagnant pool of water. There under the overhang of a mesquite smoldered a campfire, an occasional wisp of smoke drifting up in the hot, still air. We dismounted a little distance from the camp. I fished a blanket from my roll and followed the boys. There was a profusion of the man's boot tracks, but few of the girl's moccasins. Here was the imprint of their bedroll, and tracks of the two led into the brush. I grabbed Blue's arm as he started to follow and motioned for them all to stay put. The tracks didn't go far. The girl lay where she had fallen, face first, the back of her head crushed and bloody. The large bloody rock lay nearby.

I had to hold to a mesquite bush, fighting the nausea, dizziness, anger, and sorrow that washed back and forth over me. When things had settled a little, I spread the blanket beside the girl's body and pulled her dress down over her buttocks. I gently rolled her over on the blanket. She was already getting stiff, and I almost lost it when I saw her hands clasped together across her bosom. I arranged her dress and gently brushed sand from her face and closed her eyes. Her long black hair lay about her face and shoulders.

The boys came at my call and stood quietly as Blue knelt beside the girl and wept. We wept with him. Tears of sorrow mingled with tears of anger—quiet anger filled with a terrible resolve.

In a few moments, Blue stood and said, "I must take her to her people."

"Of course, Blue Earth, we will help you," I said, my voice seeming to come from someone else and far away. Grasping the blanket corners, the three of us carried the body to the open creek bank. Gam produced a hatchet, and we cut two ash saplings and made a travois tied to Blue's pony. He seemed accustomed to the arrangement. All four of us walked, Harmon leading the pony and Gam and Blue Earth walking either side of the travois.

It was a little past noon, hot and unusually still in the brush. By the time we walked the mile back to the road, we were all soaked in sweat and thirsty. Tex had pulled the horses as far under the shade as he could, and he and the bigamist were sitting under the wagon. He had coffee and beans warming, but all we wanted was water and cooling shade.

Tex's anger showed. "One man who marries too many women and one who kills them, both showing their contempt for womanhood in their own way. I don't think they're much different from each other in the end analysis. We're sure in good company, boys." He moved away from the prisoner.

There are times when a man's natural hunger takes a back seat to other things, and this was one of those. Harmon put the food away and poured the coffee on the little fire. "Gam, you go back with Blue Earth and try to find out more about Chew, where he's going and so forth. We will go on and try t' catch him. Unless the trail's hot, we'll wait for you at Woodward. There should be several passengers there for us. Here's some money for a long box if you need it." I gave him five dollars, which would take care of all funeral expenses, if necessary. They soon left, both men walking and leading their horses.

"Tex, saddle up and let Harm drive Tumbleweed awhile. Maybe with him driving, our prisoner will live long enough for us to collect our fees." I showed him the tracks we were following and we proceeded at a slow pace, one then the other watching the ground. Near Gage, Chew left the road. "Bet he's goin' around town," Tex said.

"You think you can track him through th' brush without gettin' ambushed?"

"Shore, Lee. I'll let my Grandma's Cheyenne blood take over an' see you t'other side o' town."

"Be sure you do. If we pick up his trail there, I'll fire two shots, an' you can come on ahead."

He nodded and ducked into the brush.

I hurried to catch up with Tumbleweed. There wasn't much to Gage, a half-stocked store/real estate office and a half-dozen shanties scattered around. Lot sales were not doing any business. After refilling our water barrels—at ten cents a gallon—we moved on. It was a mile or more before we picked up Chew's trail again and I signaled Tex. Pretty soon, he appeared on the road behind us and eventually caught up.

I gained new knowledge of Chew's habits when I saw that his tracks led boldly into Woodward just after sunset. He avoided Gage, where the few people living there would take note of a traveler, but tomorrow morning, Woodward would wake up with a new visitor who came in from some unknown origin. He, being a little scrawny man, wouldn't stir much interest.

His trail went cold. Though we searched the whole town, nothing of him could be found. We didn't know the descriptions of his horses, only their tracks, and those disappeared completely in the traffic of the town. A ride up the Fort Supply road didn't reveal anything of his presence. The train presented a means for him to disappear in two directions, and we became convinced that is how our fugitive escaped.

After two days of searching and waiting on Gam, when he showed up we drove to Supply and picked up nine prisoners being held in the brig. From there, we headed east. We got a break in our search for Chew when we went back through

Woodward. Chew had been seen leaving town on the Fort Supply road. He must have bypassed Supply while we were there and gone only God knows where from there on. We reversed our tracks and returned to Supply.

There were only two trails leaving Fort Supply going north or west, the Jones and Plummer cattle trail to Dodge City, and an ill-defined trail northwest and west into No Man's Land, officially called the Public Land Strip.

No Man's Land got created by the setting of the state and territorial boundaries of four of the five states that surround it. The southern boundary of Kansas on the north was set at the 37th parallel. The Missouri Compromise dictated that no slave state could be established north of parallel 36-30, so Texas had to cede their lands north of there. The Indian Territory/Oklahoma boundary was defined by law as the 100th meridian, and the eastern boundary of New Mexico was the 103rd meridian. Colorado was ignored in the process. In spite of Cherokee claims that they owned the strip, and their attempts to extort rental from those who settled there, the Supreme Court ruled in 1885 that their claim was invalid.

Thus, the area from 36-30 to the 37th parallel and the 100th meridian to the 103rd Meridian became land claimed by or assigned to no state. No state meant no state law. There was no federal law due to a lack of interest.

The strip was in the High Plains or Llano Estacado, the Great American Desert of old—hot, dry, all sky and sand. Yet there is an attraction to this land that can't be explained. Was it the altitude, the air, the openness, or the vision that all ground rose from where you stood, making a man feel he was the center of the world? The saying that "all hell needs is water" applies also to this land. If it wasn't for the constant worry and search for water, this land would be pleasant indeed.

The only town in the whole strip was Beaver, which started out as a trading post and stop on the Jones and Plummer cattle trail. If anywhere in the country was more lawless and wild than the Indian territories, it was the Public Land Strip. Outlaws too mean and wild to stay in the I.T. gravitated to the strip. It got so bad that the few good folk got together a vigilance committee and disposed of some problems. Then they met and decided to organize the strip into a territory, and Cimarron Territory was proposed. They had their own laws and police, wrote a constitution, and petitioned Congress for recognition. There has been no encouragement from Washington.

Dodge City police had a keen interest in Mr. A.B. Chew. A telegram to the chief prompted a town search, which revealed no Abe Chew, under either of his aliases. The more we searched, the more convinced I became that the man had gone west into the Cimarron Territory.

"It looks like we are gonna have to go into the Cimarron Strip to catch our man," I said one night.

Tex was perplexed. "We're not gonna drag that wagon over there, are we?"

"Well, what do you propose t' do with all those prisoners, turn 'em all loose?" Gam asked.

"We couldn't carry enough food for such a trip, an' th' buffalo are gone." Harm was always concerned about where his fixin's were coming from.

"I've talked to the officer in charge of the Fort Supply brig, and he has agreed to take the prisoners back if we are going after Chew. Tomorrow, they are going back." The prisoners groaned. Fresh air and decent food had spoiled them. "We're gonna park the wagon and ride. Harm, make up your supplies in packs, and we will take the team for our pack mules. Those aparejos are lookin' pretty thin. Tex, find us some good hay an' stuff 'em up."

Early morning found us at the brig and we returned our prisoners. The jailer didn't notice there were ten men this time. Harm and Tex had the mules packed and we made tracks west. Beaver River is about the only source of water in the strip, and that's pretty unreliable. If there were no pools, we dug wells in the riverbed and hoped they would fill with water by morning. Sometimes they did.

Tracks didn't last long in this sandy soil and they quickly lost their distinction, just becoming a trail of indentions across the land. There were plenty of them along the river bottoms, mostly deer and elk searching for water.

"How do you know this is th' way Abe came?" Tex asked one evening.

"I don't know, but it seems this is th' only way he could go from Supply without running into country where he was looked for—maybe it's a hunch or a wild goose chase." I wasn't even sure myself.

CHAPTER 33
MIRAGES

"After a while in this business, Lee, you get a feelin' for what's goin' on an' what's liable t' be happenin'. Pay attention to your hunches an' act on 'em. You'll find them a valuable asset." Bass said as I locked up our latest arrest. While visiting the home of a bootlegger, he had lifted the lid on the flour bin and found our quarry stuffed in the flour.

We had been seeing false lakes on the horizon and knew what they were. They were interesting, made somehow by the heat waves coming off the ground, but no good for watering men and animals. One day we were startled by the image of a man and horses in the sky. They appeared overly tall, shimmering in the light—a man riding a horse and leading another.

"Which way are they goin'?" Harm asked.

"I always thought a horse's tail went on his hind end. If that's so, those horses are goin' away from us." Tex grinned.

"You can't tell from their shadows which end their tails're on," Harm argued.

"Tell you what, Harm; ride up north there about two mile an' look at that mirage from th' side an' you'll *know* which way they's a-goin'," Gam said.

"Can you do that, Lee?"

"No, I don't think so, Harm, but I can tell which direction *that* man's goin'." I pointed to the mirage of a lone rider moving north from the south.

"Well, I'll be darned," Tex said, "two mirages at once."

"It may be one mirage, Tex; looks like they will meet before long."

"Shore does, don't it?"

"Lee, that's an Injun," Gam said.

"I think you are right, and that man's hat"—pointing to our first vision—"makes it seem he's American or Mexican."

"How far away are they?" Harmon asked.

"They're over the horizon, probably twenty-five, thirty miles or so," I said.

"Th' Injun's trackin' th' white?" Gam asked.

"Not unless th' white's made a left turn." Tex chuckled.

"Th' way I sees it, that Injun gonna cross his trail in a minute er two," Gam surmised.

The images wavered and flickered and faded. "Guess we'll never know what happens now," Harm said.

"Might if we're on the same track as they are," Tex observed. I could tell that it was Tex's *determination* to find out.

"Folks might be hurtin' in Beaver if this is th' only water we can find this far down th' river," Gam said, looking in the half-filled well.

"Might be they's had time t' dig their well deeper," Tex said. "Time we was movin'."

"Anxious t' git to th' meetin' place, Tex?" Harm braced his foot against the mule's gut and pulled the cinch tighter.

We found the windblown tracks where the Indian joined the trail. Tex rode ahead to see what happened. He waited on us after riding a mile ahead. "Nothing; they didn't meet. I guess th' Injun was just travelin' th' road."

"Man not Brown." The voice came from across the road behind us and we turned to see the Indian step out of the brush, a grin on his face. It was Blue Earth.

"Blue Earth, what are you doing up here?" I asked.

"I come to get Brown."

"Is he here, Blue?" Gam asked.

"He not go to town, Lee, he stay away. I show you."

"Are you hungry, Blue?" Harm asked.

"Much water here,"—he motioned toward the river—"make good beans and rice." Blue was hungry, all right.

"Lead us to it, Blue. I'm gittin' hungry too." Tex turned into the brush and *he* led us to the river. "Blue, this is th' driest water yet," he called from the sandy bed.

Without glancing at the Texan, the Indian turned up the stream and around the next bend. We saw ahead a rock ledge the river ran over when it flowed. Below the ledge was a pool of water, and water seeped from under a layer of the ledge, cool and fresh. The Indian pony whickered a greeting to our animals from the shade of a cottonwood.

"Nice place, Blue," Tex called from behind us.

"Fire ready, Harm. I help unpack."

"When did you eat last, anyway?" Harm asked.

"Two, three days ago, ate prairie dog. Much hurry here to help you catch Brown."

"Is he close?" I asked.

"No. Far away near Buffalo Springs." To answer my questioning look, he explained, "I come here to get you."

The Five Civilized Tribes we worked with the most had become so "civilized" they had almost lost or ignored the instincts, intuitions, and spiritualism of the so-called wild Indian. These Indians, living with nature and often in harsh climates, depended much on their inner selves to guide them. Call it a sixth sense, if you wish, but that would oversimplify it, I think. For instance, Blue Earth had not followed us, he had *intercepted* us as we came from Fort Supply and he came from Norice. How did he know where we would be? How did he know where we will find Abe Brown/Chew? Ask him and he would only shrug his shoulders and say something like "I know." He doesn't try to analyze why he knows, he just accepts the knowledge as it comes to him. It's a great mystery and, sadly, a fading mystery, as the Indian race becomes more and more absorbed into the so-called civilized world.

We ate our dinner and watched as Blue ate and ate and ate his meal. When he had finished, I asked, "Blue, how far to Buffalo Springs?"

"Five days there"—he pointed just south of due west—"this many"—he held up seven fingers—"by river."

"Too dry to go cross-country." Gam was not yet used to a land without plentiful water like the Ozark hills.

"Water plenty. Only Indian know where." Blue grinned.

"We won't be killin' animals t' git there, will we?" I wasn't about to sacrifice our horses for the sake of saving time.

"No; water there," Blue insisted.

"OK, Blue, we go there." I pointed southwest. "Today we rest."

The pleasant aroma of coffee awoke me, and we were soon fed and riding west. We crossed a clear little stream about eight miles from the river and rode on another twenty miles to Kiowa Creek, where we dug for water. Our stock were able to fill themselves and graze on plentiful brown gramma grass.

The next water we found was on the headwaters of Clear Creek, twenty-two miles from Kiowa. It was twenty long sandy miles from there to Palo Duro Creek. The horses smelled water and took us to a long pool in the creek bed.

That night, Blue Earth drew us a map in the sand. "We here." He pointed to a spot on the line he had drawn for Palo Duro. West of there he drew another stream that crossed our path. "This Agua Fria—Coldwater Creek." Farther west, he drew a stream that came from the north and snaked itself east, then turned north again, apparently out of our path. "Rio Beaver, *larga distancia.*"

"How many days?" I asked.

Blue shrugged. *"Uno dia—muchos dias."*

West of the last bend of the Beaver, Blue drew another stream. It dipped south in a big curve and connected to Coldwater Creek. "Agua Fria, *larga distancia—uno o mas dias.*"

"Palo Duro, Agua Fria, Beaver, Beaver, Agua Fria agin. These streams go ever-where," Gam said.

"Why would he come 'way out here? To hide?" Harm asked.

"This is No Man's Land, Harm. Out here at the end, he has access to three states: Kansas, Colorado, and Texas, and New Mexico Territory. He can get into any kind of mischief he wants and run to the Public Land Strip and be safe from pursuit by the law. The only thing he has to fear is the provisional law at Beaver, and he's a long way from there.

"A man named William Coe—they called him Captain—appeared out here in 1864 and settled in the strip. He built himself a fort back in th' hills below Black Mesa. It was pretty big and pretty secure from invasion. Not bein' much on raisin' cattle and such work, he started appropriating things from traffic along th' Santa Fe Trail to his north and th' Cimarron Cutoff to th' south. He accumulated as many as fifty men of his ilk and they ruled the region. Got so bold that they would go into the towns in Colorado and take them over, grabbing anything they wanted and appropriating the women.

"He got caught a time or two and escaped. Mr. Charlie Goodnight had several run-ins with the gang. His cowhands were as salty as Coe's men, and the outlaws generally avoided the Goodnight outfit, though Coe swore to kill Mr. Charlie."

"Are they still out here?" asked Harm.

"Yuh think Chew's a part of th' gang?" Gam asked.

"No; they got busted up by th' army in th' sixties after they got so bad, something had to be done about them. They got so organized that they had a blacksmith's shop in one of the canyons on the North Carrizo and they would steal whole herds off th' Goodnight–Loving Trail, drive them to this canyon, and rebrand them. John Chisholm had trouble with them when he first came into th' Rio Pecos country."

"Tell 'em what happened to them, Lee," Tex, who was familiar with the gang, said.

"The army attacked the fort before they caught Coe, and got run off because the fort had three-foot-thick walls and gunports all around. It only had one door on the east end and no windows. The second or third time they came back, they caught the outlaws unawares. Their lookout on top of Robbers' Roost peak was either asleep or not there. They routed the outlaws and caught eleven of them. Coe got away. No one would say how, but between th' army an' a Colorado sheriff, the eleven were hanged on the cottonwoods along North Carrizo Creek. Heard it was quite a battle, Tex. Tell th' boys how Coe got captured."

Tex sat back and relit his pipe. "About two weeks after the fight, Coe stumbled in to the Emory Ranch and asked for food. Mrs. Emory fed him a big meal and sent him to the bunkhouse to rest. When she was sure he was asleep, she sent her son, Bud Sumpter, on his pony to catch the soldiers. They came back to the ranch and captured Coe. When he saw the lathered pony, Coe said, 'I never thought I would be captured by a woman, a boy, and a pony.' He was eventually turned over to the Pueblo sheriff for trial. That night vigilantes took Coe from the jail and hanged him, chains an' all, from a cottonwood on the bank of Fountain Creek. He was found next morning on his knees, strangled. They buried him under that tree."

"This was in 1868, I believe," I said. "Later on, they caught three of the men at Fort Nichols."

"So-o-o Chew wasn't a part of that crowd," stated Harm.

"No, he might not have been born by then," I said.

"Where could he be, then?" Gam wondered.

"Buffalo Springs," Blue Earth said.

"Or a settlement up north of there called Carrizos," said I.

"Carrizos? Where's that, Lee?" Gam asked.

" 'Bout thirty miles north of Buffalo Springs, three miles from New Mexico and six miles from Colorado, and a mighty convenient place for outlaws, I'd say. Last time I heard, it had a lunch counter and three saloons. Only thing lackin' for a bunch of thieves and highwaymen was a red light, an' I bet they have one by now."

"Hope so," Tex muttered and Gam grinned.

"Well, you can just set those hopes an' dreams aside. We're goin' to Buffalo Springs and thereabouts, and if we don't catch Chew there, we're gonna follow th' trail most likely, and that may or may not be to Carrizos." I tapped out my pipe. "Bedtime."

Buffalo Springs was on the banks of Coldwater Creek in Texas. The springs were deep and cold and welcome to all who came to them, man or beast. We camped north of the springs to give all critters room to approach and get water. There was so much hoof traffic that I despaired of finding any sign of our quarry. Blue Earth worked and scouted around the springs all day. When he came in for supper, he said with a satisfied grunt, "Abe Brown go south."

"What's south of here?" Gam asked, disbelieving anyone would chance that dry trip when Tascosa was seventy-five or more miles away and Mobeetie over a hundred miles.

I thought a moment. "Maybe he wants us t' *think* he went south."

"You think he didn't go south, Lee?" Harm asked.

"Which would you prefer, a hundred miles with no water or thirty miles?"

"Whoo-hoo, Carrizos, here we come," Gam crowed.

CHAPTER 34
CARRIZOS NO MORE

We were riding into one of those little communities that pop up around the territory, live awhile, then melt back into the ground when their usefulness is gone. Ol' Baz rode close and said, "Lee, places like this can tell you a lot of things if you're listenin', but you gotta win folks' confidence, an' you do that by bein' generous with your silver, friendly, an' not askin' questions. Always pay more than you're asked and be polite to th' ladies."

The three young bucks were impatient to go, but the animals were a little ganted and needed a chance to recruit some. I insisted on staying around the springs a couple of days to let the stock rest and graze. It would be the last thing mentioned that I needed a little rest also. Blue Earth rested with us the first day, but that night, the springs were visited by three men who came in from the north, watered, and left without visiting our camp. Morning found Blue and a portion of our oatmeal breakfast gone. He hadn't returned the third morning when we broke camp and rode north.

"Do you know where water is from here to Carrizos, Lee?" Harm asked.

"Not very well, and this time of year, what I know of is liable to be dry. We'll follow Coldwater. There's usually a pool or two up near its head."

The water was there all right, green and scummy. The horses only drank a little and snorted their dislike. The next creek was named Aqua Fria, but was not a part of the Coldwater Agua Fria. This was not a stream in the usual sense of the word, for it was so flat that it hardly flowed when it held water, which was seldom. It was just a drainage that had no outlet, just disappeared into the Llano.

Cienequilla and Carrumpa creeks come together to form the headwater of Beaver River. "Hot, dry, and flat" was all you could say about the next miles until we hit the Santa Fe Trail. We rode west along the trail until we could see the ruins of old Fort Nichols. It was a campsite for the trail and pretty used up, both in structure and forage. After a short rest, we rode north down into the breaks to South Carrizo Creek. It was a pleasant little stream, still flowing, and we spent the night on its banks. Blue Earth came in at sunrise and finished off our breakfast. "Not Abe Brown," he said by way of explanation for his absence.

We got a surprise when we rode into town that night. The store and post office had moved south of the river. It was a busy place, to be out in the middle of nowhere, with the only industry being farming and ranching—if you don't count the robbing, carousing, and fighting activities. We kept to the shadows and, after a look, rode out a ways and camped on the Cimarron River.

"What's th' plan, Lee?" Gam asked over his pipe.

"We'll split up, visit each place, and keep our eyes and ears open. We're just a bunch bound for Denver lookin' for a little entertainment and recreation along th' way. Here's a little advance on your pay. Buy a drink or two, don't call attention to yourselves and look and listen."

"You gonna let us get 'entertained'?" Gam asked.

"Business comes first, then I'll give you a couple of days off."

"It won't take me long to look this place out," Tex said. "If Chew is here, I'll be th' first one t' know."

286

Harm grunted. "You ain't never *seen* him, much less known him."

"You know, Harm, you're right in some of that, but I seen enough o' his work t' know that he'll *smell* like death, an' you-all told me what he looks like."

"Likely, he'll be different lookin' agin an' have a different name," Gam opined. "He seems t' gravitate to th' women, so I'll check out that new and shiny Red Light."

"You'll be sorry if you sample th' wares before us," Tex warned.

"There'll be no 'sampling' until the business is over," I said. I didn't worry about Gam's commitment to our mission. He would be all business until the business was taken care of, then it'd be "Katty, bar th' door."

Old man Marrs, who owned the lunch counter and adjacent saloon, was behind the counter cooking a steak when I entered his establishment. It smelled good and he said, "Butchered him this morning and just sliced this one off." He held up a large slab of meat and turned it over in his big cast-iron chuck wagon skillet. "Plenty o' fat on 'er, too."

"You convinced me, Marrs; I'll have it an' th' fixin's as may go with it." A large Mexican woman began dishing up the fixin's: tortillas, hominy, little green peas, and yams smothered in syrup. When the steak was done, Marrs plopped it on a plate and slid it under my nose.

"Now, that's a sight for a man long on camp cookin'," I said, and that was the last thing I said for some minutes. When I finished and looked up, the woman switched the empty plate for one with the biggest sopapilla I had ever seen. It had cinnamon and sugar sprinkled on top and honey oozed out of the insides when I cut into it. Luckily, the dessert side of my stomach was empty, but it took a big effort to finish the plate off.

"More?" Marrs asked.

"No-o, sir; I don't think I could take another pea."

Marrs chuckled, "Must be off your feed. I seen these hands around here take on three o' those plates in one sittin' an' be back for an early supper of th' same nature."

"Maybe I *am* off my feed some. How about another cup of coffee?"

He poured my cup full and poured one for himself. Lowering his voice, he asked, "Gonna be here long, Deputy?"

"Am I that obvious?"

"Nah. I saw you down in Muskogee a couple years ago; knew you were a deputy."

"Don't remember seein' you."

Marrs just smiled. He was like a lot of whites in Indian Territory, not wantin' t' be noticed by any deputy marshal.

"Matter of fact, Marrs, I am looking for a particular man, a woman killer. He goes by the name of Chew or Brown or likely some other name; a mousey little feller, quiet, but likely to be pretty dirty—might even be pretending to be a preacher. Loves hanging around women."

Marrs rubbed his chin in thought. A deputy knows the signs well. Marrs wasn't trying to remember the man I described. He was debating whether he should tell me what he knew or not. I waited until the debate was over. "Woman killer, is he?"

"More than one, Marrs, an' some not much past childhood." I didn't mention the murder of Tracey Price, since the murder of a deputy might raise esteem for Chew in many minds around this community.

"I could have seen a man like you describe around here, little guy, quiet, moves slow, sees a lot, might forget t' pay for his meal if you didn't watch."

"Sounds like him. How long ago did you see him?"

Marrs smiled. "Might have been at lunch, or yesterday at supper."

He was walking a narrow path between saying too much and allowing a possible woman killer to go free. It was a caution he had to take if he wanted to stay in business very long here. Any more information I would have to get myself—somewhere else.

"Well, I thank you for the meal; it was a real treat. How much do I owe you?"

"Six bits; it's pretty expensive shipping this stuff from Trinidad."

"I can understand that, an' I'd hate t' hafta ride to Trinidad for a meal like this." I laid a dollar on the counter and wandered into the saloon. Possibly because of the lunch counter, the saloon was a pretty quiet place. A man might not want a drink or two very soon after all that feed. Four cowhands were playing poker at a table in the middle of the room. The stakes were matches, but the play was hot. Otherwise, the bored tender sitting on the counter swinging his legs and watching the game had nothing to do. I tossed him a half dollar. "Get these boys a beer and one for yourself."

One of the men looked up from his cards. "Much obliged, Deputy."

"Hell's bells, might as well pin a sign on my shirt, front and back. How does a deputy look?"

All four of them laughed. "It ain't how you *look*, it's th' jingle in your pocket. No one out here has any, except deputies and gamblers, and gamblers have that look you couldn't miss."

The redhead grinned. "B'sides, we run all th' gamblers off."

Barkeep set four mugs of beer on the table. It looked warm.

"We're kind of rebels around here, Deputy, an' bein' so if you can afford a box of matches, we'll let you in th' game." The barkeeper wiped foam off his mustache with his sleeve and tossed me a penny box of matches.

"Think you boys can afford t' be seen with me?"

"Wouldn't be who we are around here if we didn't invite you t' play."

"Well, I wouldn't want t' spoil your reputation. I'll play a hand or two—until th' place gits crowded."

The four were named Red, Sol, Blackie, and Spider. Red was black-headed and dark; Sol was supposedly the wise one, but he couldn't play poker worth a darn; Blackie was a balding redhead (I didn't ask); and Spider was a tall, lanky, skinny feller.

We played for an hour before anyone else wandered in.

"Hey, Pete, yuh git tired of th' noise over there?" one of the men asked the newcomer.

"Shore was loud for a feller just in from th' Quiet," he replied.

I was doing pretty good for my level of poker playing, having only lost half my stash in an hour. "Pete, how 'bout me stakin' you to this game an' see if th' cards'll fall better for you?" I rose and offered him my chair.

"Your cards ain't th' problem with this bunch, stranger. You have t' learn t' be a good liar an' deal yourself a card or two from th' bottom like they do." He nodded his thanks and took the seat. I glanced in the filled lunchroom but saw no one familiar and left by the saloon door.

From the sound of things, Pressley's saloon was hopping. An occasional whoop from the direction of Carter's saloon and dance hall indicated business was also brisk there.

I was heading for camp when Gam called from the corner of Pressley's and motioned me to come there. "You'll never guess who I saw at th' Red Light." Without waiting for an answer, he said, "Kat."

"From Fort Reno?"

"Th' very one."

"Did she recognize you?"

"Yeah, we had a long talk. She said she had seen Chew here

in the last day or two. One of the younger girls had been complaining about someone following her around town and pestering her. Now she can't find the girl."

"Damn."

"That's what *I* said. I saw Harm in Pressley's. I'll get him an' meet you back at camp."

"OK. Tex must be at Carter's. I'll pick him up and be on out."

We had left Blue to watch camp, but he and his pony were gone when we got there. "Wonder where Blue Earth is."

"We can't find him or Chew in th' dark, Lee. What do we do now?" Harm asked.

"Not a thing we can do without light. My only hope is that somehow Blue has found out Chew is here and is tracking him. We'll track Blue in the morning and see where that leads us."

I lay down, but there was no pretense at sleep. The others must have been as energized.

"Harm, guess who I saw at the Red Light?" Gam asked.

"Your sister?" Tex asked.

"That's as good as my guess would be," Harm replied.

"Kat."

"No kiddin'." I could tell Harm had sat up.

"Shore 'nough. Hardly recognized her until I saw the mole on her left cheek."

"Damn, Gam, that mole was on her left *buttock* cheek. You been samplin' aginst orders?" Harm accused.

"Roosterin' agin' orders is a cap-i-tal offense, ain't it?" Tex asked.

"By slow strangulation, if I remember th' law right," Harm said. "Did you really see Kat tonight?"

"Shore, I did; yuh think I would lie to you?"

"Not unless you were breathin'," Harm retorted.

CHAPTER 35
ROBBERS' ROOST

The trouble is with the bench and behind it a maudlin sentimentality that forgets and condones a crime upon which the bloodstains have dried. The bench is indifferent and careless. The avarice, which is the curse of this age, has so poisoned the people that civil law for the protection of property concerns it more than the criminal law, which protects life.

This fearful condition does not exist because laws are defective. We have the most magnificent legal system in the world. The bench is not alive to its responsibilities. Courts of justice look to the shadow in the shape of technicalities instead of the substance in the form of crime. Everyone knows, too, that corrupt methods are used to defeat the administration of law.

Judge Isaac C. Parker

This close, maybe less than a day separates us from catching Chew, and he very likely has slipped us again. The man is quicksilver or has demonic senses that ward him from the danger of justice. Even before there was a light in the east, I was up brewing coffee. The boys were up by the time you could see your hand at arm's length. Horses were saddled and we had a last cup of coffee before light was enough to track by.

I had been watching a horse and rider coming our way from town. As they got closer, I determined the rider was sidesaddle, a woman. Closer, I saw it was Kat, of all people.

"Are you boys going to lollygag around all day wasting daylight?"

"Th' sun ain't up yet, Kat," Gam said.

"Well, howdy, Tex and Harm; how are you two?"

"Are you out ridin' for pleasure, Kat?" I asked.

"No, Lee, I'm out searchin' for a young friend of mine last seen riding this way with that man called Chew."

"So, they were riding north?"

"Didn't I just say that?"

"We're hopin' our tracker is on their trail and he has left sign for us to follow, only we don't have cat eyes, so we wait for the sun." I sure didn't need any woman tellin' me what to do an' when t' do it.

"Here's Blue's sign, Lee." Harm had found a shock of grass twisted together and bent north.

We spread out and rode north watching for signs. Blue was faithful to leave them often, and we had little trouble following.

Dry Cimarron, they call her further downstream; when we got near, we could hear her roar, bank full and still rising. It often happens this way. Some torrent in the mountains breaks loose and sends a flood down the river, where never a drop of rain fell. Sometimes it builds into a wall three-, four-, ten-feet high and rolling as fast as a horse can run. Pity anything caught in that.

We found Blue Earth sitting on the bank watching the water rise, wary that it could sneak around behind and strand him on an island that would crumble and wash away from under him.

"Man cross here before water." Blue pointed to vague tracks into the water.

"Where would he be going out here?" Kat asked.

"May be he go there." Blue pointed with his chin.

I stared at the hillside through the trees, searching for the sign Blue had seen. At the top I made out what seemed a corner of a building or wall. It didn't go very high.

"Some sort of building, Lee," Tex said.

"Nothing we can do but wait for the water to fall," I said. "Might as well make ourselves at home." But none of us were "at home" knowing our quarry might be at hand, within shouting distance yet untouchable. We watched the river recede until it was back within its banks but still frothing and rolling, carrying all kinds of debris with it. I walked the bank, watching the water. A little below the crossing, the water spread out in a large pool and it seemed to be flowing a little slower. It looked shallow, only wading depth, until somewhere in the middle, where the old channel was. I watched the water awhile until the urge to try it was too strong to resist so I sat down and took my boots off. I shoved my gun down in the bottom of one boot and stuffed my pants into the top. With my cartridge belt in the other boot and the rest of my clothes stuffed tight on top, I tied the boots together and hung them around my neck.

The water was cool and not deep for quite a ways. When it was halfway up my chest, a treetop came floating down on me, and I tied my boots high on a dry limb and pushed the tree into the current. We were in the main channel, and I found myself swimming and trying to push the tree across the current. It carried me downstream a long ways. I could hear the crash of water falling over some obstruction down below. Push as I might, it seemed the tree was determined to resist and stay out in the current. Some obstruction on the bottom caught the tree and rolled it over. My boots disappeared under the water. The tree slowed and stopped. We washed up against a logjam that had built on a huge cottonwood that had fallen across the river when the bank washed out from under its roots. It had backed the water up and made the little lake where I waded in. Likely, the water was still piling up behind the dam, and more and more debris was piling against the dam.

I felt along the tree limbs with my feet, feeling for the boots and hoping they were still there. The water began to froth and sting. Alkali. It choked me when I breathed and stung my eyes. I was desperate to find my boots and dove under, pulling myself along the limbs of the tree. A boot bumped my arm and I grabbed it. The knot was tangled around the limb, and I was running out of air. I bit down on the boot top and with both hands broke the limb below the knot and clawed for the top.

My first gasp for air filled my lungs with fumes from the frothy water and choked me. I clung to the limbs and struggled to stay above water. A breeze brushed by, and I was able to get fresh air into my chest. It was easy pulling myself along the piled brush and out of the main flow. Here the water was fresher and didn't sting.

The bank was a vertical wall. The only way up was to climb the roots of the fallen tree. Once on top of the root ball, I had to jump across a gap to the bank. My feet crumbled the edge of the bank and I fell, grasping for anything I could reach to keep from falling into that gap between roots and bank. Clawing and digging, I made solid ground and lay there, muddy and sandy and exhausted.

It was some moments before my energy returned enough for me to sit up and take stock. When I pulled my pants out of the boot, they were wet but not soaked. I pulled my shirt out of my other boot and dried it good. My gun was mostly dry. At least the sand didn't get in it, and the mechanism worked. My belt hadn't fared so well. Most of the shells would probably be no good. At best, I had five good shells in the gun.

I must have looked a sight, naked and covered with dirt and sand. There was a trickle of blood here and there, but nothing bad that I could tell. My trip down the river had taken me past the mouth of a stream that flowed between Chew's crossing and the ruins of that building up on the hilltop. Hopeful that it was

295

dry, I hobbled toward it with only a pause here and there to remove sandspurs from my feet. The stream was full of water. As I watched, it rose some. This was backwater from the dammed-up lake, a good place to wash off and dress.

My wet pants were clinging and binding, and I left my shirt off for that reason. Funny, but being naked felt pretty good. Nothing to bind or pull, unconfined. Maybe I was meant to be an Indian—maybe there was Indian blood in me from some shadowy ancestor.

The climb up the hill was steep and rocky, and there was much slipping. I made no attempt to be quiet, but moved as fast as I could. The top of the bank was so steep, all I had to do was lean forward to lie down. The ruined building was about fifty yards away. This west and south side seemed the most complete. There were no windows, only gun slots arranged along the wall. It looked like the east end of the building was pretty whole, most of the damage being on the west end where the roof sagged down into the ruins.

The place was quiet and seemed deserted. As I started to rise, a horse walked around the east corner of the building and began cropping grass along the wall. It was Abe Chew's big racehorse dragging a rope.

A woman came around the corner carrying the picket end of the rope and made a halfhearted attempt to drive it in the ground. She was disheveled, and her torn dress hung loose and open. She kept trying to hold it together as she worked. Once she stopped and pulled a spur from her bare foot.

I scrambled up the bank and waved both arms, but she didn't see me and returned to the building. It seemed to take forever to run across that ground to the building. When my breath was back, I walked out and removed the picket rope from the horse and shooed him away. At least Chew would have to ride a horse more our speed if he somehow got away.

There must be some kind of entrance on the east end of the building. I chanced a glance into one of the gunports and saw nothing, but heard sounds of a struggle. The girl gave a little cry and I found myself racing around the east corner of the building. There was a gap in the middle of the wall where once there had been a door. I dove through it in time to see Chew standing over the woman, raising a big rock above his head with both hands. My first shot smashed into his hand and the rock, causing it to fall and the woman to ward it off with her hands. My second shot, meant for his filthy heart, busted his thighbone. The man screamed like a girl and fell backwards on the rubble. The barrel of my gun laid against his head stopped the wailing, and I turned to help the girl up. "I'm Deputy Lee Sowell, ma'am."

Her knees buckled and she clung to me, crying and shaking.

"He was going to kill me," she said, and anger gave her body strength. She leapt onto the man as he was coming to and beat him about the head and face. Chew tried to defend himself with his one good hand, but couldn't stay the fury above him. When I became concerned that she would damage her hands, I pulled her off him and her anger turned to pain and anguish. She leaned against me and wept great sobs. The anger began to rise again, and I led her away from the man. Chew's bedroll was rolled out. There was blood on it, both old and fresh. His rifle was propped against his saddle, and I picked it up as we passed.

A noise at the entry made me look up—and into the familiar muzzle of a shotgun. "It's me, Harm, don't shoot." The muzzle withdrew and Harmon peeked around the wall. "You OK, Lee? We found your hat hangin' on a limb, high and dry, and thought the river swallowed you."

"Looks like it tried to and spit him back out," Tex said from the opposite side of the door.

"Where's Gam?" I asked.

"He and Blue are lookin' for yer body down by th' dam," Harm said.

Tex stepped away and fired two quick shots into the ground. "That's th' signal t' tell them we found your ass." He grinned.

"Mollie, are you all right, girl?" Kat jumped down from her horse, and Mollie rushed to her.

I took Kat's horse, stripped the wet saddle and blanket from him, and rubbed him down with it. He seemed content to crop the grass, and I went back to the building. "How was the crossing, Kat?"

"It was swimming, but we made it."

I noticed her clothes were dry—had not been wet at all.

"Wish I had been there to help you across." I grinned.

"I'm sure you do." She smiled.

Mollie seemed to be mostly whole except for a split lip and bruises we could see. I left the two women and went to see if Harm needed help patching up Chew. He had wrapped Chew's hand and a finger lay beside the man. Already, his leg had swelled until the pants were drawn tight and Tex was kneeling on Chew's shoulders, holding his good arm so he would not interfere with Harm as he slit the pants leg.

Harm looked up as I knelt beside him. "He hasn't bled much, Lee."

"Too bad. His blood's so black, it doesn't run too much."

Chew stopped his whimpering and opened his eyes. "Why did you shoot me?"

"The first time was to stop you from murdering that girl. The second time was when I missed your heart, Chew. I should have got closer and hit it with a third shot."

"Why do you want to kill me?" he whined.

I started counting on my fingers, "A family of five here in th' strip, a fourteen-year-old girl in the Creek Nation, a deputy

U.S. marshal and his posse. That's nine; a Kiowa girl from Rainy Mountain School, an' th' kidnapping and attempted murder of Miss Mollie. That's eleven that we know of."

Tex grabbed Chew's hair and pulled his head back. "How many more are there, or have you lost count?"

"There's those alley killin's in Dodge City," Harm said.

"Too bad you won't be able to walk to the gallows with that busted leg, Chew, but I'm sure there are plenty of people willing t' carry you there."

"Hey, there's plenty o' rocks here, why don't we get rid of him th' way he did all those girls?" Tex asked.

"Wait a minnit, Tex," Gam called from the door. His gun and belt were dry, but the rest of him dripped, and his boots sloshed when he walked. "Glad t' see you're well—an' dry, Lee." He handed me my hat in passing. "You can't do this man like that, Tex, you know dam—" He glimpsed the women listening. ". . . darn good an' well it's my turn t' do th' prisoner in. Give me that rock an' turn him over."

"No, no, no, no," Chew screamed, "you have to take me to Judge Parker."

"We done appealed your case to a higher Judge, an' He has said you must die," Harm said.

"Either way, boys, Chew is gonna die," I said. "We'll *try* to get him back to Fort Smith, but it depends on his good behavior whether he gets there or not."

"I'll be good," Chew whined. "I'm hurt. There's some laudanum in my bedroll. I need some."

I turned to the women, "Mollie, did Chew give you some laudanum?"

We heard horses and looked to see Blue leading our horses. "River must be down," Tex opined.

Blue Earth entered the ruins and saw Chew lying there. For an instant, I thought he would spring on him and end our responsibilities right there, but with visible effort he controlled his emotions and looked away. "We'll see he gets what he deserves, Blue," I said.

"River going down," he said, and walked out.

Harm rose. "Hold on, Blue; let's cook."

It took them only a few minutes to get a fire going outside the ruins and coffee boiling. Harmon poured rice into another pot and added a couple of cans of tomatoes and a fresh jalapeno pepper to the mixture. We gathered around and shared our cups and plates. Mollie seemed much better, and even laughed some at the boys' antics.

"What is this place, I wonder?" Harm asked no one in particular.

"Looks like a fort to me," Gam said. "Those walls are a good three foot thick."

"Yeah, an' not a window anywhere," Tex observed.

"Nothin' but those gun loops for ventilation," Gam said.

"I'm guessin' this is Captain Bill Coe's Robbers' Roost," I said.

"Seems like a good candidate for it, don't it?" Tex said.

"Yes, this *is* Robbers' Roost," Kat said. "An old Mexican sheep rancher that lived on the flat where Texiquetti Creek joins the Cimarron told early settler Ab Easley about it. No one could get to them until the army came."

"Was Easley in th' fort at th' time?" I asked.

"You can ask him yourself," Kat retorted. "The fort supplies building stones for some of the buildings around here now."

Gam wandered over to the rubble of the building, kicking stones and pushing aside the roof. We heard him exclaim something, but didn't pay attention until he walked back to the fire. "Lookee what I found," he said, tossing a rusty cannonball from hand to hand.

"Back away from th' fire with that thing," I called a little louder than necessary.

Gam backed away and asked, "What's the matter, Lee?"

"Look that ball over real good and see if it has a hole bored in it."

Gam rolled the ball in his hands several times and said, "Don't see one . . . yuh thought it had powder in it?"

"I wouldn't want t' find out standin' over a fire, would you?"

"By th' heft of it, I'd say it was solid," Gam tossed the ball to Harmon, who spilled his coffee catching the thing.

"Da—arn, Gam, what if it exploded?" he yelled.

Tex took the ball from Harm and gave it a thorough examination. "No holes and it *feels* solid."

"Did any of you boys ever look up the word 'darn' in *Webster's Dictionary*?" Kat asked.

"Did any of us ever *see* a dic-tion-ary?" Tex asked, a rhetorical question, answer obvious.

Kat ignored the interruption. "It means 'damn,' so you might as well use th' real thing as not. It all means th' same."

"I-I never knowed," Harm stammered.

"A hefty dose of th' gentle sex would do your manners good." I laughed.

I admired Kat's frankness and at the same time recognized that this woman was more than what she appeared. She was educated, and by her manners came from a higher station in life than what she now lived. I gained a new respect for her.

We had completely ignored Abe Chew but now his whining drew our attention. "What do you want, Chew?" I called.

"Laudanum," he replied.

"Can't give it to you. It would probably kill you, an' we want t' see that pleasure for ourselves," Tex replied.

I am sure Chew was in a lot of pain, and I'm just as sure that if it were any person other than Abe Chew, all of us would have had more mercy for him. The fact that we didn't spoke of our horror at the things this monster had done, not of our hard hearts to ordinary mankind. I was tired, really tired. Before I realized it, I had fallen asleep leaning against my saddle.

CHAPTER 36
THESE OWNERS SHALL BE QUIT

"We git so caught up in this business of catchin' people for th' money in it that we forget that it's about what's right and just. That feller got judged by someone b'sides Judge Parker an' he got what he deserved. Halleluiah an' amen. I'm goin' to supper." And that's just what Ol' Baz did.

—*From Chapter Seven,* Death in a Narrow Place

People were stirring. I woke up to find the sun had hidden behind Black Mesa and a long cool evening had begun. "River's still too high to get Chew across, and th' ladies don't want t' git wet, Lee, so I guess we'll hafta wait an' see how she looks in th' mornin'," Gam said as he handed me a plate of beans and rice.

"Another meal without meat. Can't go much longer like this," I said.

"If that river don't go down tonight, I'm goin' huntin' in th' mornin'," Tex vowed "An' I ain't gonna worry if my elk has a brand on his rump."

They had splinted Chew's leg and moved him to his filthy bed. He was in such pain, they relented and gave him laudanum. "It was either that or listen to him groan and yell all night," Harm said. So far, he showed no sign of infections.

Both women were familiar with camp life and made themselves handy, but they insisted on rolling out Harm's bed between our beds for safety's sake. Even here and especially with Abe Chew in our midst, we set our watches, and by full dark all was quiet. Kat lay down on the side of their bed next to me and I chuckled when after she struggled under the covers, she plopped her dress on top of the bed.

My swim must have taken more out of me than I realized, for I drifted into a dreamless sleep. It must have been after midnight when someone tapped on my shoulder. "Scoot over, Lee. Mollie has all the covers." I remember muttering something and turning over on the cold side of the blankets. There was a draft when the covers lifted and Kat lay with her back against my back.

A sharp pain struck my calves, and I was wide awake. "Dang, woman, those are the coldest feet I ever felt."

"Sh-h-h-h. Go to sleep and no funny stuff."

"A man who's been without female companionship for months and months an' some voluptuous woman slips into his bed in the middle of the night and he's supposed to behave? What kind of devilish torture is that?"

"This is not the time, nor the place, Lee Sowell. *Go back to sleep.*"

Like I could sleep, but it was nice to feel her warmth against my back. Gradually, her feet warmed, but she didn't move them away. I could get used to this . . . An elbow gently poked my ribs and I awoke. "It's almost time for your watch, Lee. Get up and dress before someone finds us and spreads the word to th' world."

I scooted out from under the covers and pulled on my pants and boots. I was sitting there when Harm found me. He started to tap Kat on the shoulder and I said, "Here I am, Harm."

"Who's this?" he whispered.

"Mollie got all the covers an' Kat came over here an' got me up." It was the truth, but a little out of order. I picked up my rifle and rounded the camp. Everything looked in order, the horses dozed, and all was quiet. I went into the building to check on Chew. He was resting easy under the influence of the laudanum. In th' dim moonlight, his face looked hideous with dark holes where the eyes were; his sunken cheeks and pale skin made his face look like a skull.

It was my custom as last watch to stoke up the fire and put the coffee on. After that, I walked to the edge of the bank and listened to the river, still hidden in the dark valley. It seemed to me the water over the dam wasn't as loud. Hopefully, we could cross today.

"Breakfast reminds me much about supper last night," Tex said.

Gam snapped his fingers. "I *knew* I had seen this b'fore. Thanks for rememberin', Tex."

"When does your hunt start, Tex?" I asked as I waited for Kat to finish her breakfast on my plate.

"Soon's I determine that river can't be crossed."

"We have to rig up something to get Chew across and to town."

"Th' pack mules are used to carryin' a stretcher. We could get some poles outta that logjam an' rig one up," Gam said.

"Say, where's Blue Earth?" Tex asked.

"I saw him get up an' leave right after Lee put th' coffee on." Kat dished a plate of food and brought it to me.

"You sure you're through?" I asked Kat.

"Yes, Lee, I'm sure. Even if that river's still swimming, I'm going back to town and dish up me a *variety* of food for tonight."

"Gets awful borin' without meat, don't it? But Harm does a good job with what little he has." I couldn't let my cook get discouraged.

"All you got t' do t' appreciate Harm's cookin' is let Gam cook you a meal." Tex chuckled.

"You ain't never had any repeat customers after they eat what *you* cook up, either," Gam shot back.

No one mentioned Chew or looked in on him. He was my prisoner and my entire responsibility as far as they were concerned. Breakfast over, we all walked over to the top of the bank to look at the river. "I believe it's down enough, Mollie. Feel like goin' t' home?" Gam asked.

Mollie smiled. "It's not exactly home, but I'll be glad to get there and away from here."

The boys found two long poles for the stretcher and we returned to the fire. I went into the ruins to see to Chew and get him ready to move. Something about Chew lying on his side and his utter stillness gave me pause, and I approached him with what I guess you could call caution.

The covers were pulled high over his pillow and when I rolled him on his back and pulled the covers down, the pillow was empty. Abe Chew's head was gone!

I pulled the covers back and discovered his belly had been slit open and his bowels drawn. His genitals were gone. The sight and smell were overwhelming. I covered the body and turned away, struggling to keep my breakfast down.

"What's takin' you so long, Lee? He givin' you trouble?" Tex and Kat stood at the door.

"No, he's no trouble at all, just out of his head a little."

"My gosh, Lee, you're pale as a ghost. Do you feel all right?" Kat grasped my arm and I didn't feel so jittery.

Tex had walked to the bed and stopped and stared. "Good Lord Almighty, he's plumb out of his head, Kat. It's gone."

"His head's *gone*?"

"It was Blue. Blue Earth cut off his head, and he's takin' it back to Snow Flower's people!" Tex was shouting with glee.

I didn't mention that was not all he had done, not wanting Kat—or Mollie, for that matter—to know. Gamlin and Harmon were standing in the doorway and went to the bed to see for themselves. I put my arm around Kat and directed her reluctant steps to the door. "You don't have to see it to believe it, Kat. You can take my word for it."

"I'm not some squeamish ninny, Lee Sowell. I've seen a lot of things in my time."

"You don't need that image to haunt your dreams in years to come."

In spite of her bluster, she was trembling, and I sat her down on one of the saddles.

Mollie was staring at us, pale as a sheet. "Is he dead?"

"Yes, Mollie, he'll never rape or murder again." I hadn't caught myself soon enough, and the words indelicate for ladies' ears had tumbled out. "Get Kat a cloth to wash her face and neck before she faints." I squeezed Kat's arm to stop her protests. "Nothing like getting busy helping someone to get your mind off bad things," I whispered.

The three boys were still at the body when I returned to the ruins. "Did you see what he did down below?"

"Yes, and Chew was alive when that happened," I said.

"How do you know that?" Tex had overcome his nausea, but Gam and Harm both looked pale still.

"He bled."

"He would have screamed; he was a screamer."

"Blue Earth knew how to prevent that without killing him. Blue wanted Chew to feel and know everything happening to him up until the moment he cut his throat."

"I guess that's a good enough reason t' always stay on th' good side of the Ki-o-ways." Tex didn't grin when he said it.

"Are we goin' after him?"

"No, Gam, the man has exacted the only justice he knew for the crimes Chew committed, and I'm satisfied with that."

"That's one ox that won't gore again, will he, Lee?"

"And *these* 'owners' shall be quit, Harm. Someone get a shovel. We got a buryin' t' do."

"And his blood is on no one's hands," Harm said.

We picked a spot for the grave and had just begun digging when four riders topped the hill and rode toward us. "We thought you had been gone long enough, an' you might need some help." It was my four poker partners: Spider, Red, Blackie, and Sol.

"Just waitin' for the river t' go down so's it won't get our skirts wet," I replied. "We caught our kidnapper and Mollie is safe."

"Well, yer skirts'll stay dry now," Blackie said.

"Say, that looks an awful lot like a grave you're markin' out there. Someone die?" Red asked.

"Injun friend of our'n took Abe Chew's head to Rainy Mountain," Gam explained.

"Chew didn't survive th' operation," Tex added.

"Shore looks like you folks had a time of it," Red said.

"Yeah. Why don't you let us take care o' th' buryin', an' you-all git across that river while it's below skirt-soakin' level. We'll meet you in town for a celebration?" Sol suggested.

I nodded. "We'll help you dig th' grave first."

"That'd be 'most all th' ceremony, an' it's time Spider got re-acquainted with th' blister end of a shovel," Blackie opined.

"We'll take care of th' buryin'. You folks go start th' party an' we'll catch up," Sol urged.

"Well, I for one will take you up on the proposition," Gam said. "Diggin' graves can git t' be a trial when you ride with Lee."

Harm handed Spider the shovel. "Don't burn up th' handle, now."

"I might *break* it over Blackie's head," Spider grumbled.

Both women and Harm were packin' up gear, and Gam and Tex were rounding up the cavvy. "Looks like we're takin' you up on th' deal before dinner," I said. "Nobody here has any great love for this place. Just to keep th' record straight, all damage except th' bullet holes was done by our Indian guide in revenge for Chew murderin' a young Kiowa girl. Justice has been served as far as I'm concerned."

"We can understand that," Red said.

He might think again when he sees th' remains, I thought.

"Just roll him up in his bedroll and throw him in th' hole. I ain't gonna say anything over that grave, 'cept, 'Well done, Injun.' " Some white men would not countenance an Indian killing a white, even if th' man deserved it. Blue Earth would be safer if he were not associated with this event.

"If his possibles bag should roll out, bring it to me. There may be someone in his family we can notify—and spread th' joy, quite likely."

"Will do, Mr. Lee."

"See you at Marrs's. I'm settin' 'em up."

CHAPTER 37
FLORENCE ARISES

The Cimarron was quite calm by the time we crossed her after midmorning. Kat took some ribbing about crossing the flood and keeping her clothes dry. She didn't mind and gave as much as she got. We left the three possemen setting up camp while I escorted the ladies to town and went over to Marrs's and made arrangements for a big meal and celebration. I sat at a secluded table and wrote out my report on the Chew case. It was always a chore without Harm helping, but this time I did it so I could include some remarks he didn't need to see. When I left Marrs, there was a fresh hindquarter of beef being cut up for steaks and such, and ribs were in the smokehouse.

The walk to the post office was pleasant; there was no weight on my shoulders. E. E. Hubbard had built a general store on the south side of the Cimmaron and his wife had a corner of her husband's store for the post office. She was pleasant and friendly and we had a nice conversation. When she took my report to weigh, she looked at the return address and exclaimed, "Oh, Deputy Sowell, this is not Carrizos."

"It isn't?"

"No, Carrizos was on the other side of the river and when we moved over here, we named the post office Florence after our daughter."

No one remembers now why Carrizos ceased to be and Florence became. Quite likely, it was because the bulk of potential customers for Hubbard's store were on the south side of the river. A little village grew up around the post office and store. Three saloons were in the village, a lunch counter and saloon owned by a man named Marrs; and two other saloons, one owned by a Pressley and the other by a man named Carter. In 1892 Fairchild B. Drew owned the store. He filed on a homestead a mile east of Florence, platted the south forty acres into a townsite, and moved his store there. The saloons followed, and the need arose to name the new community because the saloons could not be named.

At the suggestion of a recent resident, the town was named after Kenton, Ohio, and in those days of phonetic spelling, the town became Kinton. Later on, somebody kicked the "i" out and made it an "e."

I met the posse on my way to camp. They were washed and in clean clothes. "I brought your clean clothes, Lee; th' river's just right for bathin' if you hurry. We pulled the plug in it," Harm said.

"Probably be dry tomorrow," Tex grumbled.

I folded my paperwork and stowed it. "Thanks, I'll go take care of that chore; bar's open for beer only." As I passed by the Red Light, Kat called to me, "Come here, Lee. I have something for you."

She took my reins and led us around back to a two-room cabin behind the building. "This is my house. You won't have to go to the river to get a bath if you don't want to."

"Sounds good to me, Kat," I said and grabbed my saddlebags as she held the door for me. The front room was a combination sitting room and kitchen, and there in the middle of the floor was a tub of water.

"Get yourself undressed and I'll get the hot water," she said.

I was standing in the middle of a tub of cold water when she poured in a pan of boiling-hot water. Then with another kettle, she poured water only a little cooler over my head and shoulders. Tossing me a cloth and bar of Pears soap, she said, "Scrub," and disappeared into the bedroom. I scrubbed a week's worth of dirt off and sat in that tub and soaked until it cooled and Kat returned with a towel.

"Your clothes are laid out in the bedroom," she said and followed me into the room. "But I thought you might enjoy something else before you dressed."

"I certainly would, ma'am." This time, her feet were warm.

I was away from Marrs's longer than I intended. When Kat and I got there, the party was in full swing. Mollie had brought some of her friends; the four poker players were there and, by their hilarity, must have been there some time. Marrs had the pan hot and threw two steaks in when he saw us enter. He motioned when they were ready and I whispered, "How much is this costing me?" when I picked up the plates.

"Plenty," he said and grinned happily. He knew I would be inserting some silver into the local economy. We had the lunchroom to ourselves, but the saloon side was filling up with other people. They seemed as festive as we were. When we were full of steak and ribs, our crowd drifted into the bar to a warm greeting by the crowd. Word of our captive had obviously spread, and among these people, at least, the news of his early demise was welcome.

Red motioned me to the bar and called for the attention of the crowd. When all was quiet, he sat up on the bar to be above the crowd and said, "We found Chew's possibles when we went to bury him and when we looked inside, found a bag with these in it." He held up a board on which were tacked seventeen locks of hair, each tied with a ribbon and a tag attached on which was written a name. "The man had kept a record and token from each victim." A murmur something like a growl went through the crowd. "Now, some of us would rather not receive a visit from a U.S. deputy marshal, but this visit by Lee Sowell is just what we needed. The work he and his posse did the last two days—and no telling how many days before—is more than welcome by any reasonable man, no matter which side of th' law he's on."

Shouts of "Hear, hear" and "Amen" were heard from the crowd.

"Tonight we celebrate the capture and demise of a monster who has preyed among us. In recognition of that fact, Deputy Sowell has declared a truce and will not arrest any miscreants until he has his tumbleweed wagon back in order." He grinned at me, and what could I do but agree? Th' deed was done.

Mollie received special attention from the crowd. That pleased her very much and helped her shed the horror of the last couple of days.

Marrs ran low on the hard stuff and had to buy several bottles from Pressley or Carter at th' seller's price. When he came back from his buying trip, both saloon owners came with him. Save for Marrs's place and the Red Light, the whole town was shut down.

As the evening wore on, I noticed an unusual number of men leaving by the back door and returning with empty glasses, which were promptly refilled. This was more than men leaving to relieve themselves, and my curiosity sent me out the door. At first there seemed nothing out of the ordinary, but as my eyes became adjusted to the dark, I perceived a large object hanging from a cottonwood limb a few feet from the door. A couple of men were looking at it. As I approached, I realized it was a body—the headless body of Abe Chew, a rope looped across his chest and under his arms.

"Come to view th' remains and drink a toast, dep'ty?" one of the men asked. Blackie had followed me out. Now he said, "We started to bury him, Mr. Lee, an' thought th' rest of town should

313

see and appreciate th' fruits of your labor. Do you want us to bury him when we're through?"

"I'm sure th' town would appreciate that after a day or two," I said.

It was a stellar celebration and I enjoyed it greatly. A large weight had been removed from my mind. I was even glad Chew was gone and we didn't have the responsibility of returning him to Fort Smith.

We spent a pleasant two days there. Even though it lacked the amenities of larger, more established towns, the change of pace was good for all of us. No longer did I dream of severed heads in a burial cave or a mangled head of an innocent child or woman. They seemed to fade away, replaced by pleasant thoughts and dreams of a woman with a warm heart and, sometimes, warm feet.

The second day Kat and I rode up the Cimarron Valley into New Mexico. The river flowed between high mesas of blackrock lava, their steep sides all but impassable. The vega was level or gently rolling land where the wild grasses grew in profusion. We ate our lunch in Sheep Pen Canyon. There was a nice hole of water in the river where the horses watered; such a nice hole of clear cold water that we swam awhile, then made a leisurely ride back to Kenton.

"Why hasn't someone settled that valley an' raised a million cattle?" I asked, not really needing an answer.

"Apaches, Lee, but now that they are gone into the mountains and seldom if ever roam here, the land is open for anyone to occupy."

"It's put in my mind a notion to go into th' ranchin' business, Kat; what do you think?"

"You probably would go crazy without bullets flying at you all th' time." She laughed.

"Look how high the water got in the flood. A feller'd have to build on one of those foothills t' stay dry."

"You'd have to build a fort like Captain Coe."

"Naw, th' first thing I'd build would be a bunkhouse where eight or ten men could live. It'd have a kitchen on one end an' a stove-up old vaquero cookin' for 'em. Then after a year or two when I had the money, I'd marry me a wife, an' she could build a house like she wanted. Do you think she would like that, Kat?"

"Would she have t' let you live in it too?" She laughed again.

"O' course she would; how else could she keep her feet warm?"

Our horses and I were the most anxious to move early the third morning. Tex and Gamlin were grumpy at th' best an' I would have offered to let them stay, but I was afraid they would jump at the opportunity. Harmon wasn't grumpy, because he had no hangover, but I do believe he would have stayed if given the opportunity. How long any of them would have stayed in that isolated place is another question.

Then there were the mules. They had gotten fat on the grazing the last few days and were determined that they would *not* go anywhere. Tobe shook off his pack, and Pet fooled Gam by holdin' air, an' when we started, the pack swung to her belly. She nearly tore it to pieces before we could stop her. We moved the pack to one of the horses, and I saddled Pet. We fought for a while, but I won out and she was a tired mule that night when we camped.

Twelve dry days after leaving Kenton, we rode into Fort Supply. Harmon and Tex were glad to see that tumbleweed again, much to Gamlin's disgust. The next morning when we went to pick up our prisoners, there were only nine and a bill for three days' board for a nonauthorized prisoner. They had turned the polygamist loose.

I still had that bag with the locks of hair from Chew's victims, not knowing exactly what to do with them. When we passed through Fort Gibson, I talked to the Indian agent there. We agreed that the locks should go to next of kin if possible. We solved that problem by fastening the locks on a board and hanging it in the agency headquarters. A sign above the board explained that the next of kin could claim a victim's lock and take it upon reasonable proof of kinship. Over the next four or five years, all the locks disappeared except the six locks of the pilgrims that had died in the strip.

The agent told me that one day a man stepped off the Kansas and Arkansas Valley Railway train and presented his credentials, showing that he was the brother of the murdered wife. He took those last locks and the next train back north.

We headed east, and six weeks after leaving Fort Supply, we crossed the river to Fort Smith with fifteen prisoners, no money, and no food.

CHAPTER 38
TAILHOLT ROUNDUP

Fall, 1888

We stayed in Fort Smith almost a month and it nearly drove Gamlin crazy, but I had business with Marshal Carroll and the Judge that took a little time. Tex Shipley and Harmon rode to Lake's Ferry. Tex had a notion to go on to Texas from there.

I was finishing up my business with Judge Parker and about to take my leave when he asked, "Lee, have you been hearing the talk about these train and stages robberies?"

"Yessir. Marshal Carroll has been on all of us t' put a stop to them. He threatened me this morning with a whippin' if I didn't get out of town and in the hunt."

The Judge smiled. "I have information that Pard Newman has been spreading a lot of money around Tahlequah and Tulsa—a lot more than he would get from his bootlegging operations. He has several big-spending companions that have even less reason to have money than he does. I want you to see what you can find out about their operation. Maybe we'll stop a lot of robbing."

"I'll do that, Judge, starting first thing in th' morning."

"Good, and good night to you."

Gam's gonna be happy now, I thought as I left the marshal's office with a fist full of warrants. I sent word to Greenwood for Gam to come in, and ordered Harm's grocery list filled at the mercantile. By the time Gam arrived that night, I had the stock penned and Tumbleweed loaded for a trip. We were the first customers t' cross th' ferry into the I.T. next morning.

"Where we goin', Lee?" Gam called as he sawed on the reins of two cantankerous mules.

"Lookin' for train robbers an' scalawags, Gam—whoa, there, Tobe—gonna stop by Tahlequah first, then we may go to Tulsa or Tailholt, depending on what we find."

"What's at Tailholt?"

"Suspicious characters. Harm's gonna meet us at Muskogee."

"I gotta drive this wagon all th' way—"

"I could just pay you driver's wages instead of what you're makin' if you want."

"No, that's OK."

"Don't say another word about drivin', then."

Blessed peace settled on us except for the antics of those mules. Gam fought them all day, an' by supper, his arms were sore from sawing on the lines. I hoped the mules would settle down some the second day, but that wasn't on their minds. At midmorning I relieved Gam and drove those mules hard the rest of the day. On day three, the team was tired, maybe a little sore, and for the most part behaved, but we knew their perverse minds were still thinkin' on mischief. It was just a matter of time.

Harm met us that evening on the east side of the river and Tex was with him. "Thought we had lost you, Tex," I said.

"We would have except for a pair of blue eyes," Harm said.

"I can change my mind without some girl interferin'," Tex said.

"May be that is what'll happen next time." Harm grinned.

Tahlequah was quiet. Pard Newman had blown his way through town on his way to Tulsa only the day before.

"Want t' point th' wagon tongue towards Tulsey Town, Lee?"

Gam was a little too eager to go there an' maybe that's what helped me d'cide. "No-o-o, let's check out Tailholt while we're this close an' then we'll see about goin' to Tulsa."

"I do believe it's easier t' get to Tulsa from Tahlequah than t' git to Tailholt in this wagon," Tex complained. We had to cross the Illinois River and Baron Fork and climb up the breaks on a road not much more than a single track trail. Tex was almost right; it was pretty near as hard going those twelve miles to Tailholt as it was going those sixty miles to Tulsa.

"Bein' isolated and hard to get to makes it a good place t' hide out, don't it?" Gam's observation was more a statement than a question.

"Not to mention its access to railroads an' th' state line," Harm called as his horse strained on the rope that kept Tumbleweed from toppling over into the gulley below.

I spied the top of Sugar Mountain. "Tex, see that mountain over there above th' trees? That's th' Sugar Mountains. Aim for th' north side of the mountain. Tailholt is about a mile east of them."

"You want t' drive right into town, or hide out in th' woods?"

"Hide 'er in th' woods, an' we'll ride into town on fresh horses that can 'outrun fleeing bandits,' as the yellow journalists say."

"You read that stuff?" Harm rode up coiling his rope.

"How else can he git instructions on police methods?" Gam laughed.

"Yeah, Harm," I said. "That's how I got my 'lightning-fast draw and unerring shot from the hip.' "Th' whole posse laughed at that, even those sweating mules grinned.

The nice things about the green side of the territory are the abundance of water, shade, and firewood. It wasn't hard for Tex and Harm to locate a campsite on a branch just northwest of Sugar Mountain. When we were settled, we left Harmon cooking and rode to check out Tailholt. It couldn't be called a village; it was more a settlement with no post office or real store, just a feller selling goods out of his house.

Our reception was guarded and cool. Strangers in places like this were suspect and not very welcome, especially if someone smelled "lawman" on them. Gam and Tex sat their horses while I visited with the would-be merchant on his front porch. He was barefooted, his ragged overalls reaching mid-shin and held up by a single rawhide gallus tied to the strap button on his bib. He was making shavings with a large bowie-like knife, and there was the bulge of a gun in his pocket. There had been warning of our arrival.

"Someone said you might have some canned goods for sale," I said by way of greeting.

The man studied his handiwork a moment and said, "Ain't got nothin' for sale, mister; need t' git t' town an' resupply one o' these days."

"Nothing?"

"Nothin' at all." He shifted on his stool and I noticed an M.K. & T. fob and a gold chain strung across his belly to the bulge in his watch pocket.

"Do you know what time it is?" I asked.

"Shore," he said squinting at the sun, "it be about mid-afternoon."

"I mean clock time"—nodding toward his watch pocket—"I forgot t' wind my clock an' plumb lost track."

"Clock don't run; spring's broke. I just wear it t' keep th' kids from playin' with it an' losin' it."

"Well, I shore wished you had some goods. We're runnin' short an' could use some canned termaters an' such."

"Sorry, mister, maybe next time." I left the man to his carving.

Gam chuckled. "Wouldn't even give you th' time of day."

"These places sure got a bunch of *good* horses hangin' around th' barns," Tex noted.

"I noticed, Tex; not many our stock could keep up with."

"Well fed, too, ain't they?" Gam observed.

Tex nodded. "I'd say they possibly eat better than th' folks I seen peekin' out th' doors an' windows."

"Well, what do you expect when th' store's out o' goods?" I chuckled. "That watch chain had an M.K. & T. fob on the end; I'd bet my hat that watch was th' proud possession of a conductor a few days back."

"He's gonna be awful mad when we give it back to him with a broke spring," Gamlin said, grinning.

"It may be hard t' find now that th' feller's had warning," I said.

"Cain't run far barefooted." Tex was not familiar with the people of these hills.

"Those feet are hard as whet leather. Bet he could run on nails an' not get a scratch," I replied.

"We're not gonna do much good here since we gave them warnin'," said Gam.

"I doubt any more of them leave, if they haven't left before we showed up. And I suspect there's gonna be a meeting tonight after dark."

"What d'yuh think they'd talk about, Lee, th' lack o' groceries at th' store?" Gam laughed.

"Two things we need t' do tonight; get men and horses out of camp and safe, and attend that meeting."

"I'm fer any meetin' that ain't got a preacher attached to it," Gam volunteered.

"Might be I should go," Tex said, "just in case a parson should show up."

I heeled up a trot. "Looks like we're headin' for a straw vote."

Harmon was glad we showed up; he knew the camp was being watched by more than one pair of eyes, and it made him mighty nervous. "What have we rode into, Lee?"

"We been here b'fore, Harm." I meant in hazardous situations, not Tailholt. More than once has our camp been shot at from ambush, and the good practices Bass Reeves and common sense have taught us have kept us from damage. Just before dark, all four of us made a sweep of the area around camp and flushed out our spies. We found their barefooted tracks making for the settlement and returned to camp.

"Eat up, boys, then roll out your beds and fill them like you were sleeping in them. Harm, fix your fire for the morning. Leave the coffee pot on th' fire."

I made my bed, then threw the covers back like I had gotten up for guard duty. When it was full dark, we caught up the stock, and leaving all else, walked up between the two peaks that made up Sugar Mountain. The tops of the mountain are essentially flat, and we climbed the steep side of the north peak and picketed the horses there. "Tie the horses good; we will leave them here for the night. Some of us have to be sure to be back here before daylight or we'll lose the whole bunch."

"Can't afford that since we done give away our whole camp," Gam grumbled.

"Bet they don't take Tumbleweed." Harm's voice was grim. It bothered him to think he could lose his supplies and utensils.

"I'm bettin' no one wants the wagon, and the other things can be replaced easy enough at Tahlequah, if need be," I said. "Let's get to th' town-hall meetin'. We're probably late now."

"How can you be so sure they're gonna be meetin'?" Tex asked.

"Wait a minute—Lee are you takin' *all* of us an' leavin' these horses *alone*?" Gam's voice hinted at disbelief.

"Yes, I am, Gam. I'm willin' t' risk losin' them and havin' t' track them down after I've filled that wagon with train robbers."

"After we fill it up, we're gonna have t' hunt th' countryside for all our gear—and possibly bareback." Tex was thinking out loud.

" 'Possibly bareback' might be a luxury we won't have," Gam growled.

"Probably on empty stomachs, too," Harm observed.

"Stop yer yammerin' an' head down that hill for town hall," I demanded.

There was many a stumble and muttered curse down the mountain until we came to an open pasture on the flat and the walking was easier. I donated skin off my shin in the process of finding the rail fence on the other side of the field. The road on the other side made walking easier. Only a few lights showed here and there in the cabins. Many of them were dark. The straw merchant's house was better lit; after a few instructions, we surrounded it. Gam and Tex went to the back door, and when they had time to be in place, Harm and I climbed the steps and clumped across the plank floor to the door. I peeked through a crack until my eyes were used to the light. Harm stood with his back to the light so he could guard against latecomers.

"Come on in here, feller; you don't have to be invited," our host called.

I pushed open the door and entered with two handguns drawn. Eight or nine men sat around the room and stared, too surprised to react. I quickly said, "Just sit still, men; th' place is surrounded an' there's no place t' go."

The back door opened and Gam stepped in, gun in hand.

"What do you want, Dep'ty?" our merchant growled.

"Well, first of all, I want you to stand up and unhook that conductor's watch from your trousers and lay it with your handgun and knife in the middle of the floor. Then go to the back door where the man there has some more jewelry for you to wear. On second thought, turn all your pockets wrong-side out an' let's see what else you got.

"Deputy," I said to Gam without mentioning his name, "write down this man's name and the contents of his pockets, namely, one conductor's watch and M.K. & T. fob and chain, two twenty-dollar gold pieces, one Remington pistol, and one bowie knife."

"Anything else, Mr. Merchant?" The man shook his head and went to Gam for the manacles.

I tapped the man sitting next to me. "You're next, partner. Empty 'em in th' middle there an' let's see what you got. What's your name for our records?"

He didn't answer, but someone across the room called, "Don't tell 'em, Bill Long," to everyone's amusement.

"Bill" had plenty: a watch with the initials *JRB* engraved on the cover, a diamond stick pin that would never see a tie on its present owner, and a handful of gold coins. He laid them on the floor by the other gear and moved on to Gam unbidden. Tex helped Gam apply the restraints, cuffing one prisoner to the next so that when we were finished, we had eight men shackled together in a row. Not much chance of them getting away like that.

One by one, we went through the other men in the room, picking up a considerable amount of stolen items. The men got great amusement making up names for each other, but Gam had the last laugh, because he included a description of each man in his inventory. There would be no confusion if the men chose to exchange names or make up some other name to confuse prosecutors.

We had the men return to the main room and be seated. Now, don't think because I tell you this in a few words that the operation was easy. There were several struggles and more than one of the prisoners had a lump or two and an aching head.

At dawn, Tex and Harm went for the wagon and camp gear, while Gam and I made a house-to-house search for loot. There was plenty of it; almost every house had something that linked to a robbery somewhere—so much evidence that I sent Harm and Tex skitterin' for Dutch Mills in Arkansas, where they telegraphed Marshal Carroll for reinforcements. In a couple of days, deputies began arriving, and we soon had the problem surrounded. There were a few more arrests, and by the time we were all ready to leave the village of Tailholt, there was a severe shortage of menfolk.

Harm and Tex were just north of Van Buren with Tumbleweed and the prisoners when we caught up with them. It was a good haul and put a stop to train robbin' for a while. Pard Newman must have gotten word of the raid, for he disappeared and we only heard from him by notes he left here and there threatening mayhem on me and my posse.

CHAPTER 39
NEW BEGINNINGS

We delivered our prisoners to the jail and got warrants made out for them while Harm and Tex stowed th' wagon and penned the stock. There was a letter in my mail addressed in a neat female hand and postmarked Woodward, I.T.

Gam grinned. "Want I should read that to you, Lee?"

"I can read it for myself, thank you." I found a corner away from his prying eyes and opened the letter. It read:

August 2, 1888

Dear Deputy Sowell:

I write this appealing for your considerable assistance in a matter of great importance to me. I have recently filed on a section of land in the Cimarron Valley, New Mexico Territory, below Black Mesa. My problem is that I have no cattle for the range and no manpower to develop the land so I can prove up my claim. Is there any way you could assist me? I confess to a dearth of ready cash, but there are other compensations you may find more to your satisfaction. I am a good cook and have experience handling stock. At this time, I am having a bunkhouse built on a hill not far from Sheep Pen Canyon and that lovely stretch of the river we enjoyed on our visit there.

In anticipation of your assent to my rescue, I have taken the liberty of filing for a section adjoining mine in your name. There is an abundance of grass here, as you know, and if I had a mixed herd of a hundred head or so, I would soon have a fine herd of cattle. Another herd of the same size would serve your needs also.

Please reply as soon as possible, care of General Delivery, Florence, Oklahoma. I am most in need of your assistance.

Sincerely, and with Love,
Katherine Ingram

I grinned. No dust gathers on her saddle. For me, there was no question about my desire or intention. In fact, the time spent here in town before our last trip into the I.T. was in preparation for this moment.

Marshal Carroll came out of his office and congratulated us for our work breaking up the Newman gang and related that Judge Parker had requested the honor of our presence in his court after trial closing time.

"We in some kind of trouble, Lee?" a worried Gam asked.

"Ain't we always?" I didn't tell him that I expected the summons. It would keep him occupied until we met the Judge. Harm and Tex were in a sweat to head for Lake's Ferry. I got my bank drafts, and we went downtown to get them cashed and distributed. Then I treated the boys to a meal at Heinie's and we returned to the courthouse just as court adjourned for the day.

Marshal Carroll met us in the hall. "Let's wait until the crowd thins out a little before we go in."

"Oh-h-h lordy, we must be in trouble big if th' marshal's goin' in too." Gam groaned.

"Maybe not, Gam," Tex said.

Harm looked concerned. "Do you know what this is all about, Lee?"

"I may have some idea, but I won't say."

Harm whispered to Tex, "You don't think he heard about . . ."

"Sh-h-h-h," Tex said, cutting his eyes toward me.

My eyebrows raised. "Something I need t' know, Harm?" I pretended concern.

"No, it's nothin', Lee," Tex put in.

"Better not be," I muttered as if to myself, but loud enough for the boys to hear.

Gam was dancin' from foot to foot. I stood behind him to cut off any stampeding he might be contemplatin'. Just in time, the bailiff opened the door. "The Judge will see you now."

We entered the empty courtroom and I had to punch Tex and motion for him to remove his hat. "Have a seat, gentlemen. I will be ready for you in a moment. Bailiff, come here, please." There was a whispered conversation, and the bailiff nodded and left the room. "Now, gentlemen, I think congratulations are in order for your work in breaking up a bunch of train robbers. I understand you did a good job.

"Marshal Carroll, if you will do the honors, please."

A board creaked under the marshal's foot as he opened the gate between audience and court. There was no other sound in the room. I don't think the boys were breathing. "Gamlin Stein, will you please step forward."

The boy looked pale as a sheet. I smiled at him as he stood and passed me. The two men approached the bench. "Judge Parker, this is Gamlin Stein. He has been highly recommended for deputy U.S. marshal and I would commend him to you for the administration of his oath of office."

There were two big sighs of relief from beside me, and Tex gave me a sharp elbow in the ribs. "You knew, didn't you?" he accused.

"Sh-h-h."

The bailiff had returned and handed Marshal Carroll a Bible.

"Gamlin Stein, place your hand on the Bible. Do you swear . . ." The oath was administered and Gamlin so swore.

There were the usual papers to sign, and when time came for the pinning of the badge, I stepped forward and offered the one I had ordered made for the occasion to Marshal Carroll. "No, Lee, I think you should do the honors."

I pinned the badge to his shirt without drawing blood and shook his hand, "Congratulations, Gam; you'll make a good lawman."

"T-thanks, Lee; this is all a big surprise."

Tex and Harmon were standing at the gate, hesitant to enter until Judge Parker motioned them in. They shook Gam's hand and slapped his back.

The Judge rapped his gavel lightly. "Gentlemen, it's time for my supper, and I declare this meeting satisfactorily concluded." He stood, and as he left the room said, "Bailiff, you may secure the room." It was our message to leave, which we promptly did.

Marshal Carroll left us at his office door and we proceeded to the nearest watering hole.

"Lee, you could have told us what was happening and saved us a lot of worry," Harmon scolded.

"Yeah, Lee, what was *that* all about?" Tex asked.

"I wanted to see if your consciences were clear, and I detected no small amount of concern on you-all's part. Isn't there something you need to tell *me*?"

"No!" came three answers, and we all laughed.

"I spent that time last month getting this all set up, Gam, and I have to say that the marshal was as assured as I was that you were ready to be a deputy. Make a good one."

"I'll shore try, Lee."

"I offered my resignation last month, but th' marshal would have none of it. Instead, I will be a deputy at large and won't have to tow ol' Tumbleweed around with me. That letter I got was from Kat. She has taken up a claim in New Mexico Territory and filed for one in my name next to her land. She needs cattle, and I suppose I will be going to Kansas to find us both a herd."

"Just throw 'em all in together, Lee. That's th' way that story will end." Tex laughed. "Think I'd better go with you an' show you how t' herd an' nurture cow people."

"You're welcome t' come along."

"Harmon looked at Gam. "Think you'll be needin' a cook and driver?"

"Shore will, Harm. Think you know of one available?"

"I'll look around for one."

"Fine print in your contract stip-i-lates you are not to cook anything," I said to Gam.

"It don't either." He rustled through his papers, then gave up the search. "I'll look at it later." We all had a good laugh at that.

"Gam, I'm makin' you a gift of ol' Tumbleweed, what's left of her. I'm keepin' my two mules an' Pet an' Tobe. All I want from th' wagon is about three of th' manacles an' maybe a small coffee pot an' Dutch oven."

"Pot's gotta be big enough fer two," Tex interjected.

"The marshal's got you a packet of warrants, an' he would like you to be out as soon as you can. That don't mean you can't take a couple or more days t'rest and resupply. Harm an' Tex will want t' have some time at th' ferry. You need to take your posse into account when plannin' your work."

"Yeah, remember that, Gam." Harm smiled.

"You can get by, th' two o' you, but it's better if you have a third man. He can wait till you are more established. Keep good records an' stay alert and smart. Watch out for Pard Newman. He'll be on th' prod after we cleaned up on his kinfolk." I didn't need to say all that except for my conscience's sake.

★　★　★　★　★

Turnin' loose of the deputy work an' lettin' Gam and Harm go it alone is a lot like settin' your kid on a horse th' first time. You feel responsible and want to trot alongside t' catch th' kid if he should fall, but in th' end, he's gotta ride on his own, an' so will these boys. The time for gradual letting go had passed, an' it was best I get out of th' way—and that's just what I did.

Tex was set on visitin' at th' ferry. He would take th' M.K. & T. to Baxter Springs, Kansas, where we would meet in a month. From there, it was just a matter of picking up a couple hundred head of cattle and getting them to th' Cimarron Valley. It took a couple of days t' settle up business in town. Early one morning, I rounded up my stock an' struck out for Liberty Springs, Arkansas.

ABOUT THE AUTHOR

James D. Crownover is the author of the double Western Writers of America Spur Award–winning *Wild Ran the Rivers*. He makes his home in Elm Springs, Arkansas, with his wife, Carol, and Duchess, a spell-checking bullmastiff. His favorite things are spending time with grandchildren, woodworking, traveling back roads, and writing. His special interest is in the adventures of the unrecognized pioneers who in the process of making a place for themselves, built a great nation where individual freedom and initiative thrive.

The employees of Five Star Publishing hope you have enjoyed this book.

Our Five Star novels explore little-known chapters from America's history, stories told from unique perspectives that will entertain a broad range of readers.

Other Five Star books are available at your local library, bookstore, all major book distributors, and directly from Five Star/Gale.

Connect with Five Star Publishing

Visit us on Facebook:
   https://www.facebook.com/FiveStarCengage

Email:
   FiveStar@cengage.com

For information about titles and placing orders:
   (800) 223-1244
   gale.orders@cengage.com

To share your comments, write to us:
   Five Star Publishing
   Attn: Publisher
   10 Water St., Suite 310
   Waterville, ME 04901